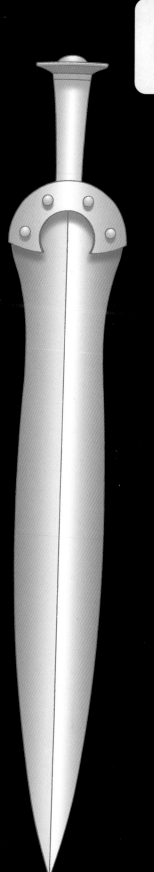

THE SWORD

AIR

JOSHUA LUNA
Story, Script, Layouts, Letters

JONATHAN LUNA
Story, Illustrations, Book Design

SPECIAL THANKS TO:

Rommel Calderon
Randy Castillo
Dan Dos Santos
Timothy Ingle
Jenn Kao
Marc Lombardi
Jordan Millner
Dawn Smith
Victoria Stein
Giancarlo Yerkes

IMAGE COMICS, INC.

Robert Kirkman Chief Operating Officer
Erik Larsen Chief Financial Officer
Todd McFarlane President
Marc Silvestri Chief Executive Officer
Jim Valentino Vice-President
Eric Stephenson Publisher
Todd Martinez Sales & Licensing Coordinator
Betsy Gomez PR & Marketing Coordinator
Branwyn Bigglestone Accounts Manager
Sarah deLaine Administrative Assistant
Tyler Shainline Production Manager
Drew Gill Art Director
Jonathan Chan Production Artist
Monica Howard Production Artist
Vincent Kukua Production Artist

www.imagecomics.com
www.lunabrothers.com

THE SWORD, VOL. 4: AIR
ISBN: 978-1-60706-168-7
First Printing

International Rights Representative: Christine Jensen (christine@gfloystudio.com)

PRINTED IN KOREA

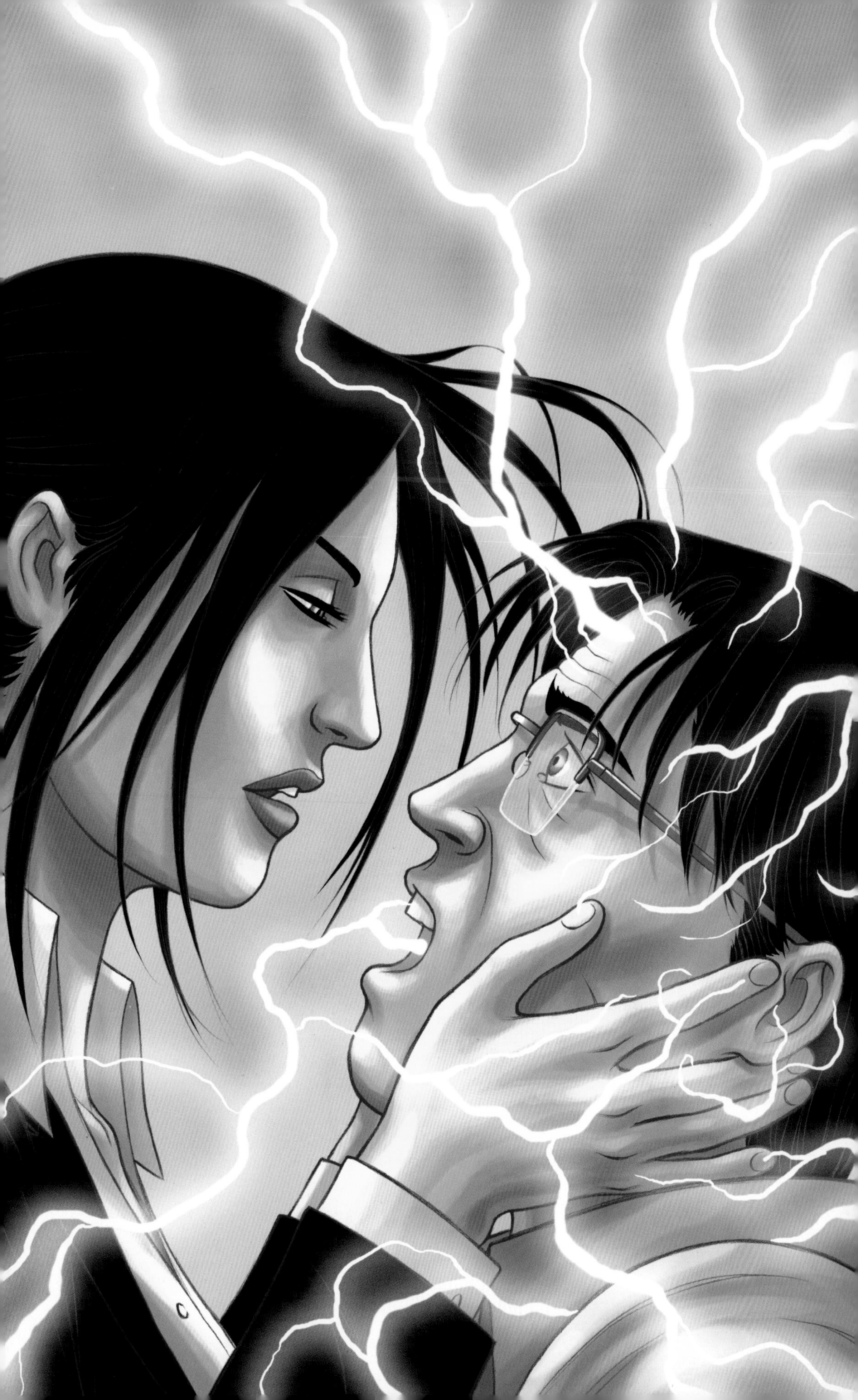

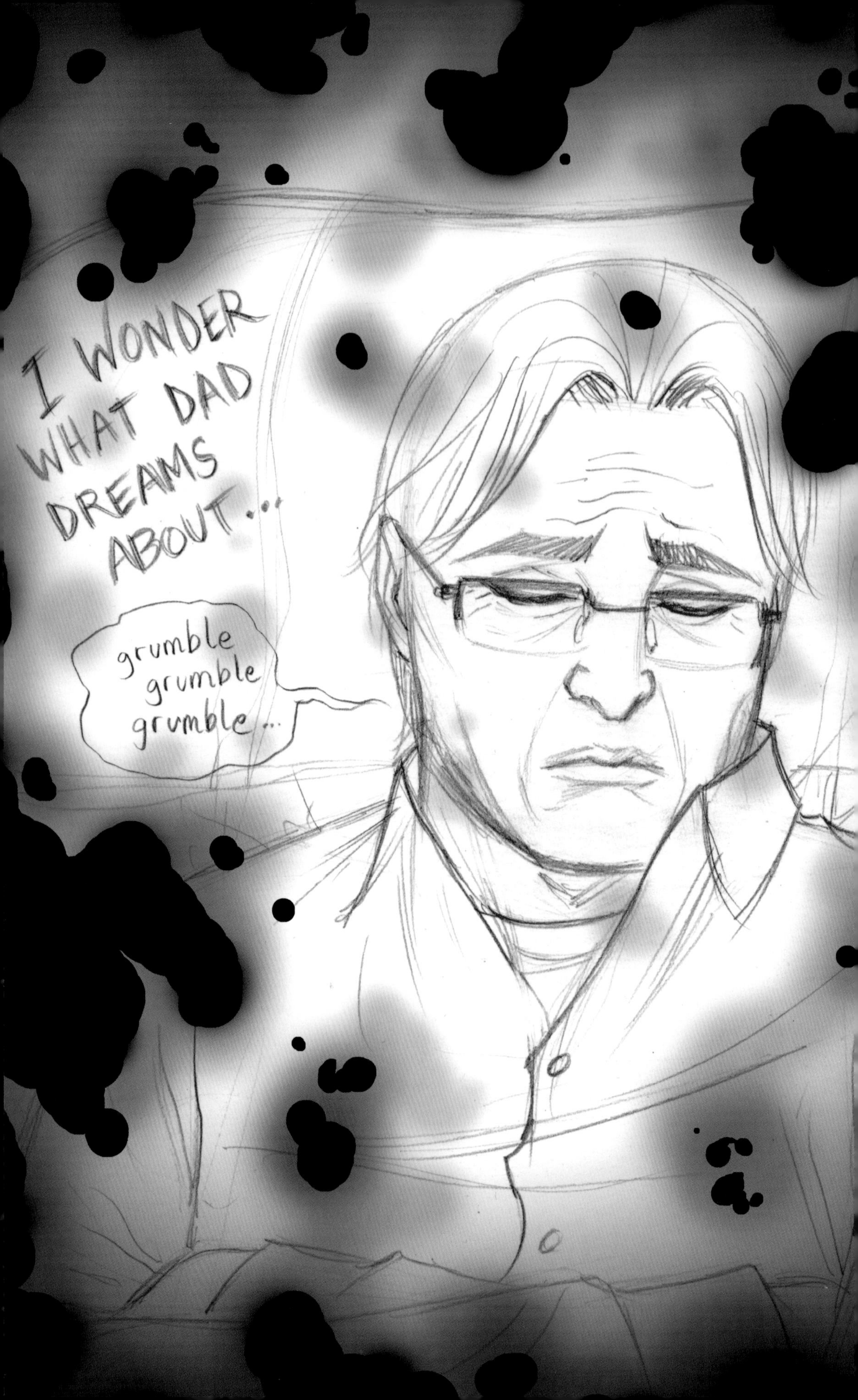
I WONDER WHAT DAD DREAMS ABOUT...
grumble grumble grumble...

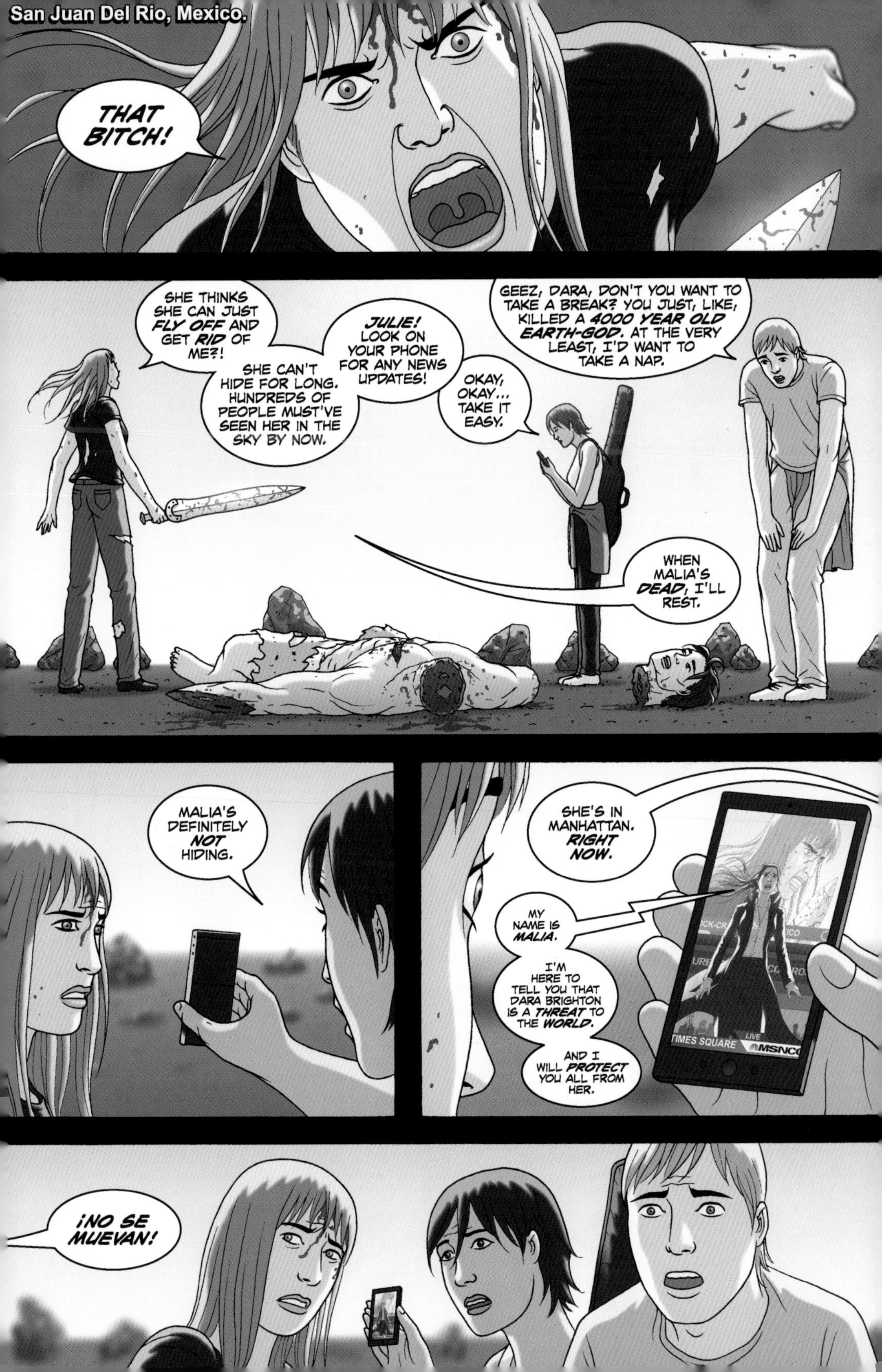
San Juan Del Rio, Mexico.
THAT BITCH!
SHE THINKS SHE CAN JUST FLY OFF AND GET RID OF ME?!
SHE CAN'T HIDE FOR LONG. HUNDREDS OF PEOPLE MUST'VE SEEN HER IN THE SKY BY NOW.
JULIE! LOOK ON YOUR PHONE FOR ANY NEWS UPDATES!
OKAY, OKAY... TAKE IT EASY.
GEEZ, DARA, DON'T YOU WANT TO TAKE A BREAK? YOU JUST, LIKE, KILLED A 4000 YEAR OLD EARTH-GOD. AT THE VERY LEAST, I'D WANT TO TAKE A NAP.
WHEN MALIA'S DEAD, I'LL REST.
MALIA'S DEFINITELY NOT HIDING.
SHE'S IN MANHATTAN. RIGHT NOW.
MY NAME IS MALIA.
I'M HERE TO TELL YOU THAT DARA BRIGHTON IS A THREAT TO THE WORLD.
AND I WILL PROTECT YOU ALL FROM HER.
TIMES SQUARE
LIVE
MSNC
¡NO SE MUEVAN!

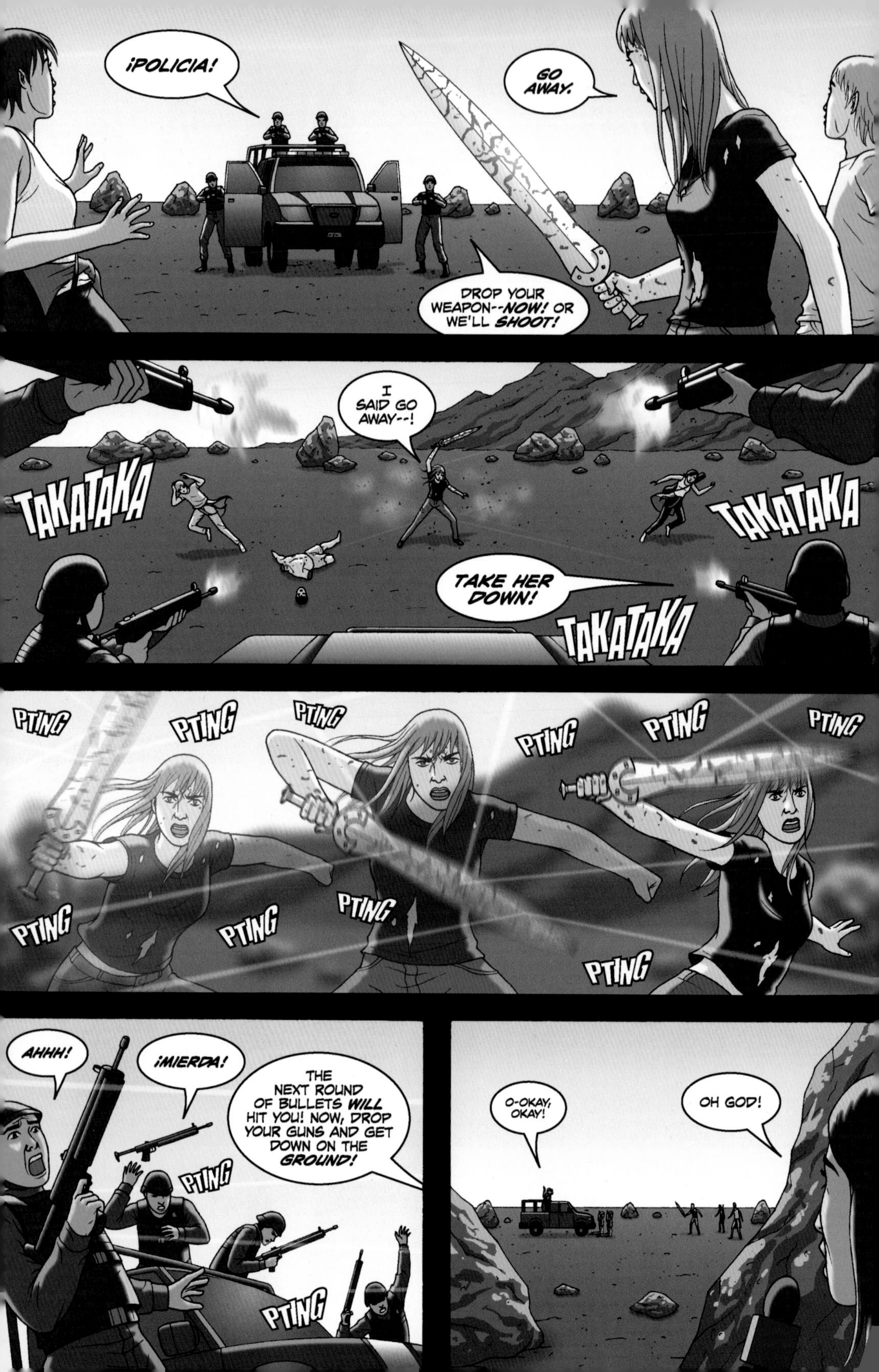
¡POLICIA!
GO AWAY.
DROP YOUR WEAPON--NOW! OR WE'LL SHOOT!
I SAID GO AWAY--!
TAKATAKA
TAKATAKA
TAKE HER DOWN!
TAKATAKA
PTING
PTING
PTING
PTING
PTING
PTING
PTING
PTING
PTING
PTING
AHHH!
¡MIERDA!
THE NEXT ROUND OF BULLETS WILL HIT YOU! NOW, DROP YOUR GUNS AND GET DOWN ON THE GROUND!
PTING
PTING
O-OKAY, OKAY!
OH GOD!

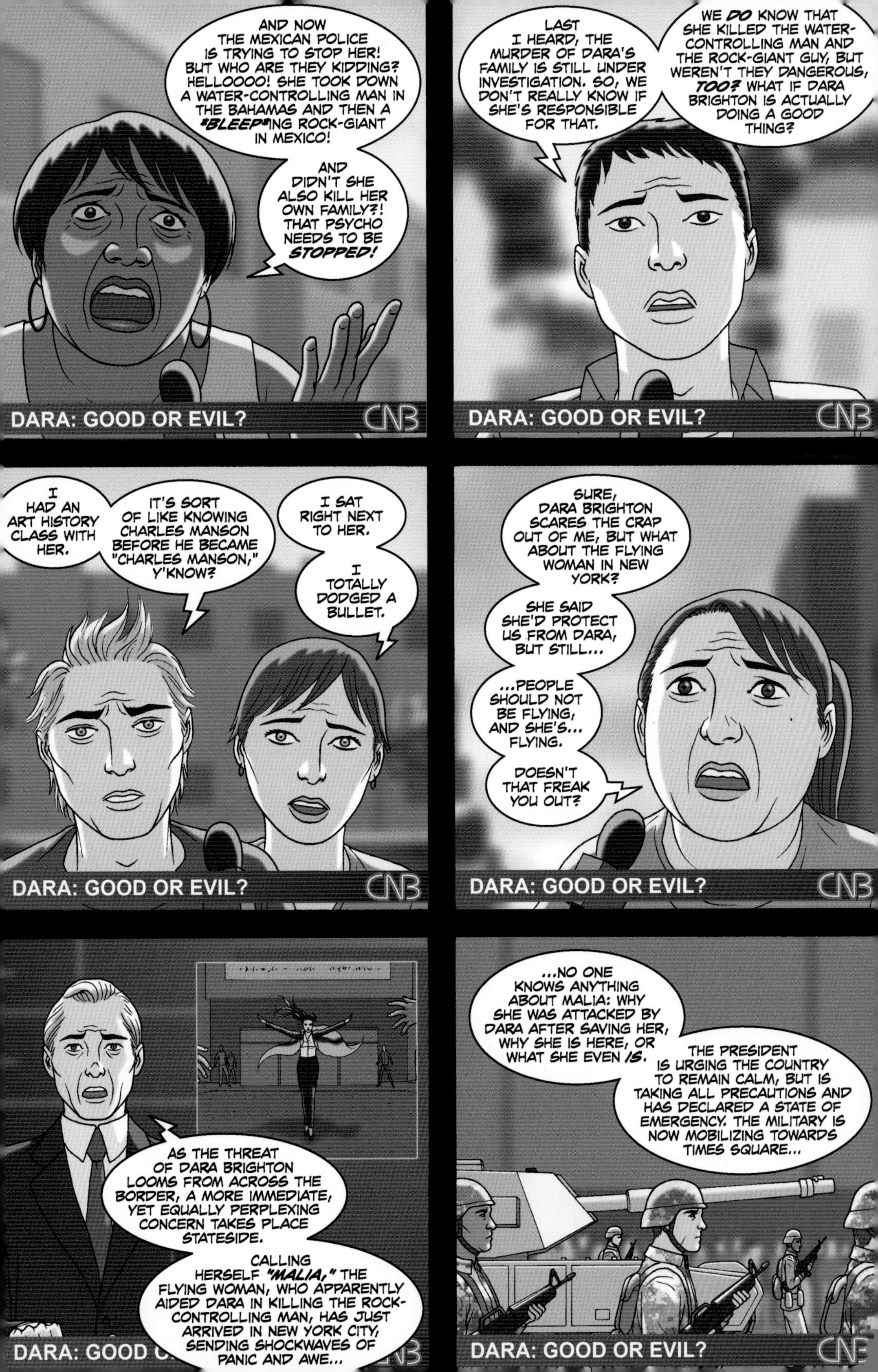
AND NOW THE MEXICAN POLICE IS TRYING TO STOP HER! BUT WHO ARE THEY KIDDING? HELLOOOO! SHE TOOK DOWN A WATER-CONTROLLING MAN IN THE BAHAMAS AND THEN A *BLEEP*ING ROCK-GIANT IN MEXICO!
AND DIDN'T SHE ALSO KILL HER OWN FAMILY?! THAT PSYCHO NEEDS TO BE STOPPED!
DARA: GOOD OR EVIL?
CNB
LAST I HEARD, THE MURDER OF DARA'S FAMILY IS STILL UNDER INVESTIGATION. SO, WE DON'T REALLY KNOW IF SHE'S RESPONSIBLE FOR THAT.
WE DO KNOW THAT SHE KILLED THE WATER-CONTROLLING MAN AND THE ROCK-GIANT GUY, BUT WEREN'T THEY DANGEROUS, TOO? WHAT IF DARA BRIGHTON IS ACTUALLY DOING A GOOD THING?
DARA: GOOD OR EVIL?
CNB
I HAD AN ART HISTORY CLASS WITH HER.
IT'S SORT OF LIKE KNOWING CHARLES MANSON BEFORE HE BECAME "CHARLES MANSON," Y'KNOW?
I SAT RIGHT NEXT TO HER.
I TOTALLY DODGED A BULLET.
DARA: GOOD OR EVIL?
CNB
SURE, DARA BRIGHTON SCARES THE CRAP OUT OF ME, BUT WHAT ABOUT THE FLYING WOMAN IN NEW YORK?
SHE SAID SHE'D PROTECT US FROM DARA, BUT STILL...
...PEOPLE SHOULD NOT BE FLYING, AND SHE'S... FLYING.
DOESN'T THAT FREAK YOU OUT?
DARA: GOOD OR EVIL?
CNB
AS THE THREAT OF DARA BRIGHTON LOOMS FROM ACROSS THE BORDER, A MORE IMMEDIATE, YET EQUALLY PERPLEXING CONCERN TAKES PLACE STATESIDE.
CALLING HERSELF "MALIA," THE FLYING WOMAN, WHO APPARENTLY AIDED DARA IN KILLING THE ROCK-CONTROLLING MAN, HAS JUST ARRIVED IN NEW YORK CITY, SENDING SHOCKWAVES OF PANIC AND AWE...
DARA: GOOD O
...NO ONE KNOWS ANYTHING ABOUT MALIA: WHY SHE WAS ATTACKED BY DARA AFTER SAVING HER, WHY SHE IS HERE, OR WHAT SHE EVEN IS.
THE PRESIDENT IS URGING THE COUNTRY TO REMAIN CALM, BUT IS TAKING ALL PRECAUTIONS AND HAS DECLARED A STATE OF EMERGENCY. THE MILITARY IS NOW MOBILIZING TOWARDS TIMES SQUARE...
DARA: GOOD OR EVIL?
CNB

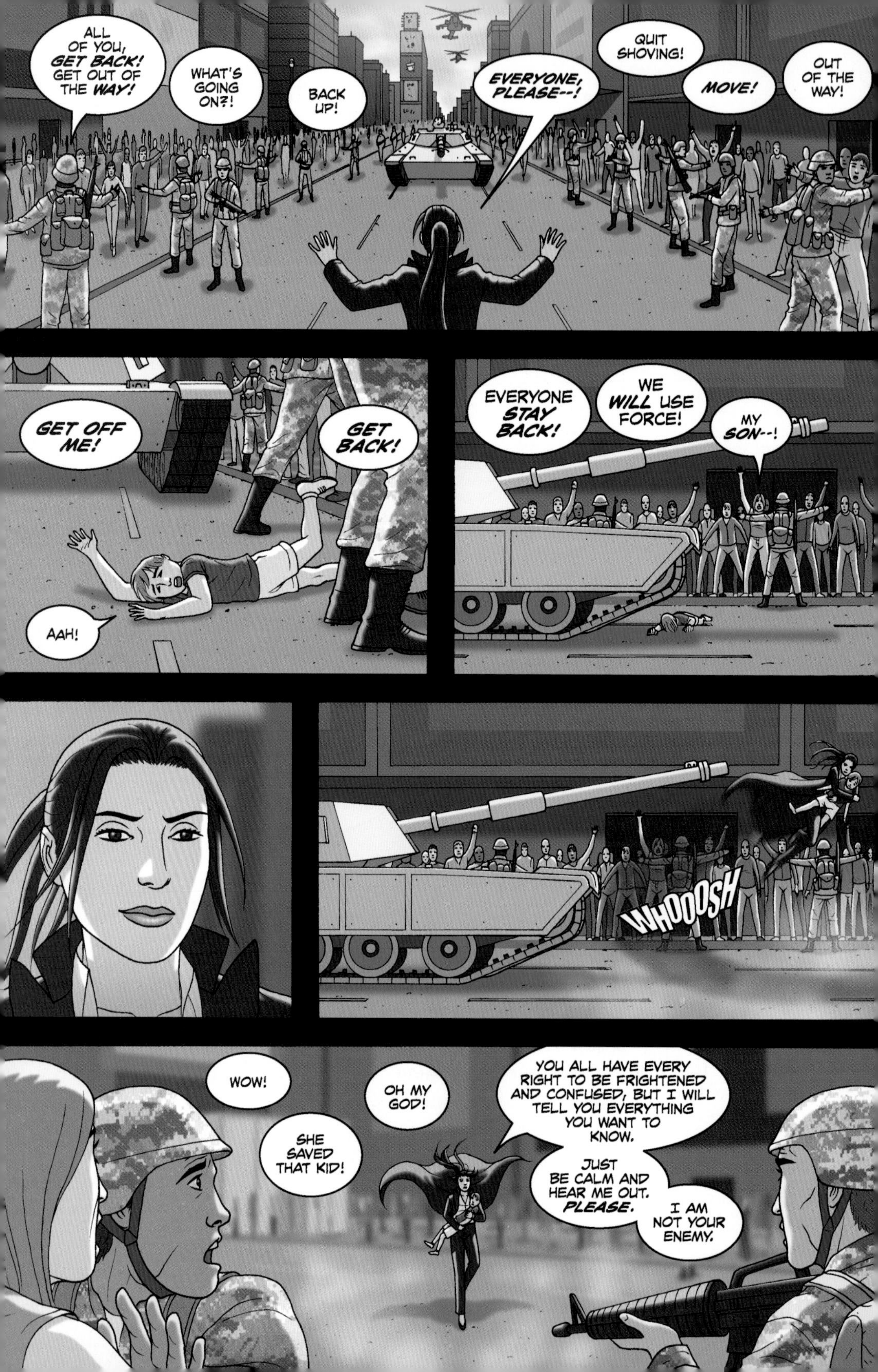
ALL OF YOU, GET BACK! GET OUT OF THE WAY!
WHAT'S GOING ON?!
BACK UP!
EVERYONE, PLEASE--!
QUIT SHOVING!
MOVE!
OUT OF THE WAY!
GET OFF ME!
GET BACK!
AAH!
EVERYONE STAY BACK!
WE WILL USE FORCE!
MY SON--!
WHOOOSH
WOW!
SHE SAVED THAT KID!
OH MY GOD!
YOU ALL HAVE EVERY RIGHT TO BE FRIGHTENED AND CONFUSED, BUT I WILL TELL YOU EVERYTHING YOU WANT TO KNOW.
JUST BE CALM AND HEAR ME OUT. PLEASE.
I AM NOT YOUR ENEMY.

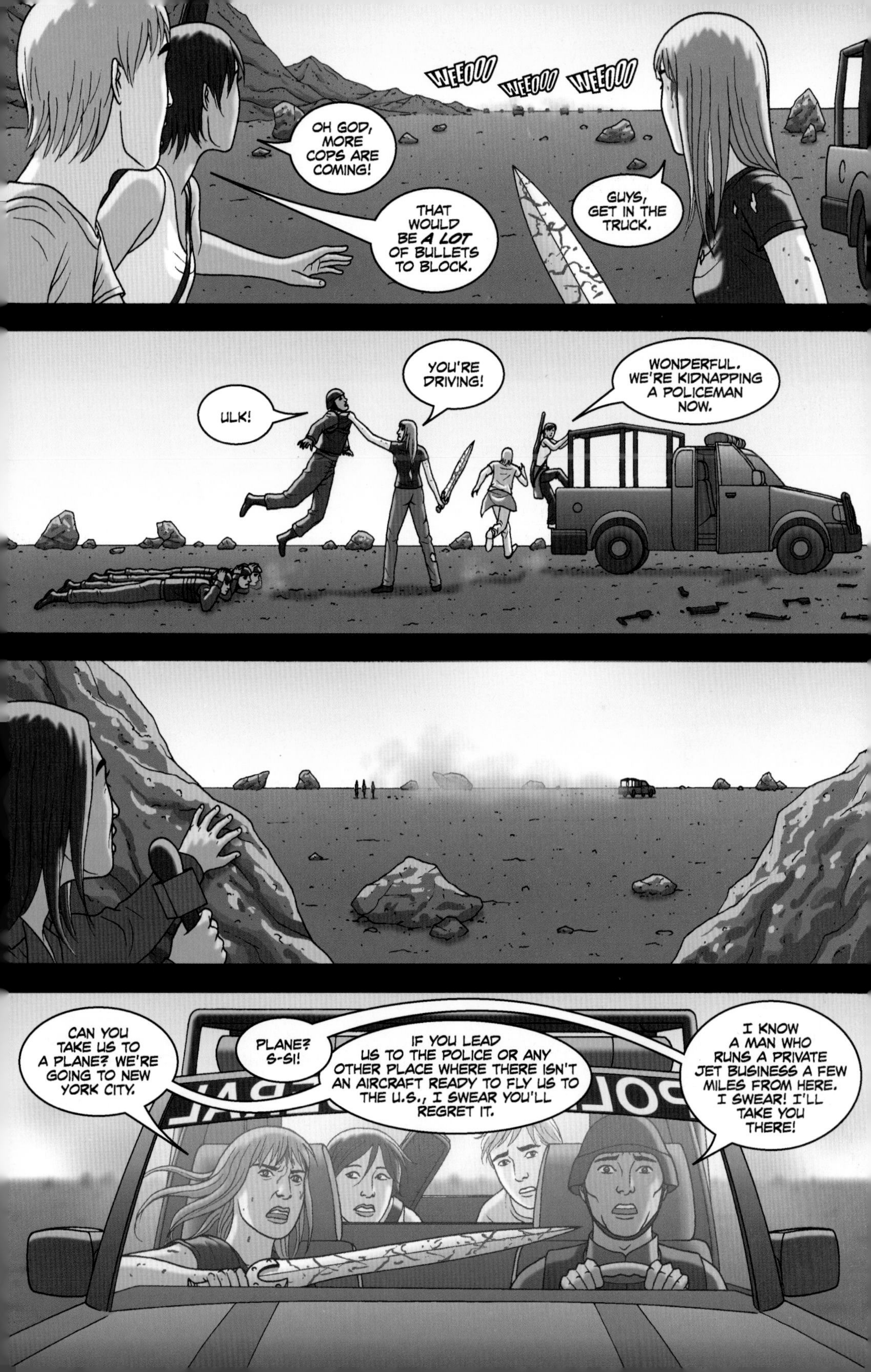
WEEOOO
WEEOOO
WEEOOO
OH GOD, MORE COPS ARE COMING!
THAT WOULD BE *A LOT* OF BULLETS TO BLOCK.
GUYS, GET IN THE TRUCK.
ULK!
YOU'RE DRIVING!
WONDERFUL. WE'RE KIDNAPPING A POLICEMAN NOW.
CAN YOU TAKE US TO A PLANE? WE'RE GOING TO NEW YORK CITY.
PLANE? S-SI!
IF YOU LEAD US TO THE POLICE OR ANY OTHER PLACE WHERE THERE ISN'T AN AIRCRAFT READY TO FLY US TO THE U.S., I SWEAR YOU'LL REGRET IT.
I KNOW A MAN WHO RUNS A PRIVATE JET BUSINESS A FEW MILES FROM HERE. I SWEAR! I'LL TAKE YOU THERE!

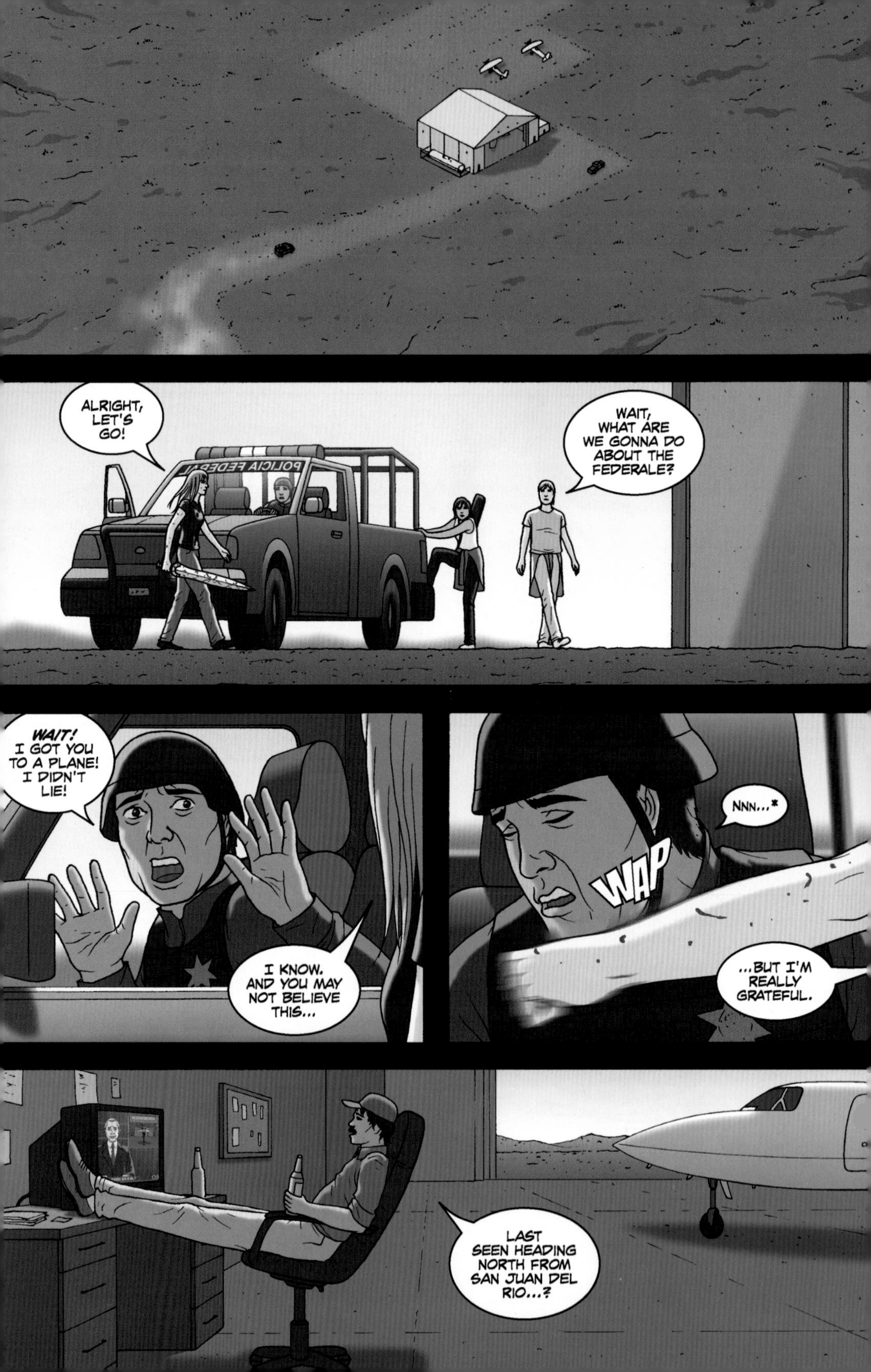

POLICIA FEDERAL
ALRIGHT, LET'S GO!
WAIT, WHAT ARE WE GONNA DO ABOUT THE FEDERALE?
WAIT! I GOT YOU TO A PLANE! I DIDN'T LIE!
I KNOW. AND YOU MAY NOT BELIEVE THIS...
NNN...*
WAP
...BUT I'M REALLY GRATEFUL.
LAST SEEN HEADING NORTH FROM SAN JUAN DEL RIO...?

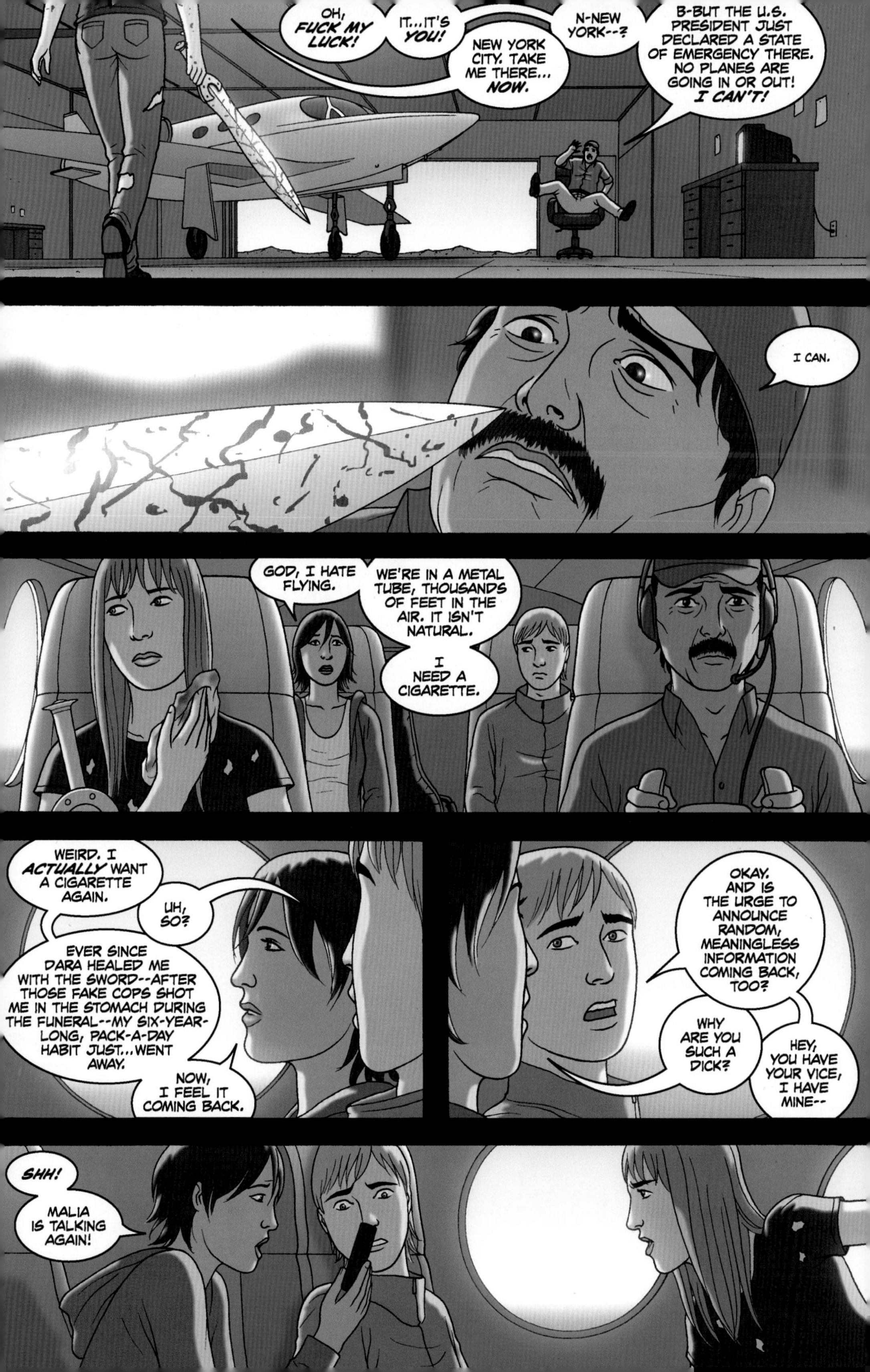
OH, FUCK MY LUCK!
IT...IT'S YOU!
NEW YORK CITY. TAKE ME THERE... NOW.
N-NEW YORK--?
B-BUT THE U.S. PRESIDENT JUST DECLARED A STATE OF EMERGENCY THERE. NO PLANES ARE GOING IN OR OUT! I CAN'T!
I CAN.
GOD, I HATE FLYING.
WE'RE IN A METAL TUBE, THOUSANDS OF FEET IN THE AIR. IT ISN'T NATURAL.
I NEED A CIGARETTE.
WEIRD. I ACTUALLY WANT A CIGARETTE AGAIN.
UH, SO?
EVER SINCE DARA HEALED ME WITH THE SWORD--AFTER THOSE FAKE COPS SHOT ME IN THE STOMACH DURING THE FUNERAL--MY SIX-YEAR-LONG, PACK-A-DAY HABIT JUST...WENT AWAY.
NOW, I FEEL IT COMING BACK.
OKAY. AND IS THE URGE TO ANNOUNCE RANDOM, MEANINGLESS INFORMATION COMING BACK, TOO?
WHY ARE YOU SUCH A DICK?
HEY, YOU HAVE YOUR VICE, I HAVE MINE--
SHH!
MALIA IS TALKING AGAIN!

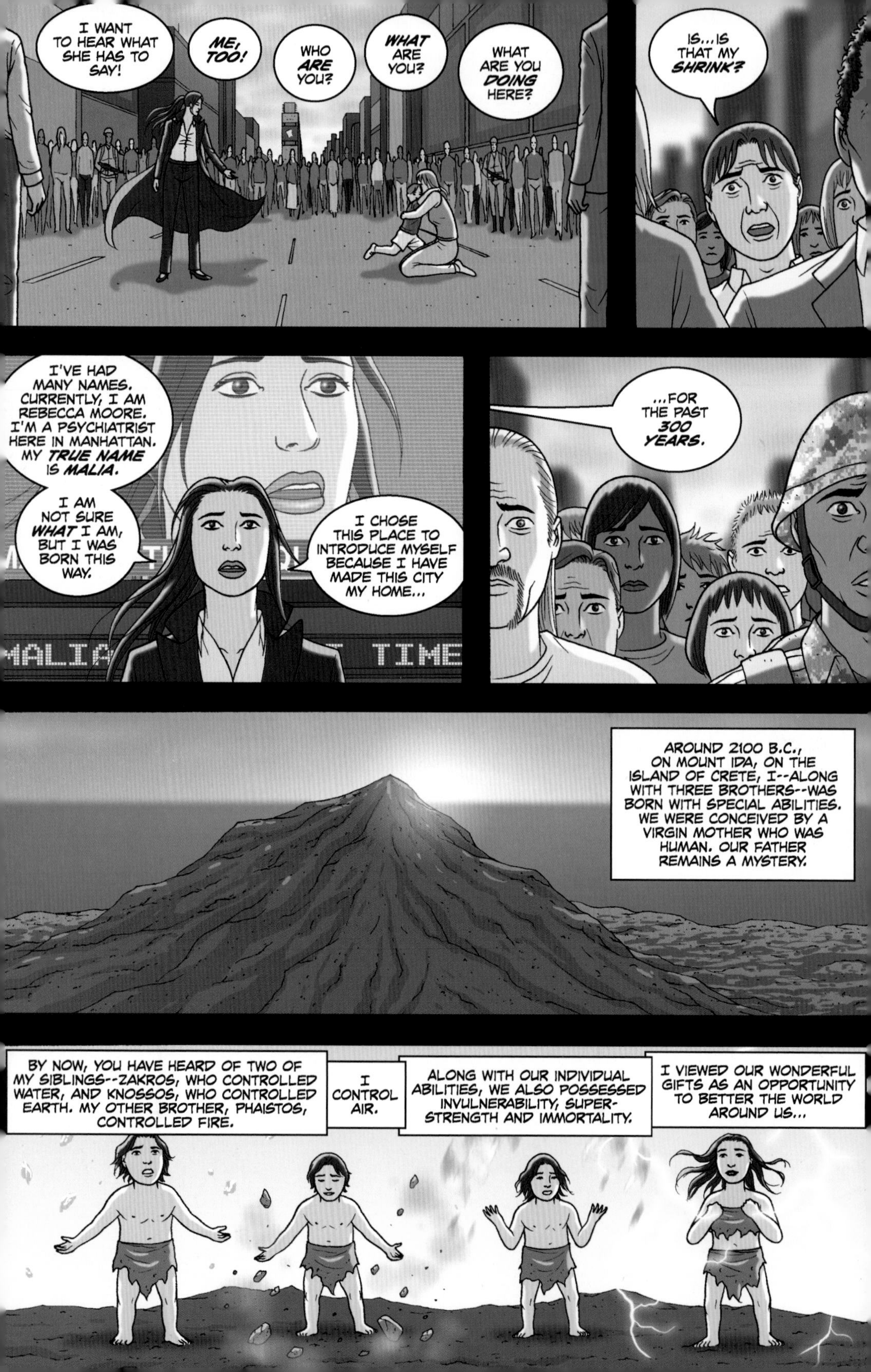
I WANT TO HEAR WHAT SHE HAS TO SAY!
ME, TOO!
WHO ARE YOU?
WHAT ARE YOU?
WHAT ARE YOU DOING HERE?
IS...IS THAT MY SHRINK?
I'VE HAD MANY NAMES. CURRENTLY, I AM REBECCA MOORE. I'M A PSYCHIATRIST HERE IN MANHATTAN. MY TRUE NAME IS MALIA.
I AM NOT SURE WHAT I AM, BUT I WAS BORN THIS WAY.
I CHOSE THIS PLACE TO INTRODUCE MYSELF BECAUSE I HAVE MADE THIS CITY MY HOME...
MALIA
TIME
...FOR THE PAST 300 YEARS.
AROUND 2100 B.C., ON MOUNT IDA, ON THE ISLAND OF CRETE, I--ALONG WITH THREE BROTHERS--WAS BORN WITH SPECIAL ABILITIES. WE WERE CONCEIVED BY A VIRGIN MOTHER WHO WAS HUMAN. OUR FATHER REMAINS A MYSTERY.
BY NOW, YOU HAVE HEARD OF TWO OF MY SIBLINGS--ZAKROS, WHO CONTROLLED WATER, AND KNOSSOS, WHO CONTROLLED EARTH. MY OTHER BROTHER, PHAISTOS, CONTROLLED FIRE.
I CONTROL AIR.
ALONG WITH OUR INDIVIDUAL ABILITIES, WE ALSO POSSESSED INVULNERABILITY, SUPER-STRENGTH AND IMMORTALITY.
I VIEWED OUR WONDERFUL GIFTS AS AN OPPORTUNITY TO BETTER THE WORLD AROUND US...

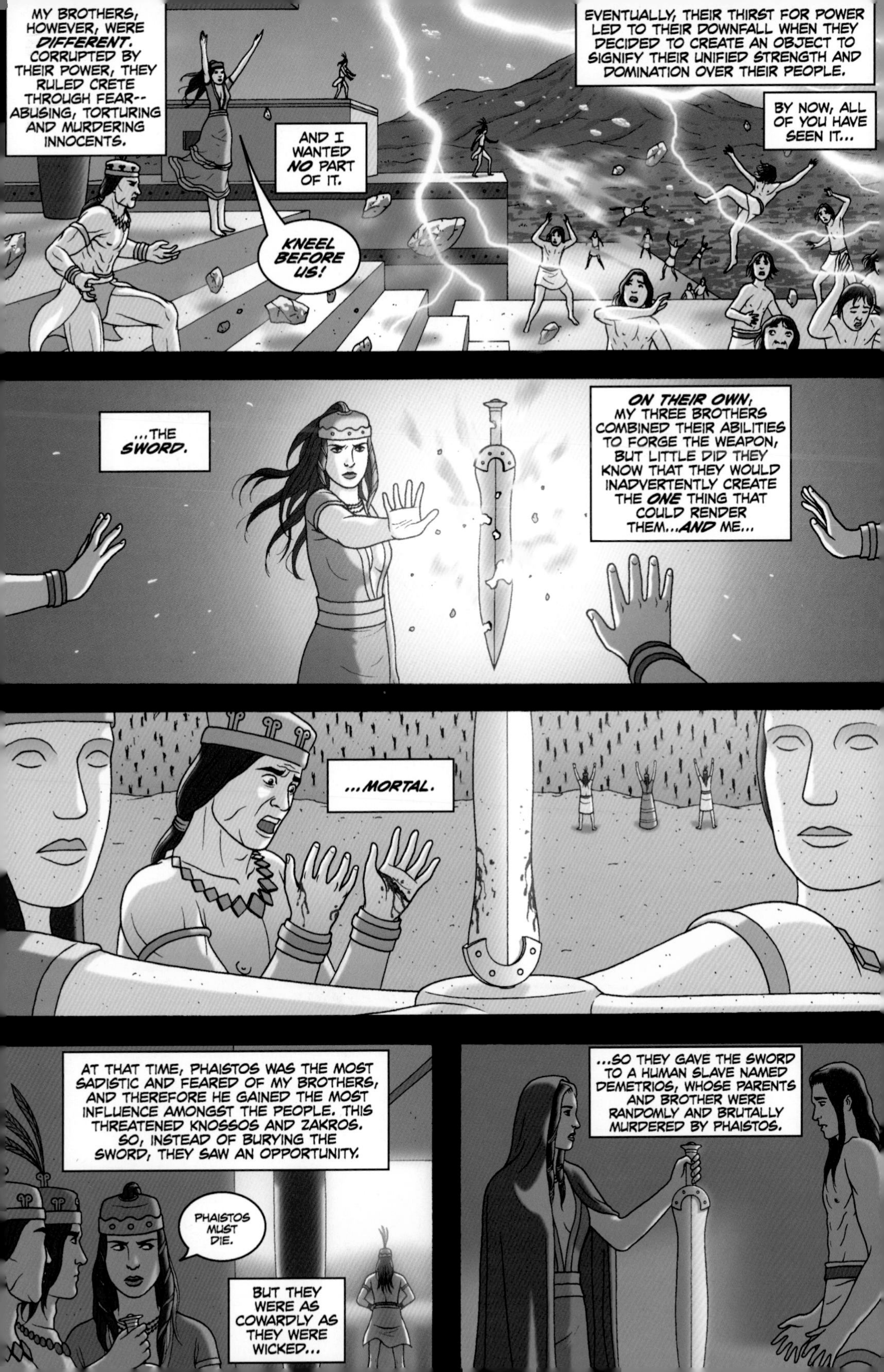
MY BROTHERS, HOWEVER, WERE DIFFERENT. CORRUPTED BY THEIR POWER, THEY RULED CRETE THROUGH FEAR--ABUSING, TORTURING AND MURDERING INNOCENTS.
AND I WANTED NO PART OF IT.
KNEEL BEFORE US!
EVENTUALLY, THEIR THIRST FOR POWER LED TO THEIR DOWNFALL WHEN THEY DECIDED TO CREATE AN OBJECT TO SIGNIFY THEIR UNIFIED STRENGTH AND DOMINATION OVER THEIR PEOPLE.
BY NOW, ALL OF YOU HAVE SEEN IT...
...THE SWORD.
ON THEIR OWN, MY THREE BROTHERS COMBINED THEIR ABILITIES TO FORGE THE WEAPON, BUT LITTLE DID THEY KNOW THAT THEY WOULD INADVERTENTLY CREATE THE ONE THING THAT COULD RENDER THEM...AND ME...
...MORTAL.
AT THAT TIME, PHAISTOS WAS THE MOST SADISTIC AND FEARED OF MY BROTHERS, AND THEREFORE HE GAINED THE MOST INFLUENCE AMONGST THE PEOPLE. THIS THREATENED KNOSSOS AND ZAKROS. SO, INSTEAD OF BURYING THE SWORD, THEY SAW AN OPPORTUNITY.
PHAISTOS MUST DIE.
BUT THEY WERE AS COWARDLY AS THEY WERE WICKED...
...SO THEY GAVE THE SWORD TO A HUMAN SLAVE NAMED DEMETRIOS, WHOSE PARENTS AND BROTHER WERE RANDOMLY AND BRUTALLY MURDERED BY PHAISTOS.

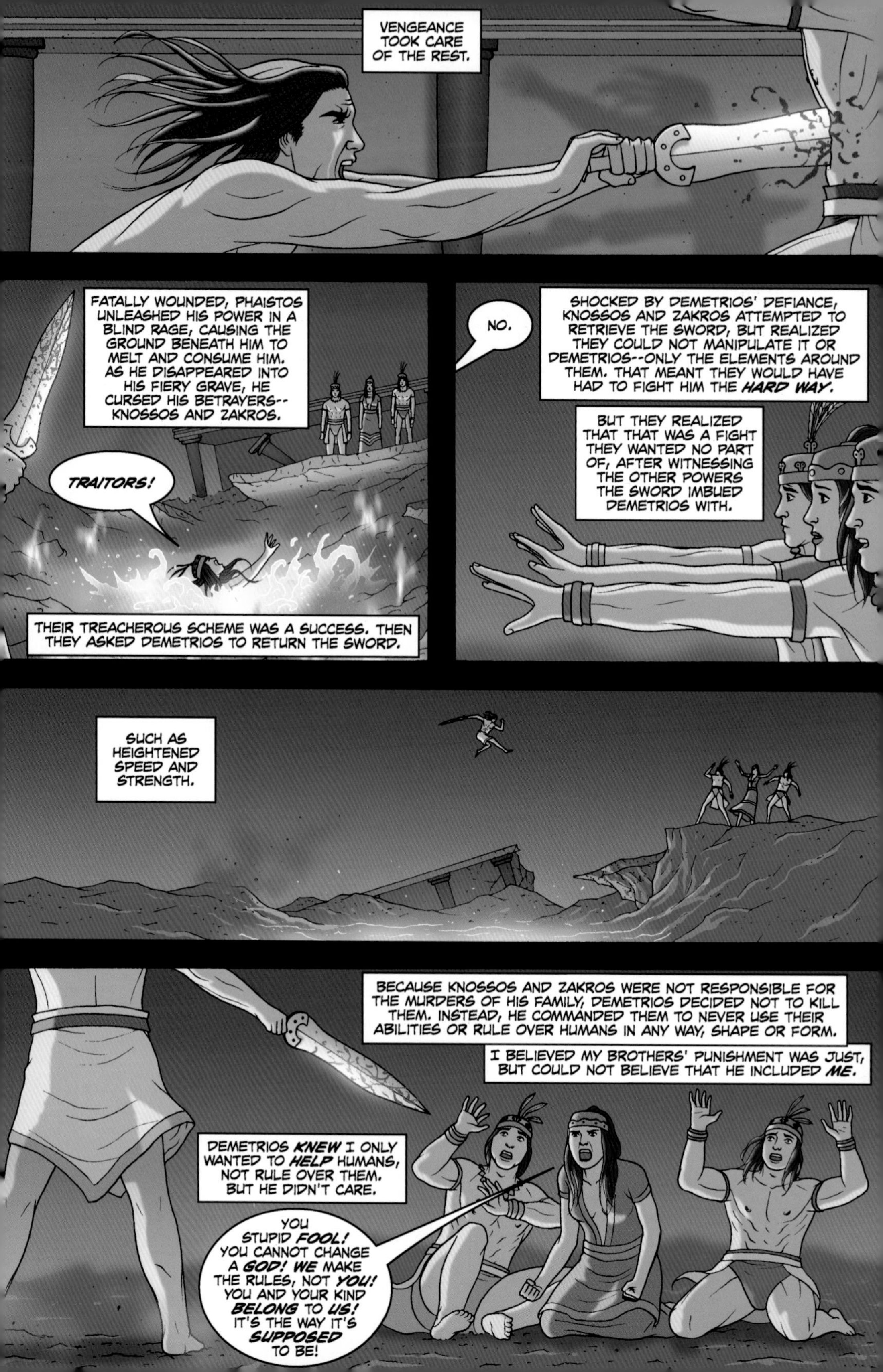
VENGEANCE TOOK CARE OF THE REST.
FATALLY WOUNDED, PHAISTOS UNLEASHED HIS POWER IN A BLIND RAGE, CAUSING THE GROUND BENEATH HIM TO MELT AND CONSUME HIM. AS HE DISAPPEARED INTO HIS FIERY GRAVE, HE CURSED HIS BETRAYERS--KNOSSOS AND ZAKROS.
TRAITORS!
THEIR TREACHEROUS SCHEME WAS A SUCCESS. THEN THEY ASKED DEMETRIOS TO RETURN THE SWORD.
NO.
SHOCKED BY DEMETRIOS' DEFIANCE, KNOSSOS AND ZAKROS ATTEMPTED TO RETRIEVE THE SWORD, BUT REALIZED THEY COULD NOT MANIPULATE IT OR DEMETRIOS--ONLY THE ELEMENTS AROUND THEM. THAT MEANT THEY WOULD HAVE HAD TO FIGHT HIM THE HARD WAY.
BUT THEY REALIZED THAT THAT WAS A FIGHT THEY WANTED NO PART OF, AFTER WITNESSING THE OTHER POWERS THE SWORD IMBUED DEMETRIOS WITH.
SUCH AS HEIGHTENED SPEED AND STRENGTH.
BECAUSE KNOSSOS AND ZAKROS WERE NOT RESPONSIBLE FOR THE MURDERS OF HIS FAMILY, DEMETRIOS DECIDED NOT TO KILL THEM. INSTEAD, HE COMMANDED THEM TO NEVER USE THEIR ABILITIES OR RULE OVER HUMANS IN ANY WAY, SHAPE OR FORM.
I BELIEVED MY BROTHERS' PUNISHMENT WAS JUST, BUT COULD NOT BELIEVE THAT HE INCLUDED ME.
DEMETRIOS KNEW I ONLY WANTED TO HELP HUMANS, NOT RULE OVER THEM. BUT HE DIDN'T CARE.
YOU STUPID FOOL! YOU CANNOT CHANGE A GOD! WE MAKE THE RULES, NOT YOU! YOU AND YOUR KIND BELONG TO US! IT'S THE WAY IT'S SUPPOSED TO BE!

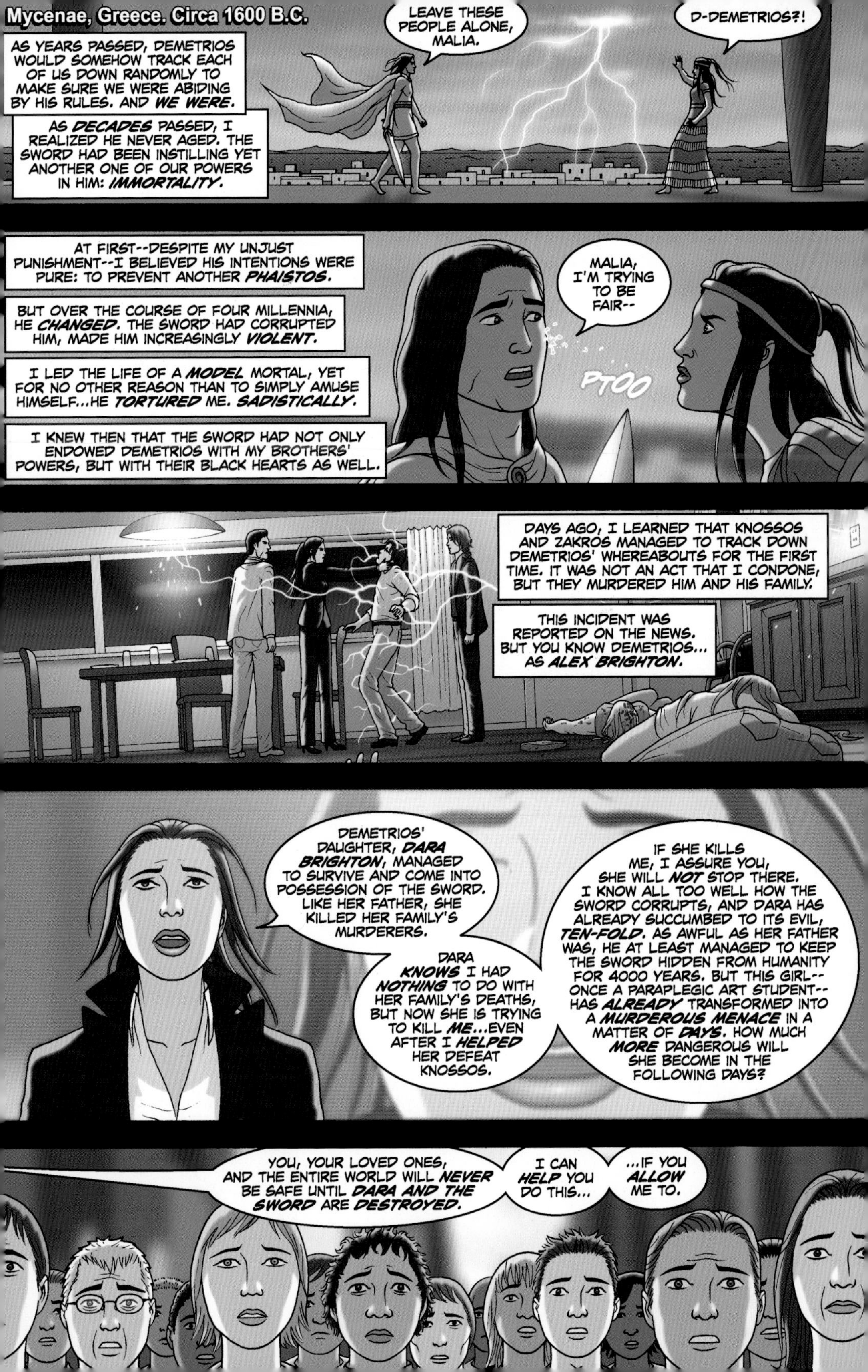

Mycenae, Greece. Circa 1600 B.C.
AS YEARS PASSED, DEMETRIOS WOULD SOMEHOW TRACK EACH OF US DOWN RANDOMLY TO MAKE SURE WE WERE ABIDING BY HIS RULES. AND WE WERE.
AS DECADES PASSED, I REALIZED HE NEVER AGED. THE SWORD HAD BEEN INSTILLING YET ANOTHER ONE OF OUR POWERS IN HIM: IMMORTALITY.
LEAVE THESE PEOPLE ALONE, MALIA.
D-DEMETRIOS?!
AT FIRST--DESPITE MY UNJUST PUNISHMENT--I BELIEVED HIS INTENTIONS WERE PURE: TO PREVENT ANOTHER PHAISTOS.
BUT OVER THE COURSE OF FOUR MILLENNIA, HE CHANGED. THE SWORD HAD CORRUPTED HIM, MADE HIM INCREASINGLY VIOLENT.
I LED THE LIFE OF A MODEL MORTAL, YET FOR NO OTHER REASON THAN TO SIMPLY AMUSE HIMSELF...HE TORTURED ME. SADISTICALLY.
I KNEW THEN THAT THE SWORD HAD NOT ONLY ENDOWED DEMETRIOS WITH MY BROTHERS' POWERS, BUT WITH THEIR BLACK HEARTS AS WELL.
MALIA, I'M TRYING TO BE FAIR--
PTOO
DAYS AGO, I LEARNED THAT KNOSSOS AND ZAKROS MANAGED TO TRACK DOWN DEMETRIOS' WHEREABOUTS FOR THE FIRST TIME. IT WAS NOT AN ACT THAT I CONDONE, BUT THEY MURDERED HIM AND HIS FAMILY.
THIS INCIDENT WAS REPORTED ON THE NEWS. BUT YOU KNOW DEMETRIOS... AS ALEX BRIGHTON.
DEMETRIOS' DAUGHTER, DARA BRIGHTON, MANAGED TO SURVIVE AND COME INTO POSSESSION OF THE SWORD. LIKE HER FATHER, SHE KILLED HER FAMILY'S MURDERERS.
DARA KNOWS I HAD NOTHING TO DO WITH HER FAMILY'S DEATHS, BUT NOW SHE IS TRYING TO KILL ME...EVEN AFTER I HELPED HER DEFEAT KNOSSOS.
IF SHE KILLS ME, I ASSURE YOU, SHE WILL NOT STOP THERE. I KNOW ALL TOO WELL HOW THE SWORD CORRUPTS, AND DARA HAS ALREADY SUCCUMBED TO ITS EVIL, TEN-FOLD. AS AWFUL AS HER FATHER WAS, HE AT LEAST MANAGED TO KEEP THE SWORD HIDDEN FROM HUMANITY FOR 4000 YEARS. BUT THIS GIRL--ONCE A PARAPLEGIC ART STUDENT--HAS ALREADY TRANSFORMED INTO A MURDEROUS MENACE IN A MATTER OF DAYS. HOW MUCH MORE DANGEROUS WILL SHE BECOME IN THE FOLLOWING DAYS?
YOU, YOUR LOVED ONES, AND THE ENTIRE WORLD WILL NEVER BE SAFE UNTIL DARA AND THE SWORD ARE DESTROYED.
I CAN HELP YOU DO THIS...
...IF YOU ALLOW ME TO.

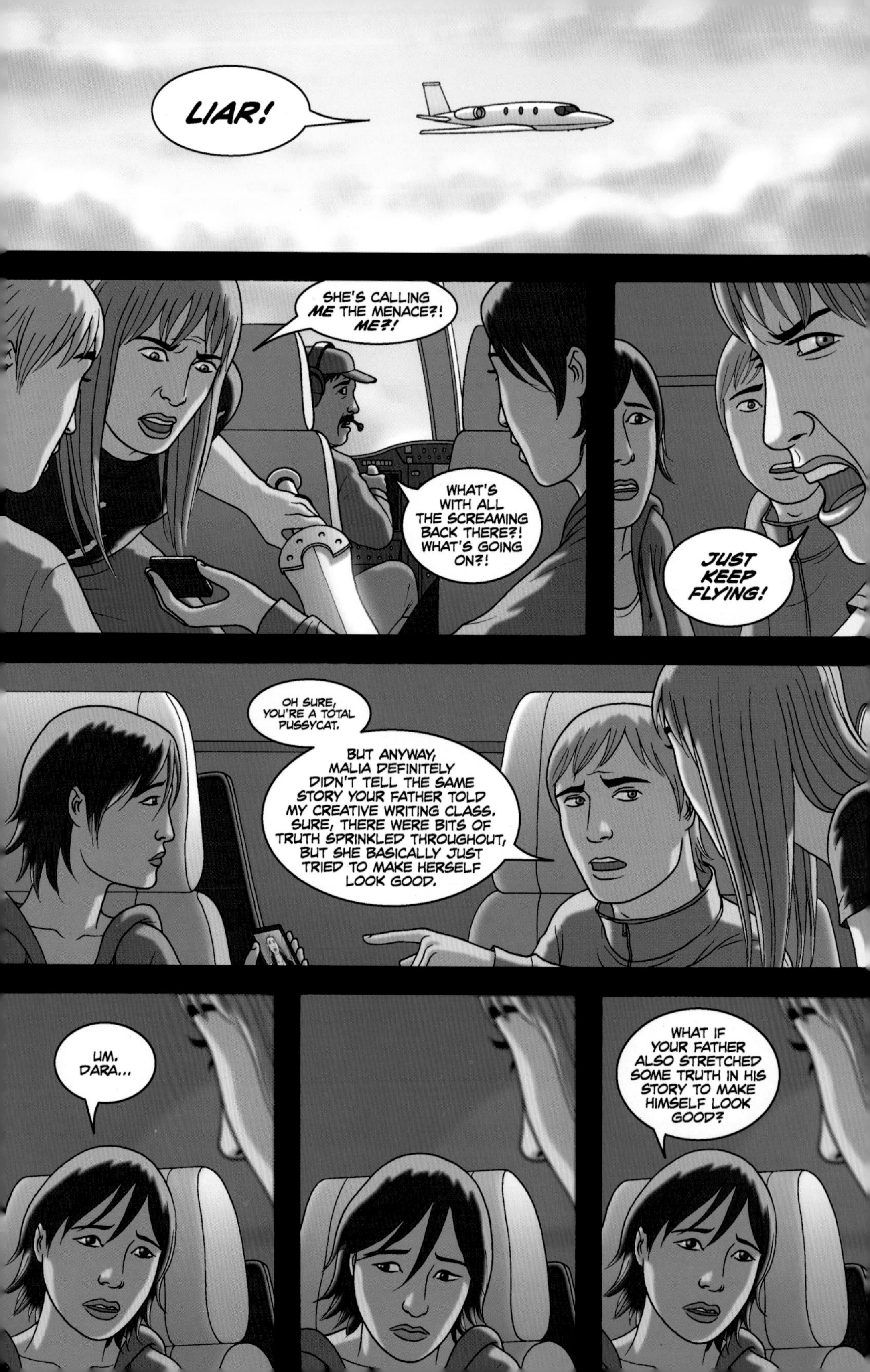
LIAR!
SHE'S CALLING ME THE MENACE?! ME?!
WHAT'S WITH ALL THE SCREAMING BACK THERE?! WHAT'S GOING ON?!
JUST KEEP FLYING!
OH SURE, YOU'RE A TOTAL PUSSYCAT.
BUT ANYWAY, MALIA DEFINITELY DIDN'T TELL THE SAME STORY YOUR FATHER TOLD MY CREATIVE WRITING CLASS. SURE, THERE WERE BITS OF TRUTH SPRINKLED THROUGHOUT, BUT SHE BASICALLY JUST TRIED TO MAKE HERSELF LOOK GOOD.
UM. DARA...
WHAT IF YOUR FATHER ALSO STRETCHED SOME TRUTH IN HIS STORY TO MAKE HIMSELF LOOK GOOD?

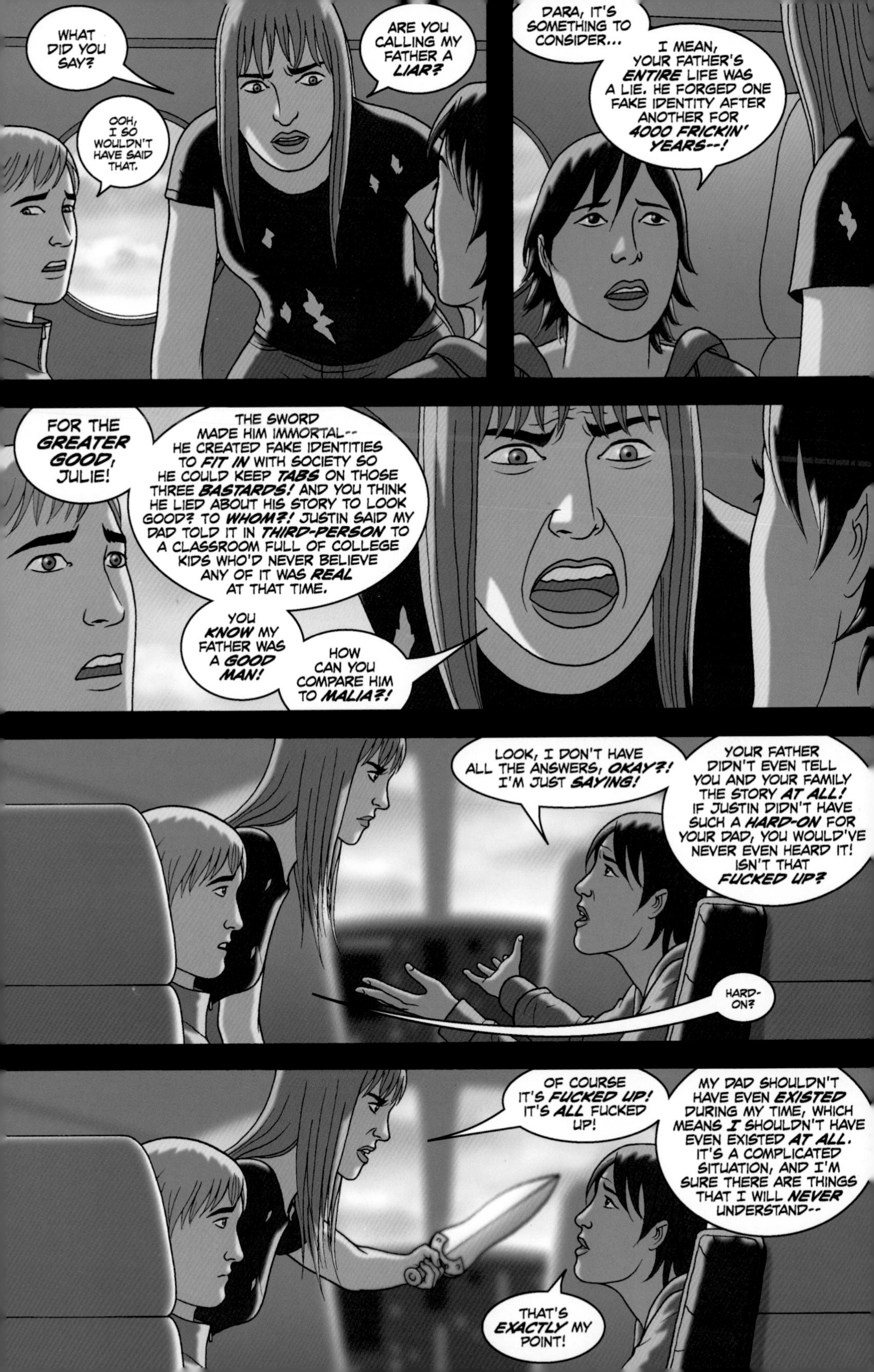
WHAT DID YOU SAY?
OOH, I SO WOULDN'T HAVE SAID THAT.
ARE YOU CALLING MY FATHER A *LIAR?*
DARA, IT'S SOMETHING TO CONSIDER...
I MEAN, YOUR FATHER'S *ENTIRE* LIFE WAS A LIE. HE FORGED ONE FAKE IDENTITY AFTER ANOTHER FOR *4000 FRICKIN' YEARS--!*
FOR THE *GREATER GOOD*, JULIE!
THE SWORD MADE HIM IMMORTAL-- HE CREATED FAKE IDENTITIES TO *FIT IN* WITH SOCIETY SO HE COULD KEEP *TABS* ON THOSE THREE *BASTARDS!* AND YOU THINK HE LIED ABOUT HIS STORY TO LOOK GOOD? TO *WHOM?!* JUSTIN SAID MY DAD TOLD IT IN *THIRD-PERSON* TO A CLASSROOM FULL OF COLLEGE KIDS WHO'D NEVER BELIEVE ANY OF IT WAS *REAL* AT THAT TIME.
YOU *KNOW* MY FATHER WAS A *GOOD MAN!*
HOW CAN YOU COMPARE HIM TO *MALIA?!*
LOOK, I DON'T HAVE ALL THE ANSWERS, *OKAY?!* I'M JUST *SAYING!*
YOUR FATHER DIDN'T EVEN TELL YOU AND YOUR FAMILY THE STORY *AT ALL!* IF JUSTIN DIDN'T HAVE SUCH A *HARD-ON* FOR YOUR DAD, YOU WOULD'VE NEVER EVEN HEARD IT! ISN'T THAT *FUCKED UP?*
HARD-ON?
OF COURSE IT'S *FUCKED UP!* IT'S *ALL* FUCKED UP!
MY DAD SHOULDN'T HAVE EVEN *EXISTED* DURING MY TIME, WHICH MEANS *I* SHOULDN'T HAVE EVEN EXISTED *AT ALL.* IT'S A COMPLICATED SITUATION, AND I'M SURE THERE ARE THINGS THAT I WILL *NEVER* UNDERSTAND--
THAT'S *EXACTLY* MY POINT!

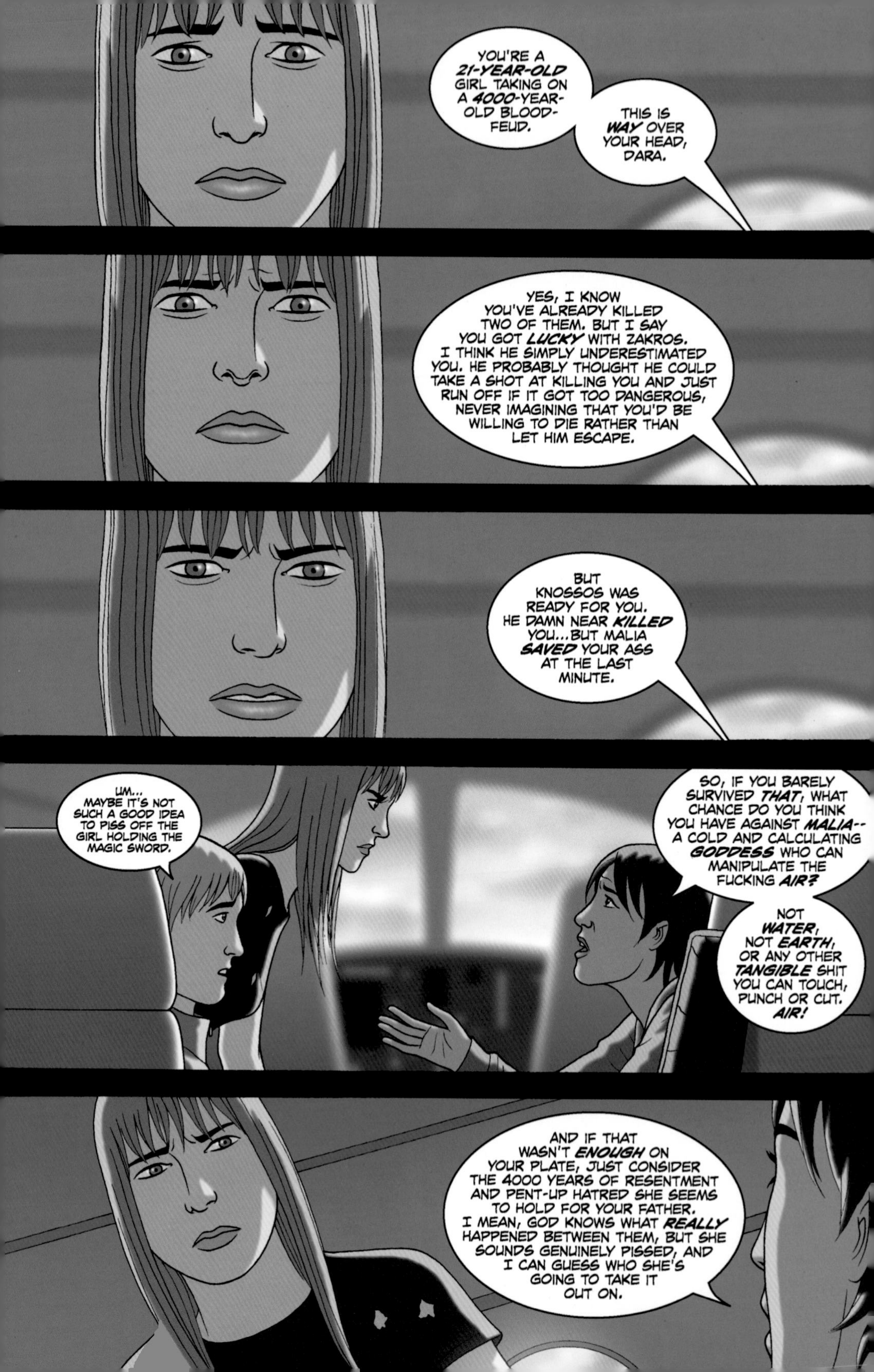
YOU'RE A 21-YEAR-OLD GIRL TAKING ON A 4000-YEAR-OLD BLOOD-FEUD.
THIS IS WAY OVER YOUR HEAD, DARA.
YES, I KNOW YOU'VE ALREADY KILLED TWO OF THEM. BUT I SAY YOU GOT LUCKY WITH ZAKROS. I THINK HE SIMPLY UNDERESTIMATED YOU. HE PROBABLY THOUGHT HE COULD TAKE A SHOT AT KILLING YOU AND JUST RUN OFF IF IT GOT TOO DANGEROUS, NEVER IMAGINING THAT YOU'D BE WILLING TO DIE RATHER THAN LET HIM ESCAPE.
BUT KNOSSOS WAS READY FOR YOU. HE DAMN NEAR KILLED YOU...BUT MALIA SAVED YOUR ASS AT THE LAST MINUTE.
SO, IF YOU BARELY SURVIVED THAT, WHAT CHANCE DO YOU THINK YOU HAVE AGAINST MALIA-- A COLD AND CALCULATING GODDESS WHO CAN MANIPULATE THE FUCKING AIR?
NOT WATER, NOT EARTH, OR ANY OTHER TANGIBLE SHIT YOU CAN TOUCH, PUNCH OR CUT. AIR!
UM... MAYBE IT'S NOT SUCH A GOOD IDEA TO PISS OFF THE GIRL HOLDING THE MAGIC SWORD.
AND IF THAT WASN'T ENOUGH ON YOUR PLATE, JUST CONSIDER THE 4000 YEARS OF RESENTMENT AND PENT-UP HATRED SHE SEEMS TO HOLD FOR YOUR FATHER. I MEAN, GOD KNOWS WHAT REALLY HAPPENED BETWEEN THEM, BUT SHE SOUNDS GENUINELY PISSED, AND I CAN GUESS WHO SHE'S GOING TO TAKE IT OUT ON.

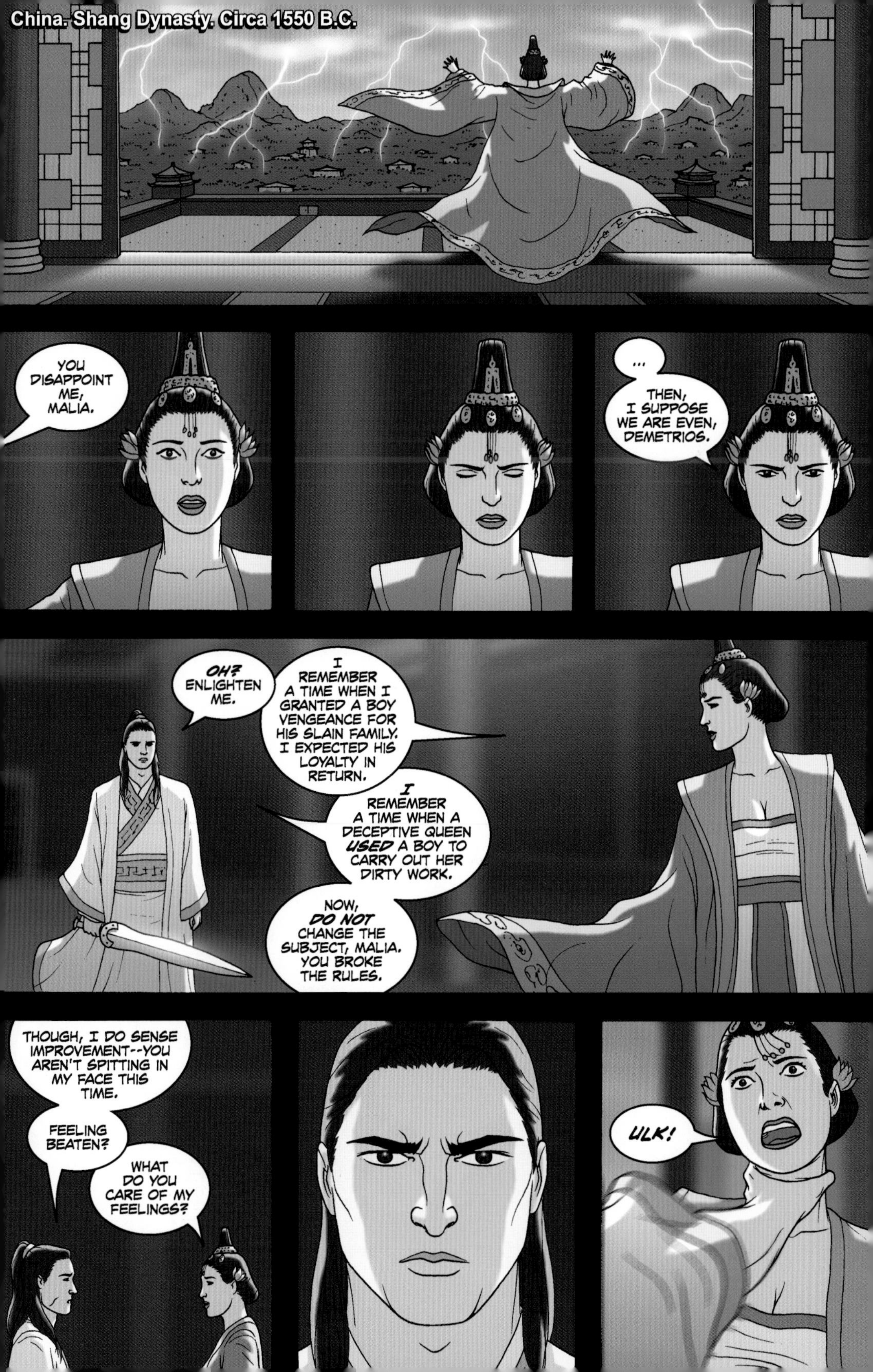
China. Shang Dynasty. Circa 1550 B.C.
YOU DISAPPOINT ME, MALIA.
...
THEN, I SUPPOSE WE ARE EVEN, DEMETRIOS.
OH? ENLIGHTEN ME.
I REMEMBER A TIME WHEN I GRANTED A BOY VENGEANCE FOR HIS SLAIN FAMILY. I EXPECTED HIS LOYALTY IN RETURN.
I REMEMBER A TIME WHEN A DECEPTIVE QUEEN USED A BOY TO CARRY OUT HER DIRTY WORK.
NOW, DO NOT CHANGE THE SUBJECT, MALIA. YOU BROKE THE RULES.
THOUGH, I DO SENSE IMPROVEMENT--YOU AREN'T SPITTING IN MY FACE THIS TIME.
FEELING BEATEN?
WHAT DO YOU CARE OF MY FEELINGS?
ULK!

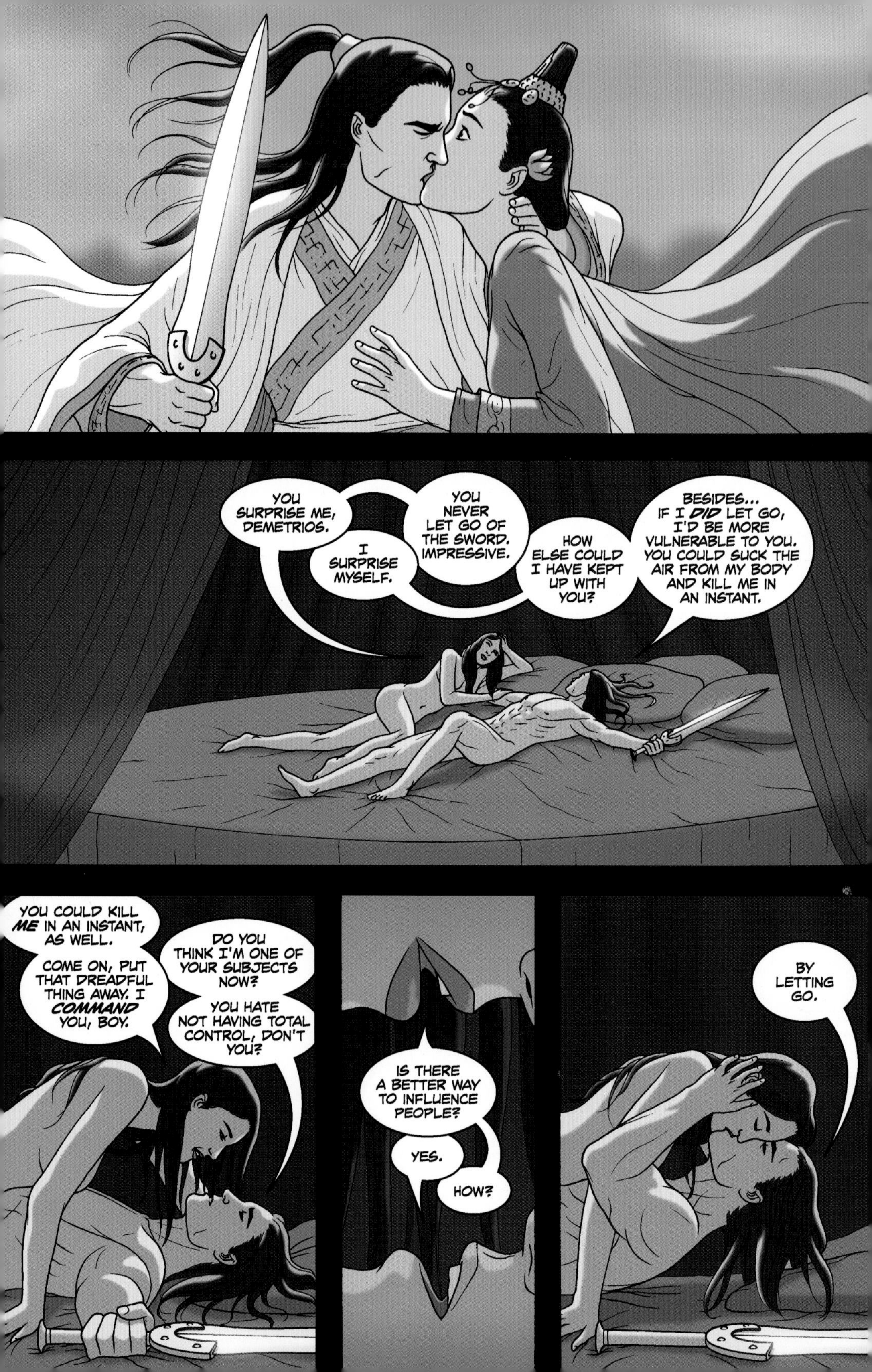

YOU SURPRISE ME, DEMETRIOS.
I SURPRISE MYSELF.
YOU NEVER LET GO OF THE SWORD. IMPRESSIVE.
HOW ELSE COULD I HAVE KEPT UP WITH YOU?
BESIDES... IF I DID LET GO, I'D BE MORE VULNERABLE TO YOU. YOU COULD SUCK THE AIR FROM MY BODY AND KILL ME IN AN INSTANT.
YOU COULD KILL ME IN AN INSTANT, AS WELL.
COME ON, PUT THAT DREADFUL THING AWAY. I COMMAND YOU, BOY.
DO YOU THINK I'M ONE OF YOUR SUBJECTS NOW?
YOU HATE NOT HAVING TOTAL CONTROL, DON'T YOU?
IS THERE A BETTER WAY TO INFLUENCE PEOPLE?
YES.
HOW?
BY LETTING GO.

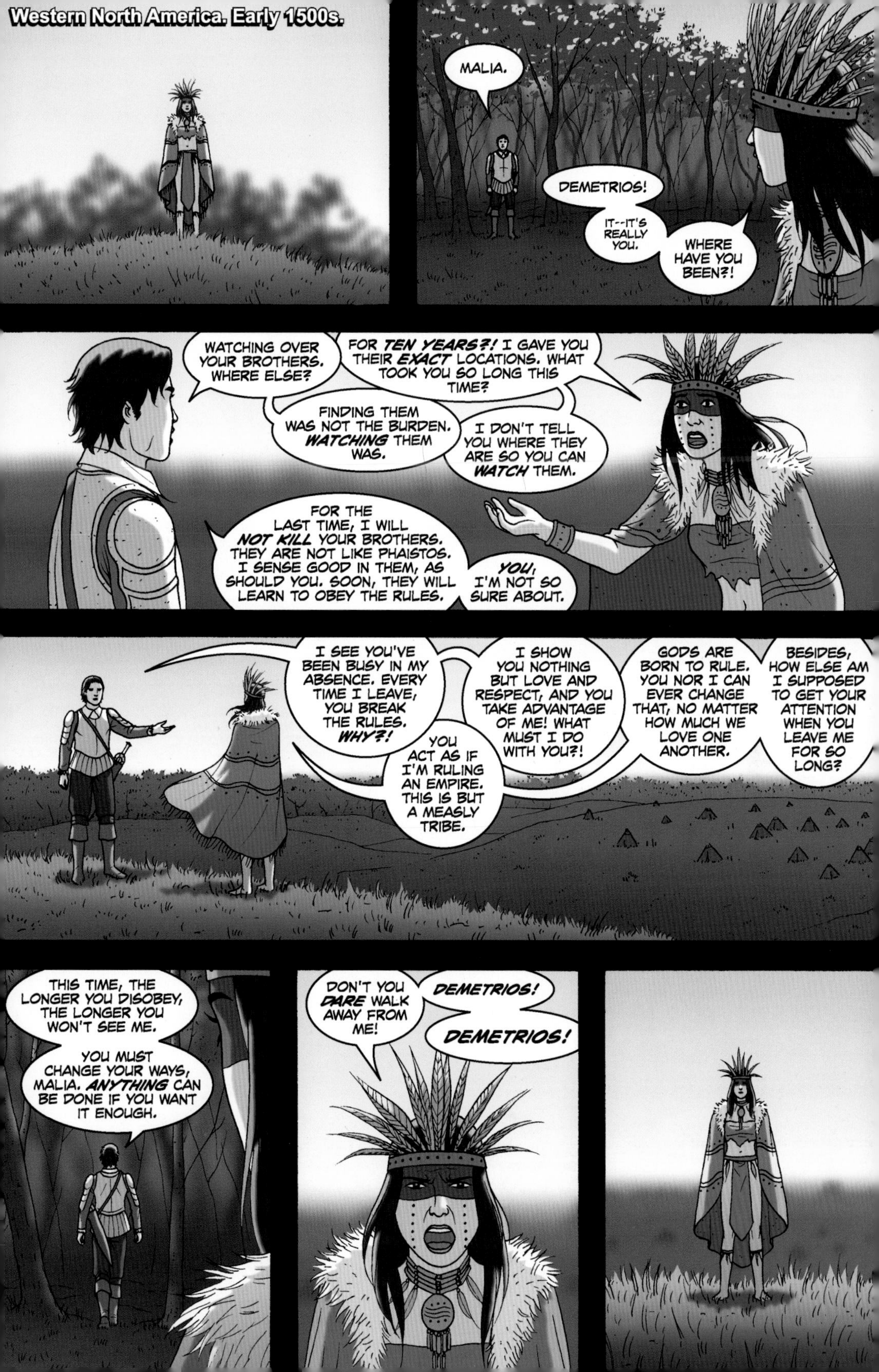
Western North America. Early 1500s.
MALIA.
DEMETRIOS!
IT--IT'S REALLY YOU.
WHERE HAVE YOU BEEN?!
WATCHING OVER YOUR BROTHERS. WHERE ELSE?
FOR *TEN YEARS?!* I GAVE YOU THEIR *EXACT* LOCATIONS. WHAT TOOK YOU SO LONG THIS TIME?
FINDING THEM WAS NOT THE BURDEN. *WATCHING* THEM WAS.
I DON'T TELL YOU WHERE THEY ARE SO YOU CAN *WATCH* THEM.
FOR THE LAST TIME, I WILL *NOT KILL* YOUR BROTHERS. THEY ARE NOT LIKE PHAISTOS. I SENSE GOOD IN THEM, AS SHOULD YOU. SOON, THEY WILL LEARN TO OBEY THE RULES.
YOU, I'M NOT SO SURE ABOUT.
I SEE YOU'VE BEEN BUSY IN MY ABSENCE. EVERY TIME I LEAVE, YOU BREAK THE RULES. *WHY?!*
YOU ACT AS IF I'M RULING AN EMPIRE. THIS IS BUT A MEASLY TRIBE.
I SHOW YOU NOTHING BUT LOVE AND RESPECT, AND YOU TAKE ADVANTAGE OF ME! WHAT MUST I DO WITH YOU?!
GODS ARE BORN TO RULE. YOU NOR I CAN EVER CHANGE THAT, NO MATTER HOW MUCH WE LOVE ONE ANOTHER.
BESIDES, HOW ELSE AM I SUPPOSED TO GET YOUR ATTENTION WHEN YOU LEAVE ME FOR SO LONG?
THIS TIME, THE LONGER YOU DISOBEY, THE LONGER YOU WON'T SEE ME.
YOU MUST CHANGE YOUR WAYS, MALIA. *ANYTHING* CAN BE DONE IF YOU WANT IT ENOUGH.
DON'T YOU *DARE* WALK AWAY FROM ME!
DEMETRIOS!
DEMETRIOS!

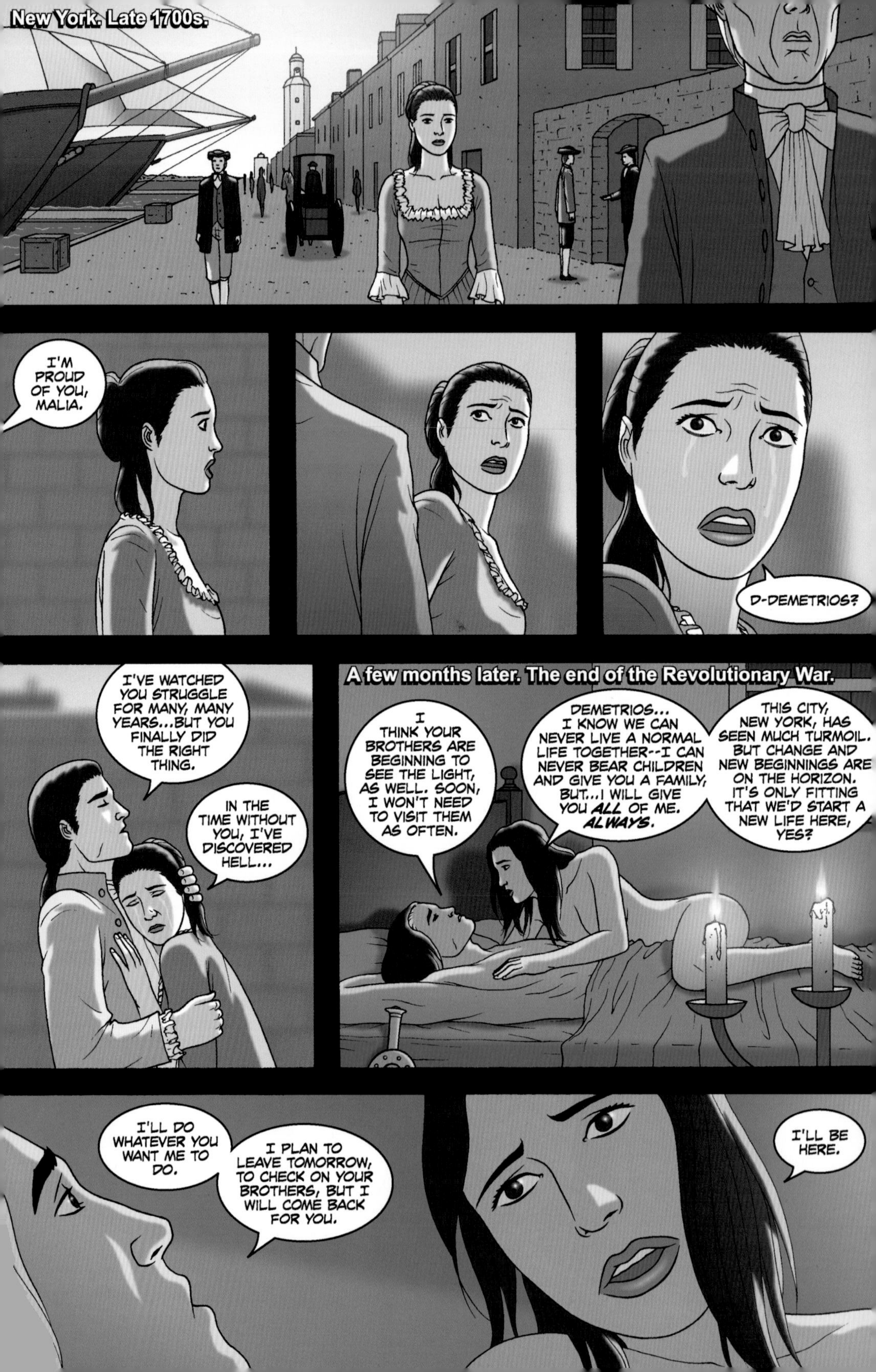
New York. Late 1700s.
I'M PROUD OF YOU, MALIA.
D-DEMETRIOS?
I'VE WATCHED YOU STRUGGLE FOR MANY, MANY YEARS...BUT YOU FINALLY DID THE RIGHT THING.
IN THE TIME WITHOUT YOU, I'VE DISCOVERED HELL...
A few months later. The end of the Revolutionary War.
I THINK YOUR BROTHERS ARE BEGINNING TO SEE THE LIGHT, AS WELL. SOON, I WON'T NEED TO VISIT THEM AS OFTEN.
DEMETRIOS... I KNOW WE CAN NEVER LIVE A NORMAL LIFE TOGETHER--I CAN NEVER BEAR CHILDREN AND GIVE YOU A FAMILY, BUT...I WILL GIVE YOU ALL OF ME. ALWAYS.
THIS CITY, NEW YORK, HAS SEEN MUCH TURMOIL. BUT CHANGE AND NEW BEGINNINGS ARE ON THE HORIZON. IT'S ONLY FITTING THAT WE'D START A NEW LIFE HERE, YES?
I'LL DO WHATEVER YOU WANT ME TO DO.
I PLAN TO LEAVE TOMORROW, TO CHECK ON YOUR BROTHERS, BUT I WILL COME BACK FOR YOU.
I'LL BE HERE.

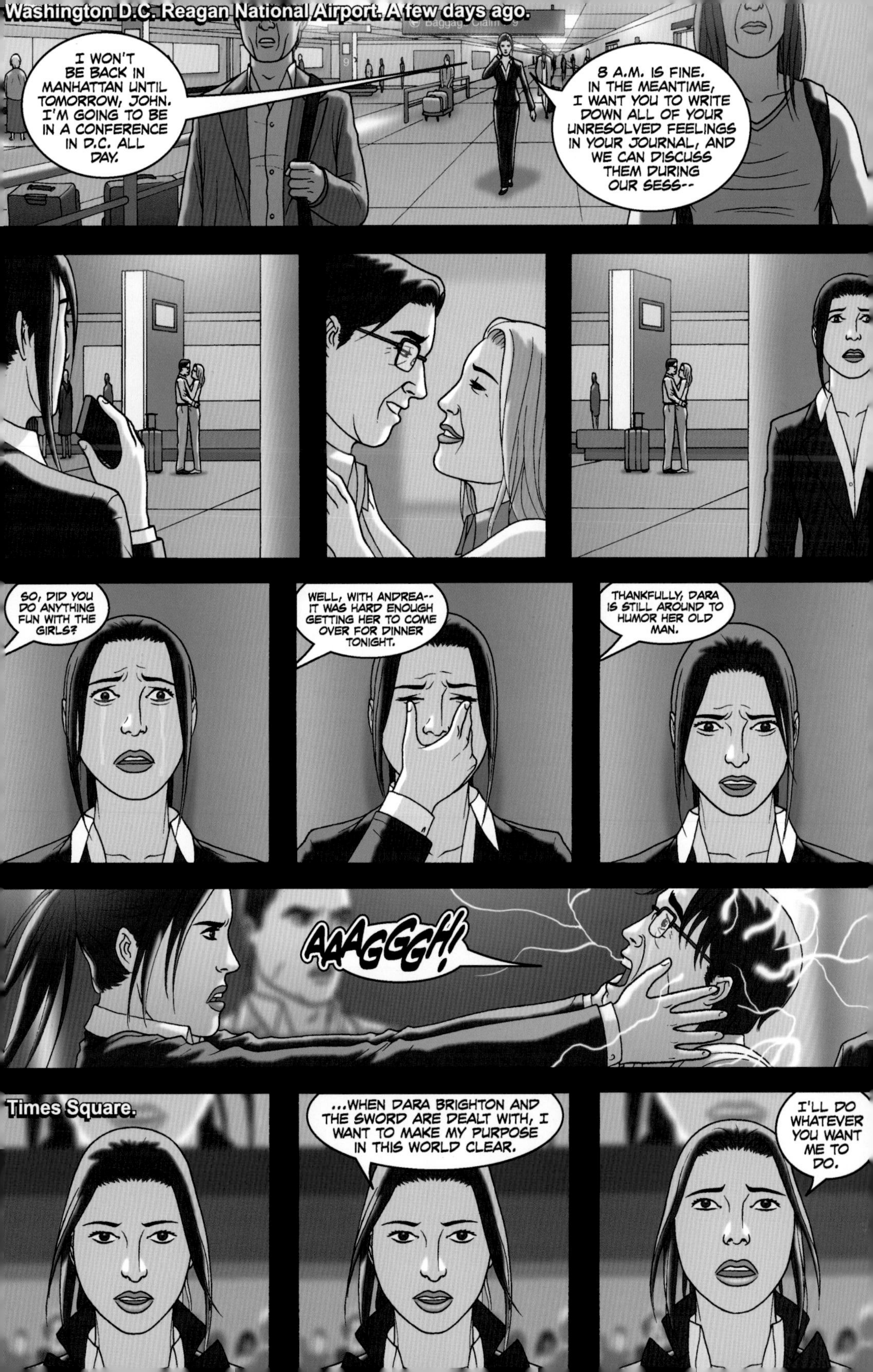
Washington D.C. Reagan National Airport. A few days ago.
I WON'T BE BACK IN MANHATTAN UNTIL TOMORROW, JOHN. I'M GOING TO BE IN A CONFERENCE IN D.C. ALL DAY.
8 A.M. IS FINE. IN THE MEANTIME, I WANT YOU TO WRITE DOWN ALL OF YOUR UNRESOLVED FEELINGS IN YOUR JOURNAL, AND WE CAN DISCUSS THEM DURING OUR SESS--
SO, DID YOU DO ANYTHING FUN WITH THE GIRLS?
WELL, WITH ANDREA-- IT WAS HARD ENOUGH GETTING HER TO COME OVER FOR DINNER TONIGHT.
THANKFULLY, DARA IS STILL AROUND TO HUMOR HER OLD MAN.
AAAGGGH!
Times Square.
...WHEN DARA BRIGHTON AND THE SWORD ARE DEALT WITH, I WANT TO MAKE MY PURPOSE IN THIS WORLD CLEAR.
I'LL DO WHATEVER YOU WANT ME TO DO.

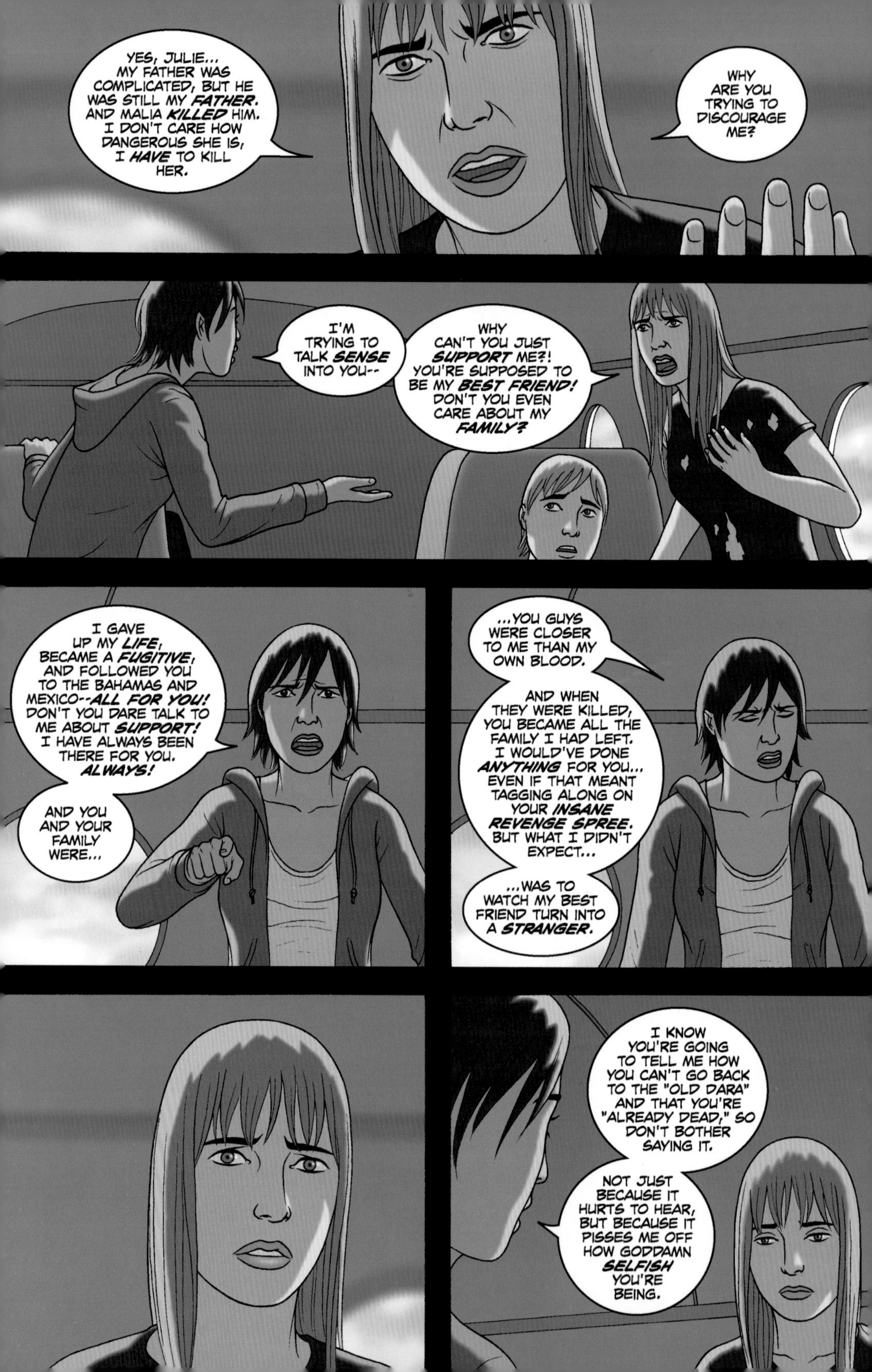
YES, JULIE... MY FATHER WAS COMPLICATED, BUT HE WAS STILL MY FATHER. AND MALIA KILLED HIM. I DON'T CARE HOW DANGEROUS SHE IS, I HAVE TO KILL HER.
WHY ARE YOU TRYING TO DISCOURAGE ME?
I'M TRYING TO TALK SENSE INTO YOU--
WHY CAN'T YOU JUST SUPPORT ME?! YOU'RE SUPPOSED TO BE MY BEST FRIEND! DON'T YOU EVEN CARE ABOUT MY FAMILY?
I GAVE UP MY LIFE, BECAME A FUGITIVE, AND FOLLOWED YOU TO THE BAHAMAS AND MEXICO--ALL FOR YOU! DON'T YOU DARE TALK TO ME ABOUT SUPPORT! I HAVE ALWAYS BEEN THERE FOR YOU. ALWAYS!
AND YOU AND YOUR FAMILY WERE...
...YOU GUYS WERE CLOSER TO ME THAN MY OWN BLOOD.
AND WHEN THEY WERE KILLED, YOU BECAME ALL THE FAMILY I HAD LEFT. I WOULD'VE DONE ANYTHING FOR YOU... EVEN IF THAT MEANT TAGGING ALONG ON YOUR INSANE REVENGE SPREE. BUT WHAT I DIDN'T EXPECT...
...WAS TO WATCH MY BEST FRIEND TURN INTO A STRANGER.
I KNOW YOU'RE GOING TO TELL ME HOW YOU CAN'T GO BACK TO THE "OLD DARA" AND THAT YOU'RE "ALREADY DEAD," SO DON'T BOTHER SAYING IT.
NOT JUST BECAUSE IT HURTS TO HEAR, BUT BECAUSE IT PISSES ME OFF HOW GODDAMN SELFISH YOU'RE BEING.

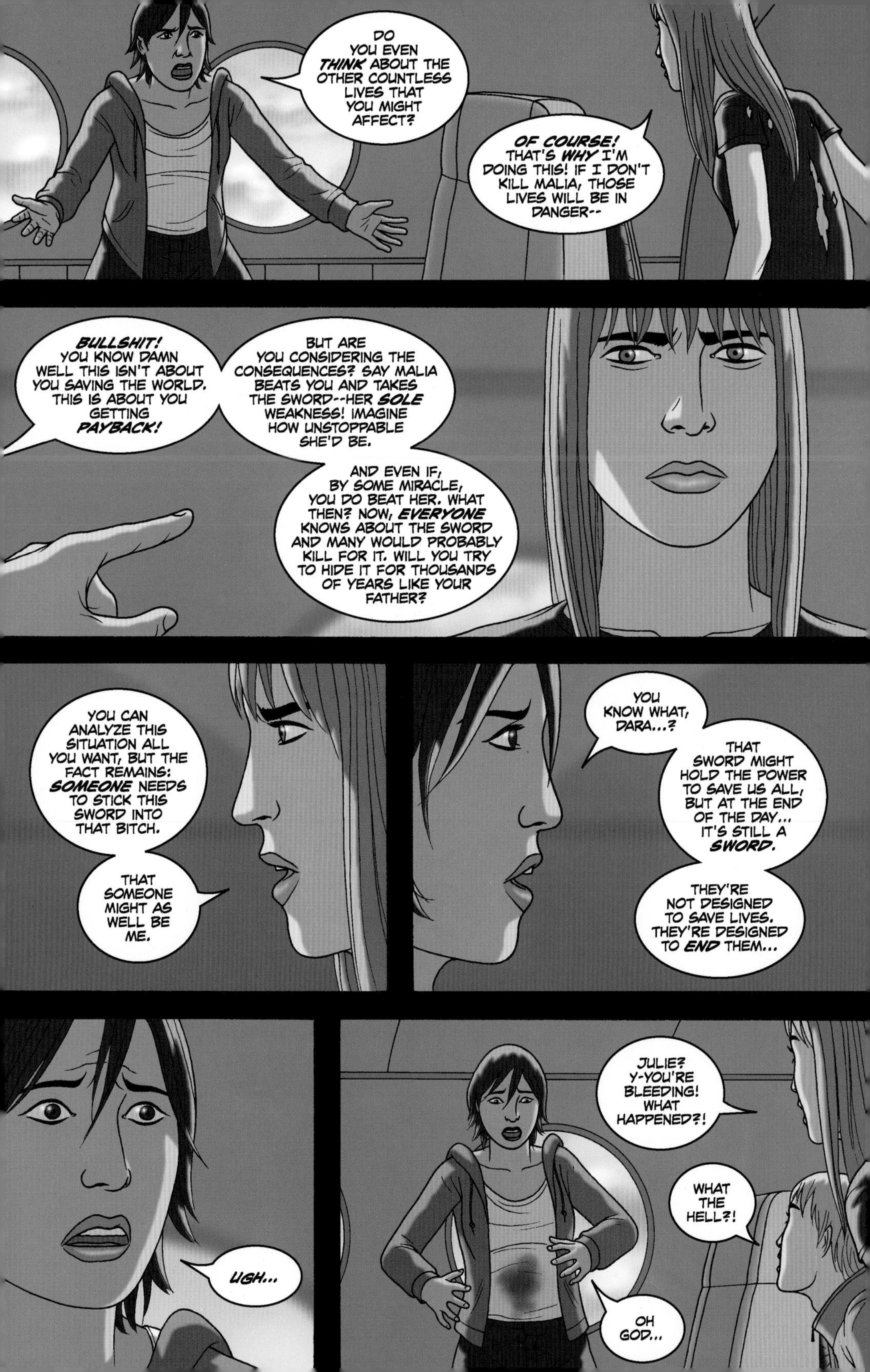
DO YOU EVEN THINK ABOUT THE OTHER COUNTLESS LIVES THAT YOU MIGHT AFFECT?
OF COURSE! THAT'S WHY I'M DOING THIS! IF I DON'T KILL MALIA, THOSE LIVES WILL BE IN DANGER--
BULLSHIT! YOU KNOW DAMN WELL THIS ISN'T ABOUT YOU SAVING THE WORLD. THIS IS ABOUT YOU GETTING PAYBACK!
BUT ARE YOU CONSIDERING THE CONSEQUENCES? SAY MALIA BEATS YOU AND TAKES THE SWORD--HER SOLE WEAKNESS! IMAGINE HOW UNSTOPPABLE SHE'D BE.
AND EVEN IF, BY SOME MIRACLE, YOU DO BEAT HER. WHAT THEN? NOW, EVERYONE KNOWS ABOUT THE SWORD AND MANY WOULD PROBABLY KILL FOR IT. WILL YOU TRY TO HIDE IT FOR THOUSANDS OF YEARS LIKE YOUR FATHER?
YOU CAN ANALYZE THIS SITUATION ALL YOU WANT, BUT THE FACT REMAINS: SOMEONE NEEDS TO STICK THIS SWORD INTO THAT BITCH.
THAT SOMEONE MIGHT AS WELL BE ME.
YOU KNOW WHAT, DARA...?
THAT SWORD MIGHT HOLD THE POWER TO SAVE US ALL, BUT AT THE END OF THE DAY... IT'S STILL A SWORD.
THEY'RE NOT DESIGNED TO SAVE LIVES. THEY'RE DESIGNED TO END THEM...
UGH...
JULIE? Y-YOU'RE BLEEDING! WHAT HAPPENED?!
WHAT THE HELL?!
OH GOD...

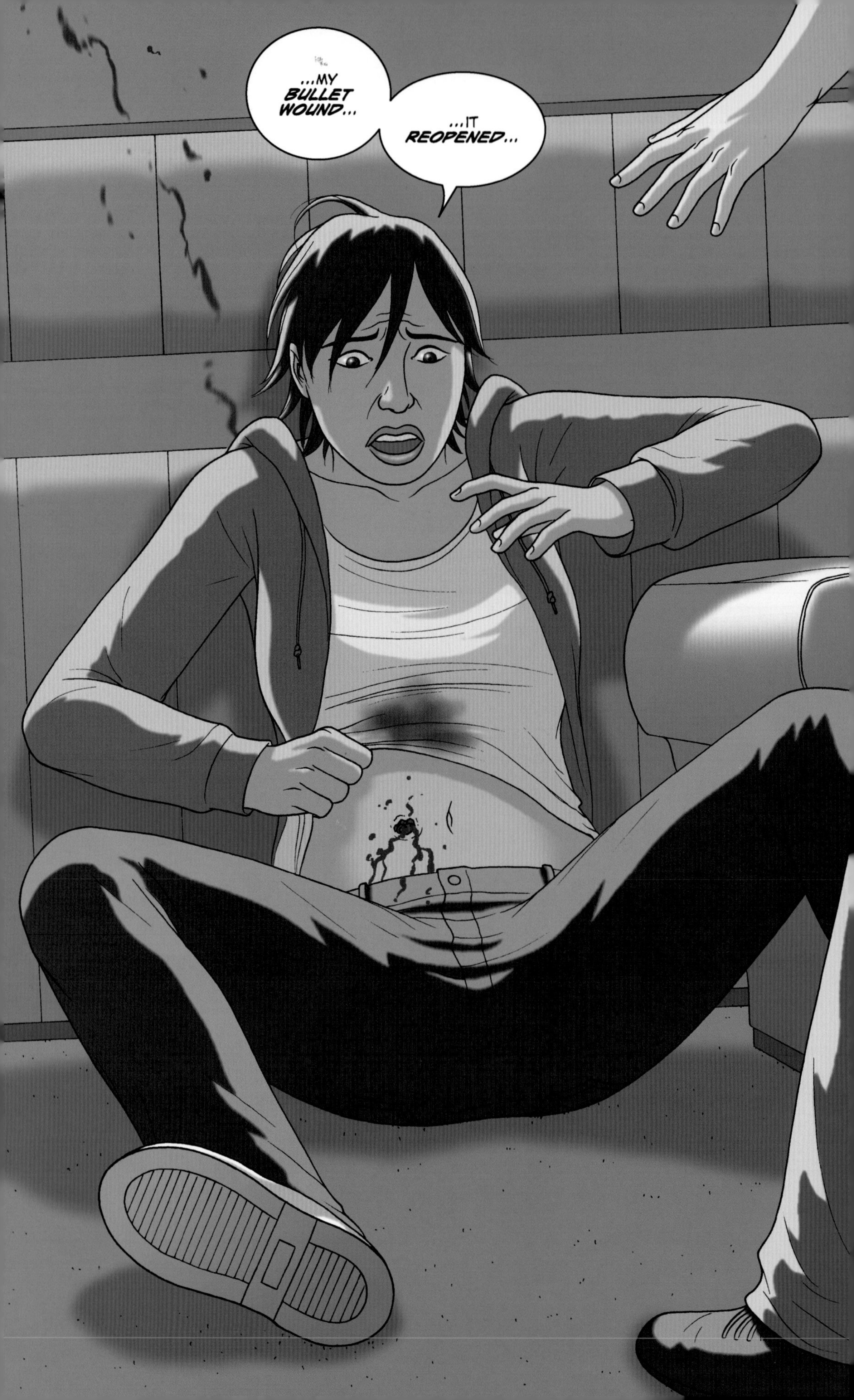
...MY BULLET WOUND...
...IT REOPENED...

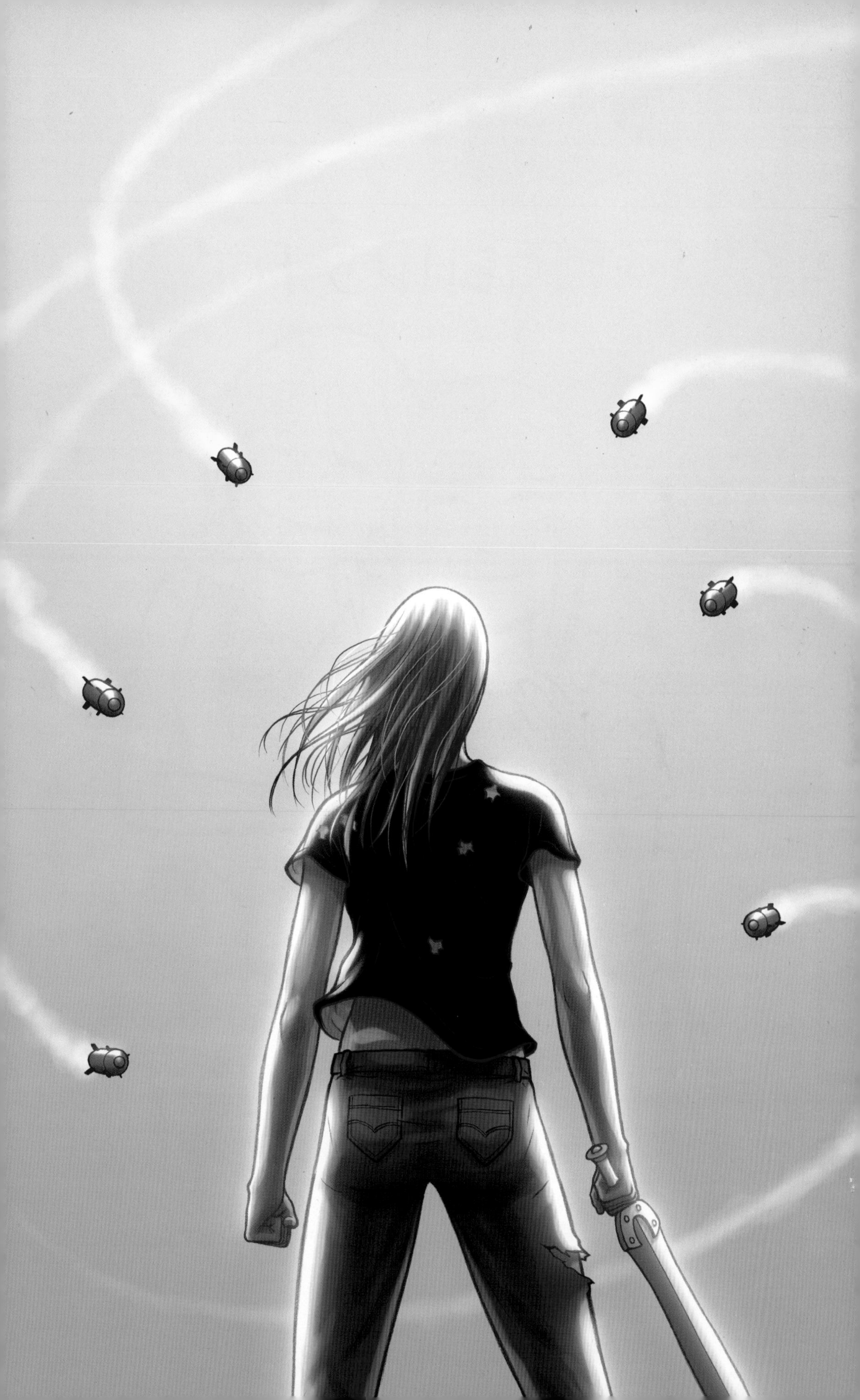

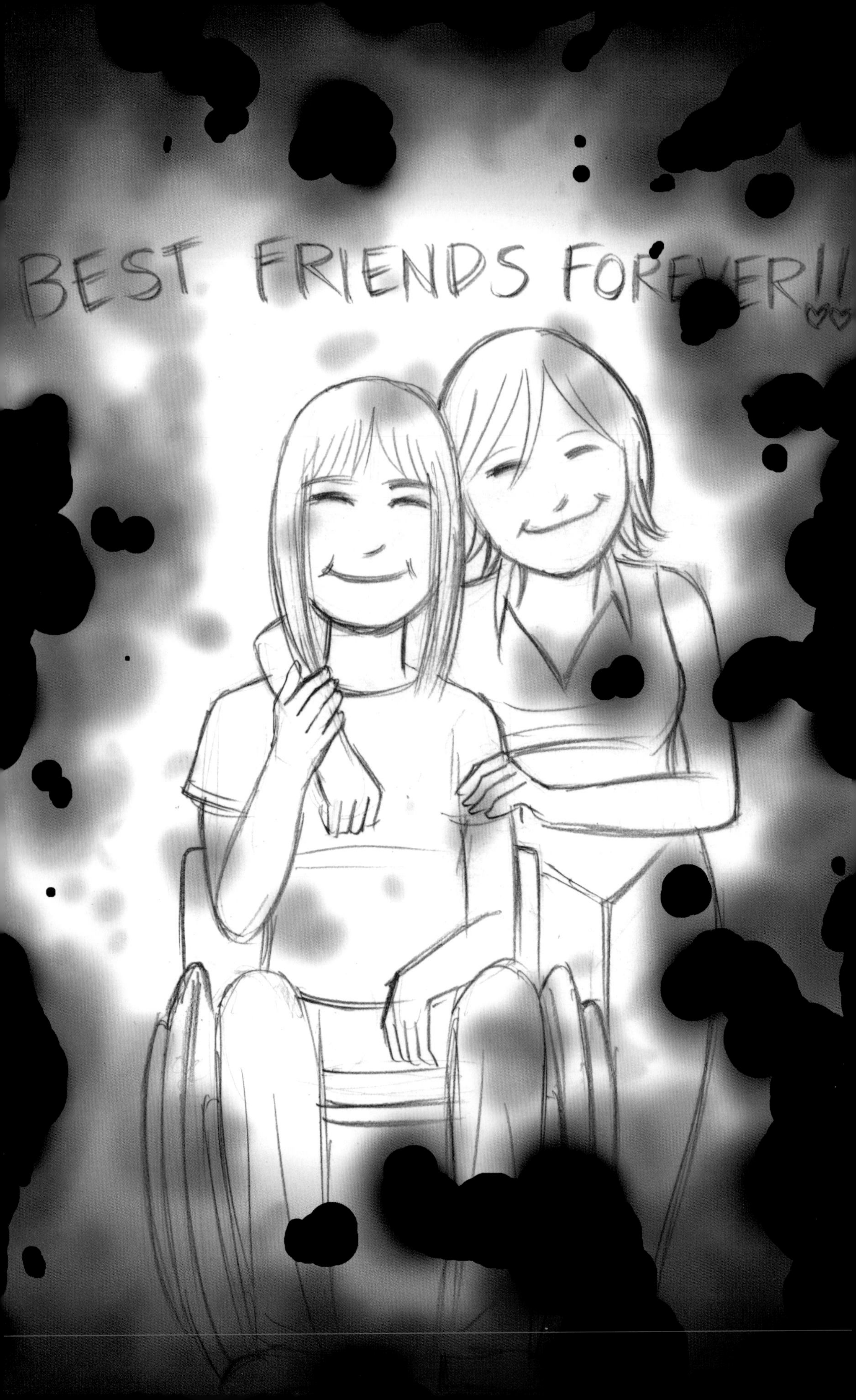
BEST FRIENDS FOREVER!!

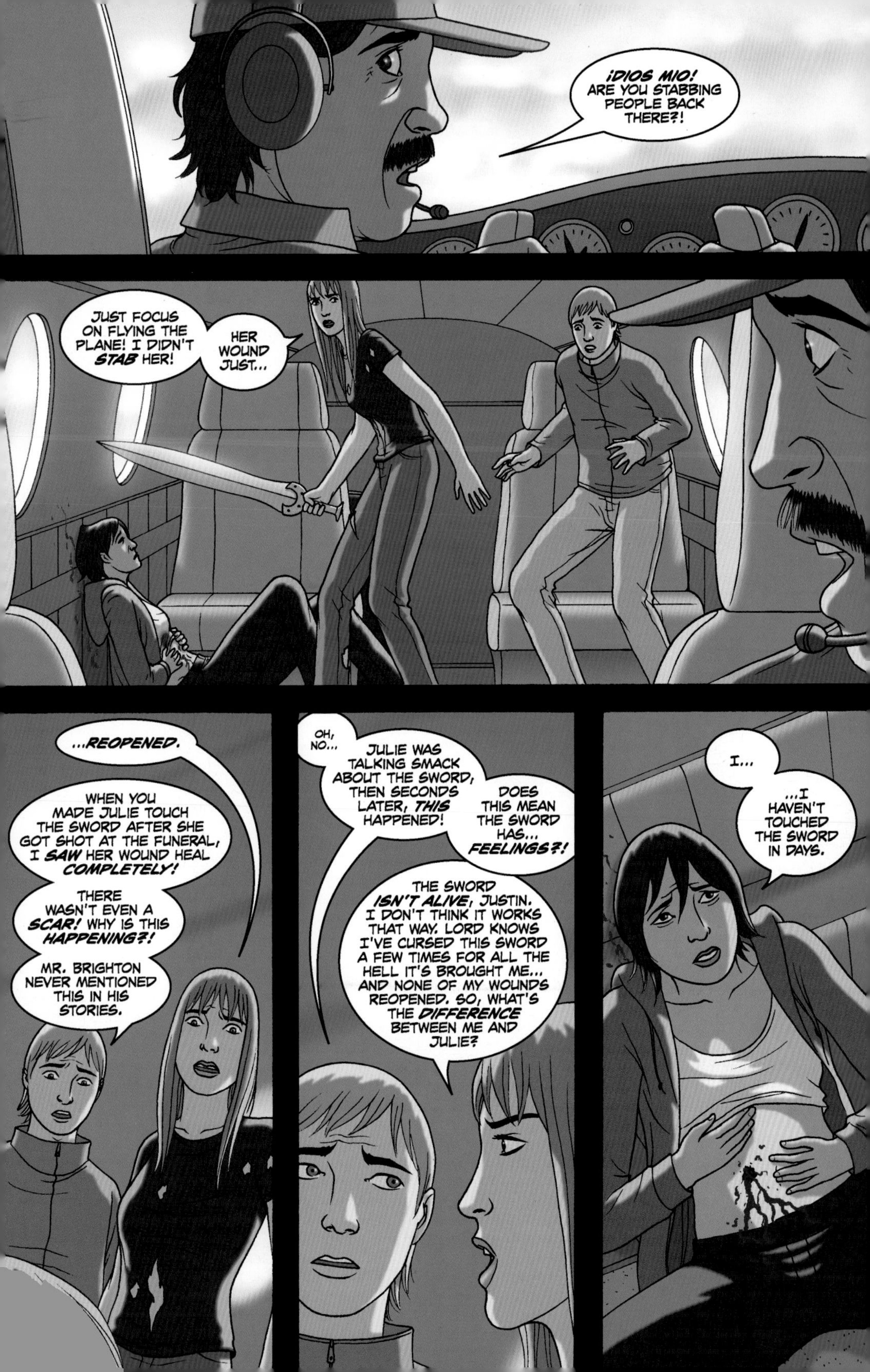
¡DIOS MIO! ARE YOU STABBING PEOPLE BACK THERE?!
JUST FOCUS ON FLYING THE PLANE! I DIDN'T *STAB* HER!
HER WOUND JUST...
...*REOPENED.*
WHEN YOU MADE JULIE TOUCH THE SWORD AFTER SHE GOT SHOT AT THE FUNERAL, I *SAW* HER WOUND HEAL *COMPLETELY!*
THERE WASN'T EVEN A *SCAR!* WHY IS THIS *HAPPENING?!*
MR. BRIGHTON NEVER MENTIONED THIS IN HIS STORIES.
OH, NO...
JULIE WAS TALKING SMACK ABOUT THE SWORD, THEN SECONDS LATER, *THIS* HAPPENED!
DOES THIS MEAN THE SWORD HAS... *FEELINGS?!*
THE SWORD *ISN'T ALIVE*, JUSTIN. I DON'T THINK IT WORKS THAT WAY. LORD KNOWS I'VE CURSED THIS SWORD A FEW TIMES FOR ALL THE HELL IT'S BROUGHT ME... AND NONE OF MY WOUNDS REOPENED. SO, WHAT'S THE *DIFFERENCE* BETWEEN ME AND JULIE?
I...
...I HAVEN'T TOUCHED THE SWORD IN DAYS.

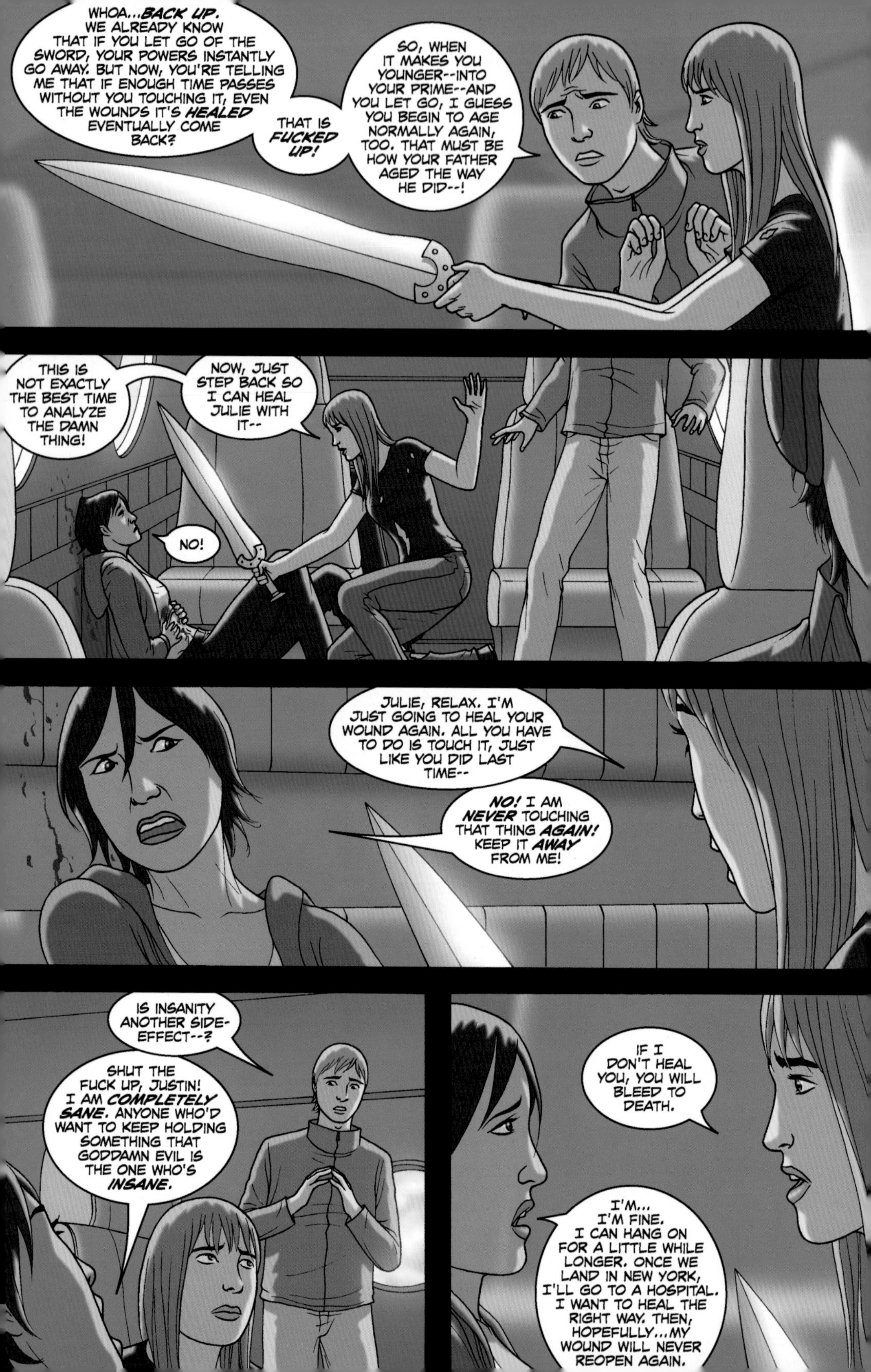
WHOA...BACK UP. WE ALREADY KNOW THAT IF YOU LET GO OF THE SWORD, YOUR POWERS INSTANTLY GO AWAY. BUT NOW, YOU'RE TELLING ME THAT IF ENOUGH TIME PASSES WITHOUT YOU TOUCHING IT, EVEN THE WOUNDS IT'S HEALED EVENTUALLY COME BACK?
THAT IS FUCKED UP!
SO, WHEN IT MAKES YOU YOUNGER--INTO YOUR PRIME--AND YOU LET GO, I GUESS YOU BEGIN TO AGE NORMALLY AGAIN, TOO. THAT MUST BE HOW YOUR FATHER AGED THE WAY HE DID--!
THIS IS NOT EXACTLY THE BEST TIME TO ANALYZE THE DAMN THING!
NOW, JUST STEP BACK SO I CAN HEAL JULIE WITH IT--
NO!
JULIE, RELAX. I'M JUST GOING TO HEAL YOUR WOUND AGAIN. ALL YOU HAVE TO DO IS TOUCH IT, JUST LIKE YOU DID LAST TIME--
NO! I AM NEVER TOUCHING THAT THING AGAIN! KEEP IT AWAY FROM ME!
IS INSANITY ANOTHER SIDE-EFFECT--?
SHUT THE FUCK UP, JUSTIN! I AM COMPLETELY SANE. ANYONE WHO'D WANT TO KEEP HOLDING SOMETHING THAT GODDAMN EVIL IS THE ONE WHO'S INSANE.
IF I DON'T HEAL YOU, YOU WILL BLEED TO DEATH.
I'M... I'M FINE. I CAN HANG ON FOR A LITTLE WHILE LONGER. ONCE WE LAND IN NEW YORK, I'LL GO TO A HOSPITAL. I WANT TO HEAL THE RIGHT WAY. THEN, HOPEFULLY...MY WOUND WILL NEVER REOPEN AGAIN.

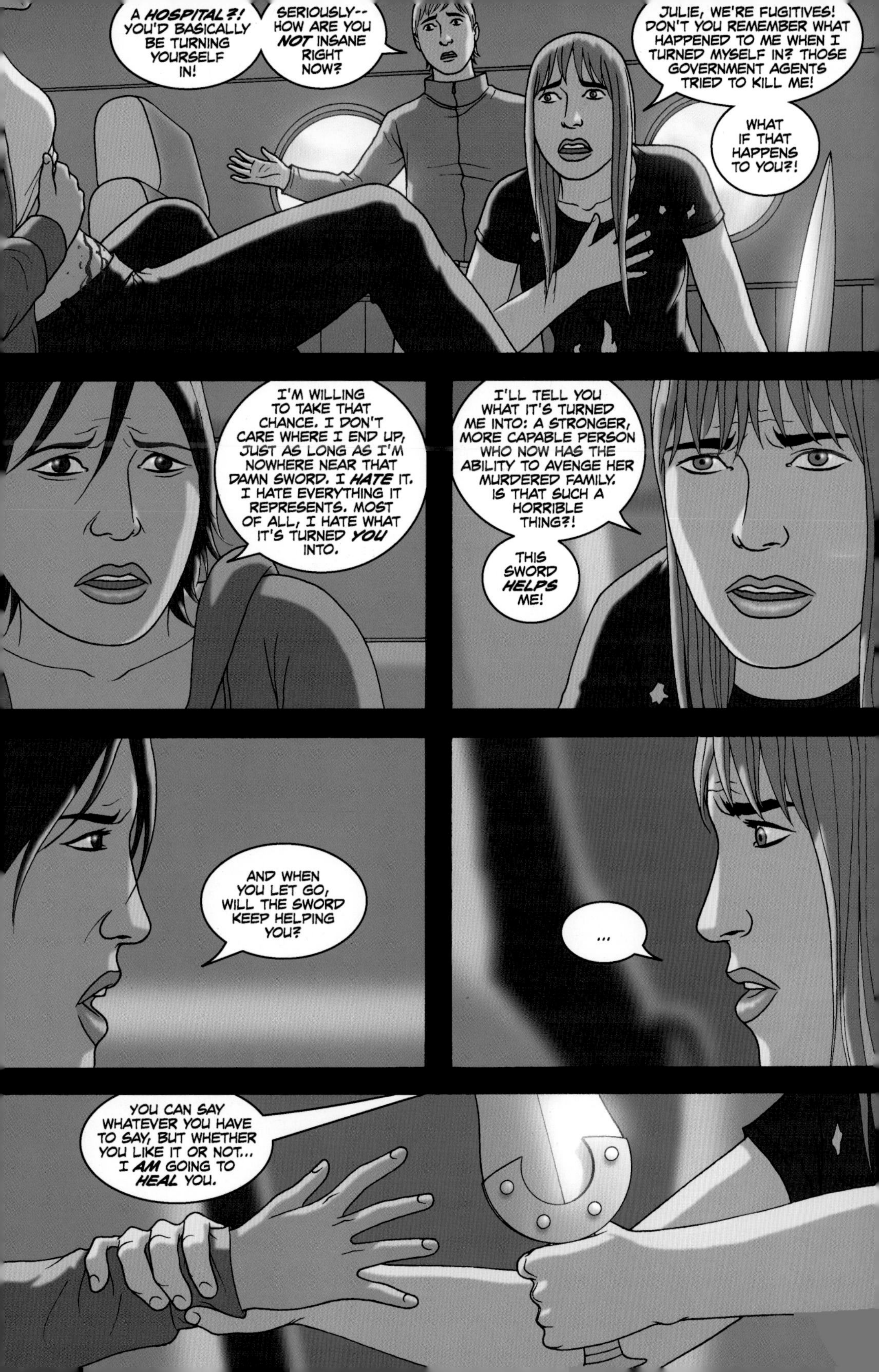
A HOSPITAL?! YOU'D BASICALLY BE TURNING YOURSELF IN!
SERIOUSLY-- HOW ARE YOU NOT INSANE RIGHT NOW?
JULIE, WE'RE FUGITIVES! DON'T YOU REMEMBER WHAT HAPPENED TO ME WHEN I TURNED MYSELF IN? THOSE GOVERNMENT AGENTS TRIED TO KILL ME!
WHAT IF THAT HAPPENS TO YOU?!
I'M WILLING TO TAKE THAT CHANCE. I DON'T CARE WHERE I END UP, JUST AS LONG AS I'M NOWHERE NEAR THAT DAMN SWORD. I HATE IT. I HATE EVERYTHING IT REPRESENTS. MOST OF ALL, I HATE WHAT IT'S TURNED YOU INTO.
I'LL TELL YOU WHAT IT'S TURNED ME INTO: A STRONGER, MORE CAPABLE PERSON WHO NOW HAS THE ABILITY TO AVENGE HER MURDERED FAMILY. IS THAT SUCH A HORRIBLE THING?!
THIS SWORD HELPS ME!
AND WHEN YOU LET GO, WILL THE SWORD KEEP HELPING YOU?
...
YOU CAN SAY WHATEVER YOU HAVE TO SAY, BUT WHETHER YOU LIKE IT OR NOT... I AM GOING TO HEAL YOU.

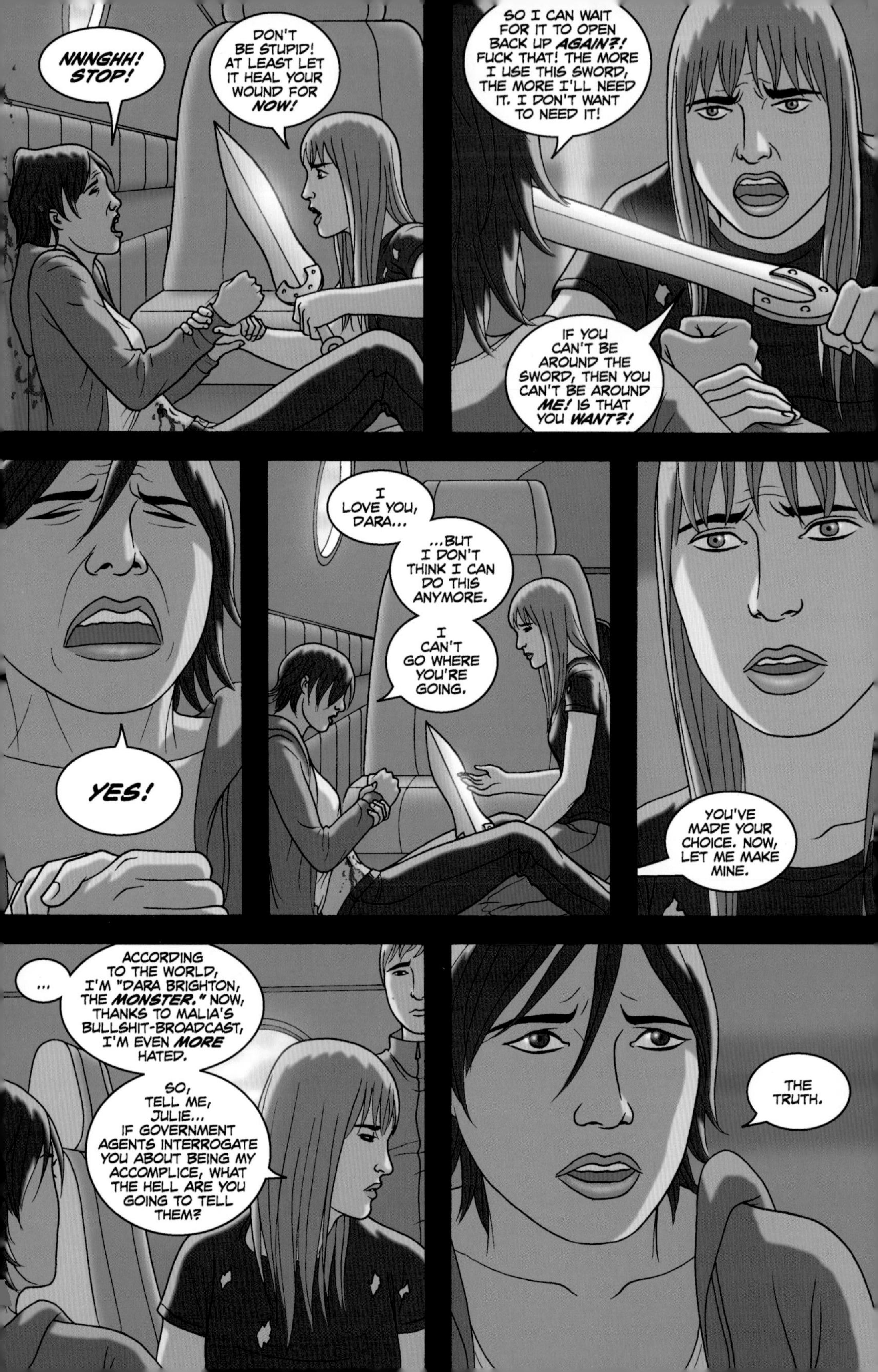
NNNGHH! STOP!
DON'T BE STUPID! AT LEAST LET IT HEAL YOUR WOUND FOR NOW!
SO I CAN WAIT FOR IT TO OPEN BACK UP AGAIN?! FUCK THAT! THE MORE I USE THIS SWORD, THE MORE I'LL NEED IT. I DON'T WANT TO NEED IT!
IF YOU CAN'T BE AROUND THE SWORD, THEN YOU CAN'T BE AROUND ME! IS THAT YOU WANT?!
YES!
I LOVE YOU, DARA...
...BUT I DON'T THINK I CAN DO THIS ANYMORE.
I CAN'T GO WHERE YOU'RE GOING.
YOU'VE MADE YOUR CHOICE. NOW, LET ME MAKE MINE.
...
ACCORDING TO THE WORLD, I'M "DARA BRIGHTON, THE MONSTER." NOW, THANKS TO MALIA'S BULLSHIT-BROADCAST, I'M EVEN MORE HATED.
SO, TELL ME, JULIE... IF GOVERNMENT AGENTS INTERROGATE YOU ABOUT BEING MY ACCOMPLICE, WHAT THE HELL ARE YOU GOING TO TELL THEM?
THE TRUTH.

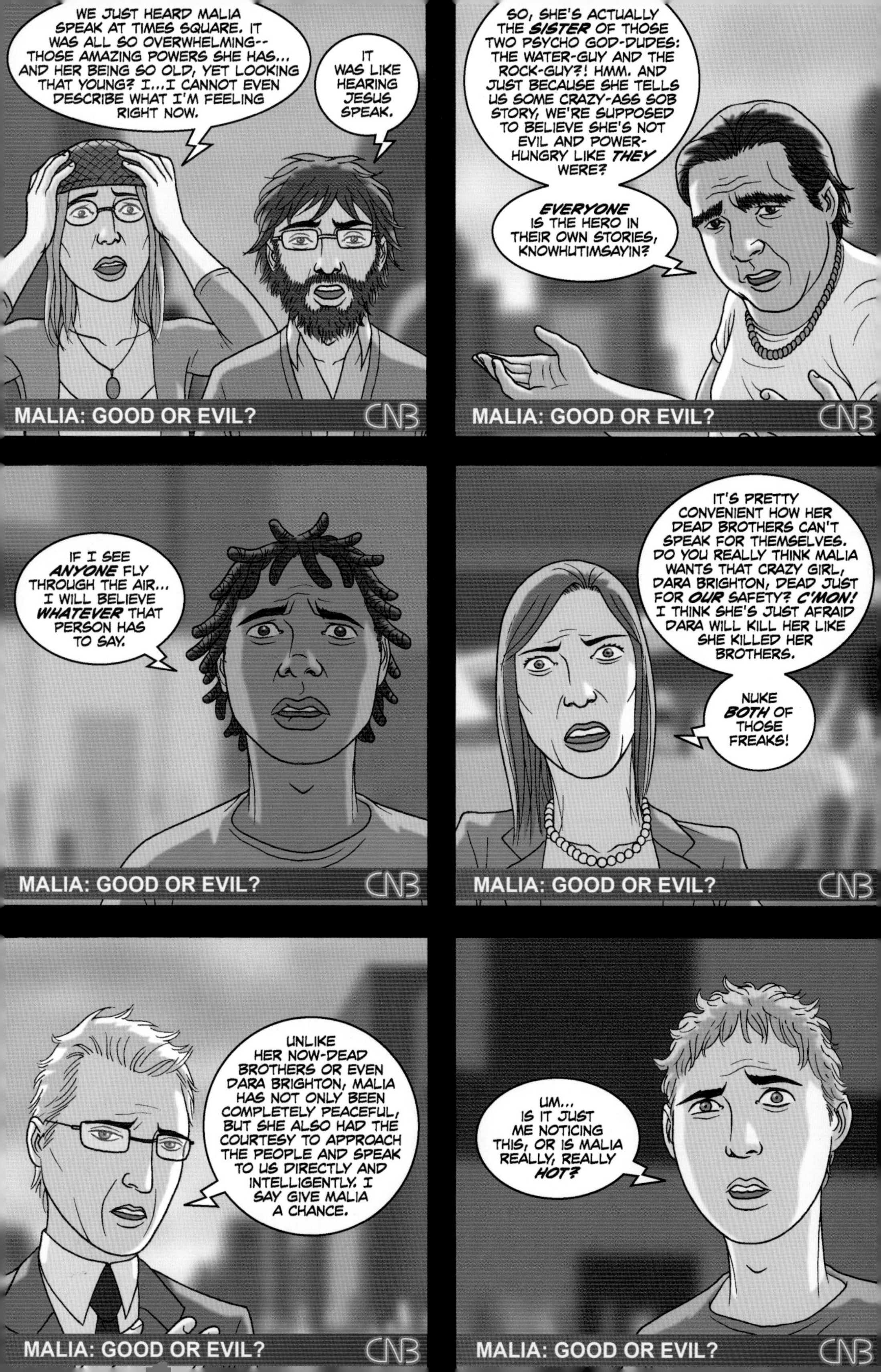
WE JUST HEARD MALIA SPEAK AT TIMES SQUARE. IT WAS ALL SO OVERWHELMING-- THOSE AMAZING POWERS SHE HAS... AND HER BEING SO OLD, YET LOOKING THAT YOUNG? I...I CANNOT EVEN DESCRIBE WHAT I'M FEELING RIGHT NOW.
IT WAS LIKE HEARING JESUS SPEAK.
MALIA: GOOD OR EVIL?
CNB
SO, SHE'S ACTUALLY THE SISTER OF THOSE TWO PSYCHO GOD-DUDES: THE WATER-GUY AND THE ROCK-GUY?! HMM. AND JUST BECAUSE SHE TELLS US SOME CRAZY-ASS SOB STORY, WE'RE SUPPOSED TO BELIEVE SHE'S NOT EVIL AND POWER-HUNGRY LIKE THEY WERE?
EVERYONE IS THE HERO IN THEIR OWN STORIES, KNOWHUTIMSAYIN?
MALIA: GOOD OR EVIL?
CNB
IF I SEE ANYONE FLY THROUGH THE AIR... I WILL BELIEVE WHATEVER THAT PERSON HAS TO SAY.
MALIA: GOOD OR EVIL?
CNB
IT'S PRETTY CONVENIENT HOW HER DEAD BROTHERS CAN'T SPEAK FOR THEMSELVES. DO YOU REALLY THINK MALIA WANTS THAT CRAZY GIRL, DARA BRIGHTON, DEAD JUST FOR OUR SAFETY? C'MON! I THINK SHE'S JUST AFRAID DARA WILL KILL HER LIKE SHE KILLED HER BROTHERS.
NUKE BOTH OF THOSE FREAKS!
MALIA: GOOD OR EVIL?
CNB
UNLIKE HER NOW-DEAD BROTHERS OR EVEN DARA BRIGHTON, MALIA HAS NOT ONLY BEEN COMPLETELY PEACEFUL, BUT SHE ALSO HAD THE COURTESY TO APPROACH THE PEOPLE AND SPEAK TO US DIRECTLY AND INTELLIGENTLY. I SAY GIVE MALIA A CHANCE.
MALIA: GOOD OR EVIL?
CNB
UM... IS IT JUST ME NOTICING THIS, OR IS MALIA REALLY, REALLY HOT?
MALIA: GOOD OR EVIL?
CNB

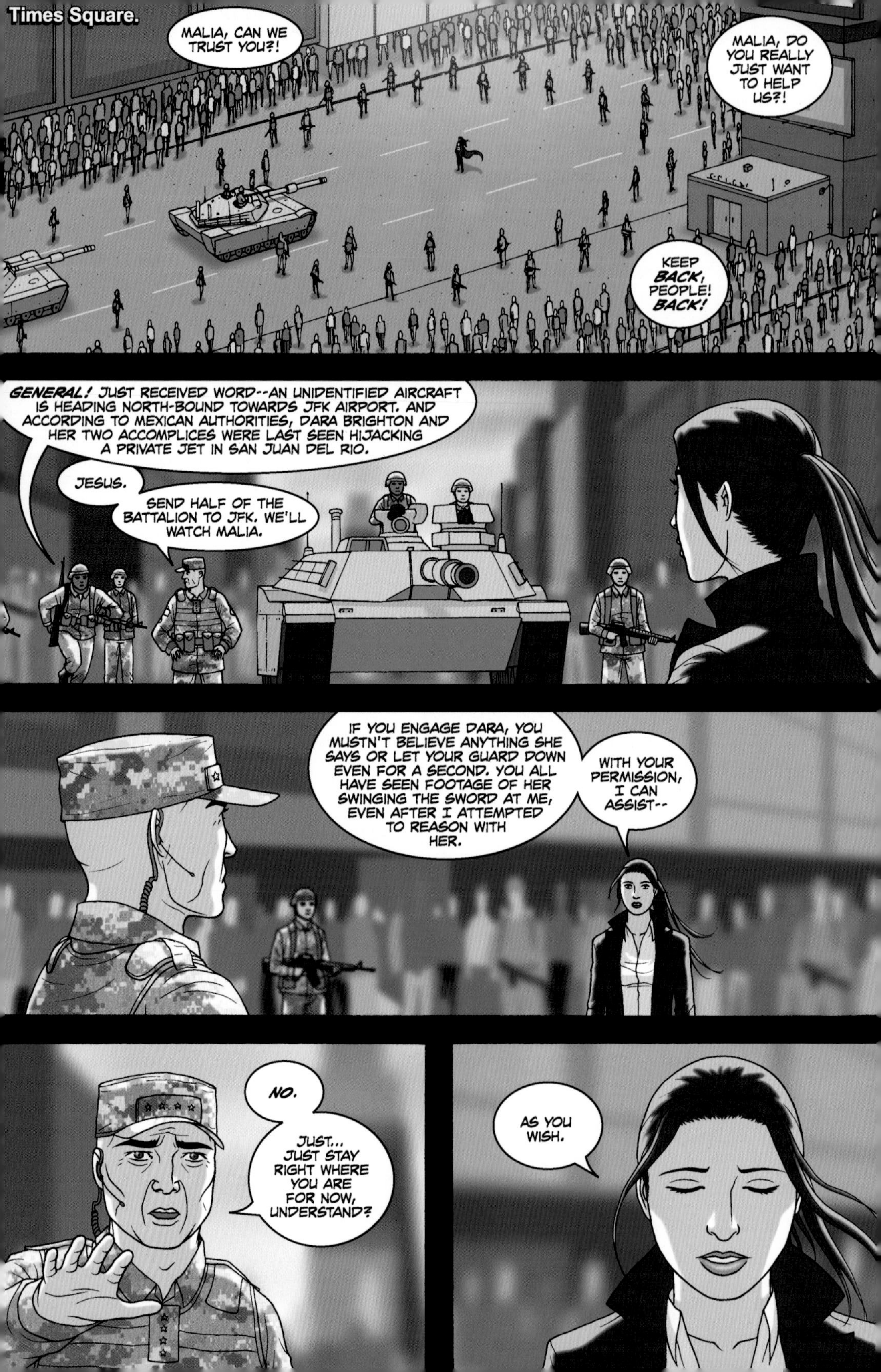
Times Square.
MALIA, CAN WE TRUST YOU?!
MALIA, DO YOU REALLY JUST WANT TO HELP US?!
KEEP BACK, PEOPLE! BACK!
GENERAL! JUST RECEIVED WORD--AN UNIDENTIFIED AIRCRAFT IS HEADING NORTH-BOUND TOWARDS JFK AIRPORT. AND ACCORDING TO MEXICAN AUTHORITIES, DARA BRIGHTON AND HER TWO ACCOMPLICES WERE LAST SEEN HIJACKING A PRIVATE JET IN SAN JUAN DEL RIO.
JESUS.
SEND HALF OF THE BATTALION TO JFK. WE'LL WATCH MALIA.
IF YOU ENGAGE DARA, YOU MUSTN'T BELIEVE ANYTHING SHE SAYS OR LET YOUR GUARD DOWN EVEN FOR A SECOND. YOU ALL HAVE SEEN FOOTAGE OF HER SWINGING THE SWORD AT ME, EVEN AFTER I ATTEMPTED TO REASON WITH HER.
WITH YOUR PERMISSION, I CAN ASSIST--
NO.
JUST... JUST STAY RIGHT WHERE YOU ARE FOR NOW, UNDERSTAND?
AS YOU WISH.

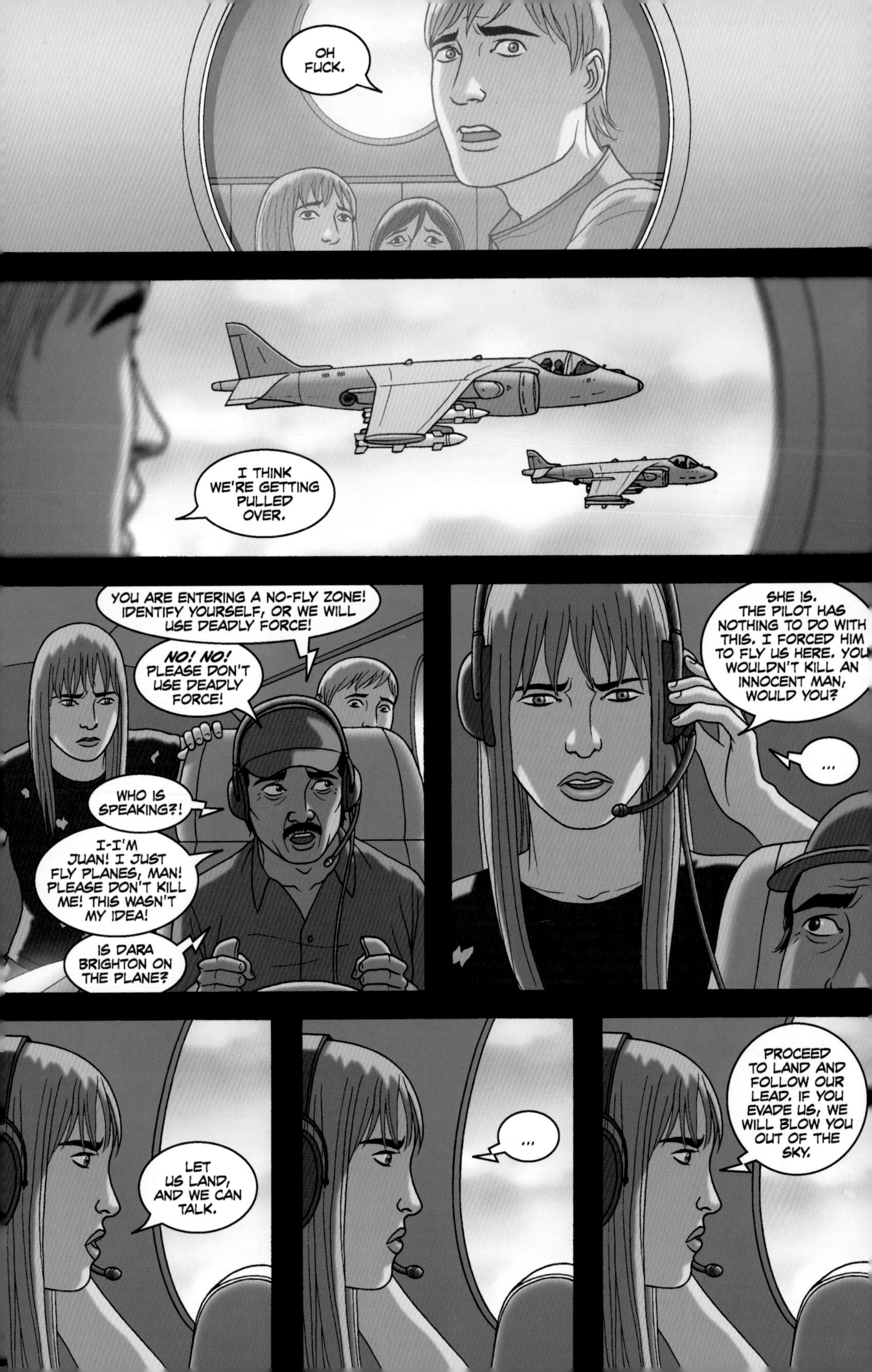
OH FUCK.
I THINK WE'RE GETTING PULLED OVER.
YOU ARE ENTERING A NO-FLY ZONE! IDENTIFY YOURSELF, OR WE WILL USE DEADLY FORCE!
NO! NO! PLEASE DON'T USE DEADLY FORCE!
WHO IS SPEAKING?!
I-I'M JUAN! I JUST FLY PLANES, MAN! PLEASE DON'T KILL ME! THIS WASN'T MY IDEA!
IS DARA BRIGHTON ON THE PLANE?
SHE IS. THE PILOT HAS NOTHING TO DO WITH THIS. I FORCED HIM TO FLY US HERE. YOU WOULDN'T KILL AN INNOCENT MAN, WOULD YOU?
...
LET US LAND, AND WE CAN TALK.
...
PROCEED TO LAND AND FOLLOW OUR LEAD. IF YOU EVADE US, WE WILL BLOW YOU OUT OF THE SKY.

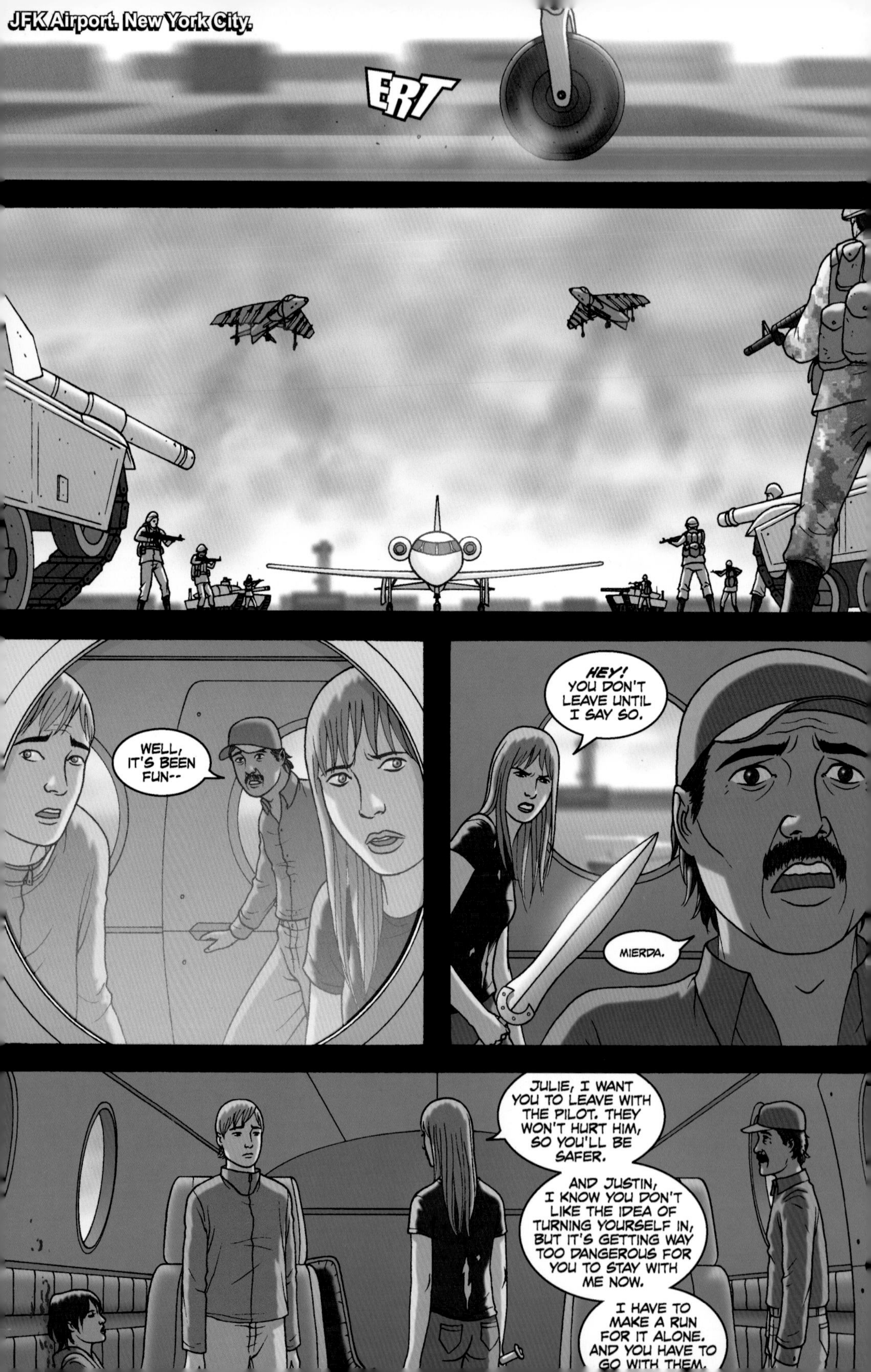
JFK Airport. New York City.
ERT
WELL, IT'S BEEN FUN--
HEY! YOU DON'T LEAVE UNTIL I SAY SO.
MIERDA.
JULIE, I WANT YOU TO LEAVE WITH THE PILOT. THEY WON'T HURT HIM, SO YOU'LL BE SAFER.
AND JUSTIN, I KNOW YOU DON'T LIKE THE IDEA OF TURNING YOURSELF IN, BUT IT'S GETTING WAY TOO DANGEROUS FOR YOU TO STAY WITH ME NOW.
I HAVE TO MAKE A RUN FOR IT ALONE. AND YOU HAVE TO GO WITH THEM.

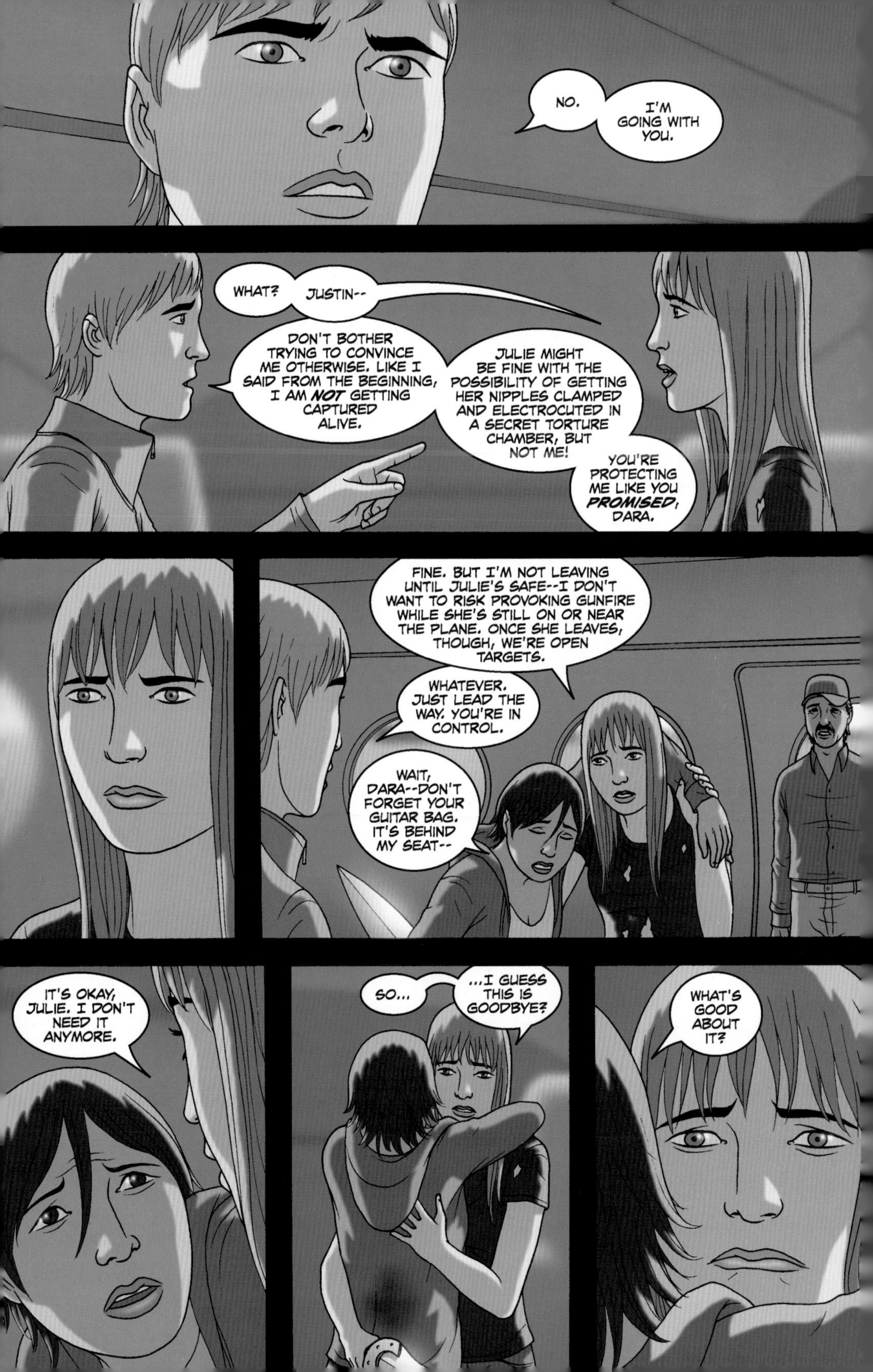
NO.
I'M GOING WITH YOU.
WHAT?
JUSTIN--
DON'T BOTHER TRYING TO CONVINCE ME OTHERWISE. LIKE I SAID FROM THE BEGINNING, I AM *NOT* GETTING CAPTURED ALIVE.
JULIE MIGHT BE FINE WITH THE POSSIBILITY OF GETTING HER NIPPLES CLAMPED AND ELECTROCUTED IN A SECRET TORTURE CHAMBER, BUT NOT ME!
YOU'RE PROTECTING ME LIKE YOU ***PROMISED***, DARA.
FINE. BUT I'M NOT LEAVING UNTIL JULIE'S SAFE--I DON'T WANT TO RISK PROVOKING GUNFIRE WHILE SHE'S STILL ON OR NEAR THE PLANE. ONCE SHE LEAVES, THOUGH, WE'RE OPEN TARGETS.
WHATEVER. JUST LEAD THE WAY. YOU'RE IN CONTROL.
WAIT, DARA--DON'T FORGET YOUR GUITAR BAG. IT'S BEHIND MY SEAT--
IT'S OKAY, JULIE. I DON'T NEED IT ANYMORE.
SO...
...I GUESS THIS IS GOODBYE?
WHAT'S GOOD ABOUT IT?

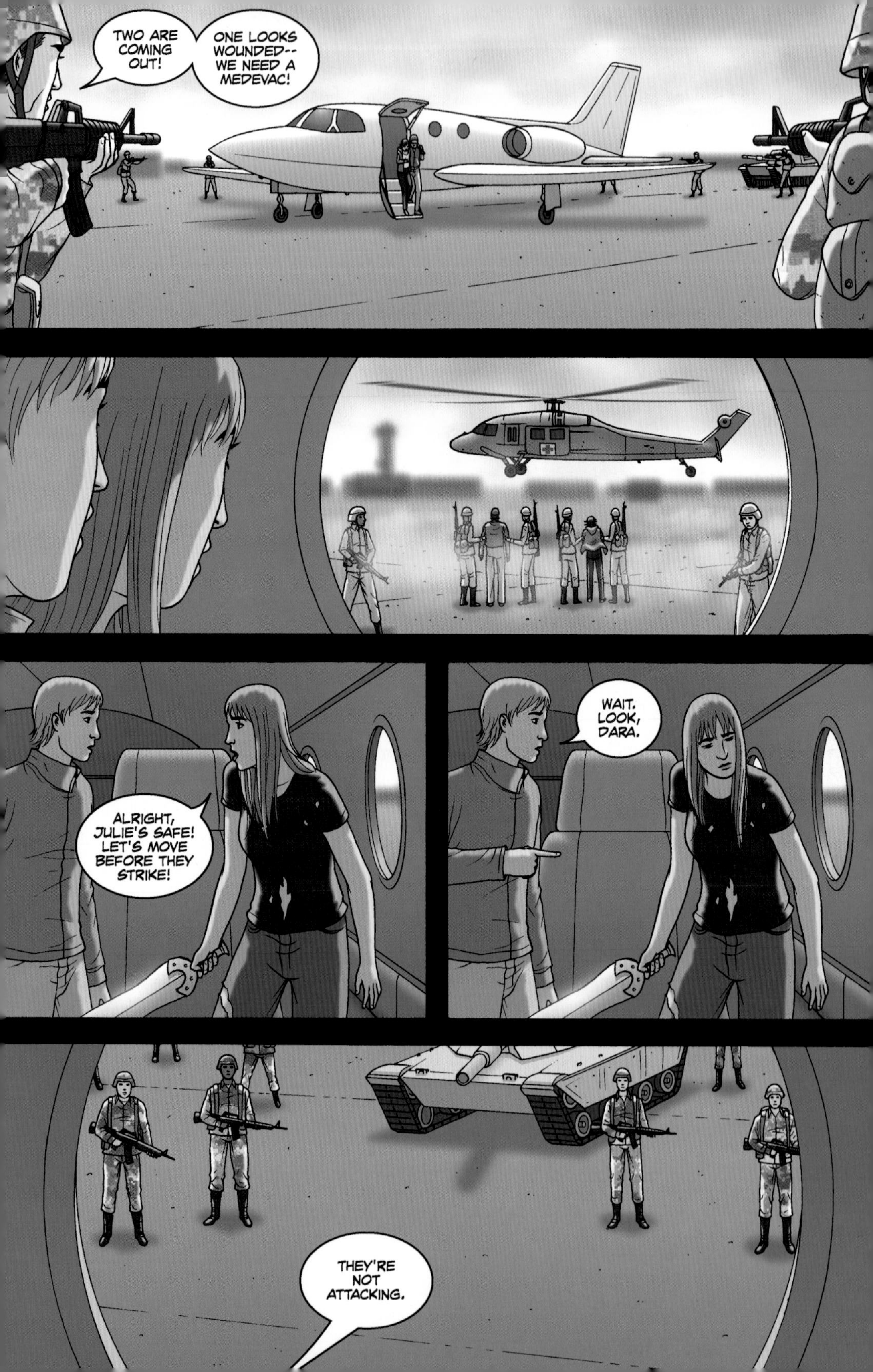
TWO ARE COMING OUT!
ONE LOOKS WOUNDED-- WE NEED A MEDEVAC!
ALRIGHT, JULIE'S SAFE! LET'S MOVE BEFORE THEY STRIKE!
WAIT. LOOK, DARA.
THEY'RE NOT ATTACKING.

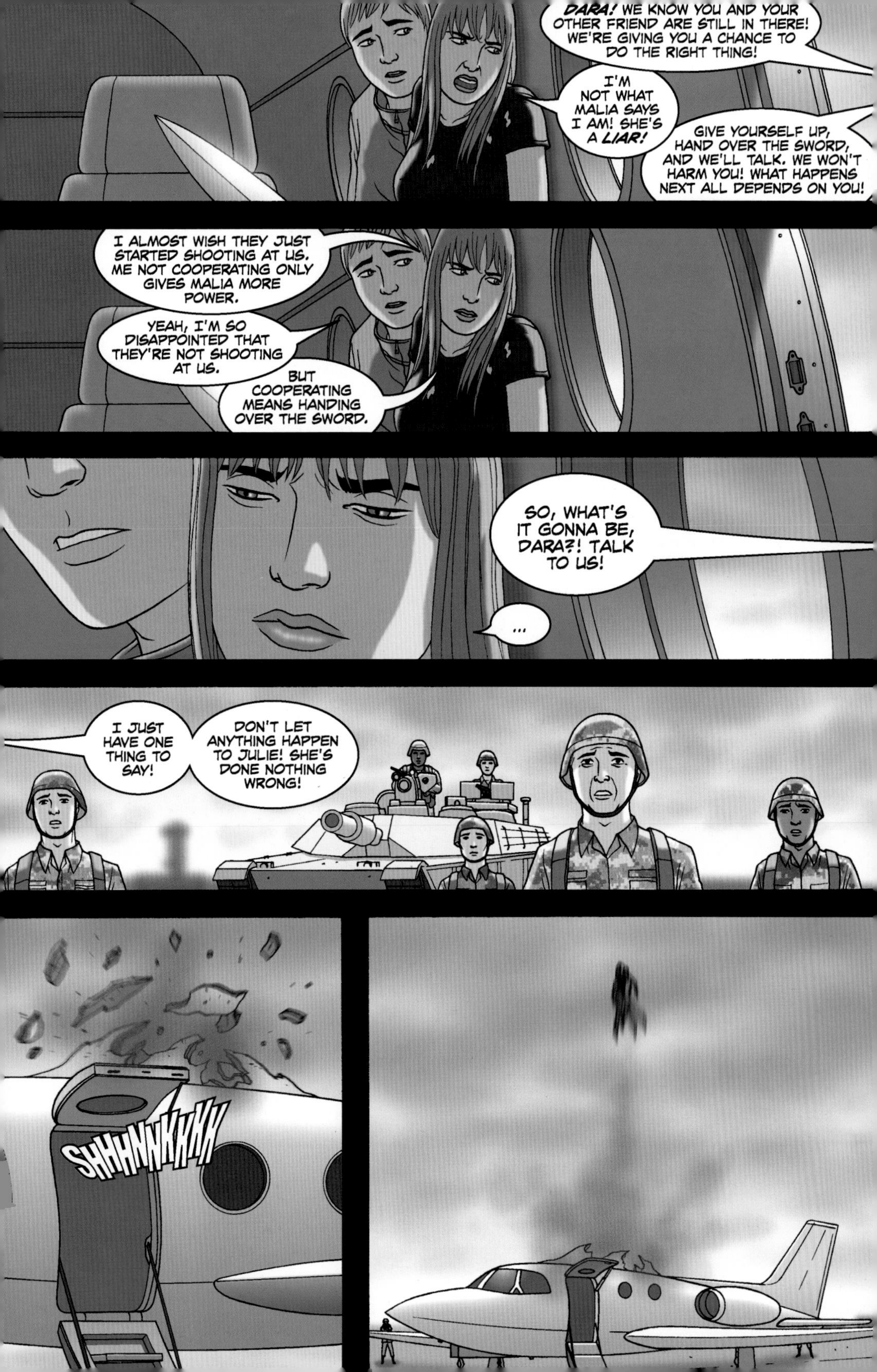
DARA! WE KNOW YOU AND YOUR OTHER FRIEND ARE STILL IN THERE! WE'RE GIVING YOU A CHANCE TO DO THE RIGHT THING!
I'M NOT WHAT MALIA SAYS I AM! SHE'S A LIAR!
GIVE YOURSELF UP, HAND OVER THE SWORD, AND WE'LL TALK. WE WON'T HARM YOU! WHAT HAPPENS NEXT ALL DEPENDS ON YOU!
I ALMOST WISH THEY JUST STARTED SHOOTING AT US. ME NOT COOPERATING ONLY GIVES MALIA MORE POWER.
YEAH, I'M SO DISAPPOINTED THAT THEY'RE NOT SHOOTING AT US.
BUT COOPERATING MEANS HANDING OVER THE SWORD.
SO, WHAT'S IT GONNA BE, DARA?! TALK TO US!
...
I JUST HAVE ONE THING TO SAY!
DON'T LET ANYTHING HAPPEN TO JULIE! SHE'S DONE NOTHING WRONG!
SHHHNNKKKK

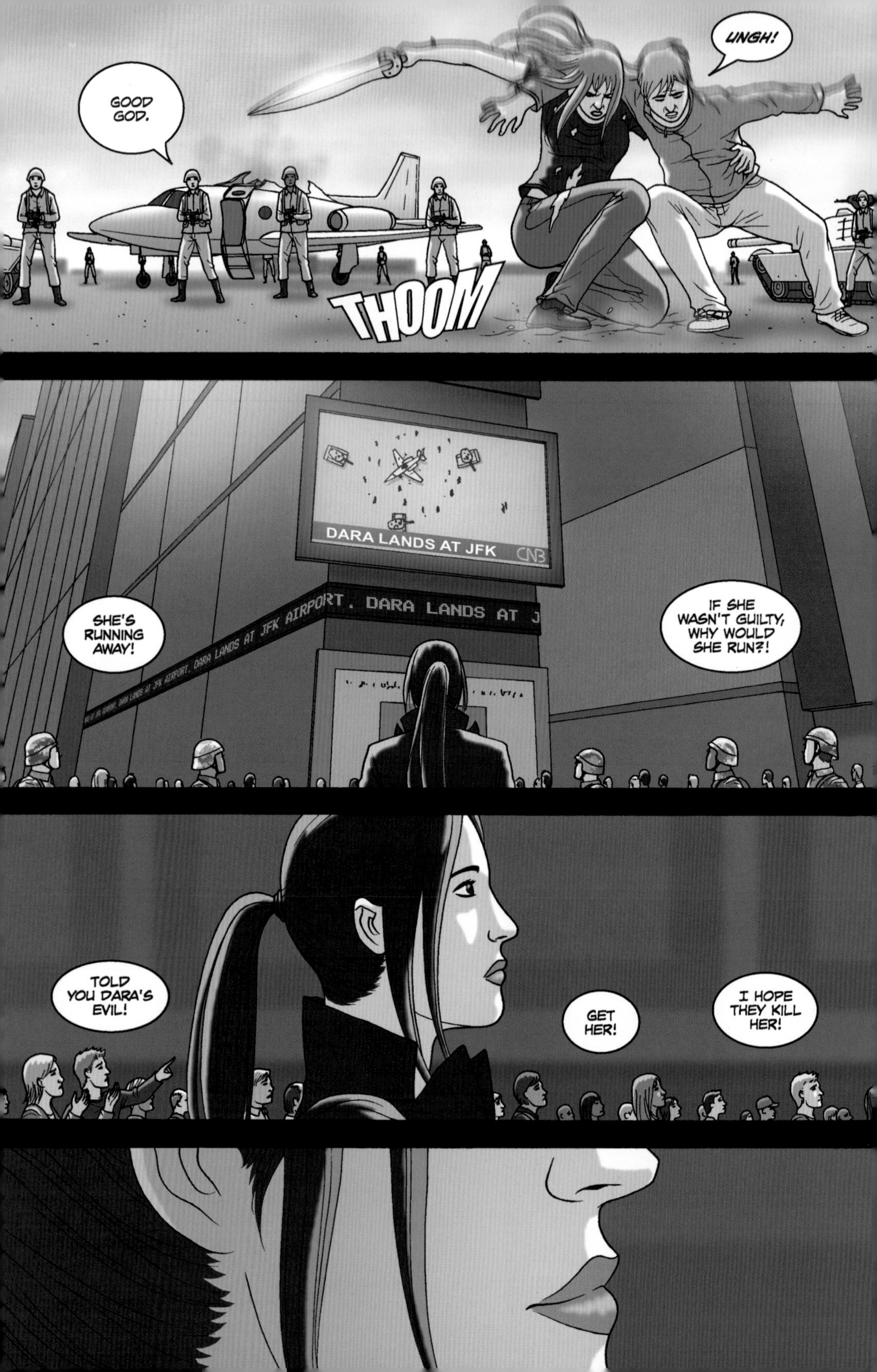
GOOD GOD.
UNGH!
THOOM
DARA LANDS AT JFK
CNB
RT. DARA LANDS AT J
DARA LANDS AT JFK AIRPORT. DARA LANDS AT JFK AIRPORT
SHE'S RUNNING AWAY!
IF SHE WASN'T GUILTY, WHY WOULD SHE RUN?!
TOLD YOU DARA'S EVIL!
GET HER!
I HOPE THEY KILL HER!

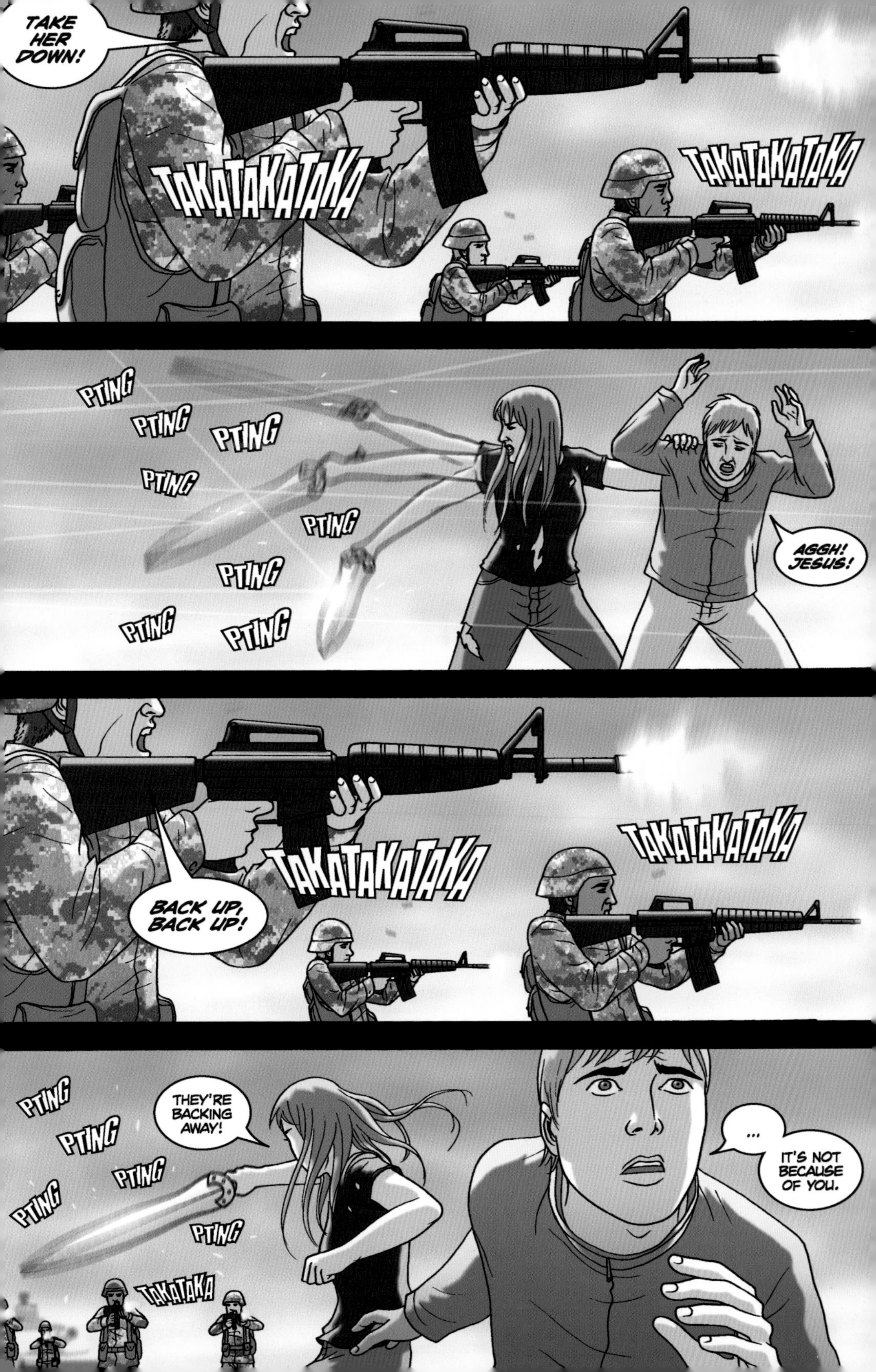
TAKE HER DOWN!
TAKATAKATAKA
TAKATAKATAKA
PTING
PTING
PTING
PTING
PTING
PTING
PTING
PTING
AGGH! JESUS!
TAKATAKATAKA
TAKATAKATAKA
BACK UP, BACK UP!
PTING
PTING
THEY'RE BACKING AWAY!
PTING
PTING
PTING
TAKATAKA
...
IT'S NOT BECAUSE OF YOU.

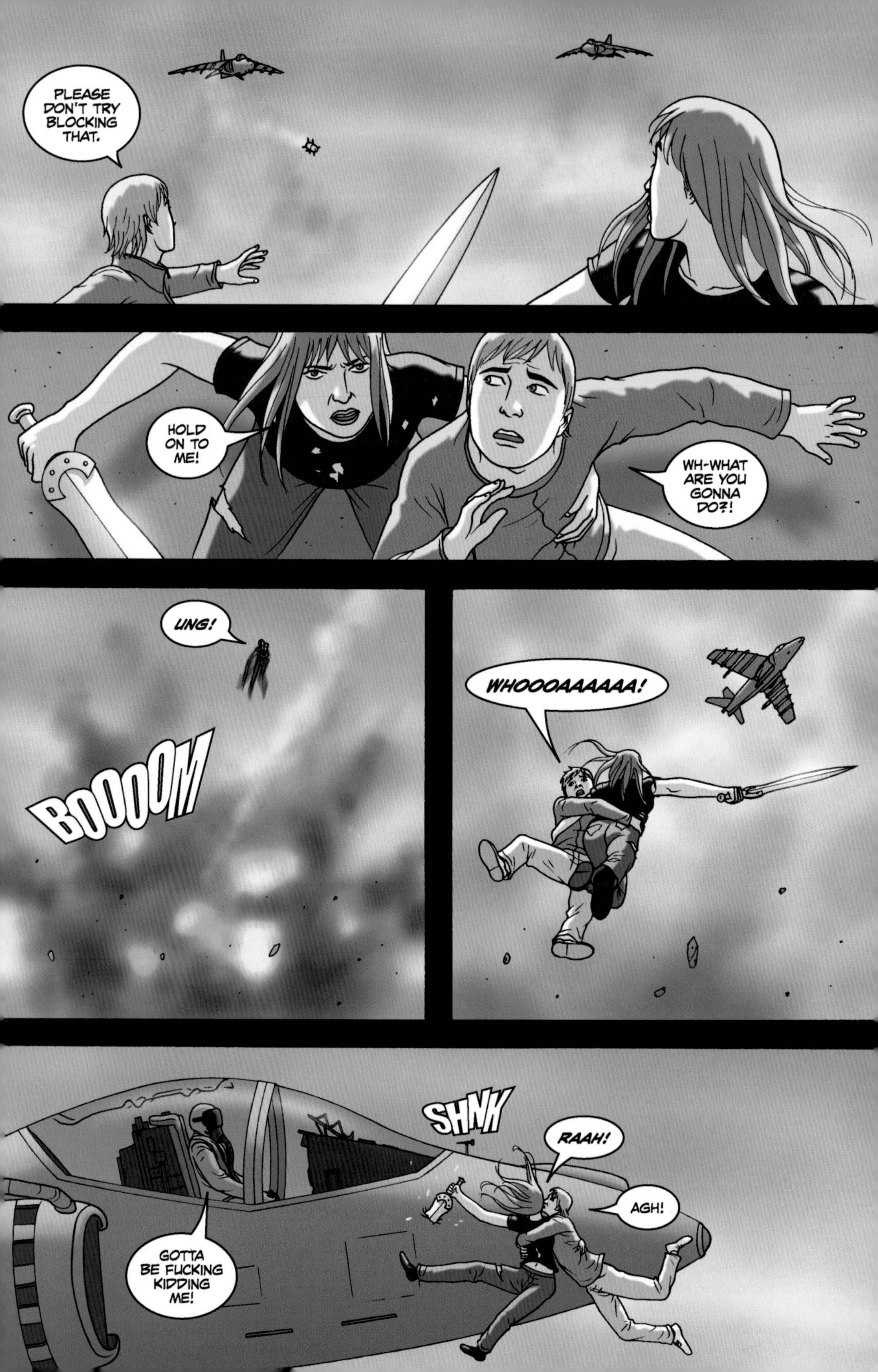
PLEASE DON'T TRY BLOCKING THAT.
HOLD ON TO ME!
WH-WHAT ARE YOU GONNA DO?!
UNG!
BOOOOM
WHOOOAAAAAA!
SHNK
RAAH!
AGH!
GOTTA BE FUCKING KIDDING ME!

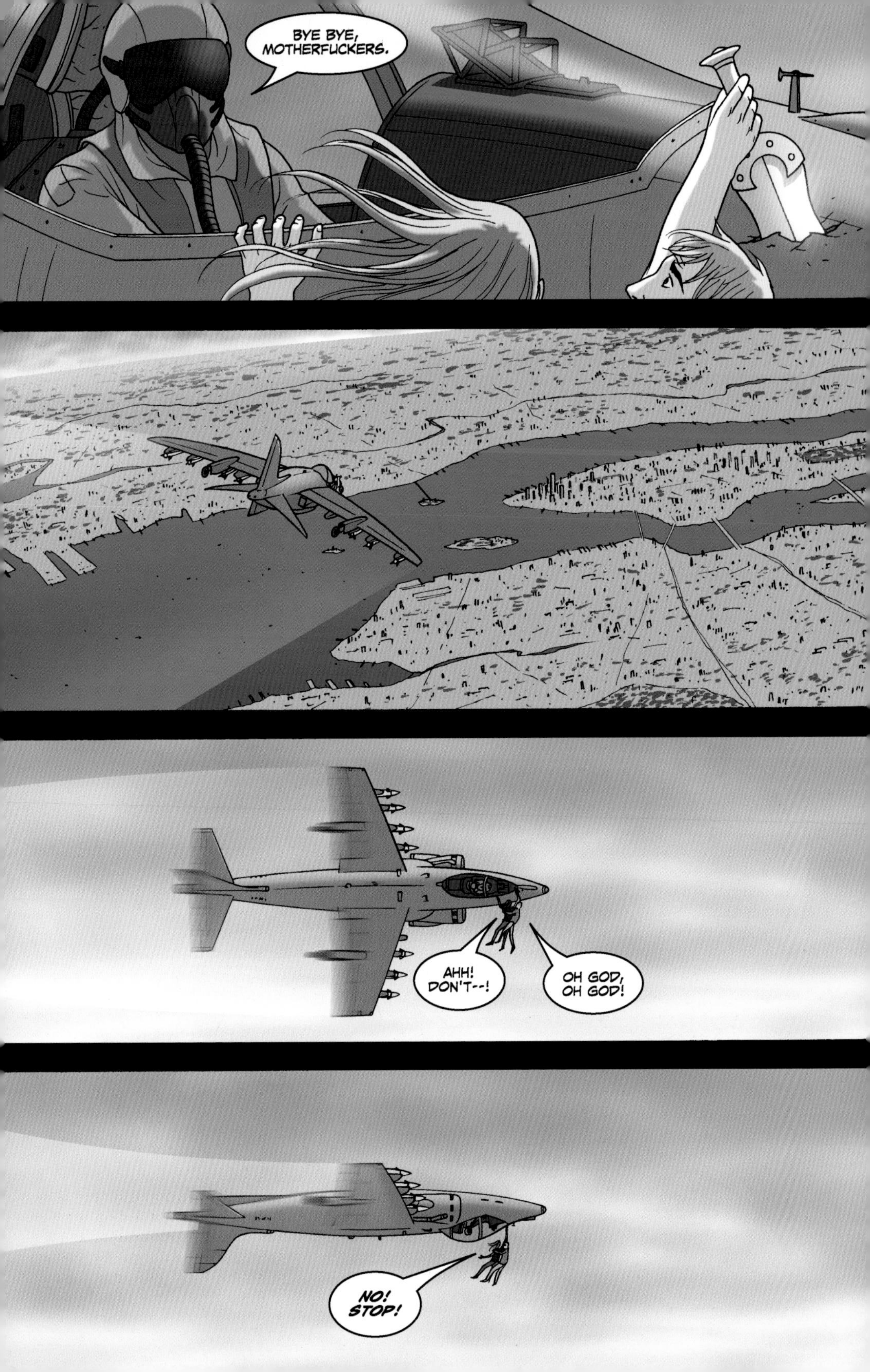
BYE BYE, MOTHERFUCKERS.
AHH! DON'T--!
OH GOD, OH GOD!
NO! STOP!

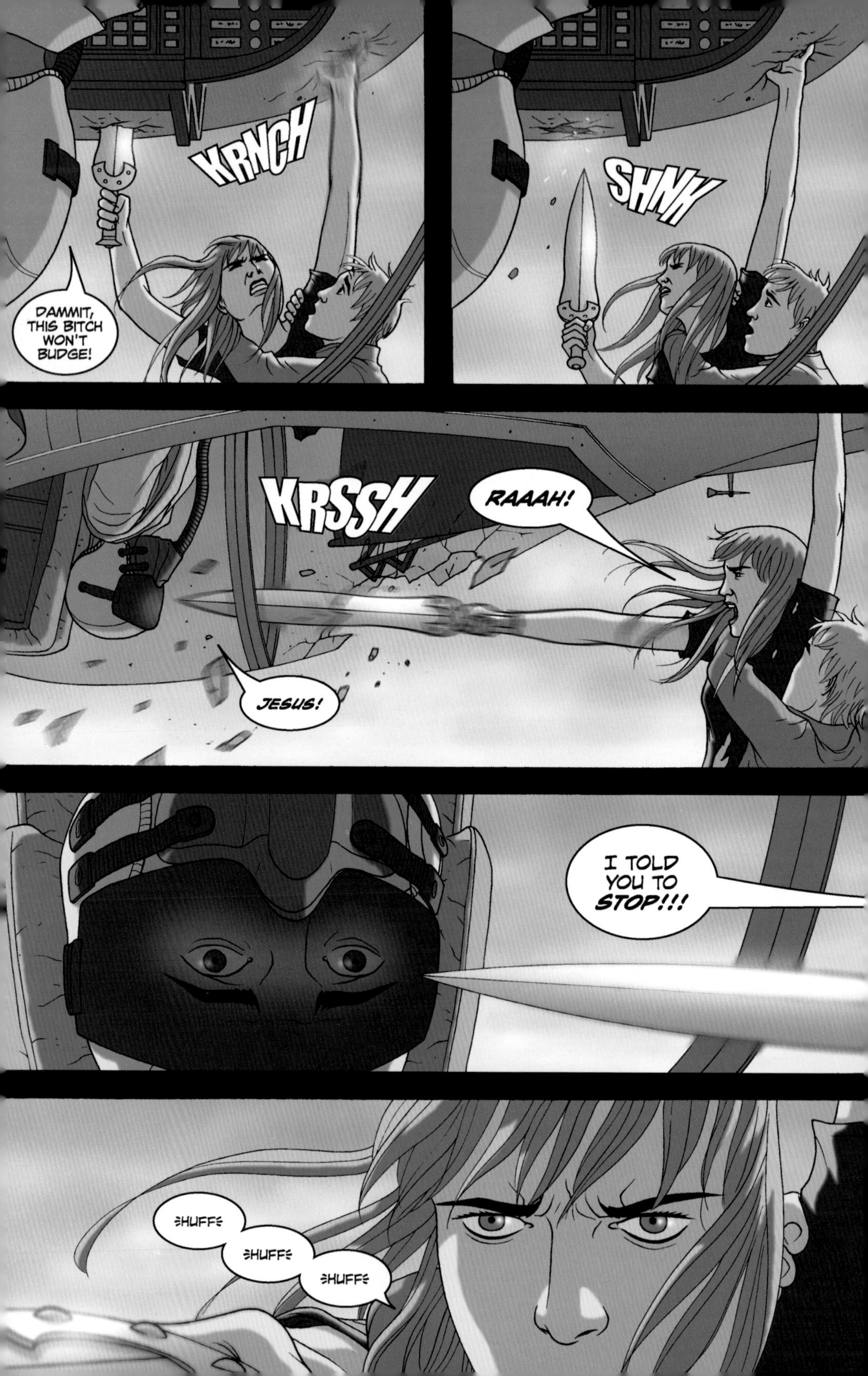
KRNCH
DAMMIT, THIS BITCH WON'T BUDGE!
SHNK
KRSSH
RAAAH!
JESUS!
I TOLD YOU TO STOP!!!
HUFF
HUFF
HUFF

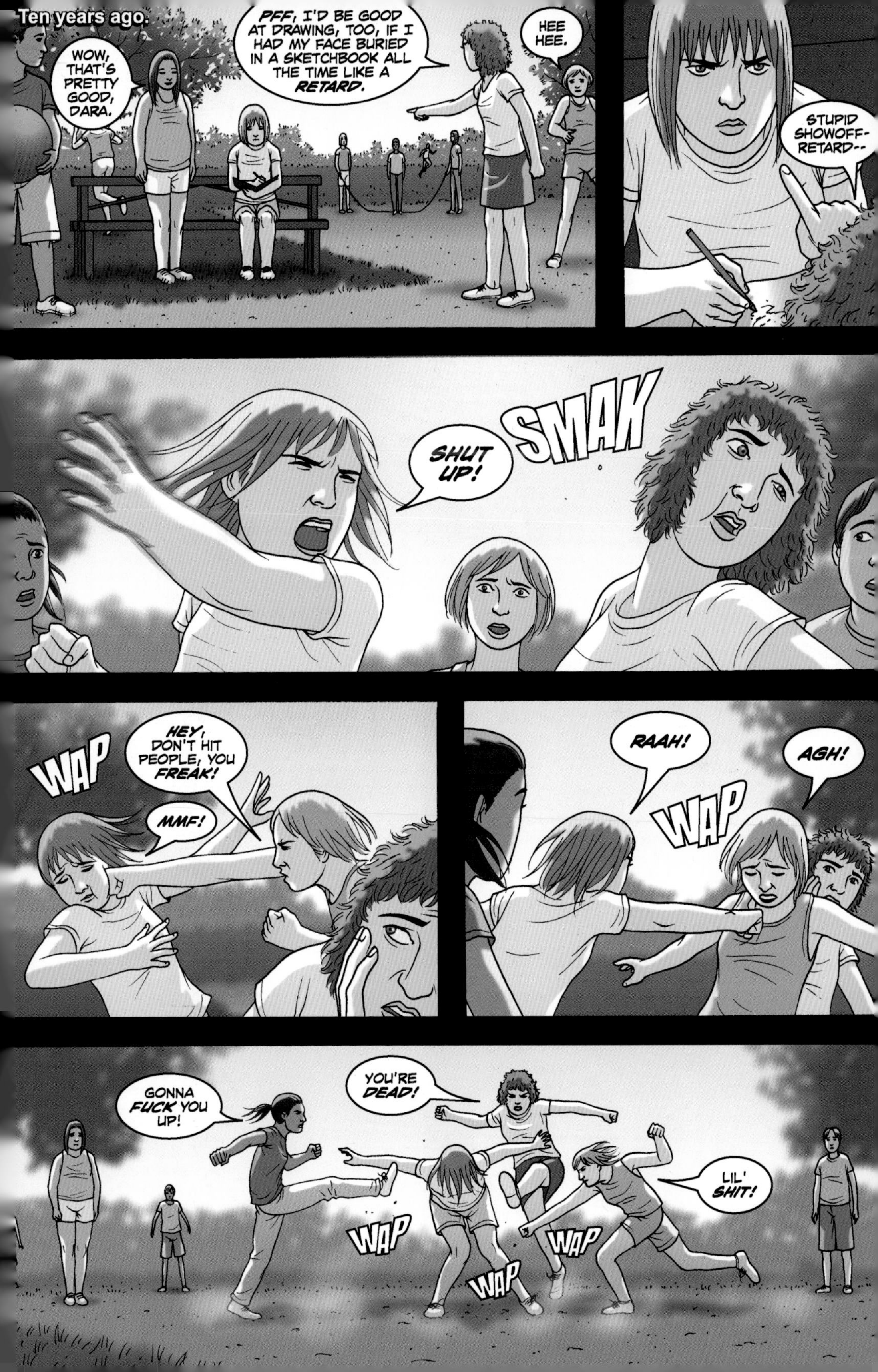
Ten years ago.
WOW, THAT'S PRETTY GOOD, DARA.
PFF, I'D BE GOOD AT DRAWING, TOO, IF I HAD MY FACE BURIED IN A SKETCHBOOK ALL THE TIME LIKE A RETARD.
HEE HEE.
STUPID SHOWOFF-RETARD--
SHUT UP!
SMAK
WAP
HEY, DON'T HIT PEOPLE, YOU FREAK!
MMF!
RAAH!
AGH!
WAP
GONNA FUCK YOU UP!
YOU'RE DEAD!
LIL' SHIT!
WAP
WAP
WAP

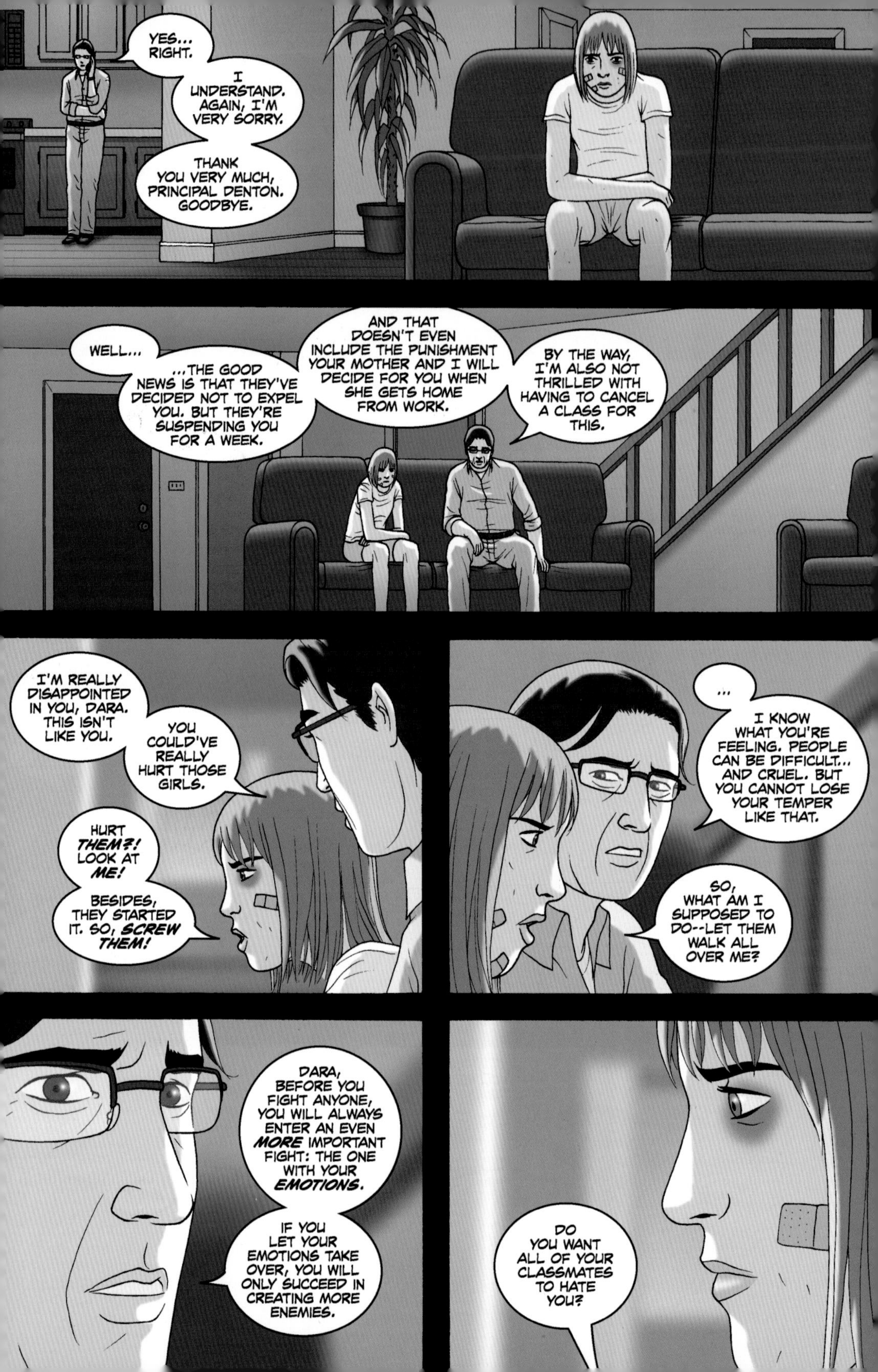
YES... RIGHT.
I UNDERSTAND. AGAIN, I'M VERY SORRY.
THANK YOU VERY MUCH, PRINCIPAL DENTON. GOODBYE.
WELL...
...THE GOOD NEWS IS THAT THEY'VE DECIDED NOT TO EXPEL YOU. BUT THEY'RE SUSPENDING YOU FOR A WEEK.
AND THAT DOESN'T EVEN INCLUDE THE PUNISHMENT YOUR MOTHER AND I WILL DECIDE FOR YOU WHEN SHE GETS HOME FROM WORK.
BY THE WAY, I'M ALSO NOT THRILLED WITH HAVING TO CANCEL A CLASS FOR THIS.
I'M REALLY DISAPPOINTED IN YOU, DARA. THIS ISN'T LIKE YOU.
YOU COULD'VE REALLY HURT THOSE GIRLS.
HURT THEM?! LOOK AT ME!
BESIDES, THEY STARTED IT. SO, SCREW THEM!
...
I KNOW WHAT YOU'RE FEELING. PEOPLE CAN BE DIFFICULT... AND CRUEL. BUT YOU CANNOT LOSE YOUR TEMPER LIKE THAT.
SO, WHAT AM I SUPPOSED TO DO--LET THEM WALK ALL OVER ME?
DARA, BEFORE YOU FIGHT ANYONE, YOU WILL ALWAYS ENTER AN EVEN MORE IMPORTANT FIGHT: THE ONE WITH YOUR EMOTIONS.
IF YOU LET YOUR EMOTIONS TAKE OVER, YOU WILL ONLY SUCCEED IN CREATING MORE ENEMIES.
DO YOU WANT ALL OF YOUR CLASSMATES TO HATE YOU?

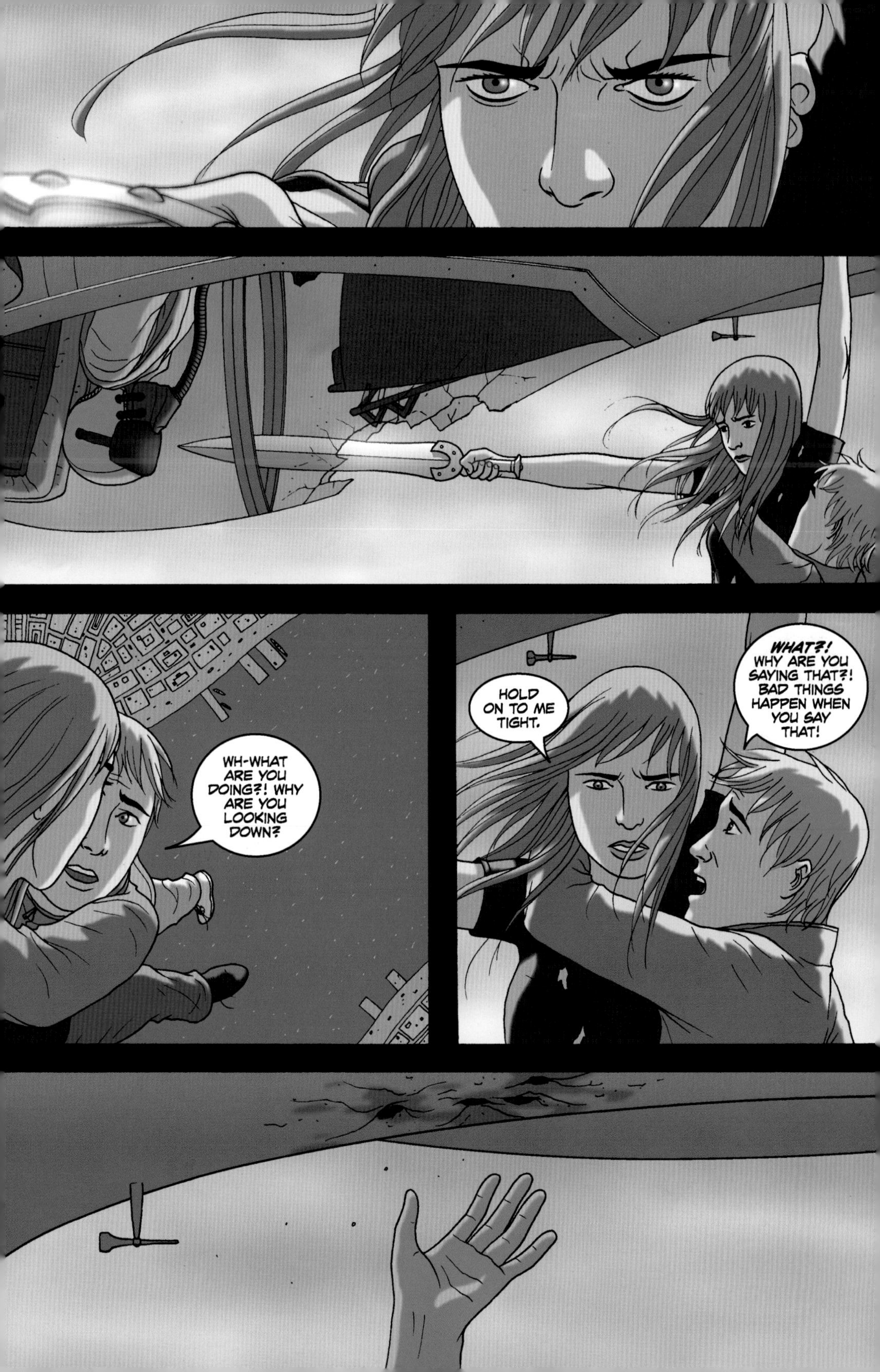
WH-WHAT ARE YOU DOING?! WHY ARE YOU LOOKING DOWN?
HOLD ON TO ME TIGHT.
WHAT?! WHY ARE YOU SAYING THAT?! BAD THINGS HAPPEN WHEN YOU SAY THAT!

I HAAAATE YOOOUUU!

SPLSSH

IN YET ANOTHER BIZARRE TWIST, WE HAVE JUST LEARNED THAT DARA AND HER REMAINING ACCOMPLICE, JUSTIN FOREMAN, HAVE LEAPT OFF OF THE JET AND DROPPED SOMEWHERE INTO THE HUDSON RIVER, ACCORDING TO EYEWITNESSES.

ACCORDING TO OUR MILITARY SOURCES, SHE CANNOT BE FOUND.

DARA BRIGHTON IS NOW ON THE LOOSE.

CNB

DARA EVADES MILITARY

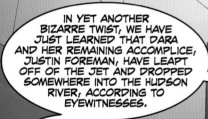

ES MILITARY. DARA EVADES MILIT

THE MILITARY IS NOW LAUNCHING A CITY-WIDE MANHUNT LIKE NEVER SEEN BEFORE.

THE PRESIDENT IS CALLING THE CAPTURE OF DARA BRIGHTON THE COUNTRY'S NUMBER ONE PRIORITY.

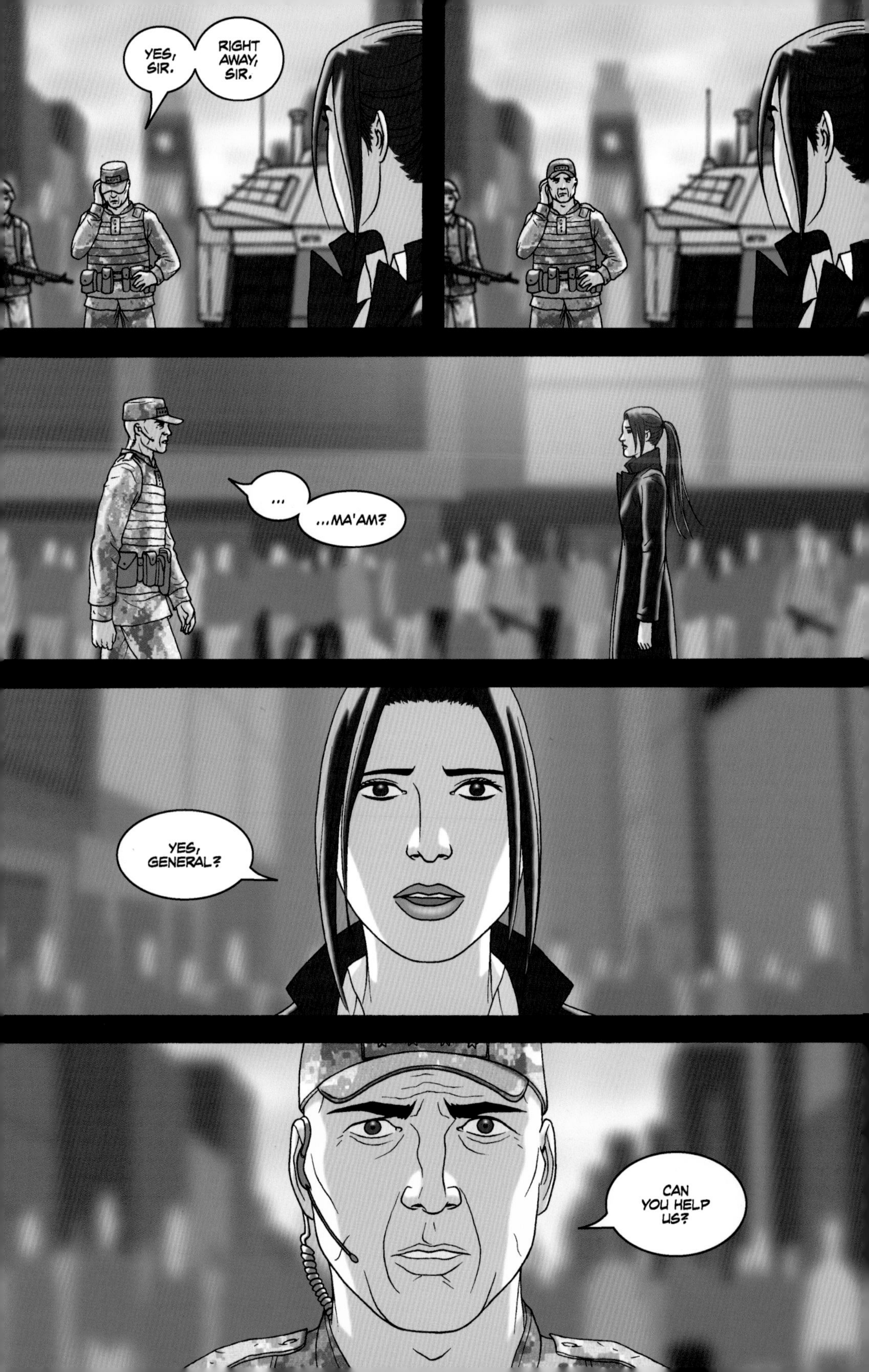
YES, SIR.
RIGHT AWAY, SIR.
...
...MA'AM?
YES, GENERAL?
CAN YOU HELP US?

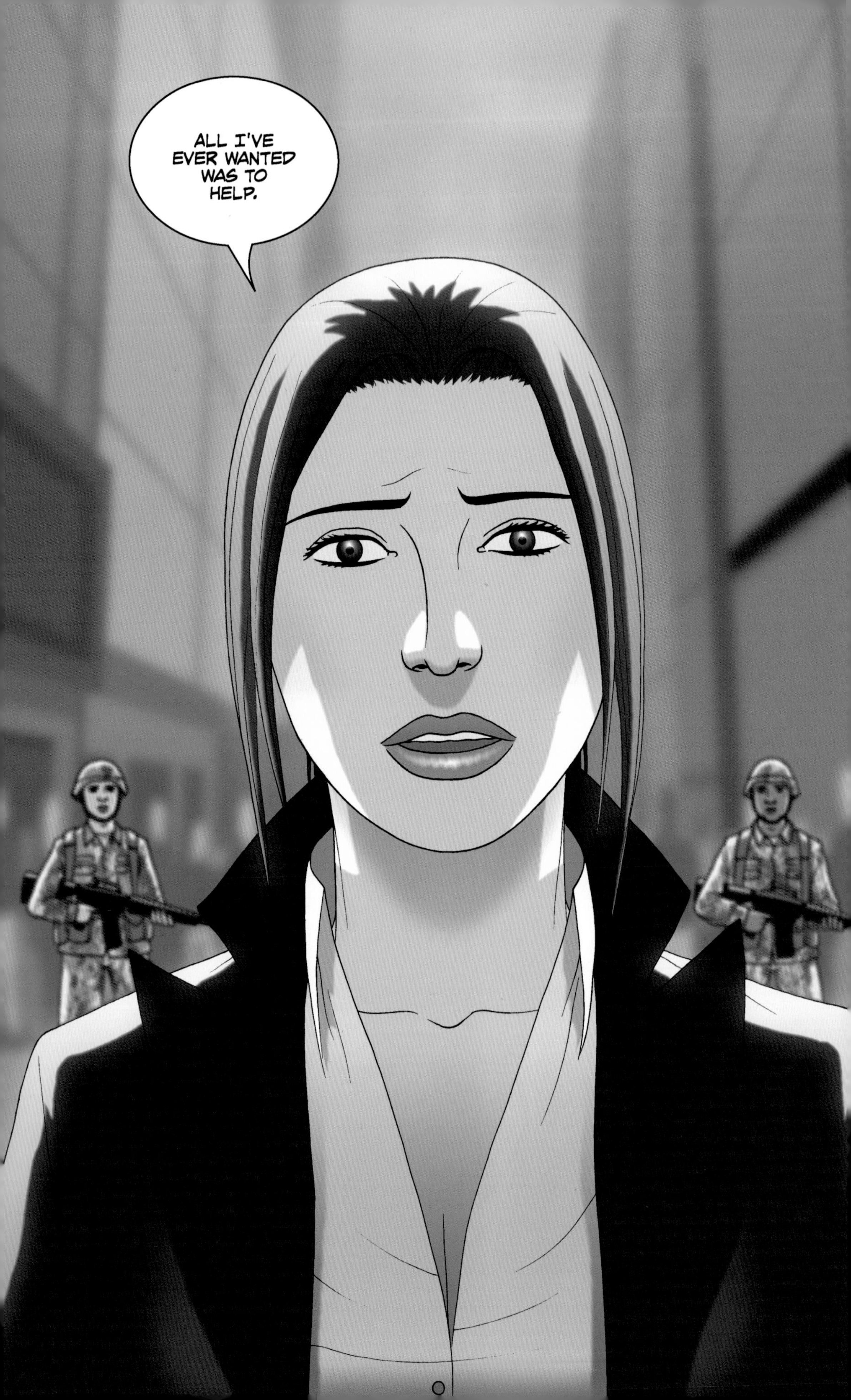
ALL I'VE EVER WANTED WAS TO HELP.

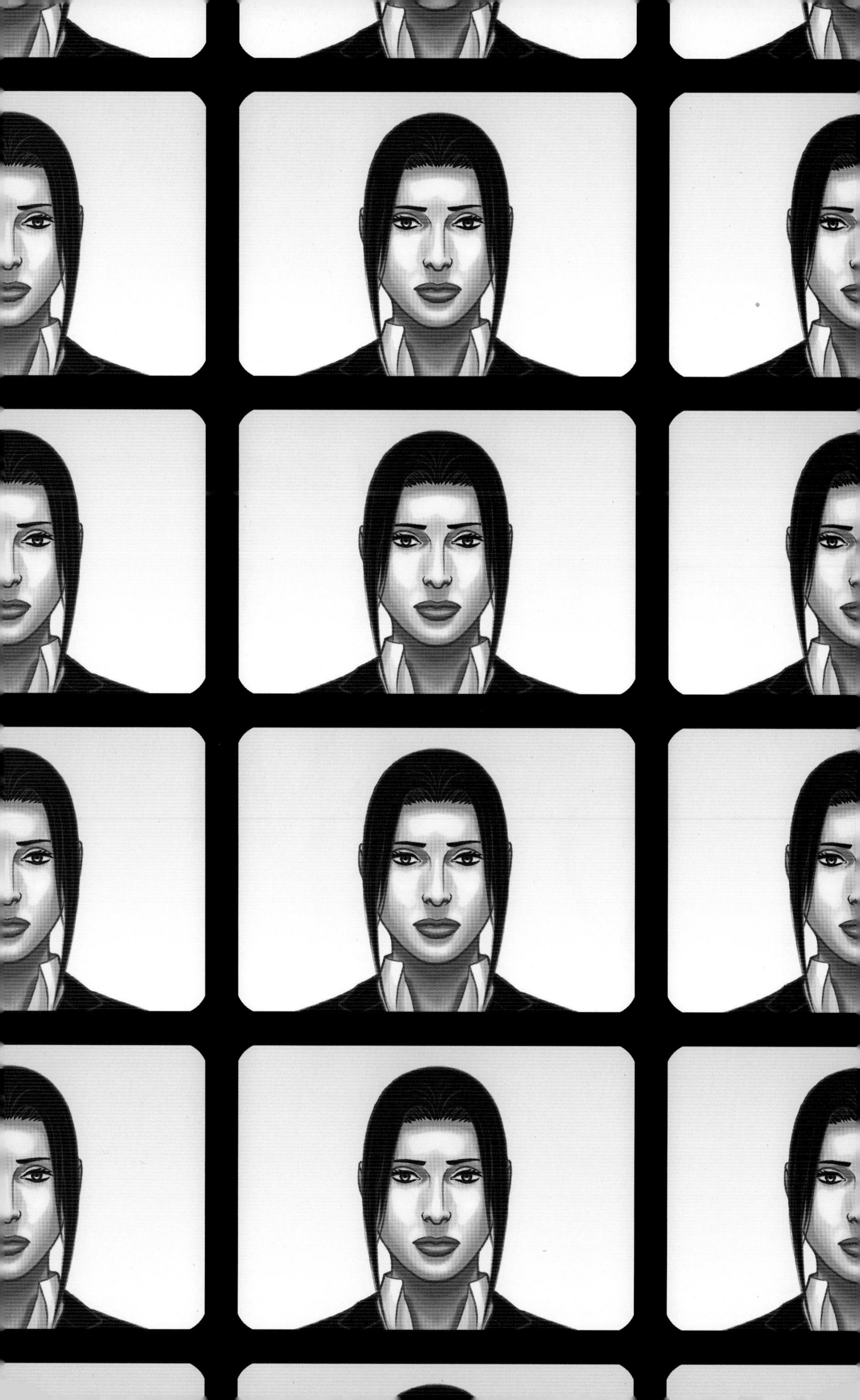

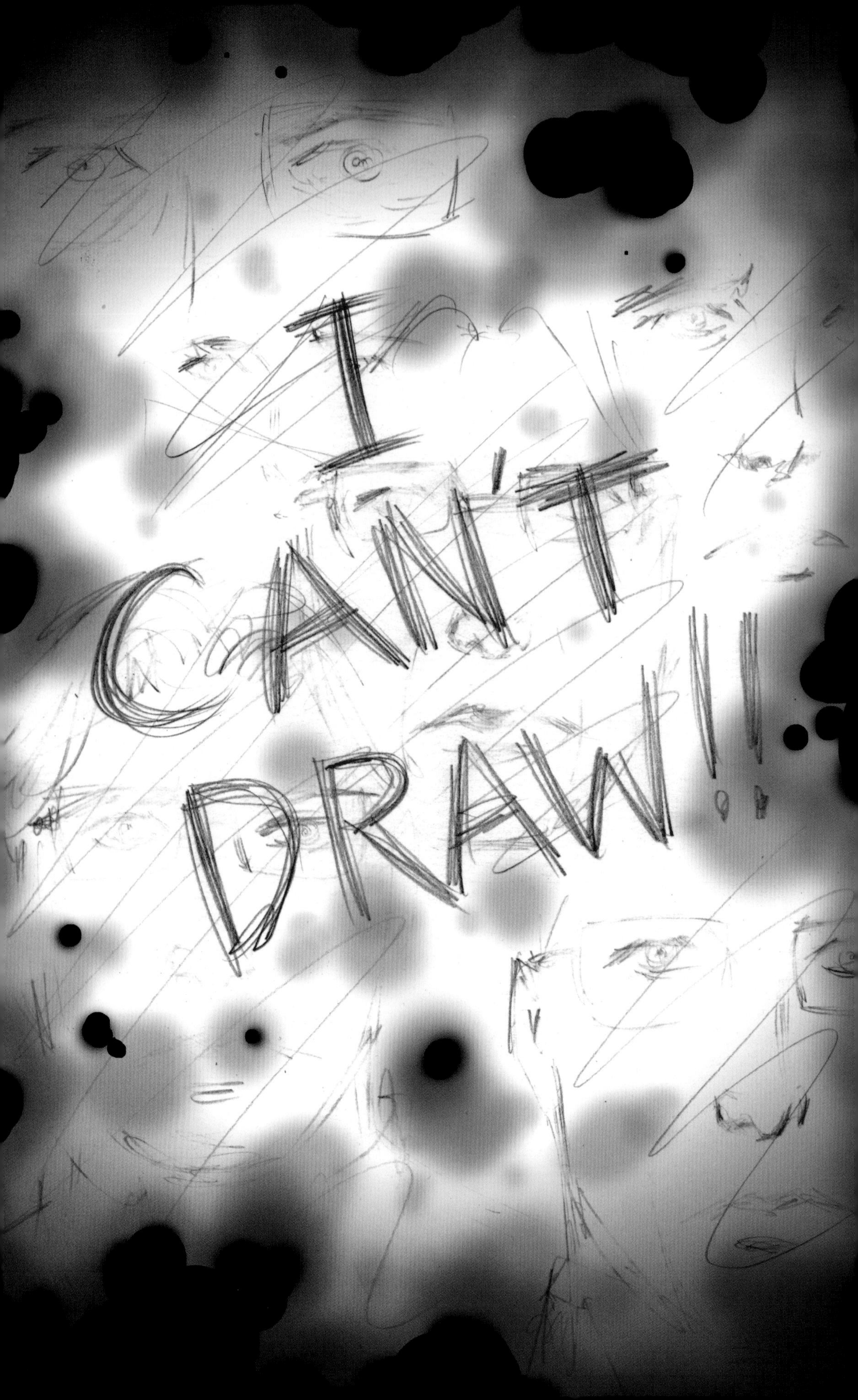
I CAN'T DRAW!!

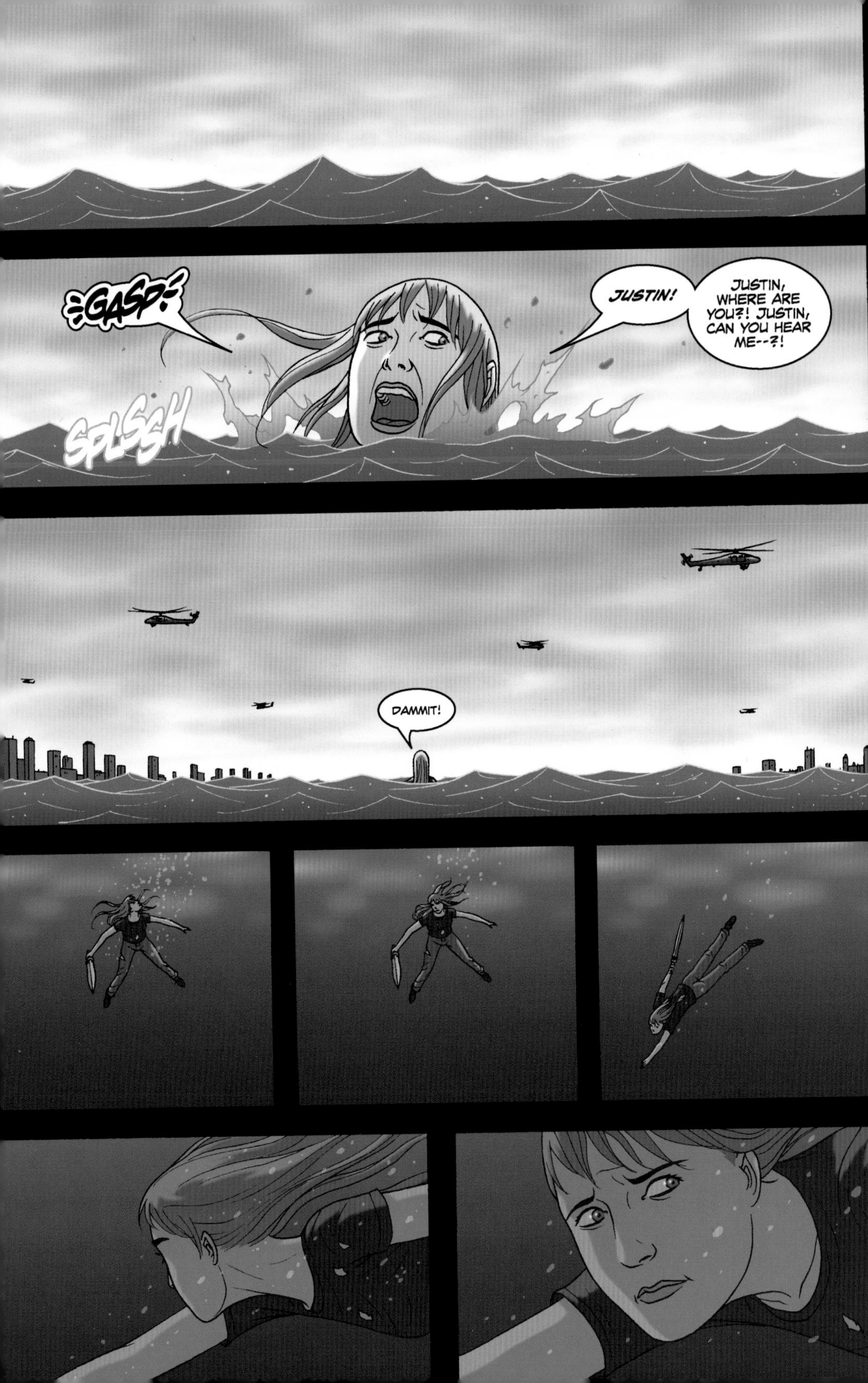
GASP
SPLSSH
JUSTIN!
JUSTIN, WHERE ARE YOU?! JUSTIN, CAN YOU HEAR ME--?!
DAMMIT!

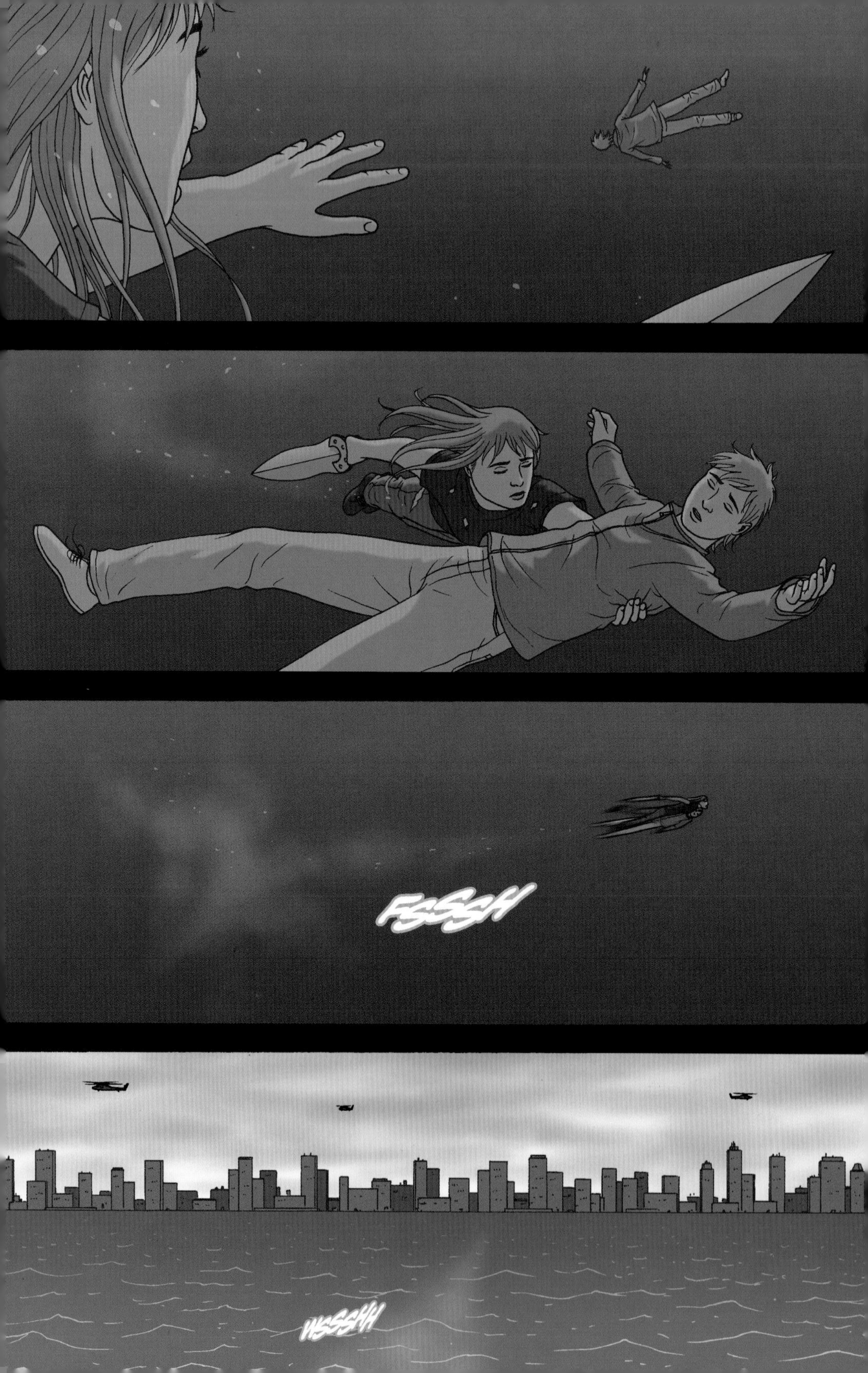
FSSSH
WSSSHH

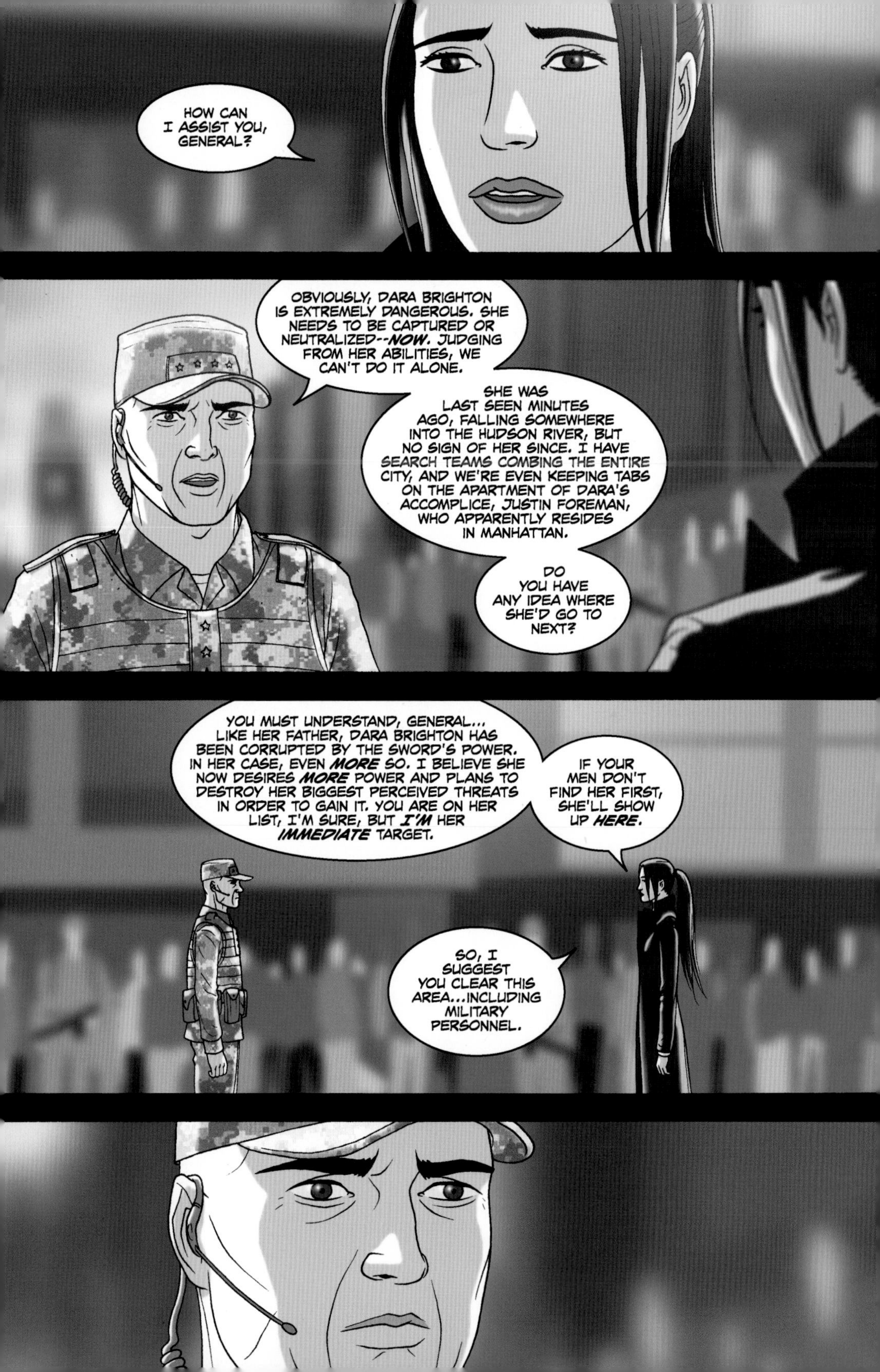
HOW CAN I ASSIST YOU, GENERAL?
OBVIOUSLY, DARA BRIGHTON IS EXTREMELY DANGEROUS. SHE NEEDS TO BE CAPTURED OR NEUTRALIZED--*NOW*. JUDGING FROM HER ABILITIES, WE CAN'T DO IT ALONE.
SHE WAS LAST SEEN MINUTES AGO, FALLING SOMEWHERE INTO THE HUDSON RIVER, BUT NO SIGN OF HER SINCE. I HAVE SEARCH TEAMS COMBING THE ENTIRE CITY, AND WE'RE EVEN KEEPING TABS ON THE APARTMENT OF DARA'S ACCOMPLICE, JUSTIN FOREMAN, WHO APPARENTLY RESIDES IN MANHATTAN.
DO YOU HAVE ANY IDEA WHERE SHE'D GO TO NEXT?
YOU MUST UNDERSTAND, GENERAL... LIKE HER FATHER, DARA BRIGHTON HAS BEEN CORRUPTED BY THE SWORD'S POWER. IN HER CASE, EVEN *MORE* SO. I BELIEVE SHE NOW DESIRES *MORE* POWER AND PLANS TO DESTROY HER BIGGEST PERCEIVED THREATS IN ORDER TO GAIN IT. YOU ARE ON HER LIST, I'M SURE, BUT *I'M* HER *IMMEDIATE* TARGET.
IF YOUR MEN DON'T FIND HER FIRST, SHE'LL SHOW UP *HERE*.
SO, I SUGGEST YOU CLEAR THIS AREA...INCLUDING MILITARY PERSONNEL.

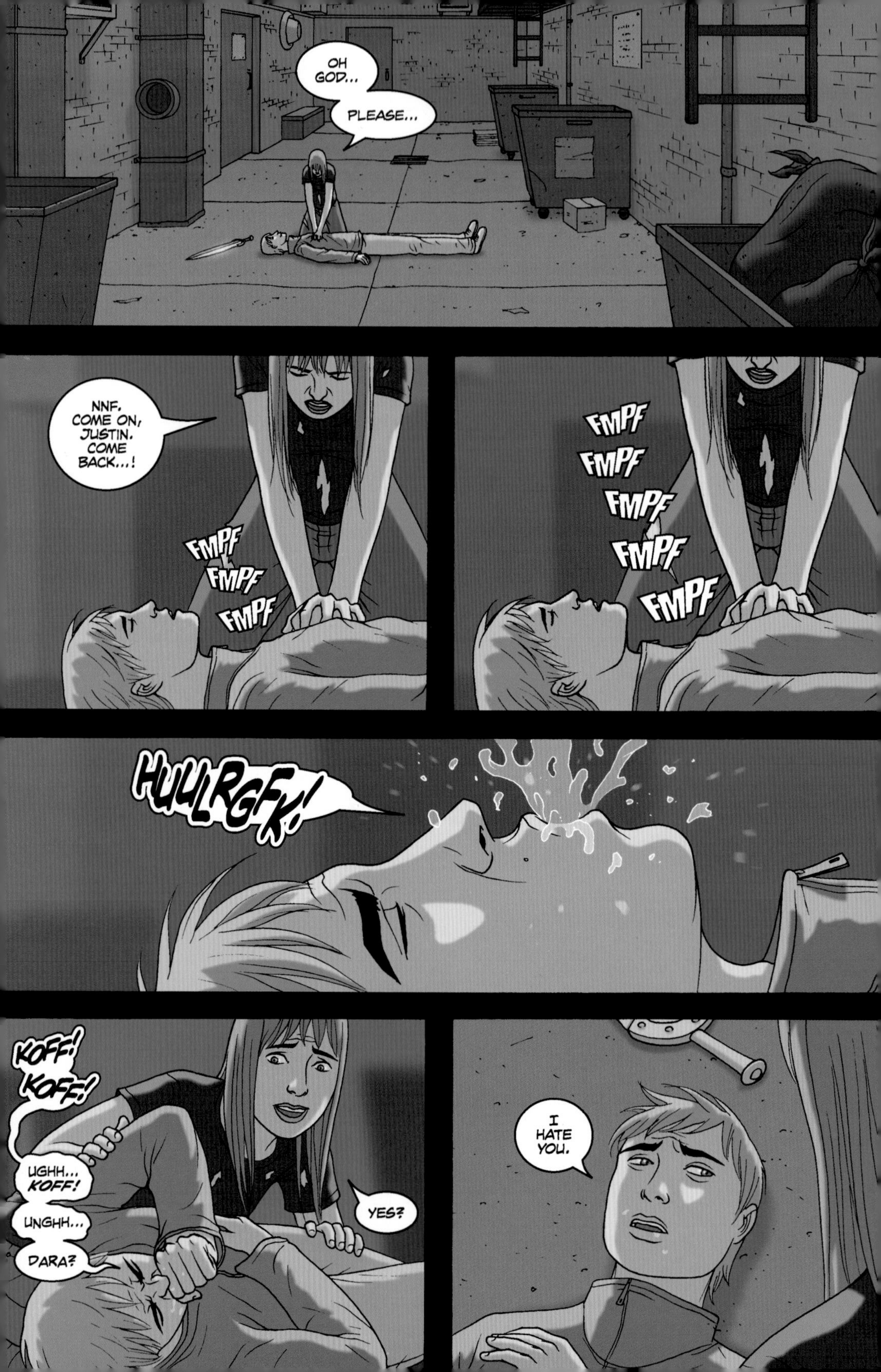
OH GOD...
PLEASE...
NNF. COME ON, JUSTIN. COME BACK...!
FMPF
FMPF
FMPF
FMPF
FMPF
FMPF
FMPF
FMPF
HUULRGFK!
KOFF! KOFF!
UGHH... KOFF!
UNGHH...
DARA?
YES?
I HATE YOU.

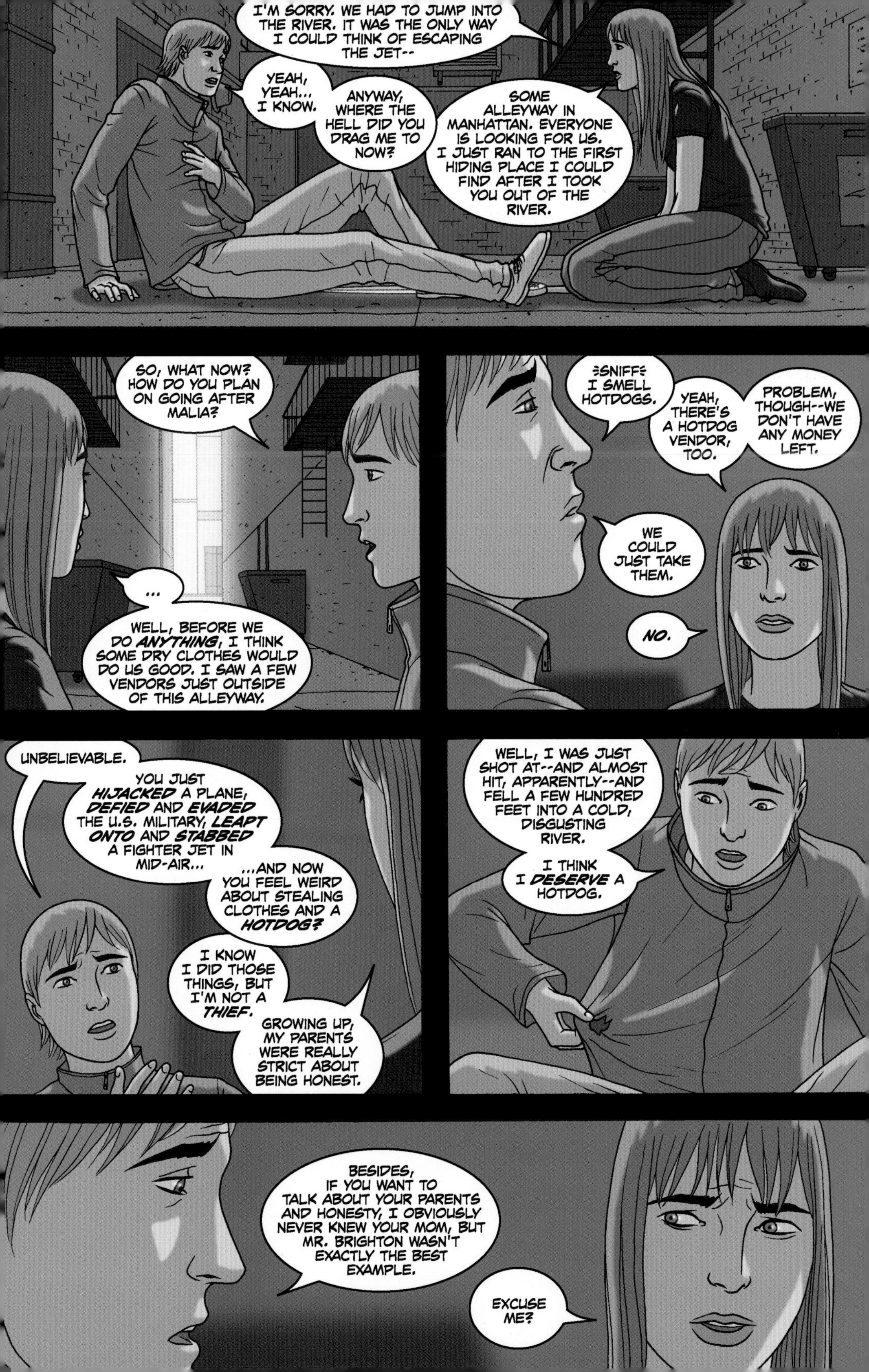
I'M SORRY. WE HAD TO JUMP INTO THE RIVER. IT WAS THE ONLY WAY I COULD THINK OF ESCAPING THE JET--
YEAH, YEAH... I KNOW.
ANYWAY, WHERE THE HELL DID YOU DRAG ME TO NOW?
SOME ALLEYWAY IN MANHATTAN. EVERYONE IS LOOKING FOR US. I JUST RAN TO THE FIRST HIDING PLACE I COULD FIND AFTER I TOOK YOU OUT OF THE RIVER.
SO, WHAT NOW? HOW DO YOU PLAN ON GOING AFTER MALIA?
...
WELL, BEFORE WE DO ANYTHING, I THINK SOME DRY CLOTHES WOULD DO US GOOD. I SAW A FEW VENDORS JUST OUTSIDE OF THIS ALLEYWAY.
SNIFF I SMELL HOTDOGS.
YEAH, THERE'S A HOTDOG VENDOR, TOO.
PROBLEM, THOUGH--WE DON'T HAVE ANY MONEY LEFT.
WE COULD JUST TAKE THEM.
NO.
UNBELIEVABLE.
YOU JUST HIJACKED A PLANE, DEFIED AND EVADED THE U.S. MILITARY, LEAPT ONTO AND STABBED A FIGHTER JET IN MID-AIR...
...AND NOW YOU FEEL WEIRD ABOUT STEALING CLOTHES AND A HOTDOG?
I KNOW I DID THOSE THINGS, BUT I'M NOT A THIEF.
GROWING UP, MY PARENTS WERE REALLY STRICT ABOUT BEING HONEST.
WELL, I WAS JUST SHOT AT--AND ALMOST HIT, APPARENTLY--AND FELL A FEW HUNDRED FEET INTO A COLD, DISGUSTING RIVER.
I THINK I DESERVE A HOTDOG.
BESIDES, IF YOU WANT TO TALK ABOUT YOUR PARENTS AND HONESTY, I OBVIOUSLY NEVER KNEW YOUR MOM, BUT MR. BRIGHTON WASN'T EXACTLY THE BEST EXAMPLE.
EXCUSE ME?

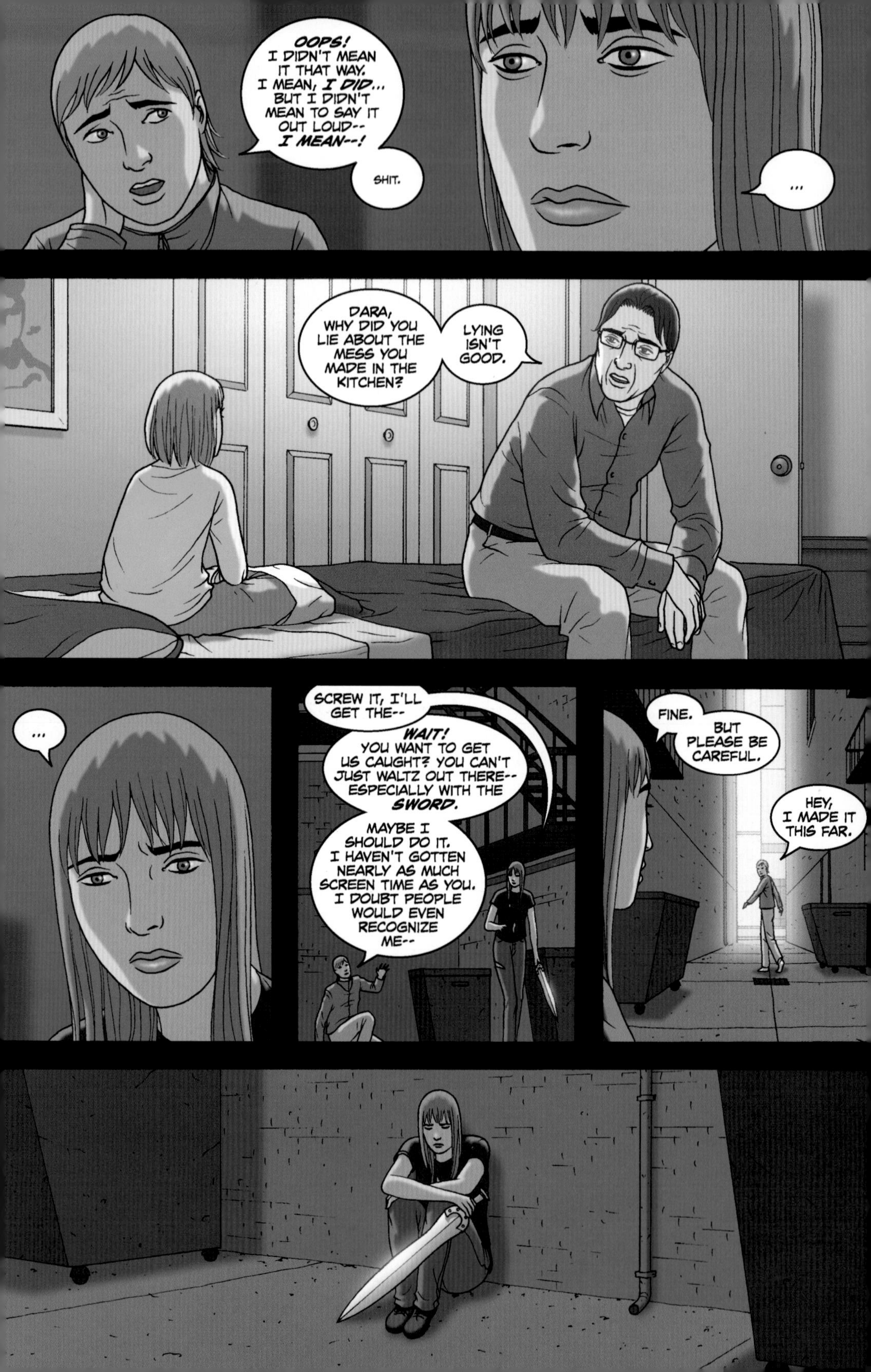
OOPS! I DIDN'T MEAN IT THAT WAY. I MEAN, I DID... BUT I DIDN'T MEAN TO SAY IT OUT LOUD-- I MEAN--!
SHIT.
...
DARA, WHY DID YOU LIE ABOUT THE MESS YOU MADE IN THE KITCHEN?
LYING ISN'T GOOD.
...
SCREW IT, I'LL GET THE--
WAIT! YOU WANT TO GET US CAUGHT? YOU CAN'T JUST WALTZ OUT THERE-- ESPECIALLY WITH THE SWORD.
MAYBE I SHOULD DO IT. I HAVEN'T GOTTEN NEARLY AS MUCH SCREEN TIME AS YOU. I DOUBT PEOPLE WOULD EVEN RECOGNIZE ME--
FINE.
BUT PLEASE BE CAREFUL.
HEY, I MADE IT THIS FAR.

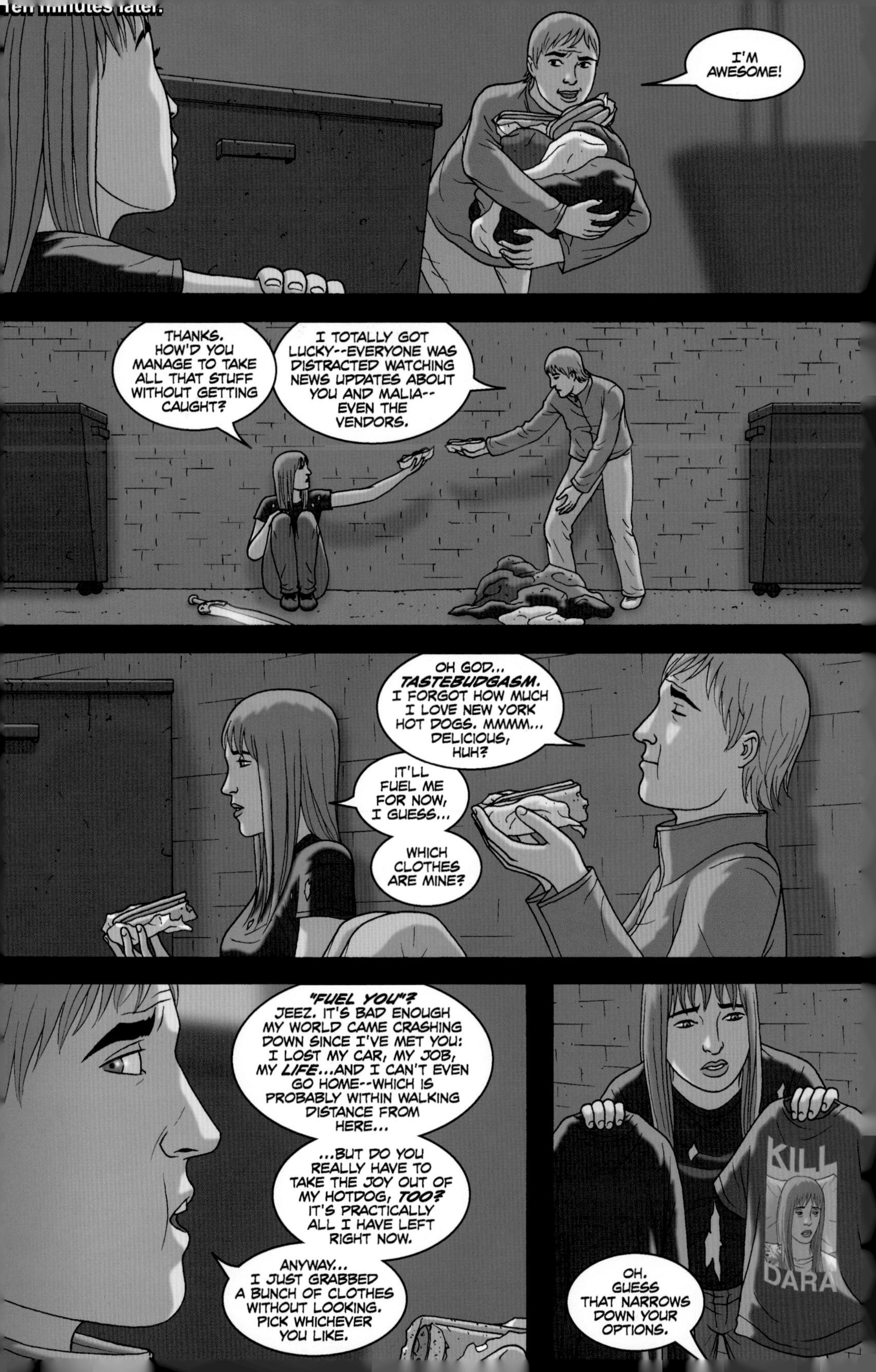
Ten minutes later.
I'M AWESOME!
THANKS. HOW'D YOU MANAGE TO TAKE ALL THAT STUFF WITHOUT GETTING CAUGHT?
I TOTALLY GOT LUCKY--EVERYONE WAS DISTRACTED WATCHING NEWS UPDATES ABOUT YOU AND MALIA--EVEN THE VENDORS.
OH GOD... TASTEBUDGASM. I FORGOT HOW MUCH I LOVE NEW YORK HOT DOGS. MMMM... DELICIOUS, HUH?
IT'LL FUEL ME FOR NOW, I GUESS...
WHICH CLOTHES ARE MINE?
"FUEL YOU"? JEEZ. IT'S BAD ENOUGH MY WORLD CAME CRASHING DOWN SINCE I'VE MET YOU: I LOST MY CAR, MY JOB, MY LIFE...AND I CAN'T EVEN GO HOME--WHICH IS PROBABLY WITHIN WALKING DISTANCE FROM HERE...
...BUT DO YOU REALLY HAVE TO TAKE THE JOY OUT OF MY HOTDOG, TOO? IT'S PRACTICALLY ALL I HAVE LEFT RIGHT NOW.
ANYWAY... I JUST GRABBED A BUNCH OF CLOTHES WITHOUT LOOKING. PICK WHICHEVER YOU LIKE.
KILL DARA
OH. GUESS THAT NARROWS DOWN YOUR OPTIONS.

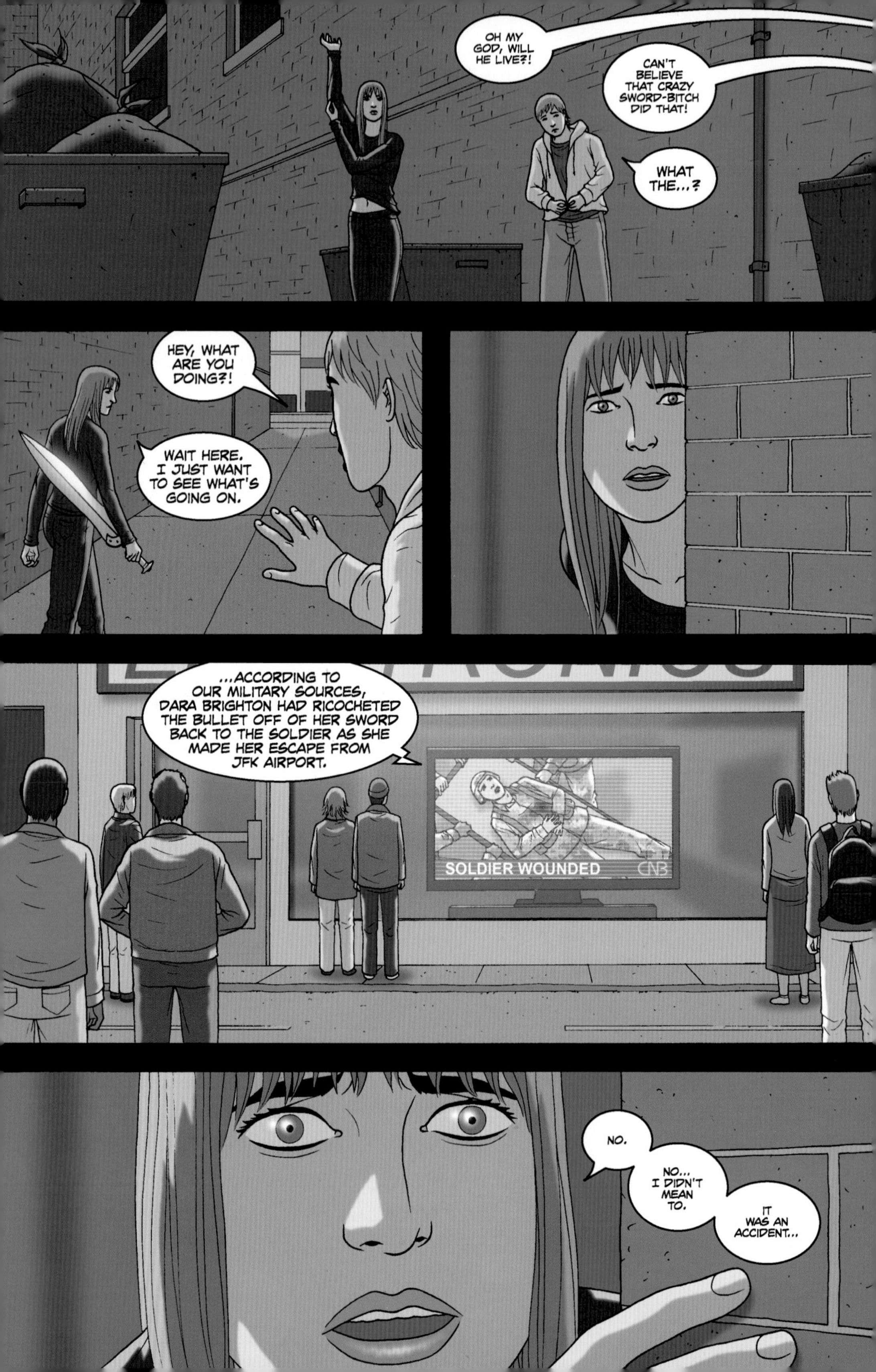
OH MY GOD, WILL HE LIVE?!
CAN'T BELIEVE THAT CRAZY SWORD-BITCH DID THAT!
WHAT THE...?
HEY, WHAT ARE YOU DOING?!
WAIT HERE. I JUST WANT TO SEE WHAT'S GOING ON.
...ACCORDING TO OUR MILITARY SOURCES, DARA BRIGHTON HAD RICOCHETED THE BULLET OFF OF HER SWORD BACK TO THE SOLDIER AS SHE MADE HER ESCAPE FROM JFK AIRPORT.
SOLDIER WOUNDED
CNB
NO.
NO... I DIDN'T MEAN TO.
IT WAS AN ACCIDENT...

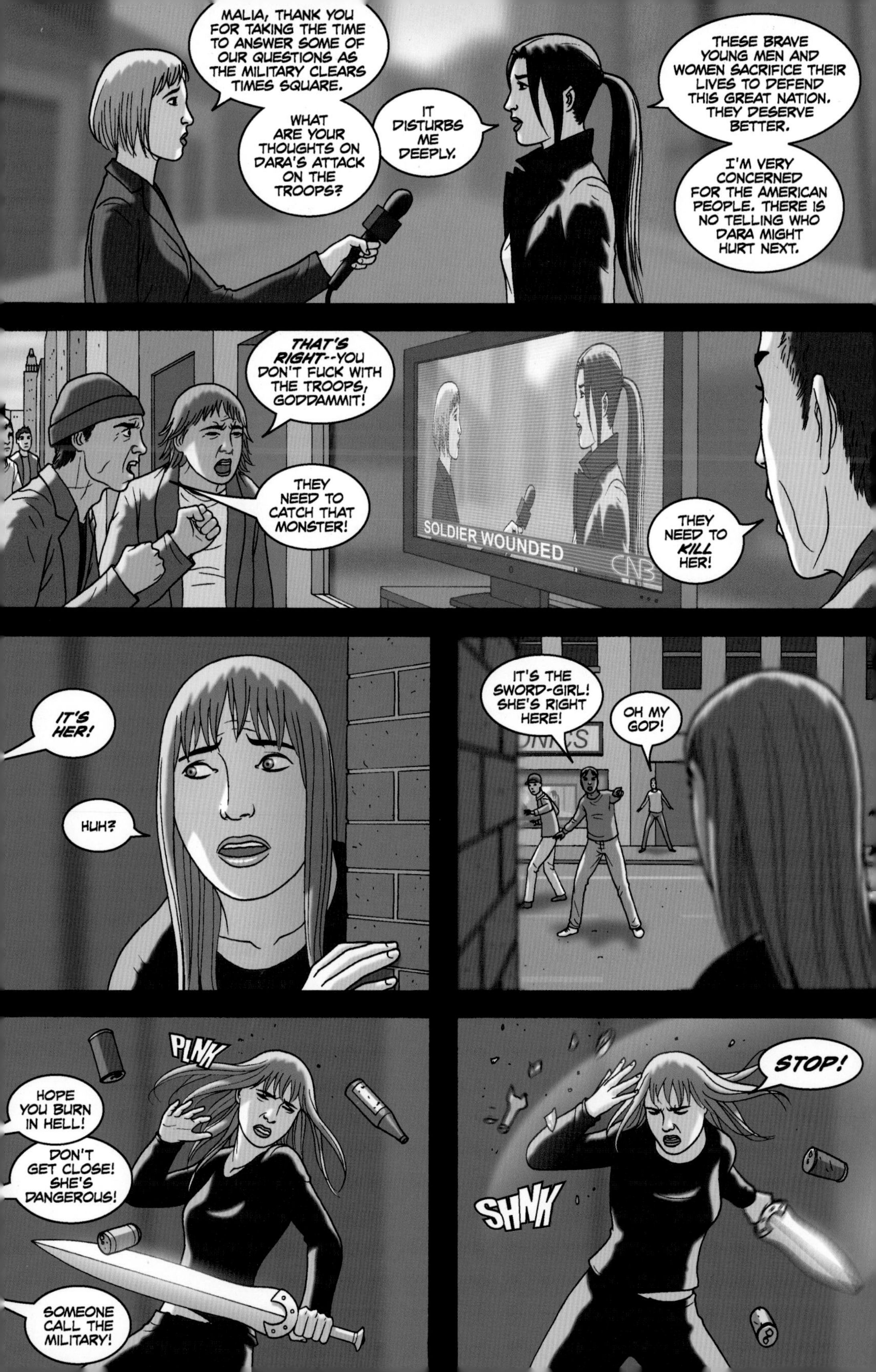

MALIA, THANK YOU FOR TAKING THE TIME TO ANSWER SOME OF OUR QUESTIONS AS THE MILITARY CLEARS TIMES SQUARE.
WHAT ARE YOUR THOUGHTS ON DARA'S ATTACK ON THE TROOPS?
IT DISTURBS ME DEEPLY.
THESE BRAVE YOUNG MEN AND WOMEN SACRIFICE THEIR LIVES TO DEFEND THIS GREAT NATION. THEY DESERVE BETTER.
I'M VERY CONCERNED FOR THE AMERICAN PEOPLE. THERE IS NO TELLING WHO DARA MIGHT HURT NEXT.
THAT'S RIGHT--YOU DON'T FUCK WITH THE TROOPS, GODDAMMIT!
THEY NEED TO CATCH THAT MONSTER!
SOLDIER WOUNDED
CNB
THEY NEED TO KILL HER!
IT'S HER!
HUH?
IT'S THE SWORD-GIRL! SHE'S RIGHT HERE!
OH MY GOD!
PLNK
HOPE YOU BURN IN HELL!
DON'T GET CLOSE! SHE'S DANGEROUS!
SOMEONE CALL THE MILITARY!
STOP!
SHNK

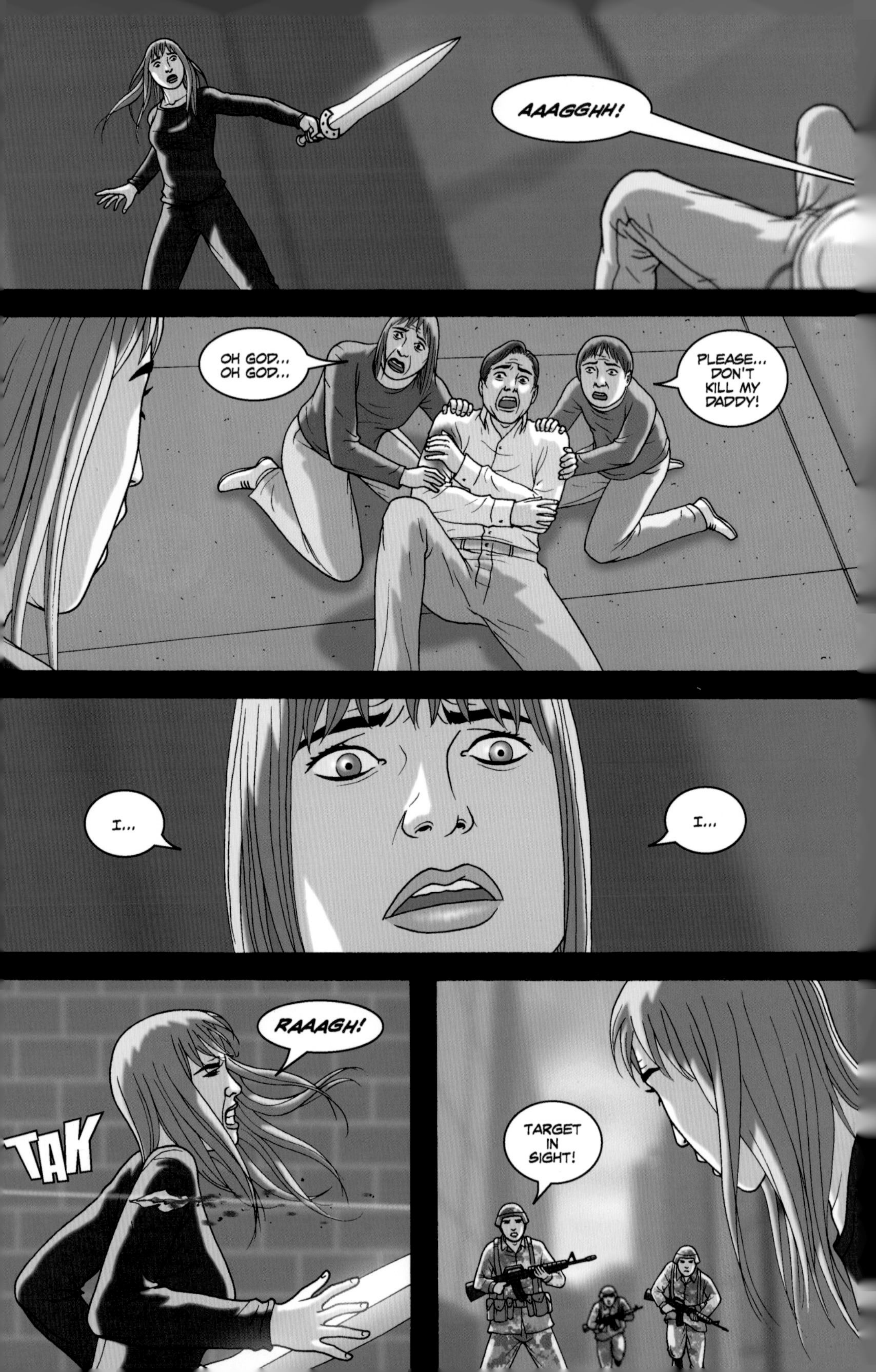
AAAGGHH!
OH GOD... OH GOD...
PLEASE... DON'T KILL MY DADDY!
I...
I...
RAAAGH!
TAK
TARGET IN SIGHT!

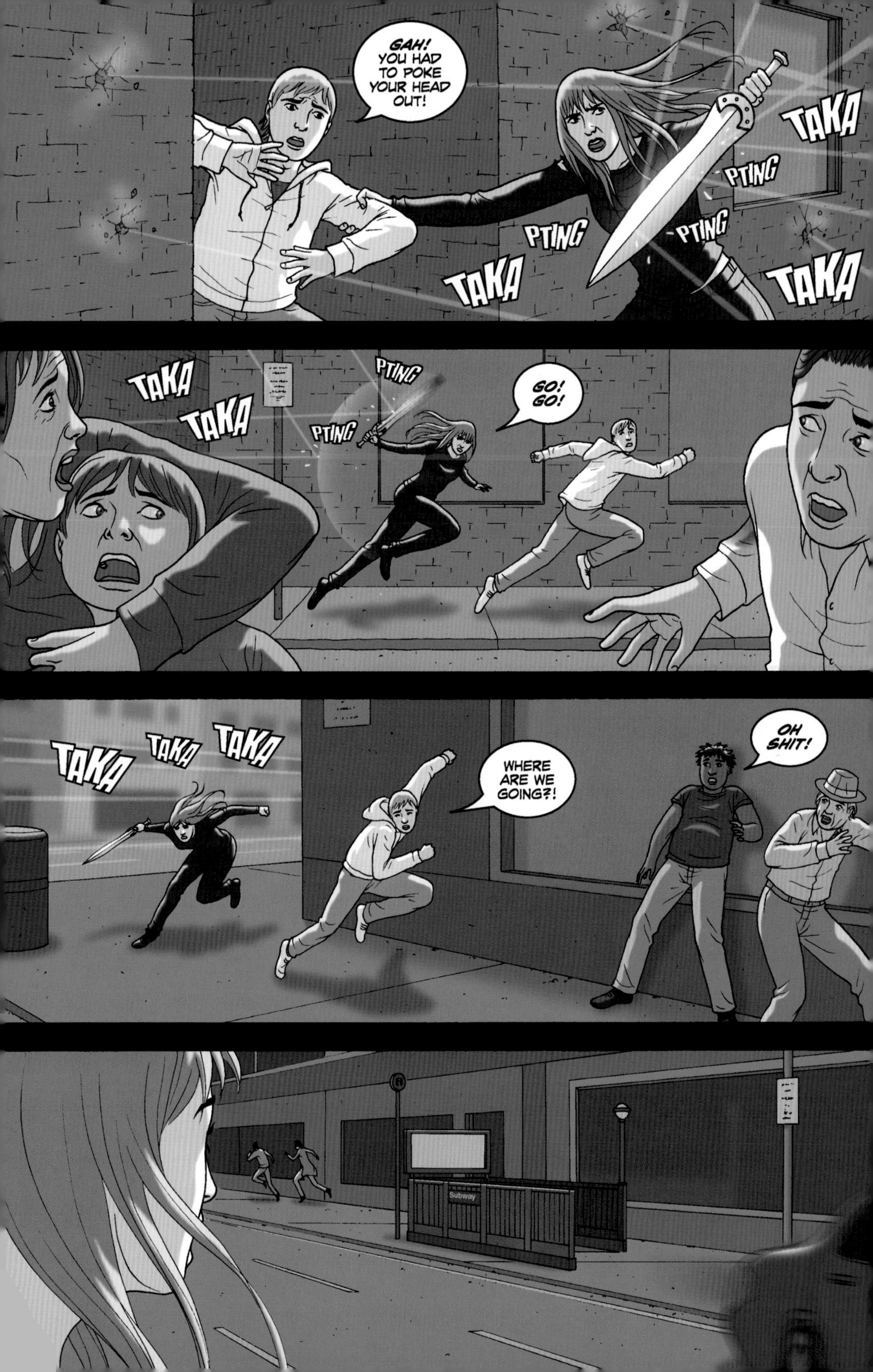
GAH! YOU HAD TO POKE YOUR HEAD OUT!
TAKA
PTING
PTING
PTING
TAKA
TAKA
TAKA
TAKA
PTING
PTING
GO! GO!
TAKA
TAKA
TAKA
WHERE ARE WE GOING?!
OH SHIT!
Subway

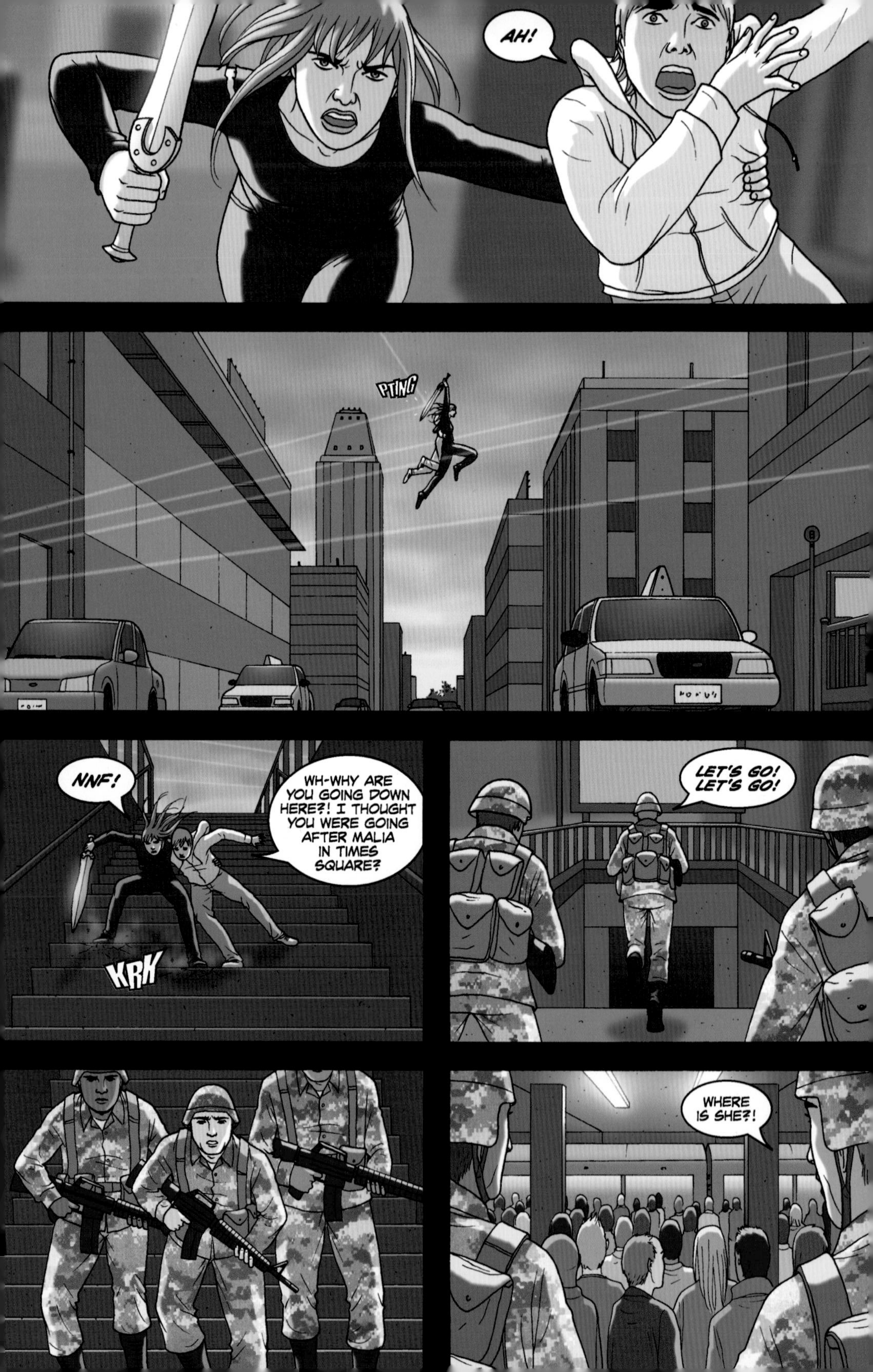
AH!
PTING
NNF!
WH-WHY ARE YOU GOING DOWN HERE?! I THOUGHT YOU WERE GOING AFTER MALIA IN TIMES SQUARE?
KRK
LET'S GO! LET'S GO!
WHERE IS SHE?!

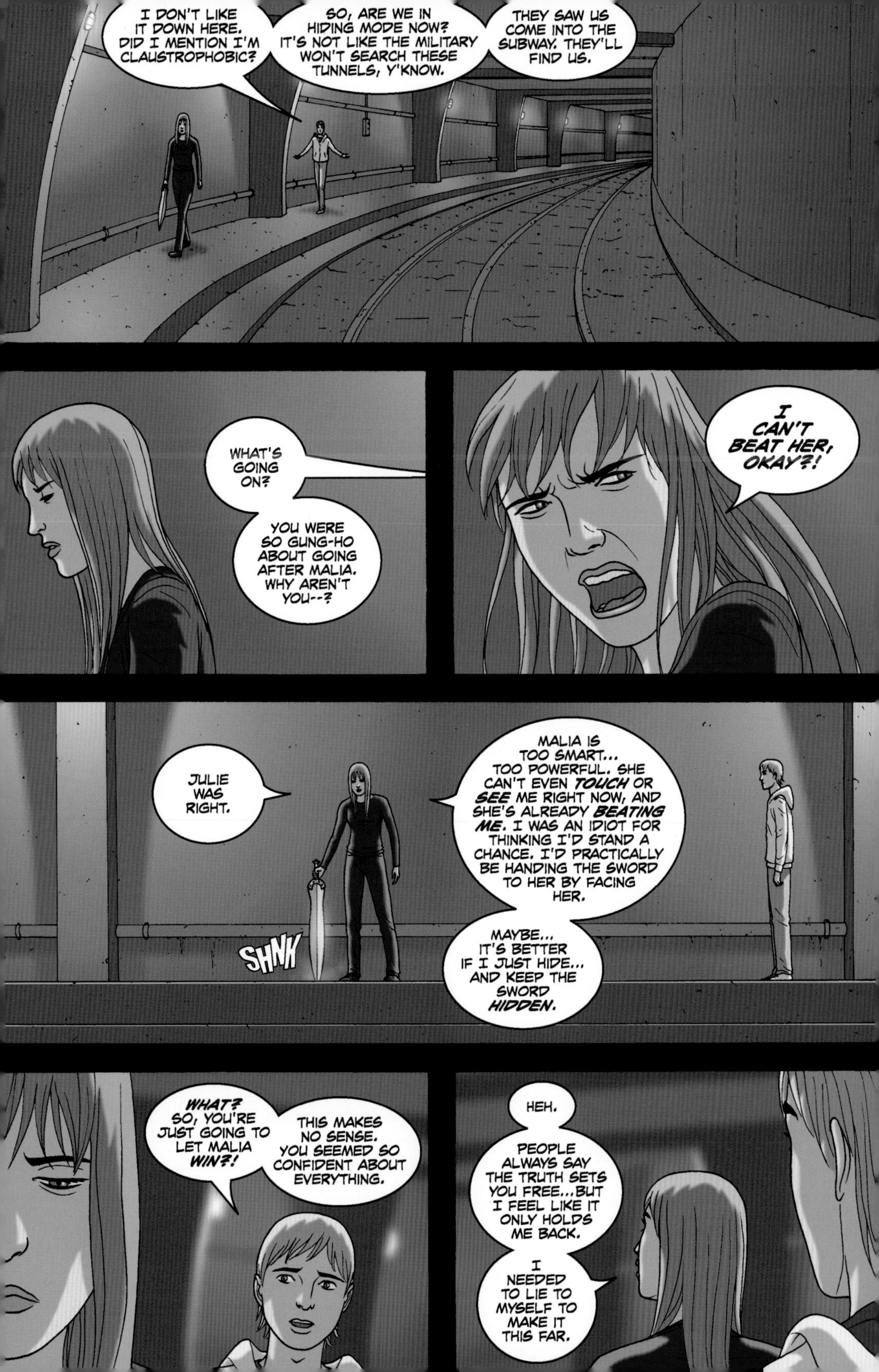
I DON'T LIKE IT DOWN HERE. DID I MENTION I'M CLAUSTROPHOBIC?
SO, ARE WE IN HIDING MODE NOW? IT'S NOT LIKE THE MILITARY WON'T SEARCH THESE TUNNELS, Y'KNOW.
THEY SAW US COME INTO THE SUBWAY. THEY'LL FIND US.
WHAT'S GOING ON?
YOU WERE SO GUNG-HO ABOUT GOING AFTER MALIA. WHY AREN'T YOU--?
I CAN'T BEAT HER, OKAY?!
JULIE WAS RIGHT.
MALIA IS TOO SMART... TOO POWERFUL. SHE CAN'T EVEN TOUCH OR SEE ME RIGHT NOW, AND SHE'S ALREADY BEATING ME. I WAS AN IDIOT FOR THINKING I'D STAND A CHANCE. I'D PRACTICALLY BE HANDING THE SWORD TO HER BY FACING HER.
SHNK
MAYBE... IT'S BETTER IF I JUST HIDE... AND KEEP THE SWORD HIDDEN.
WHAT? SO, YOU'RE JUST GOING TO LET MALIA WIN?!
THIS MAKES NO SENSE. YOU SEEMED SO CONFIDENT ABOUT EVERYTHING.
HEH.
PEOPLE ALWAYS SAY THE TRUTH SETS YOU FREE...BUT I FEEL LIKE IT ONLY HOLDS ME BACK.
I NEEDED TO LIE TO MYSELF TO MAKE IT THIS FAR.

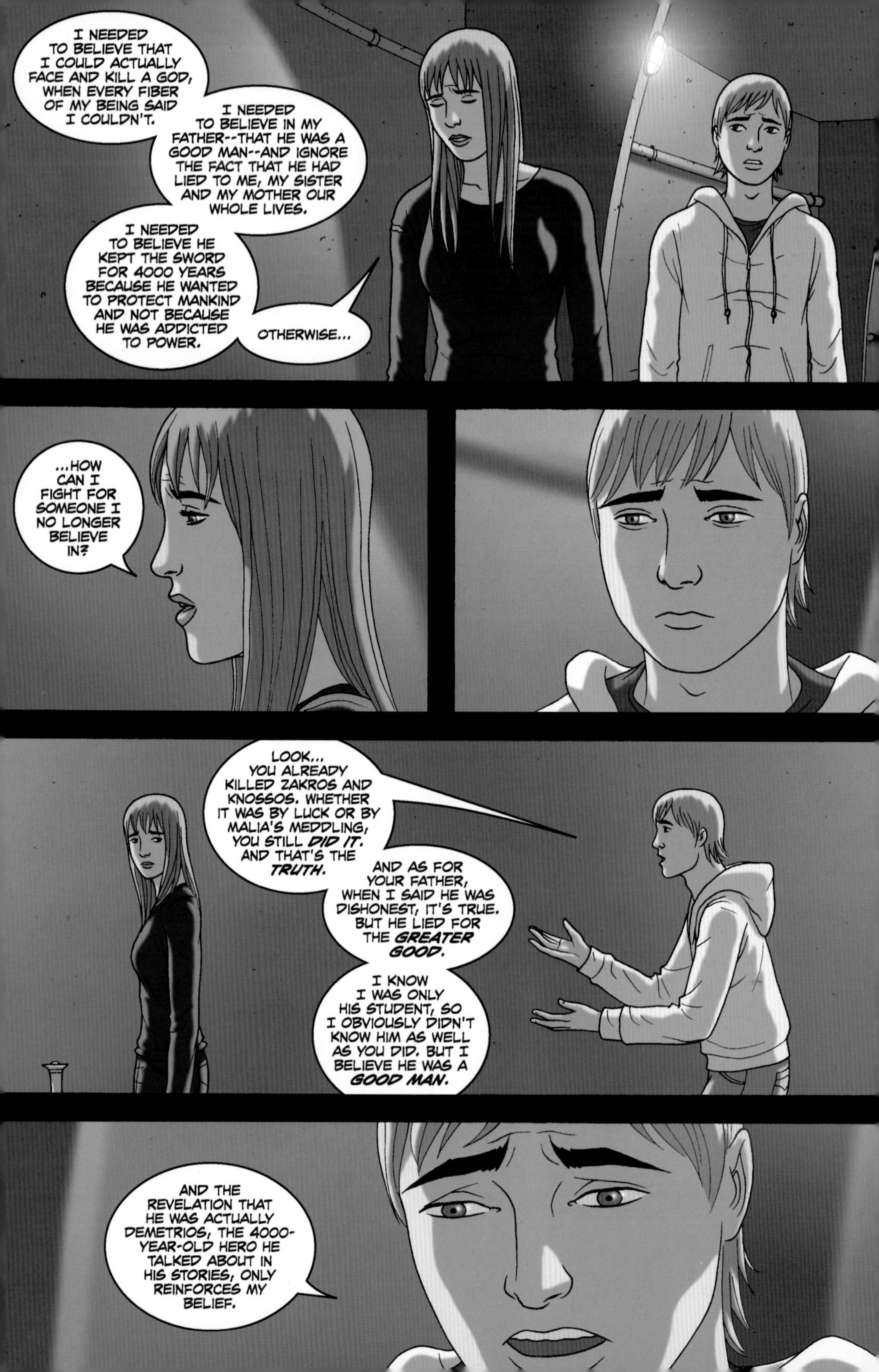
I NEEDED TO BELIEVE THAT I COULD ACTUALLY FACE AND KILL A GOD, WHEN EVERY FIBER OF MY BEING SAID I COULDN'T.
I NEEDED TO BELIEVE IN MY FATHER--THAT HE WAS A GOOD MAN--AND IGNORE THE FACT THAT HE HAD LIED TO ME, MY SISTER AND MY MOTHER OUR WHOLE LIVES.
I NEEDED TO BELIEVE HE KEPT THE SWORD FOR 4000 YEARS BECAUSE HE WANTED TO PROTECT MANKIND AND NOT BECAUSE HE WAS ADDICTED TO POWER.
OTHERWISE...
...HOW CAN I FIGHT FOR SOMEONE I NO LONGER BELIEVE IN?
LOOK... YOU ALREADY KILLED ZAKROS AND KNOSSOS. WHETHER IT WAS BY LUCK OR BY MALIA'S MEDDLING, YOU STILL *DID IT*. AND THAT'S THE *TRUTH*.
AND AS FOR YOUR FATHER, WHEN I SAID HE WAS DISHONEST, IT'S TRUE. BUT HE LIED FOR THE *GREATER GOOD*.
I KNOW I WAS ONLY HIS STUDENT, SO I OBVIOUSLY DIDN'T KNOW HIM AS WELL AS YOU DID. BUT I BELIEVE HE WAS A *GOOD MAN*.
AND THE REVELATION THAT HE WAS ACTUALLY DEMETRIOS, THE 4000-YEAR-OLD HERO HE TALKED ABOUT IN HIS STORIES, ONLY REINFORCES MY BELIEF.

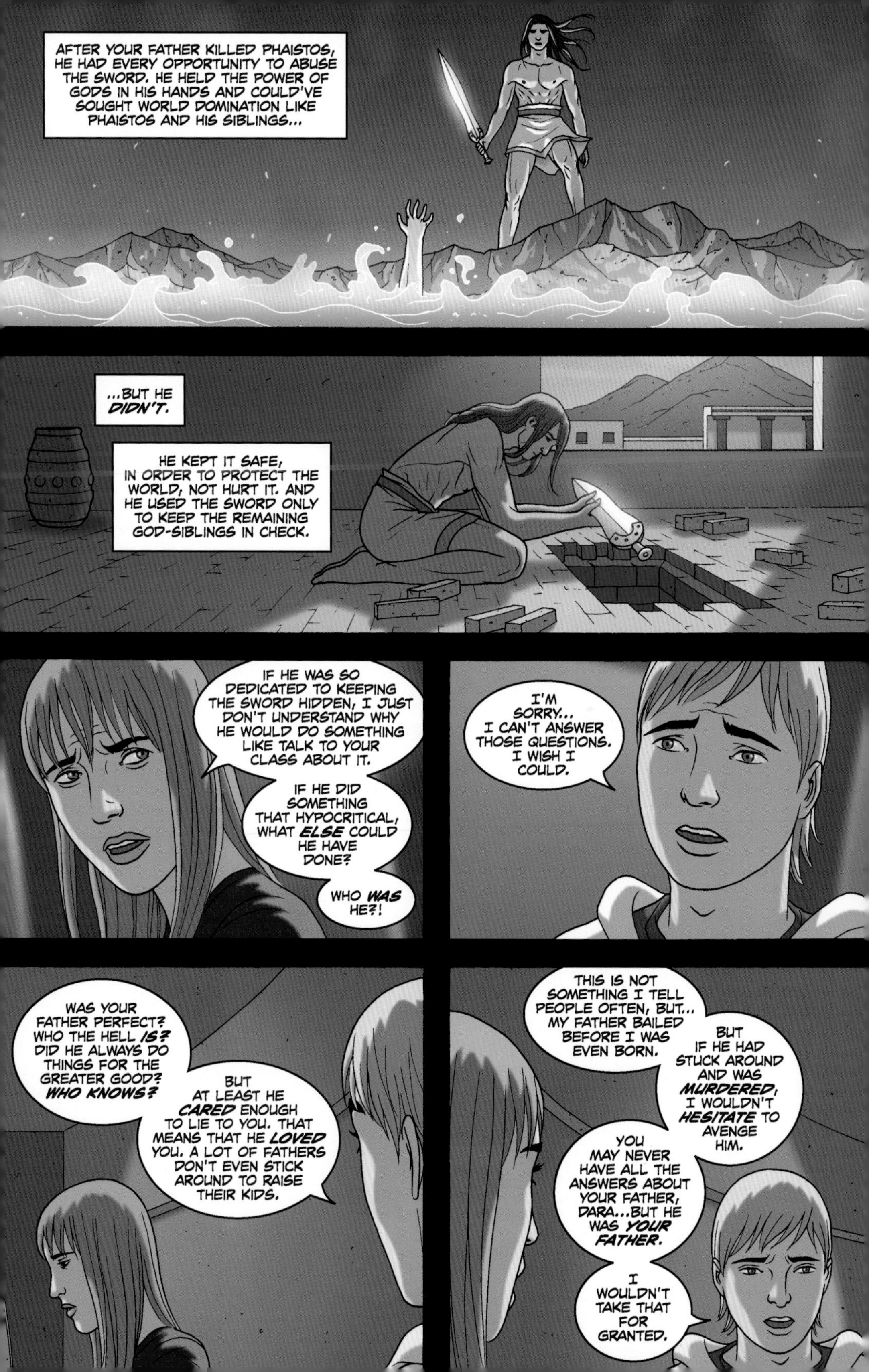
AFTER YOUR FATHER KILLED PHAISTOS, HE HAD EVERY OPPORTUNITY TO ABUSE THE SWORD. HE HELD THE POWER OF GODS IN HIS HANDS AND COULD'VE SOUGHT WORLD DOMINATION LIKE PHAISTOS AND HIS SIBLINGS...
...BUT HE DIDN'T.
HE KEPT IT SAFE, IN ORDER TO PROTECT THE WORLD, NOT HURT IT. AND HE USED THE SWORD ONLY TO KEEP THE REMAINING GOD-SIBLINGS IN CHECK.
IF HE WAS SO DEDICATED TO KEEPING THE SWORD HIDDEN, I JUST DON'T UNDERSTAND WHY HE WOULD DO SOMETHING LIKE TALK TO YOUR CLASS ABOUT IT.
IF HE DID SOMETHING THAT HYPOCRITICAL, WHAT ELSE COULD HE HAVE DONE?
WHO WAS HE?!
I'M SORRY... I CAN'T ANSWER THOSE QUESTIONS. I WISH I COULD.
WAS YOUR FATHER PERFECT? WHO THE HELL IS? DID HE ALWAYS DO THINGS FOR THE GREATER GOOD? WHO KNOWS?
BUT AT LEAST HE CARED ENOUGH TO LIE TO YOU. THAT MEANS THAT HE LOVED YOU. A LOT OF FATHERS DON'T EVEN STICK AROUND TO RAISE THEIR KIDS.
THIS IS NOT SOMETHING I TELL PEOPLE OFTEN, BUT... MY FATHER BAILED BEFORE I WAS EVEN BORN.
BUT IF HE HAD STUCK AROUND AND WAS MURDERED, I WOULDN'T HESITATE TO AVENGE HIM.
YOU MAY NEVER HAVE ALL THE ANSWERS ABOUT YOUR FATHER, DARA...BUT HE WAS YOUR FATHER.
I WOULDN'T TAKE THAT FOR GRANTED.

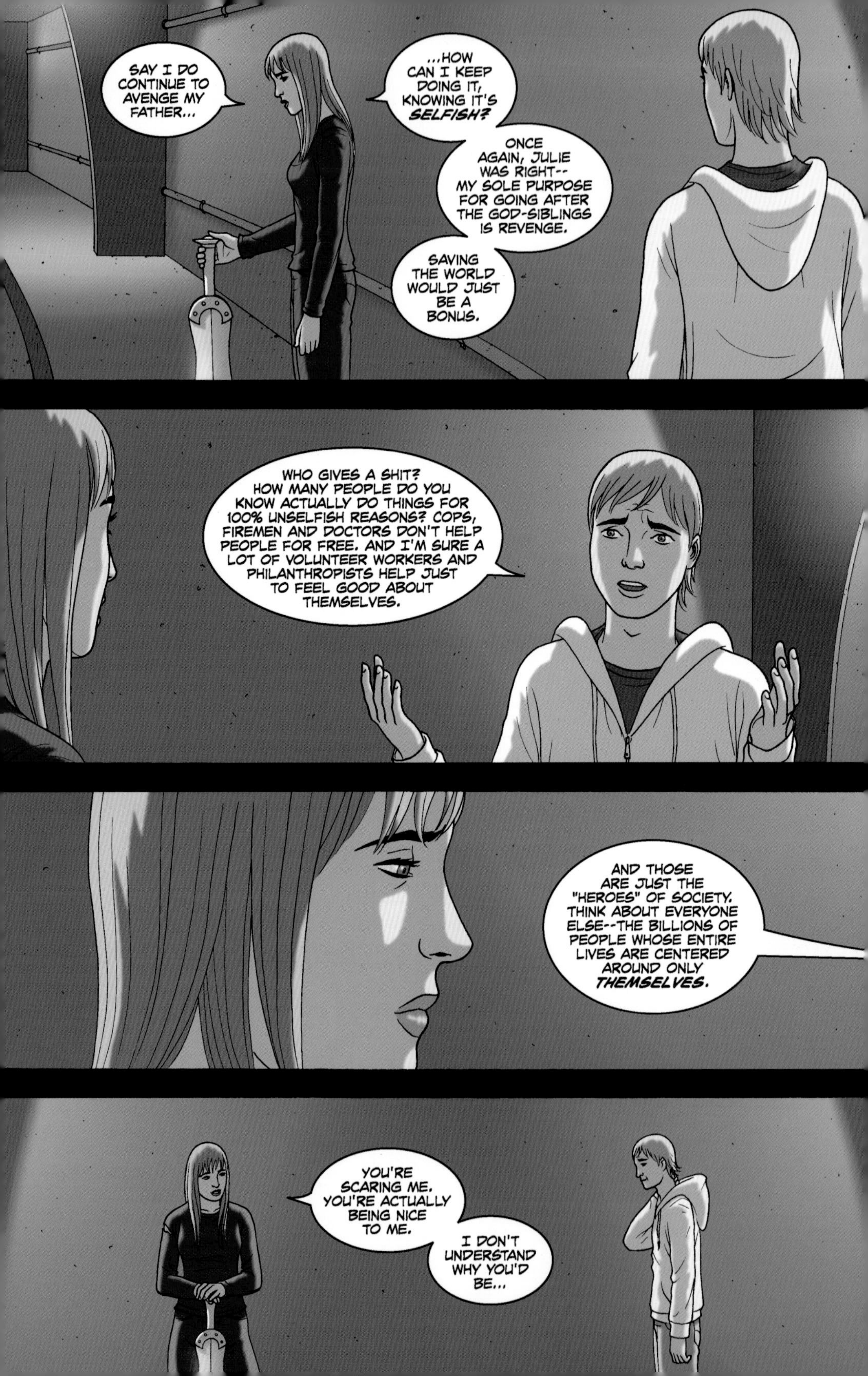
SAY I DO CONTINUE TO AVENGE MY FATHER...
...HOW CAN I KEEP DOING IT, KNOWING IT'S *SELFISH?*
ONCE AGAIN, JULIE WAS RIGHT-- MY SOLE PURPOSE FOR GOING AFTER THE GOD-SIBLINGS IS REVENGE.
SAVING THE WORLD WOULD JUST BE A BONUS.
WHO GIVES A SHIT? HOW MANY PEOPLE DO YOU KNOW ACTUALLY DO THINGS FOR 100% UNSELFISH REASONS? COPS, FIREMEN AND DOCTORS DON'T HELP PEOPLE FOR FREE. AND I'M SURE A LOT OF VOLUNTEER WORKERS AND PHILANTHROPISTS HELP JUST TO FEEL GOOD ABOUT THEMSELVES.
AND THOSE ARE JUST THE "HEROES" OF SOCIETY. THINK ABOUT EVERYONE ELSE--THE BILLIONS OF PEOPLE WHOSE ENTIRE LIVES ARE CENTERED AROUND ONLY *THEMSELVES.*
YOU'RE SCARING ME. YOU'RE ACTUALLY BEING NICE TO ME.
I DON'T UNDERSTAND WHY YOU'D BE...

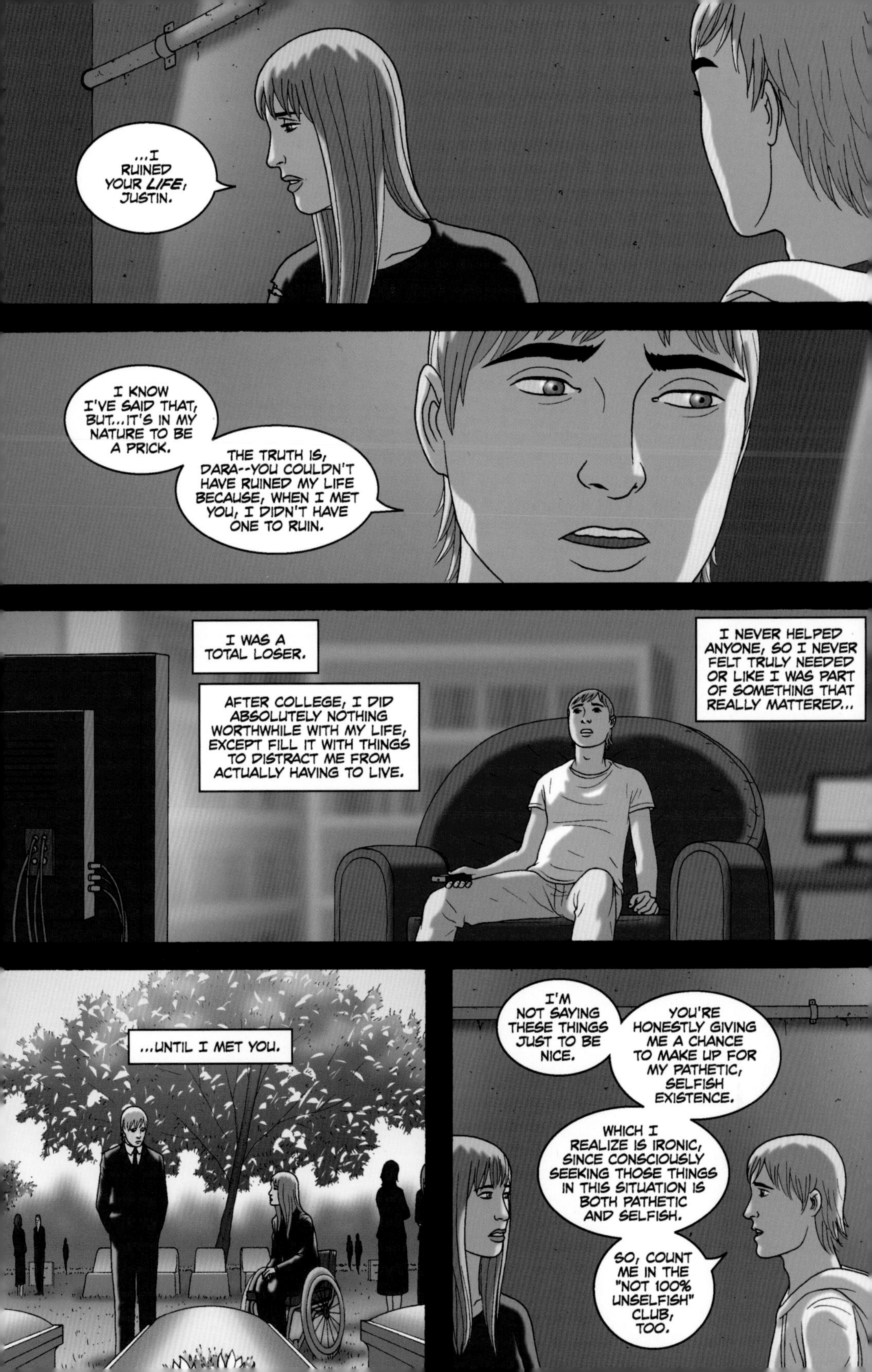
...I RUINED YOUR *LIFE*, JUSTIN.
I KNOW I'VE SAID THAT, BUT...IT'S IN MY NATURE TO BE A PRICK.
THE TRUTH IS, DARA--YOU COULDN'T HAVE RUINED MY LIFE BECAUSE, WHEN I MET YOU, I DIDN'T HAVE ONE TO RUIN.
I WAS A TOTAL LOSER.
AFTER COLLEGE, I DID ABSOLUTELY NOTHING WORTHWHILE WITH MY LIFE, EXCEPT FILL IT WITH THINGS TO DISTRACT ME FROM ACTUALLY HAVING TO LIVE.
I NEVER HELPED ANYONE, SO I NEVER FELT TRULY NEEDED OR LIKE I WAS PART OF SOMETHING THAT REALLY MATTERED...
...UNTIL I MET YOU.
I'M NOT SAYING THESE THINGS JUST TO BE NICE.
YOU'RE HONESTLY GIVING ME A CHANCE TO MAKE UP FOR MY PATHETIC, SELFISH EXISTENCE.
WHICH I REALIZE IS IRONIC, SINCE CONSCIOUSLY SEEKING THOSE THINGS IN THIS SITUATION IS BOTH PATHETIC AND SELFISH.
SO, COUNT ME IN THE "NOT 100% UNSELFISH" CLUB, TOO.

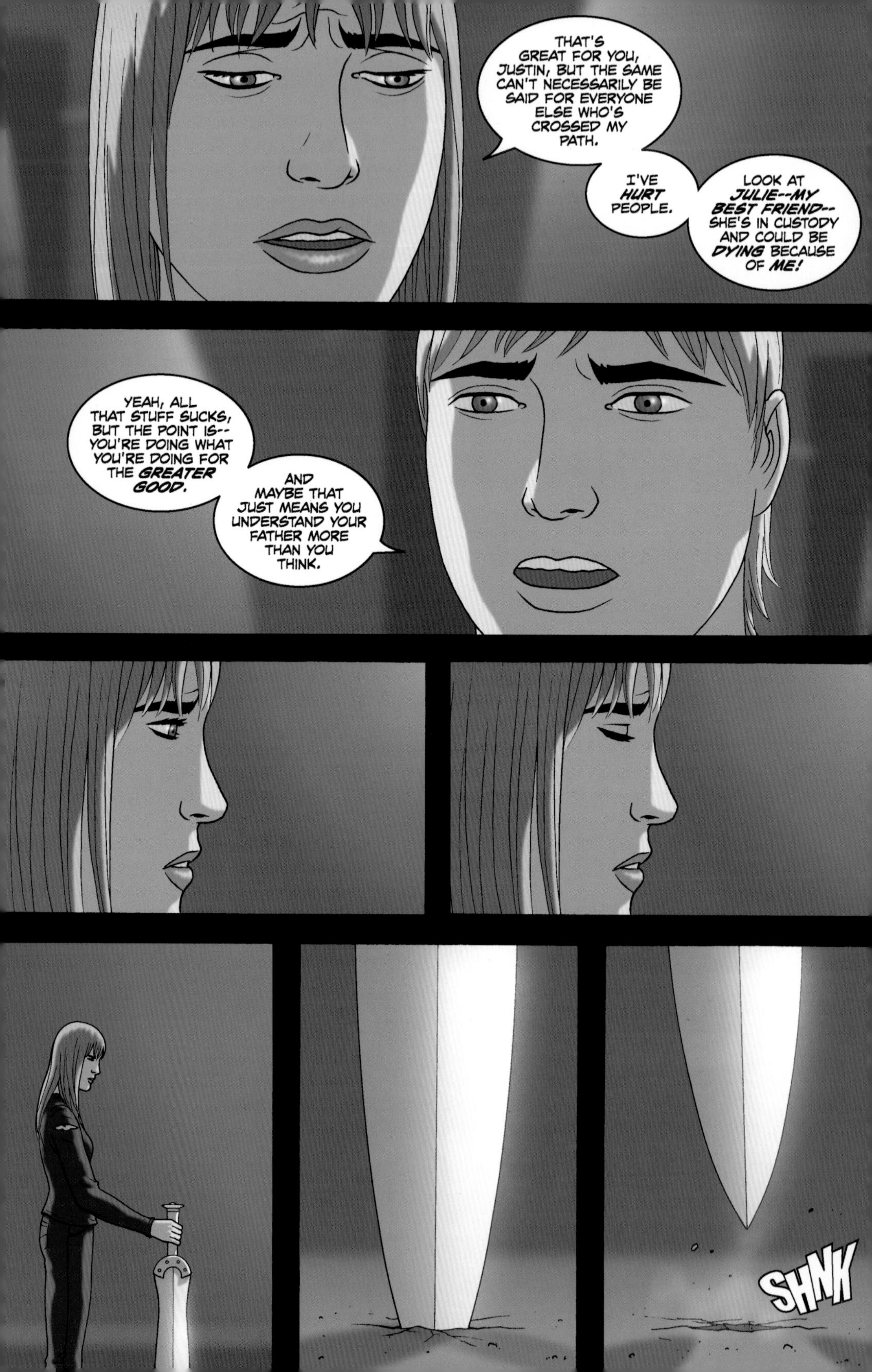
THAT'S GREAT FOR YOU, JUSTIN, BUT THE SAME CAN'T NECESSARILY BE SAID FOR EVERYONE ELSE WHO'S CROSSED MY PATH.
I'VE HURT PEOPLE.
LOOK AT JULIE--MY BEST FRIEND--SHE'S IN CUSTODY AND COULD BE DYING BECAUSE OF ME!
YEAH, ALL THAT STUFF SUCKS, BUT THE POINT IS--YOU'RE DOING WHAT YOU'RE DOING FOR THE GREATER GOOD.
AND MAYBE THAT JUST MEANS YOU UNDERSTAND YOUR FATHER MORE THAN YOU THINK.
SHNK

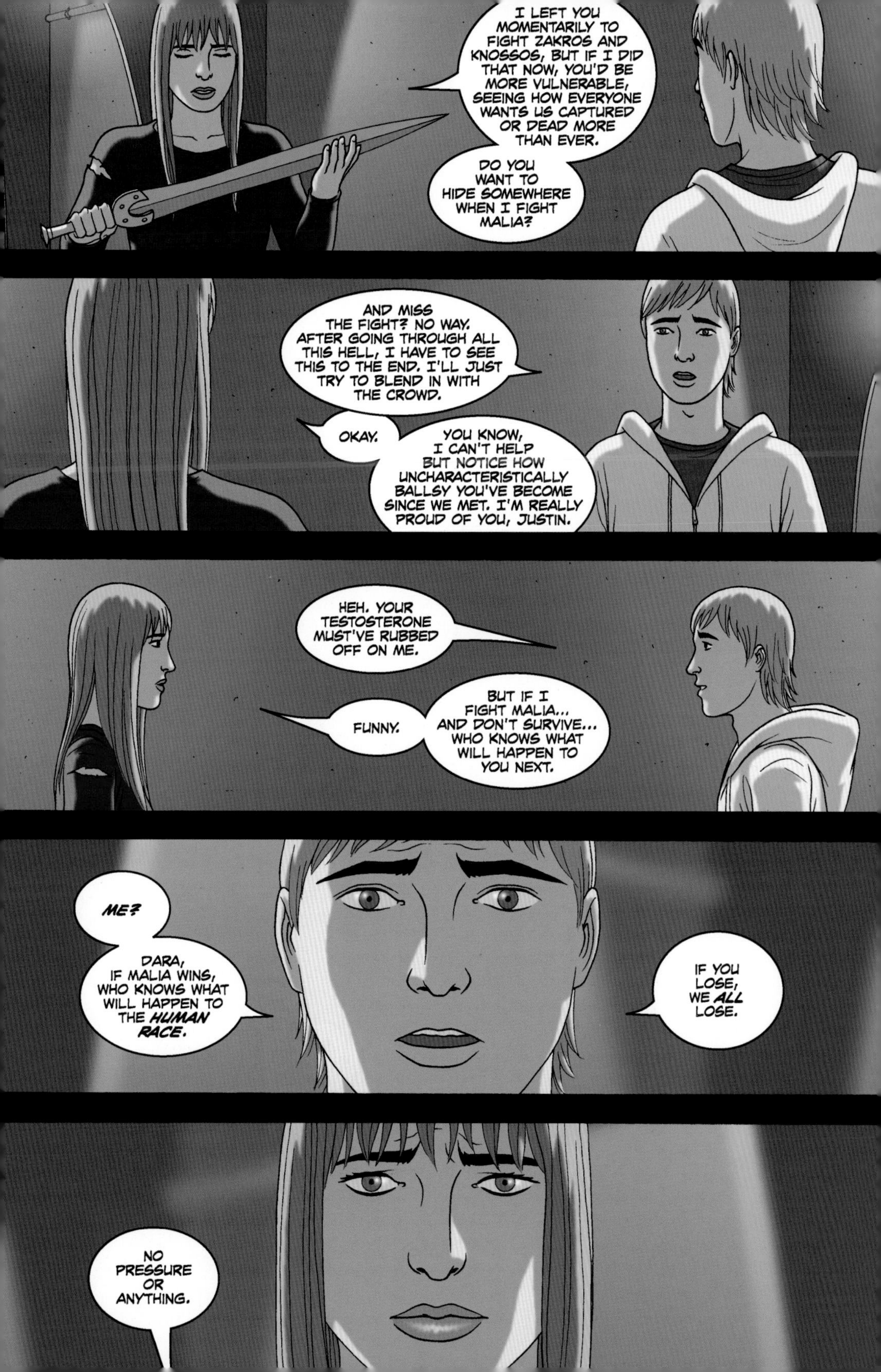

I LEFT YOU MOMENTARILY TO FIGHT ZAKROS AND KNOSSOS, BUT IF I DID THAT NOW, YOU'D BE MORE VULNERABLE, SEEING HOW EVERYONE WANTS US CAPTURED OR DEAD MORE THAN EVER.
DO YOU WANT TO HIDE SOMEWHERE WHEN I FIGHT MALIA?
AND MISS THE FIGHT? NO WAY. AFTER GOING THROUGH ALL THIS HELL, I HAVE TO SEE THIS TO THE END. I'LL JUST TRY TO BLEND IN WITH THE CROWD.
OKAY.
YOU KNOW, I CAN'T HELP BUT NOTICE HOW UNCHARACTERISTICALLY BALLSY YOU'VE BECOME SINCE WE MET. I'M REALLY PROUD OF YOU, JUSTIN.
HEH. YOUR TESTOSTERONE MUST'VE RUBBED OFF ON ME.
FUNNY.
BUT IF I FIGHT MALIA... AND DON'T SURVIVE... WHO KNOWS WHAT WILL HAPPEN TO YOU NEXT.
ME?
DARA, IF MALIA WINS, WHO KNOWS WHAT WILL HAPPEN TO THE *HUMAN RACE*.
IF YOU LOSE, WE *ALL* LOSE.
NO PRESSURE OR ANYTHING.

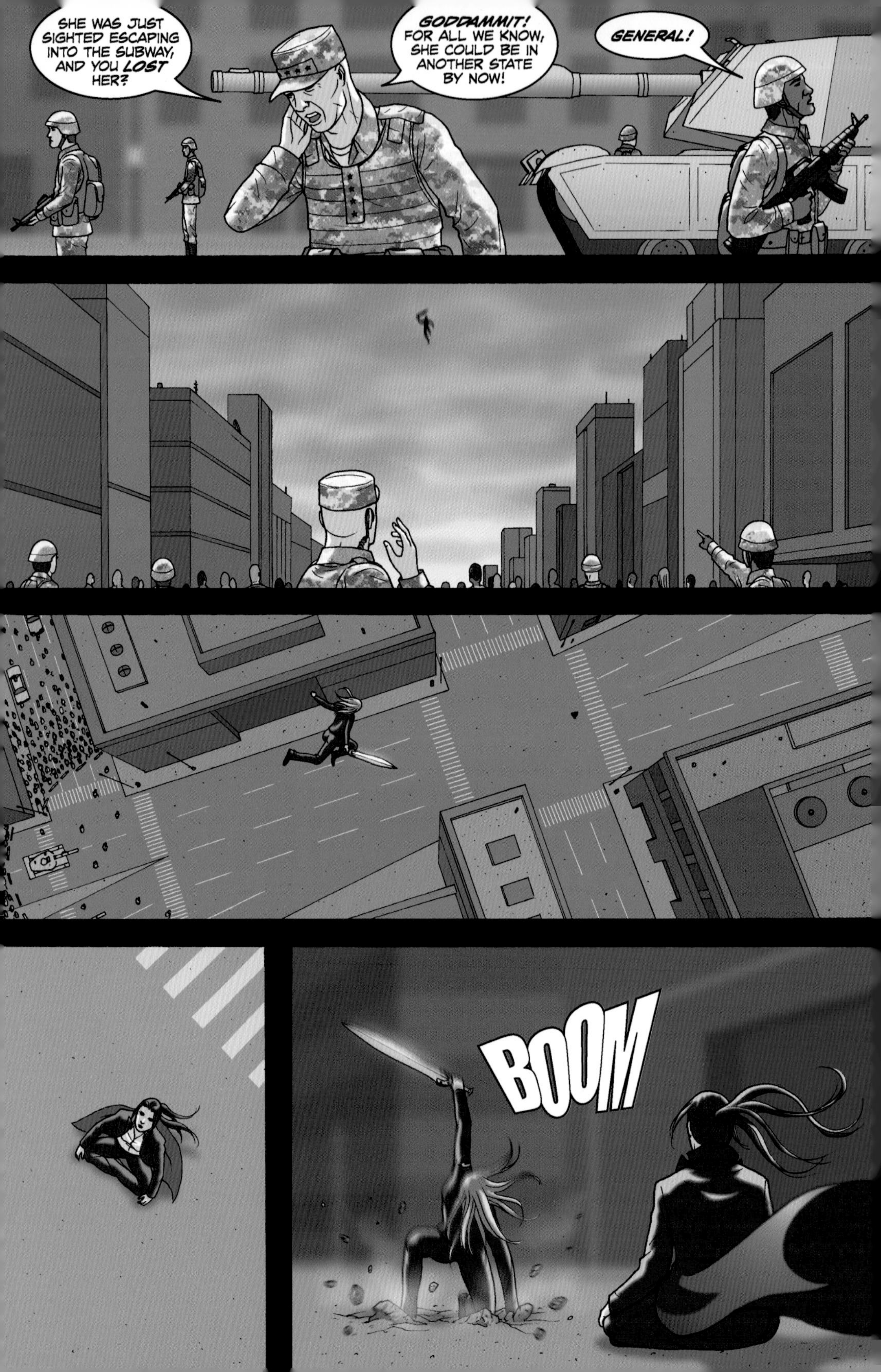
SHE WAS JUST SIGHTED ESCAPING INTO THE SUBWAY, AND YOU LOST HER?
GODDAMMIT! FOR ALL WE KNOW, SHE COULD BE IN ANOTHER STATE BY NOW!
GENERAL!
BOOM

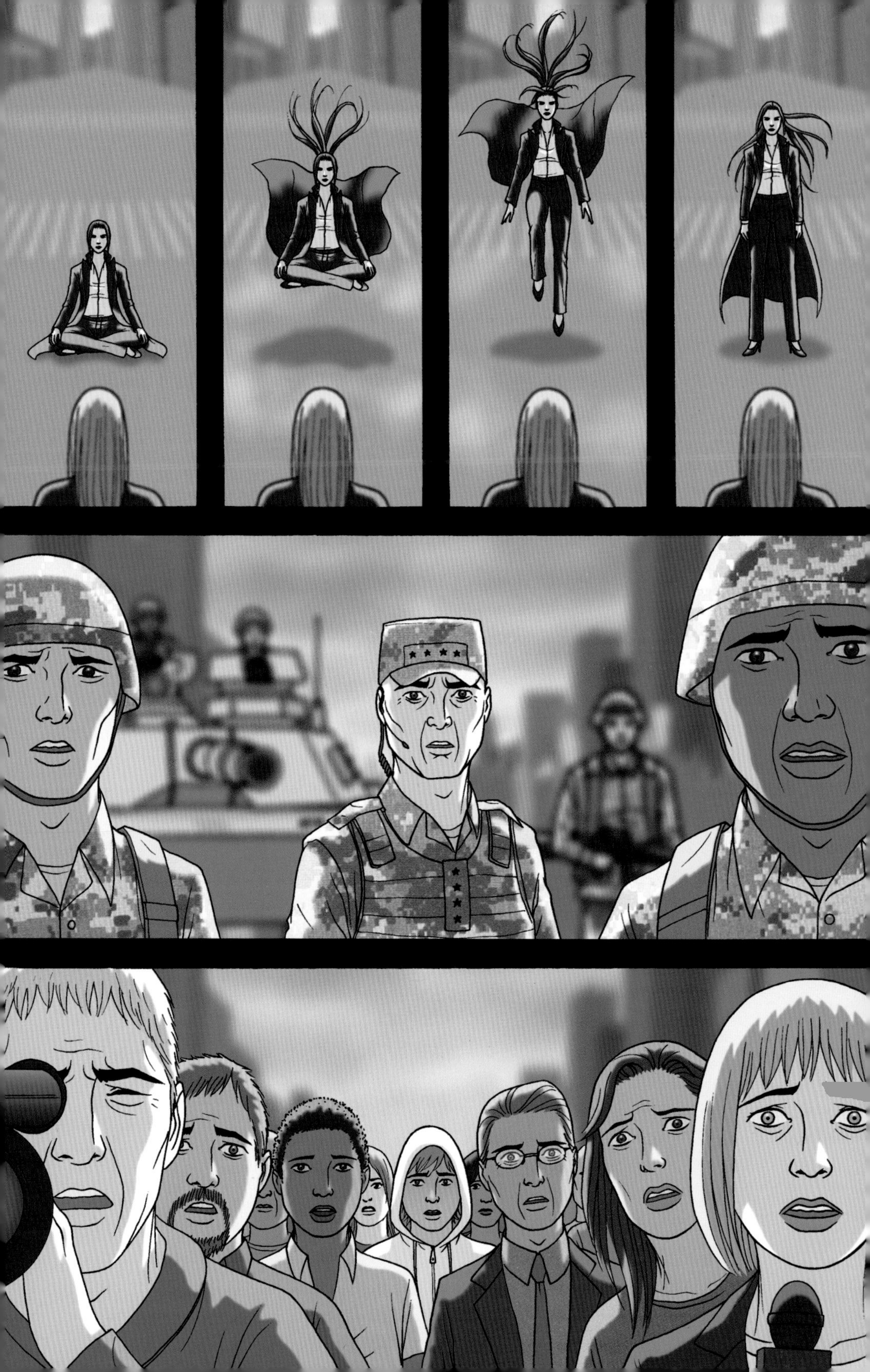

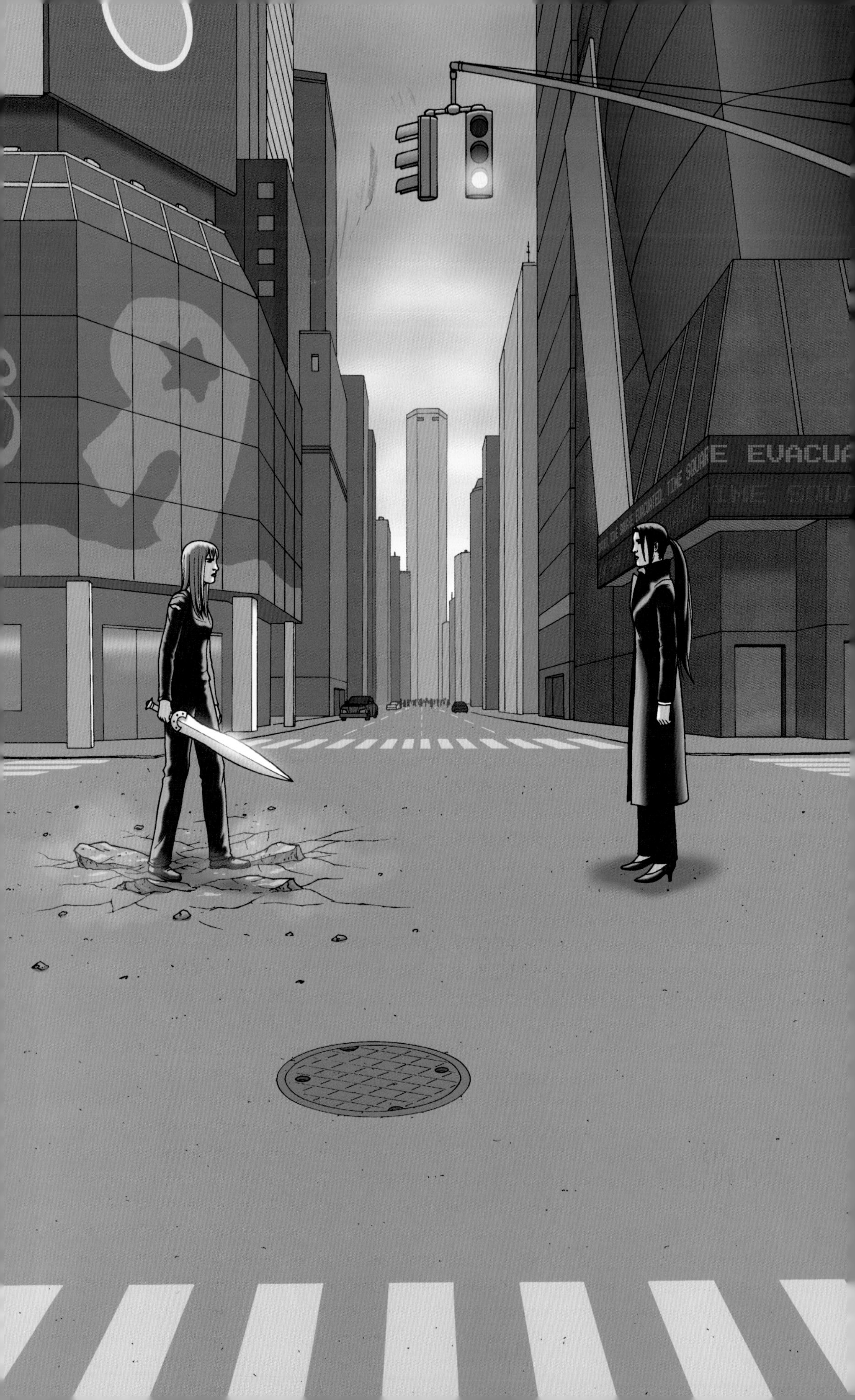
EVACUATED, TIME SQUARE EVACUA

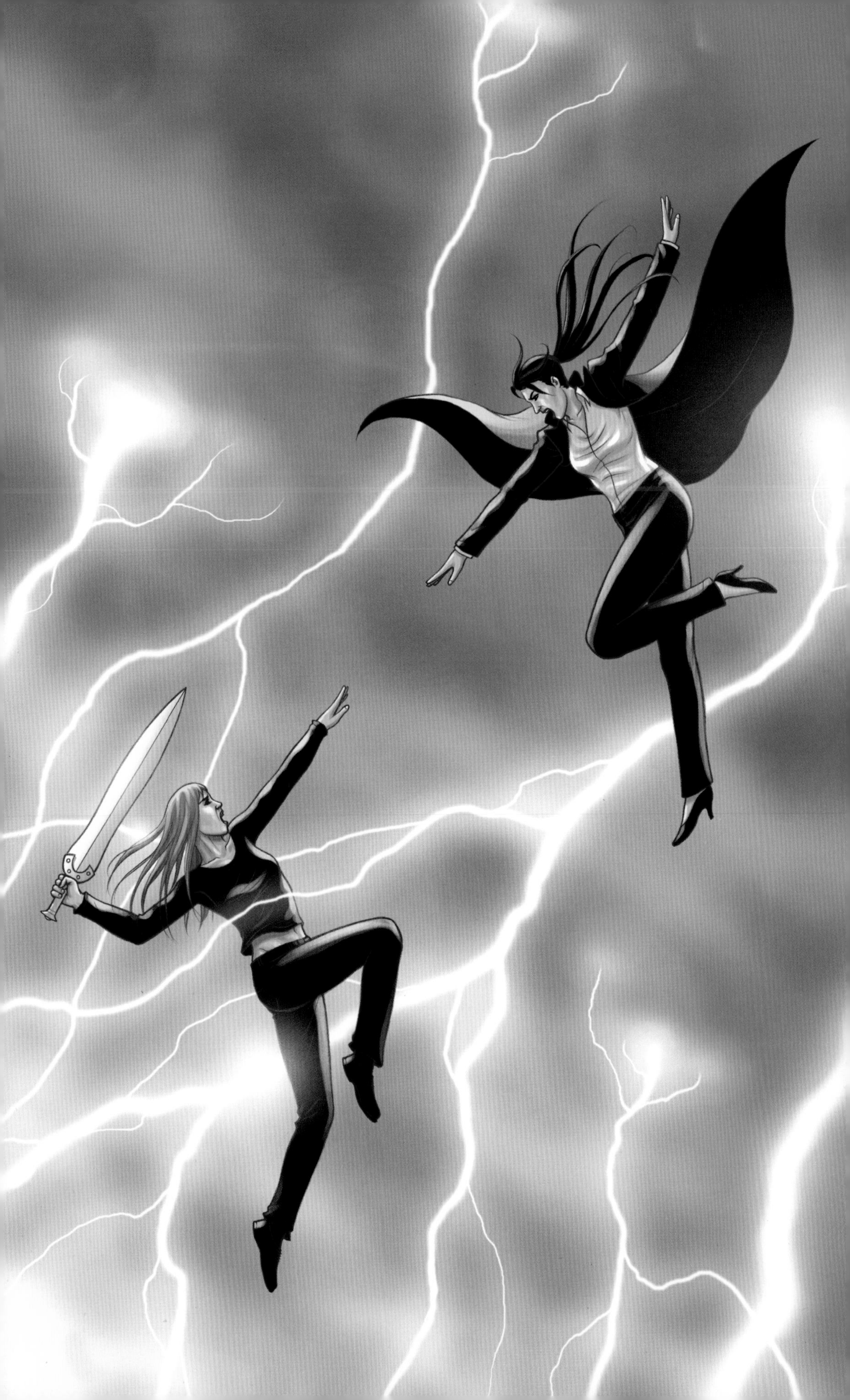

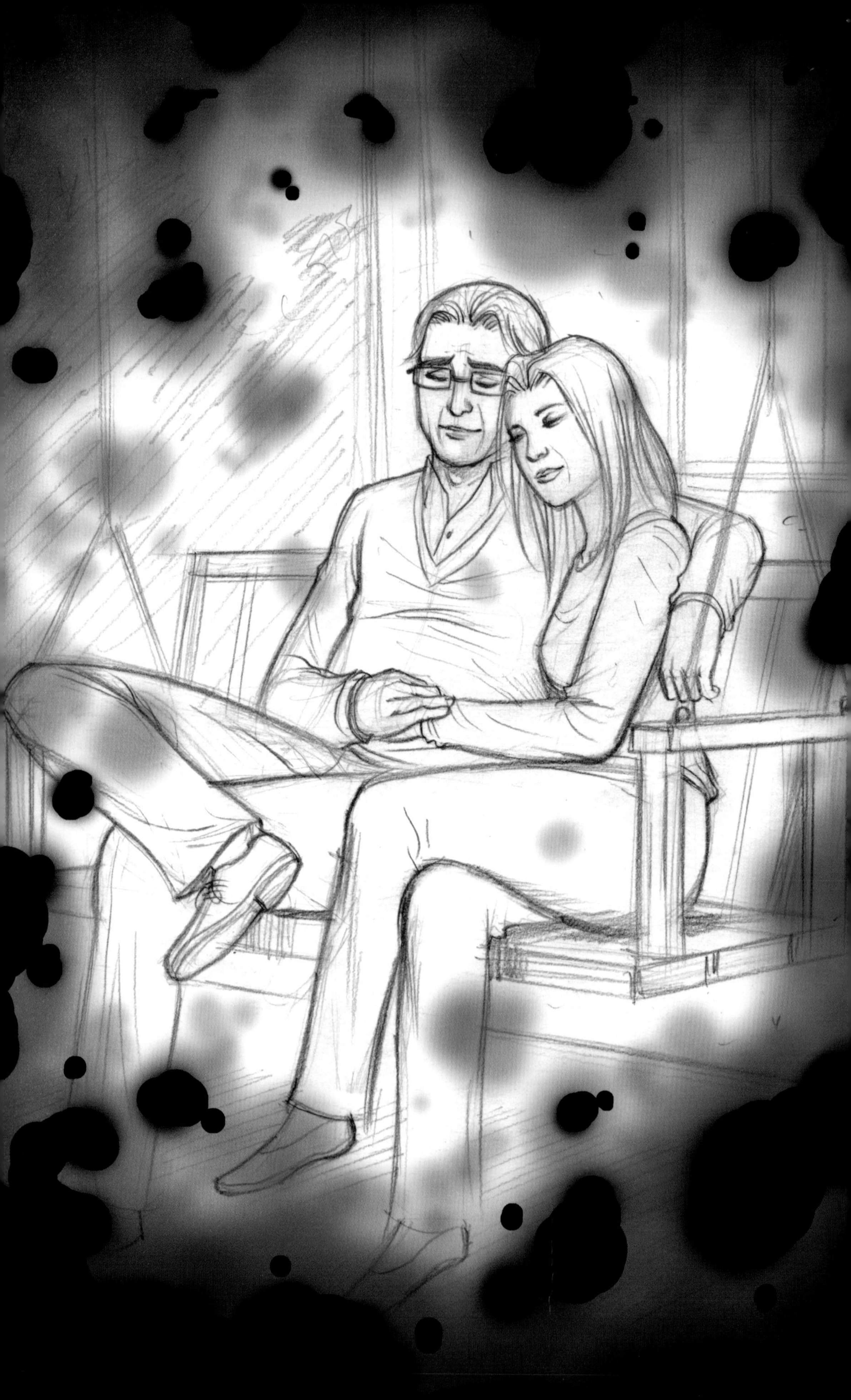

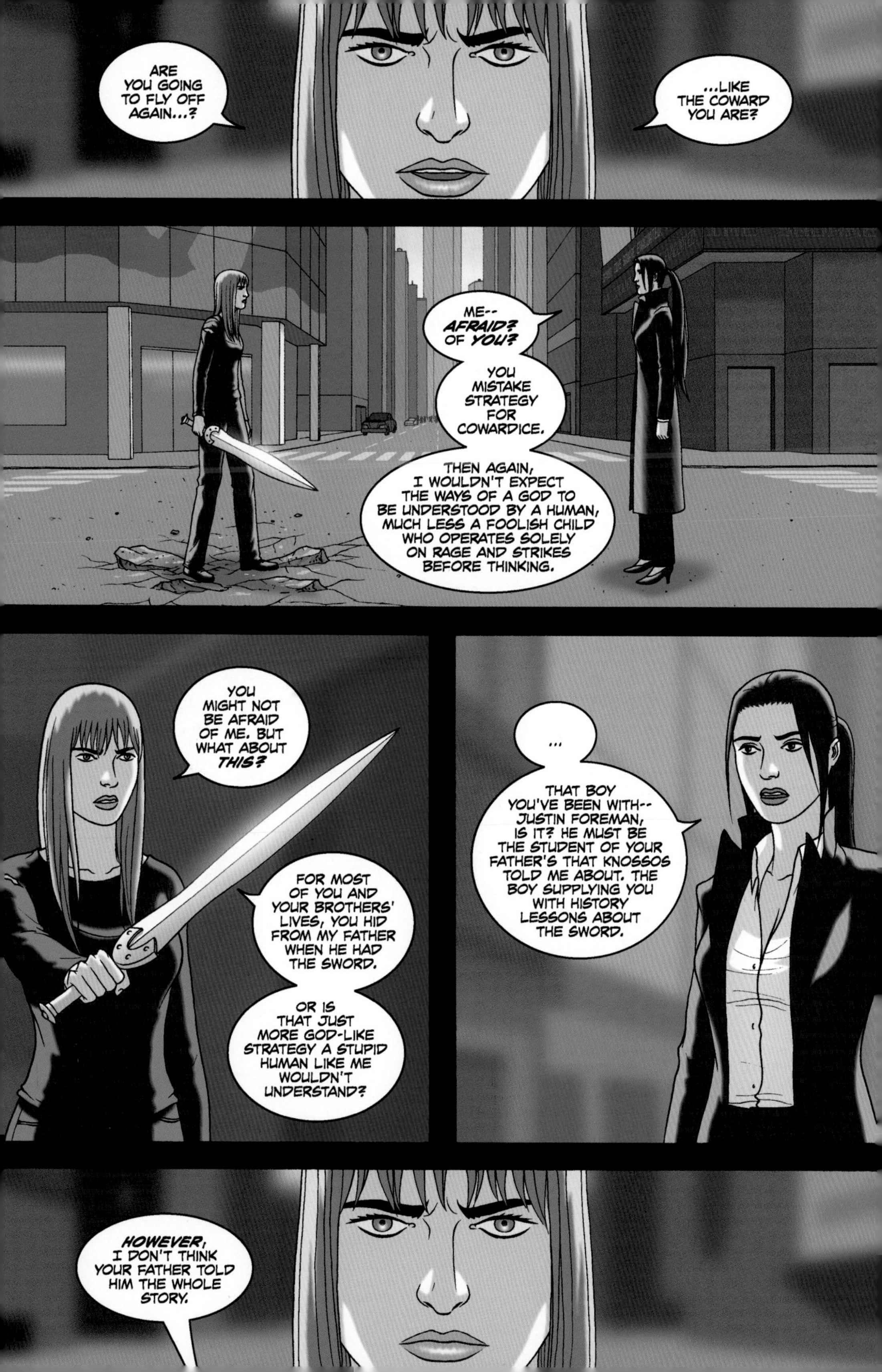

ARE YOU GOING TO FLY OFF AGAIN...?
...LIKE THE COWARD YOU ARE?
ME-- AFRAID? OF YOU?
YOU MISTAKE STRATEGY FOR COWARDICE.
THEN AGAIN, I WOULDN'T EXPECT THE WAYS OF A GOD TO BE UNDERSTOOD BY A HUMAN, MUCH LESS A FOOLISH CHILD WHO OPERATES SOLELY ON RAGE AND STRIKES BEFORE THINKING.
YOU MIGHT NOT BE AFRAID OF ME. BUT WHAT ABOUT THIS?
FOR MOST OF YOU AND YOUR BROTHERS' LIVES, YOU HID FROM MY FATHER WHEN HE HAD THE SWORD.
OR IS THAT JUST MORE GOD-LIKE STRATEGY A STUPID HUMAN LIKE ME WOULDN'T UNDERSTAND?
...
THAT BOY YOU'VE BEEN WITH-- JUSTIN FOREMAN, IS IT? HE MUST BE THE STUDENT OF YOUR FATHER'S THAT KNOSSOS TOLD ME ABOUT. THE BOY SUPPLYING YOU WITH HISTORY LESSONS ABOUT THE SWORD.
HOWEVER, I DON'T THINK YOUR FATHER TOLD HIM THE WHOLE STORY.

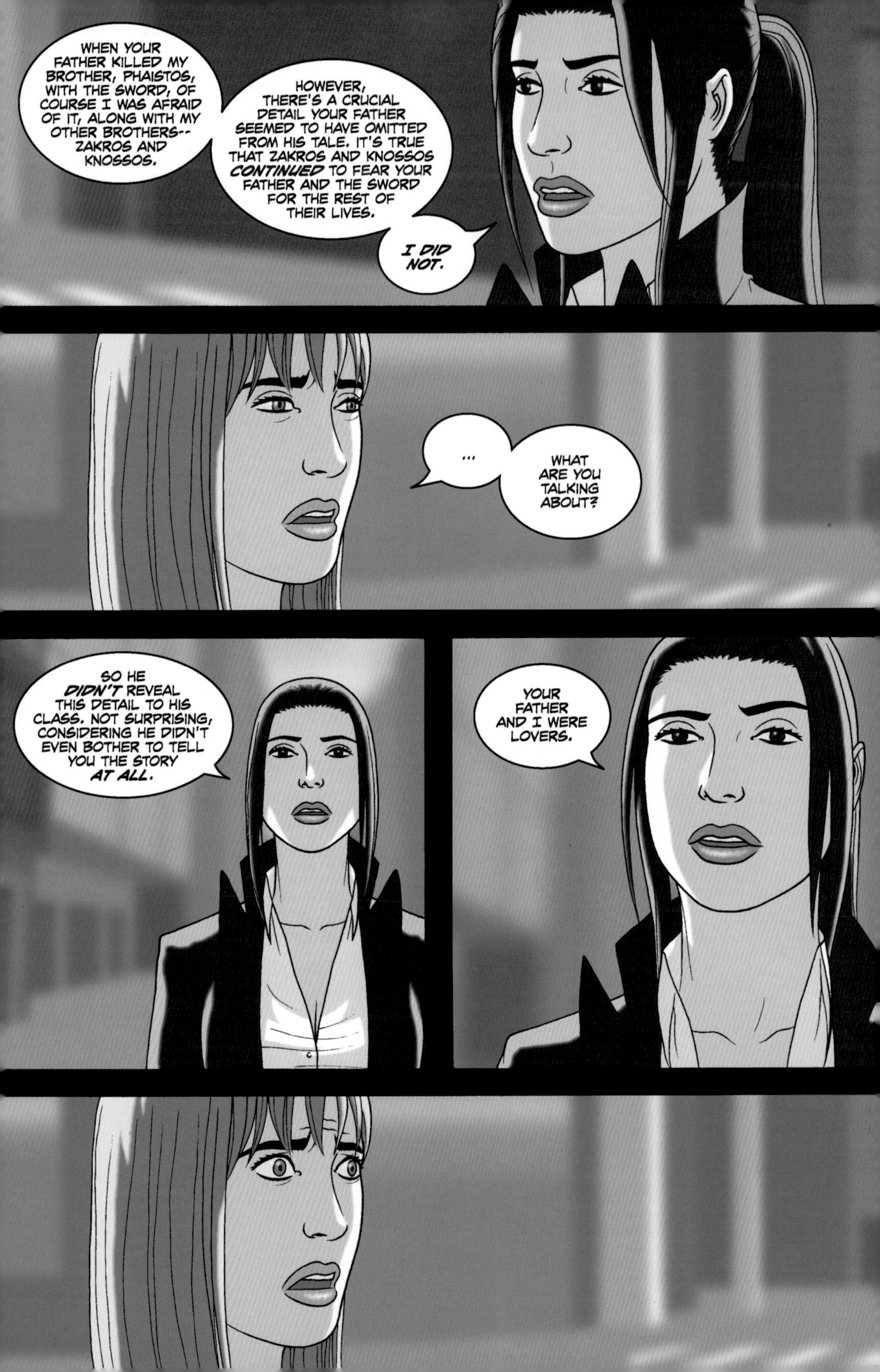
WHEN YOUR FATHER KILLED MY BROTHER, PHAISTOS, WITH THE SWORD, OF COURSE I WAS AFRAID OF IT, ALONG WITH MY OTHER BROTHERS-- ZAKROS AND KNOSSOS.
HOWEVER, THERE'S A CRUCIAL DETAIL YOUR FATHER SEEMED TO HAVE OMITTED FROM HIS TALE. IT'S TRUE THAT ZAKROS AND KNOSSOS CONTINUED TO FEAR YOUR FATHER AND THE SWORD FOR THE REST OF THEIR LIVES.
I DID NOT.
...
WHAT ARE YOU TALKING ABOUT?
SO HE DIDN'T REVEAL THIS DETAIL TO HIS CLASS. NOT SURPRISING, CONSIDERING HE DIDN'T EVEN BOTHER TO TELL YOU THE STORY AT ALL.
YOUR FATHER AND I WERE LOVERS.

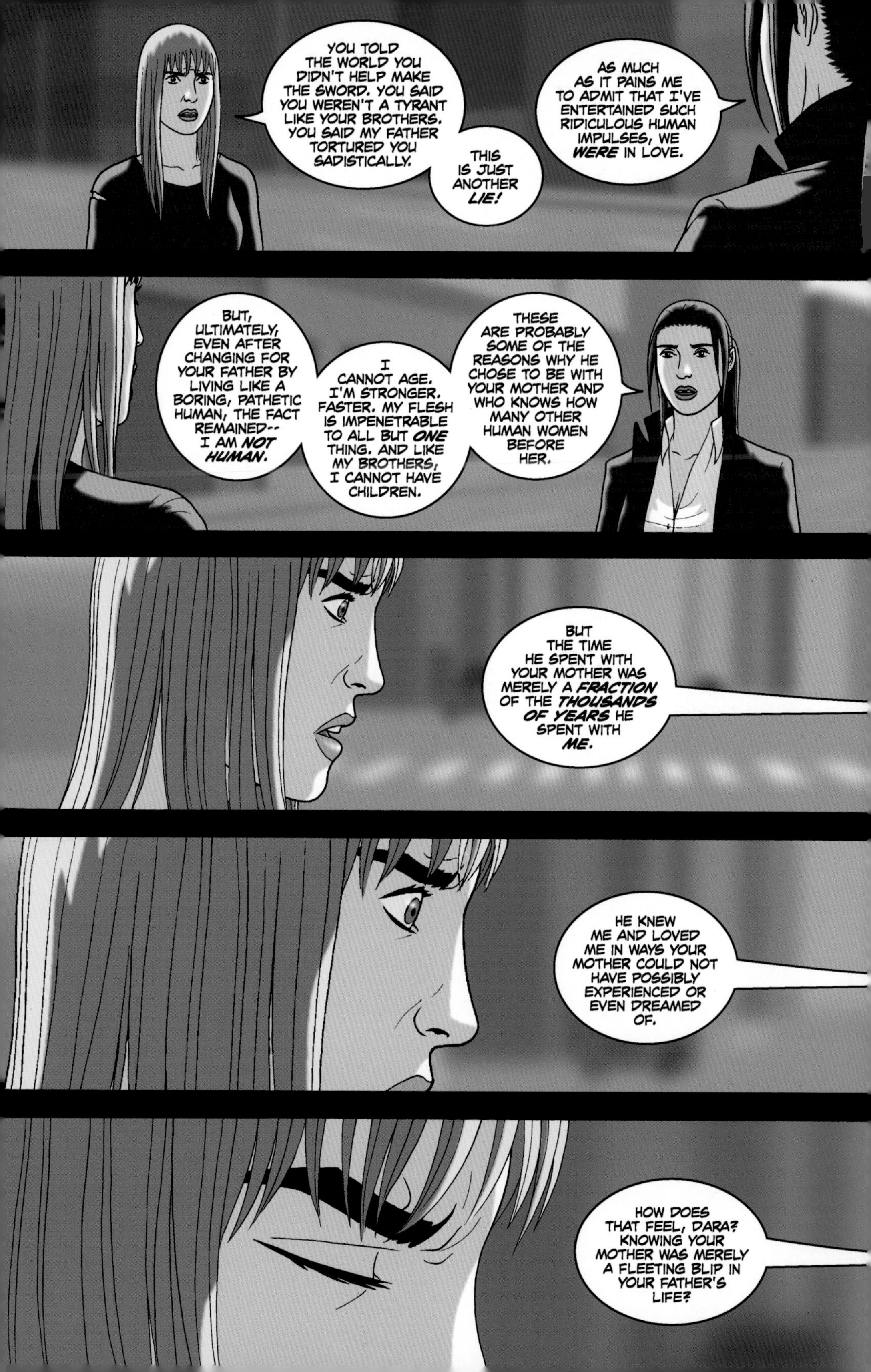
YOU TOLD THE WORLD YOU DIDN'T HELP MAKE THE SWORD. YOU SAID YOU WEREN'T A TYRANT LIKE YOUR BROTHERS. YOU SAID MY FATHER TORTURED YOU SADISTICALLY.
THIS IS JUST ANOTHER *LIE!*
AS MUCH AS IT PAINS ME TO ADMIT THAT I'VE ENTERTAINED SUCH RIDICULOUS HUMAN IMPULSES, WE *WERE* IN LOVE.
BUT, ULTIMATELY, EVEN AFTER CHANGING FOR YOUR FATHER BY LIVING LIKE A BORING, PATHETIC HUMAN, THE FACT REMAINED-- I AM *NOT HUMAN.*
I CANNOT AGE. I'M STRONGER. FASTER. MY FLESH IS IMPENETRABLE TO ALL BUT *ONE* THING. AND LIKE MY BROTHERS, I CANNOT HAVE CHILDREN.
THESE ARE PROBABLY SOME OF THE REASONS WHY HE CHOSE TO BE WITH YOUR MOTHER AND WHO KNOWS HOW MANY OTHER HUMAN WOMEN BEFORE HER.
BUT THE TIME HE SPENT WITH YOUR MOTHER WAS MERELY A *FRACTION* OF THE *THOUSANDS OF YEARS* HE SPENT WITH *ME.*
HE KNEW ME AND LOVED ME IN WAYS YOUR MOTHER COULD NOT HAVE POSSIBLY EXPERIENCED OR EVEN DREAMED OF.
HOW DOES THAT FEEL, DARA? KNOWING YOUR MOTHER WAS MERELY A FLEETING BLIP IN YOUR FATHER'S LIFE?

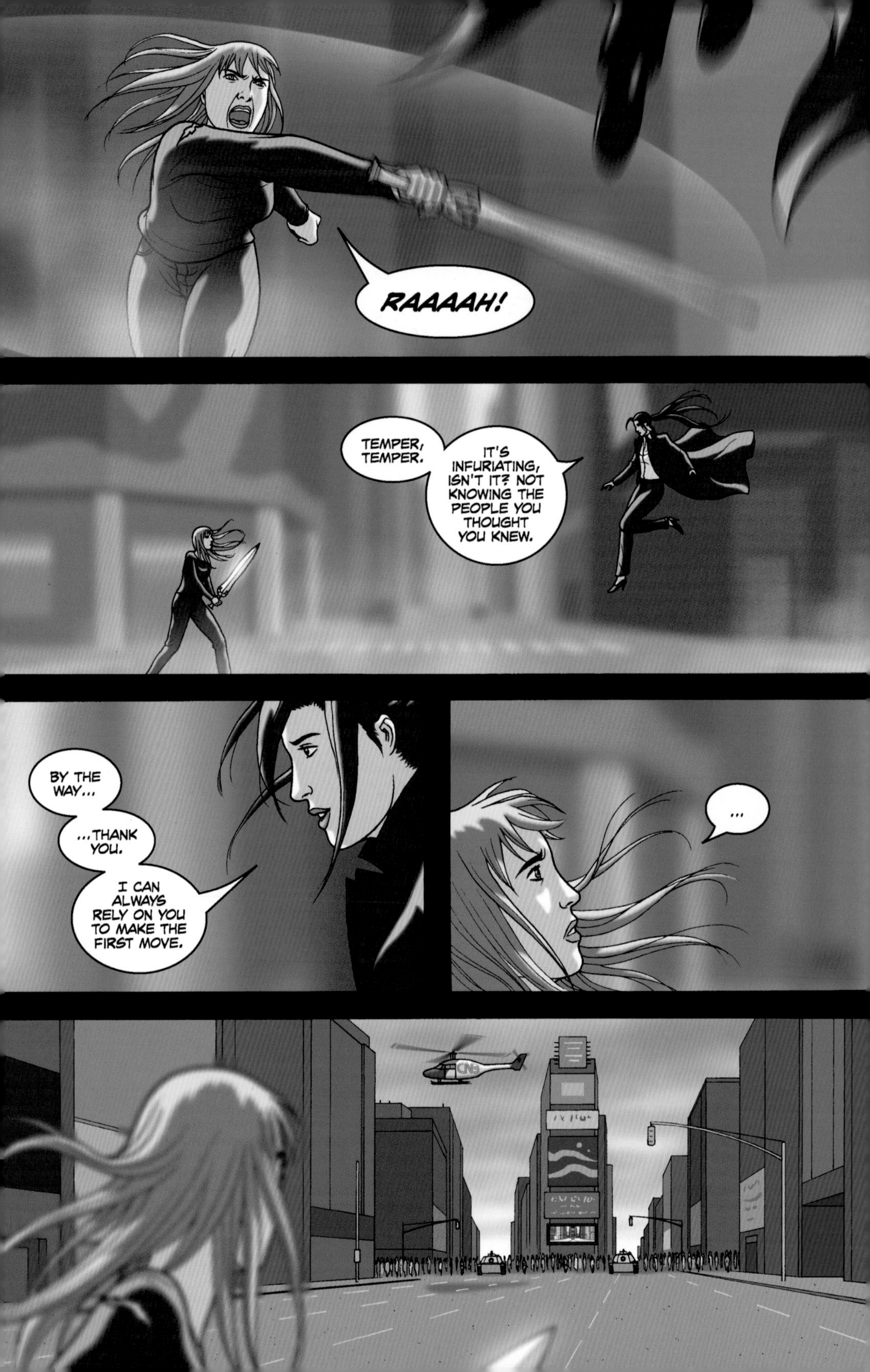
RAAAAH!
TEMPER, TEMPER.
IT'S INFURIATING, ISN'T IT? NOT KNOWING THE PEOPLE YOU THOUGHT YOU KNEW.
BY THE WAY...
...THANK YOU.
I CAN ALWAYS RELY ON YOU TO MAKE THE FIRST MOVE.
...

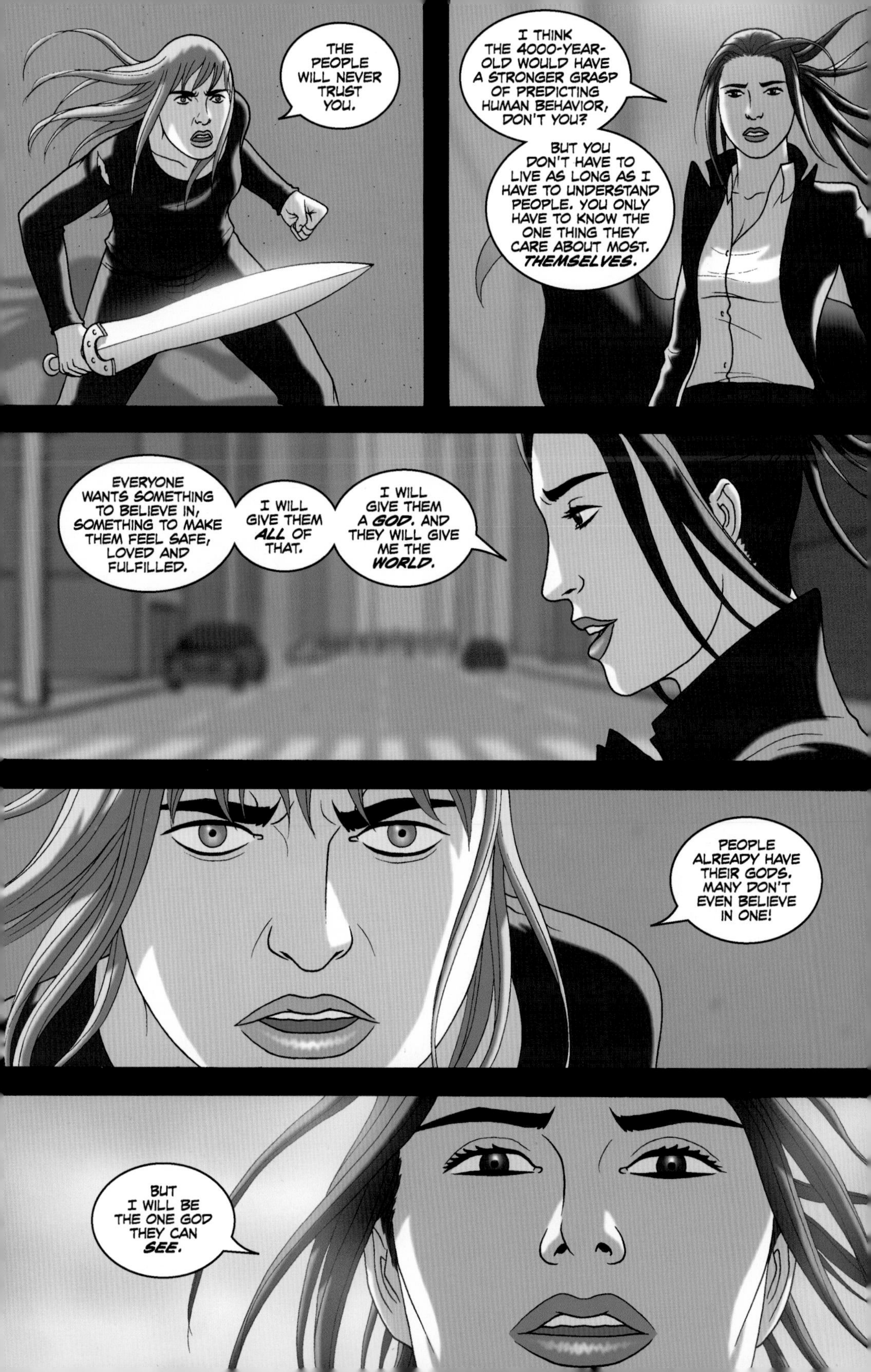
THE PEOPLE WILL NEVER TRUST YOU.
I THINK THE 4000-YEAR-OLD WOULD HAVE A STRONGER GRASP OF PREDICTING HUMAN BEHAVIOR, DON'T YOU?
BUT YOU DON'T HAVE TO LIVE AS LONG AS I HAVE TO UNDERSTAND PEOPLE. YOU ONLY HAVE TO KNOW THE ONE THING THEY CARE ABOUT MOST. ***THEMSELVES.***
EVERYONE WANTS SOMETHING TO BELIEVE IN, SOMETHING TO MAKE THEM FEEL SAFE, LOVED AND FULFILLED.
I WILL GIVE THEM ***ALL*** OF THAT.
I WILL GIVE THEM A ***GOD.*** AND THEY WILL GIVE ME THE ***WORLD.***
PEOPLE ALREADY HAVE THEIR GODS. MANY DON'T EVEN BELIEVE IN ONE!
BUT I WILL BE THE ONE GOD THEY CAN ***SEE.***

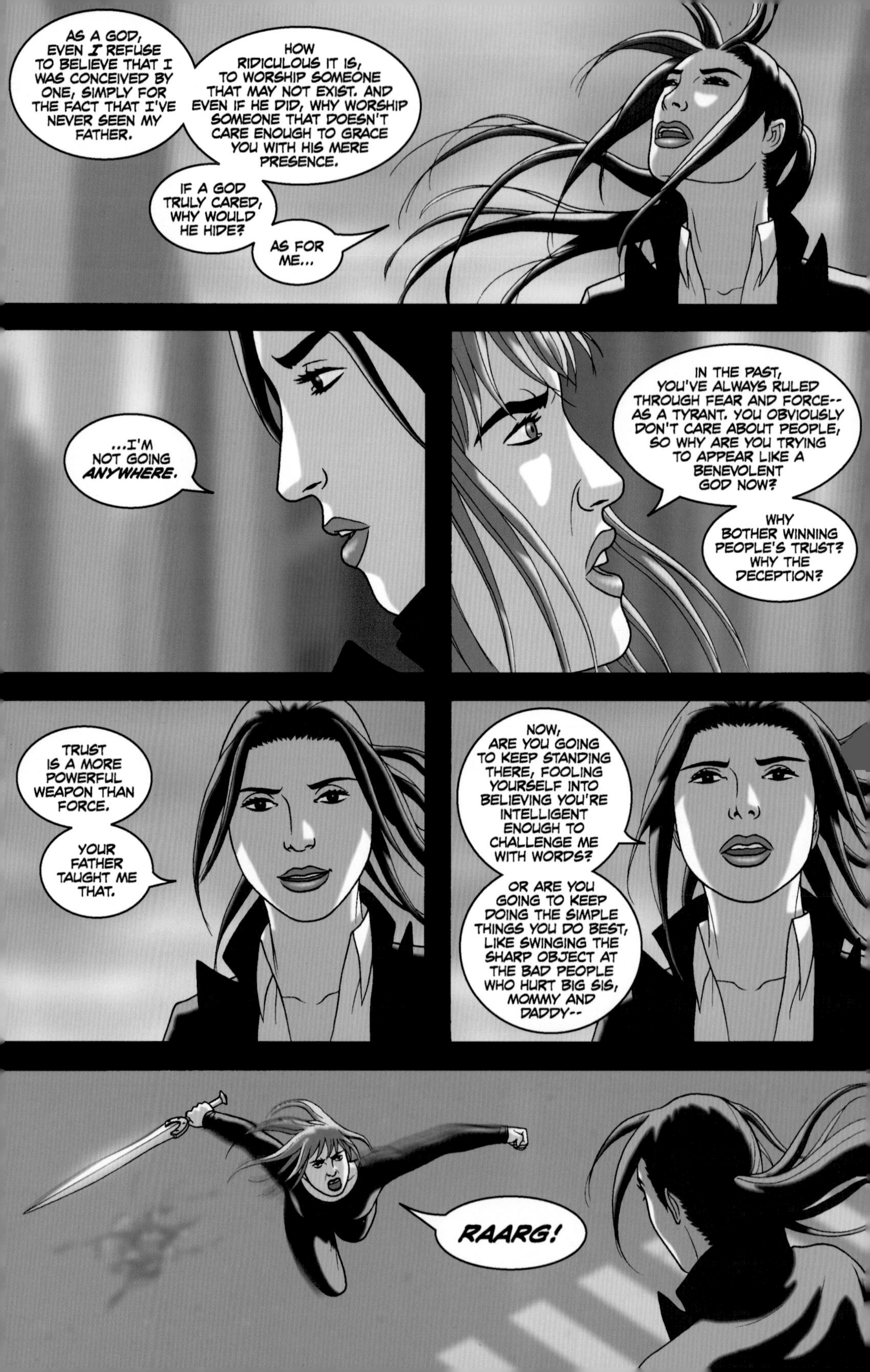
AS A GOD, EVEN I REFUSE TO BELIEVE THAT I WAS CONCEIVED BY ONE, SIMPLY FOR THE FACT THAT I'VE NEVER SEEN MY FATHER.
HOW RIDICULOUS IT IS, TO WORSHIP SOMEONE THAT MAY NOT EXIST. AND EVEN IF HE DID, WHY WORSHIP SOMEONE THAT DOESN'T CARE ENOUGH TO GRACE YOU WITH HIS MERE PRESENCE.
IF A GOD TRULY CARED, WHY WOULD HE HIDE?
AS FOR ME...
...I'M NOT GOING ANYWHERE.
IN THE PAST, YOU'VE ALWAYS RULED THROUGH FEAR AND FORCE-- AS A TYRANT. YOU OBVIOUSLY DON'T CARE ABOUT PEOPLE, SO WHY ARE YOU TRYING TO APPEAR LIKE A BENEVOLENT GOD NOW?
WHY BOTHER WINNING PEOPLE'S TRUST? WHY THE DECEPTION?
TRUST IS A MORE POWERFUL WEAPON THAN FORCE.
YOUR FATHER TAUGHT ME THAT.
NOW, ARE YOU GOING TO KEEP STANDING THERE, FOOLING YOURSELF INTO BELIEVING YOU'RE INTELLIGENT ENOUGH TO CHALLENGE ME WITH WORDS?
OR ARE YOU GOING TO KEEP DOING THE SIMPLE THINGS YOU DO BEST, LIKE SWINGING THE SHARP OBJECT AT THE BAD PEOPLE WHO HURT BIG SIS, MOMMY AND DADDY--
RAARG!

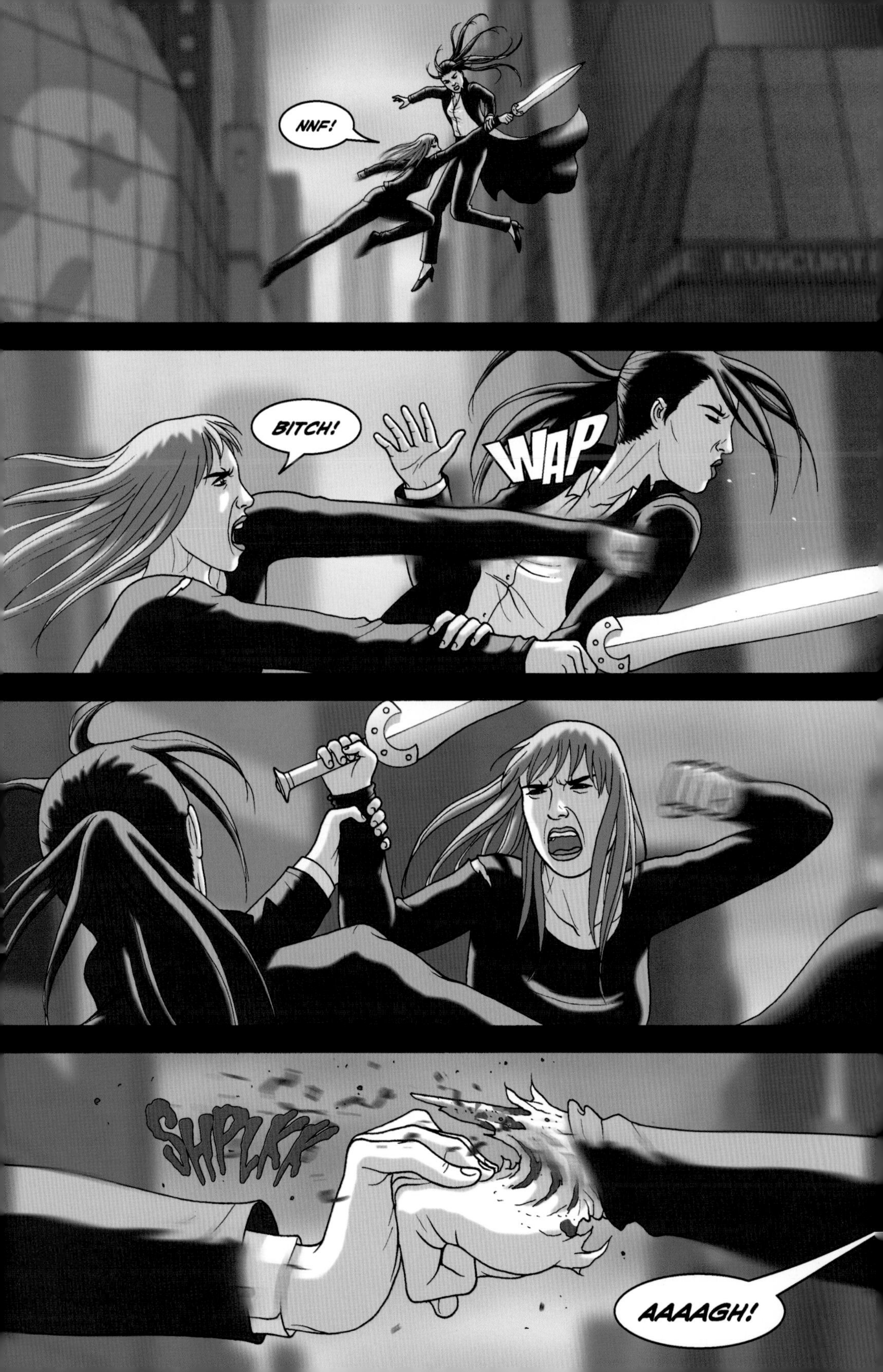
NNF!
BITCH!
WAP
SHPLKK
AAAAGH!

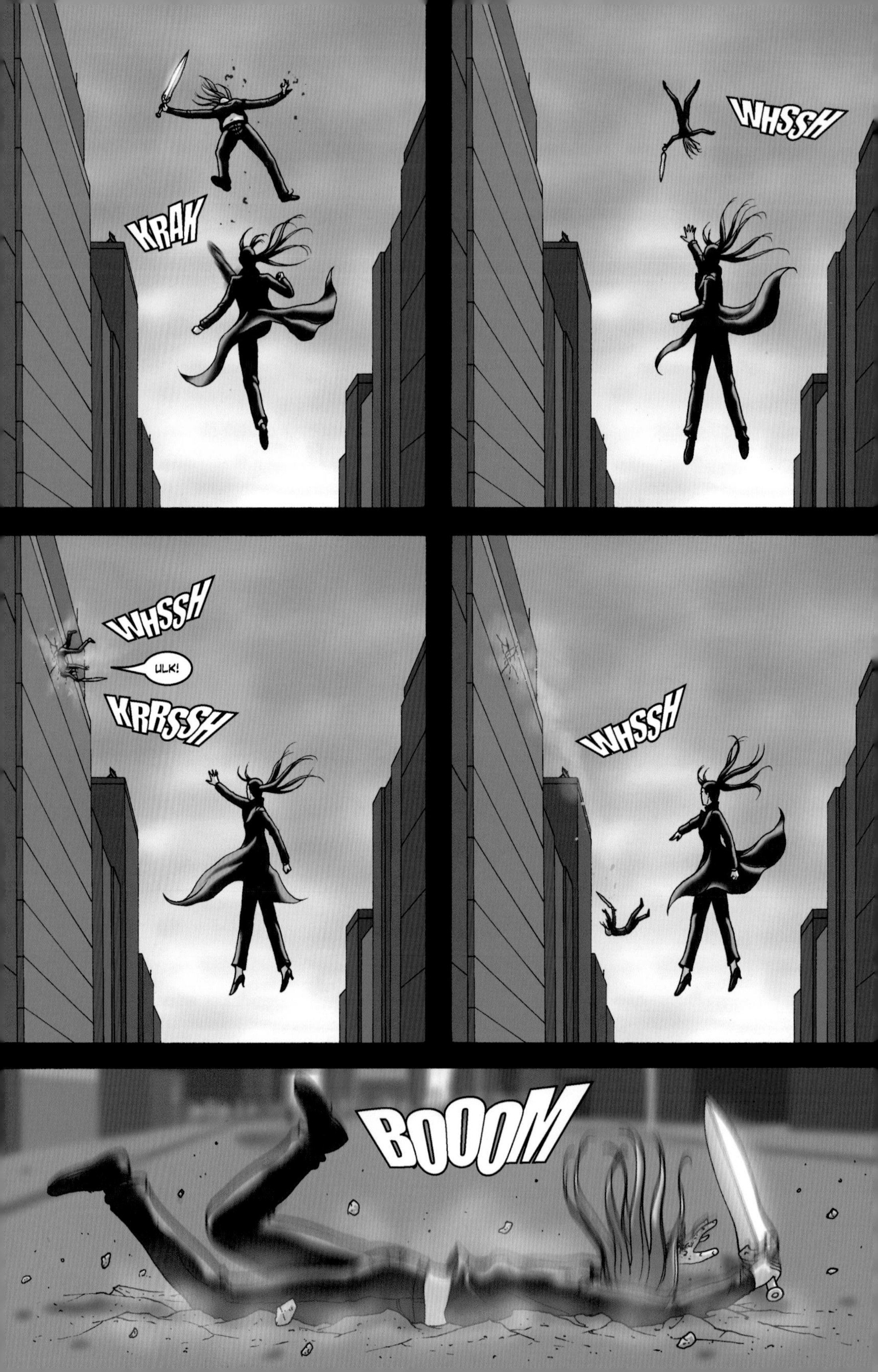
KRAK
WHSSH
WHSSH
ULK!
KRRSSH
WHSSH
BOOOM

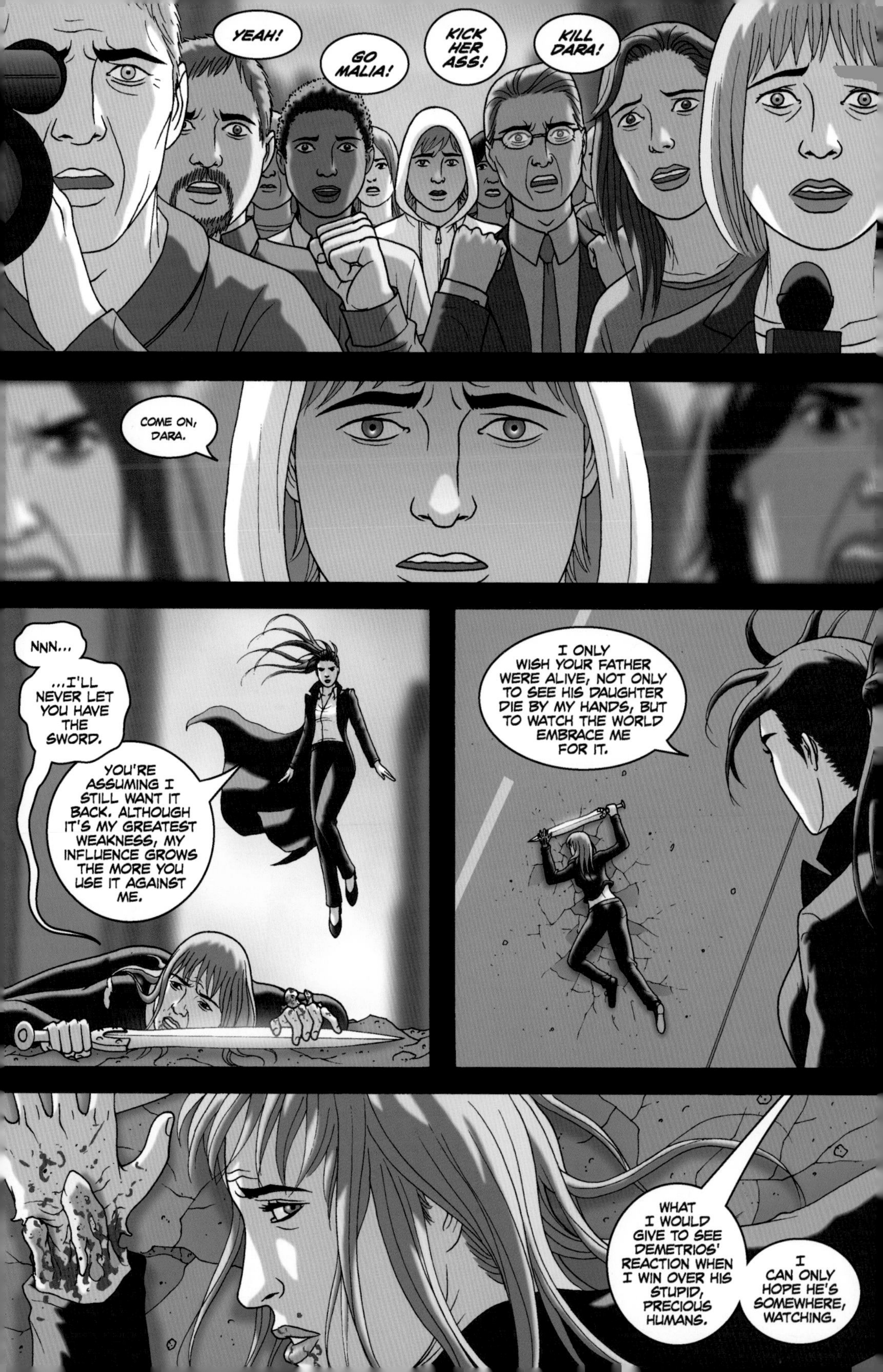
YEAH!
GO MALIA!
KICK HER ASS!
KILL DARA!
COME ON, DARA.
NNN...
...I'LL NEVER LET YOU HAVE THE SWORD.
YOU'RE ASSUMING I STILL WANT IT BACK. ALTHOUGH IT'S MY GREATEST WEAKNESS, MY INFLUENCE GROWS THE MORE YOU USE IT AGAINST ME.
I ONLY WISH YOUR FATHER WERE ALIVE, NOT ONLY TO SEE HIS DAUGHTER DIE BY MY HANDS, BUT TO WATCH THE WORLD EMBRACE ME FOR IT.
WHAT I WOULD GIVE TO SEE DEMETRIOS' REACTION WHEN I WIN OVER HIS STUPID, PRECIOUS HUMANS.
I CAN ONLY HOPE HE'S SOMEWHERE, WATCHING.

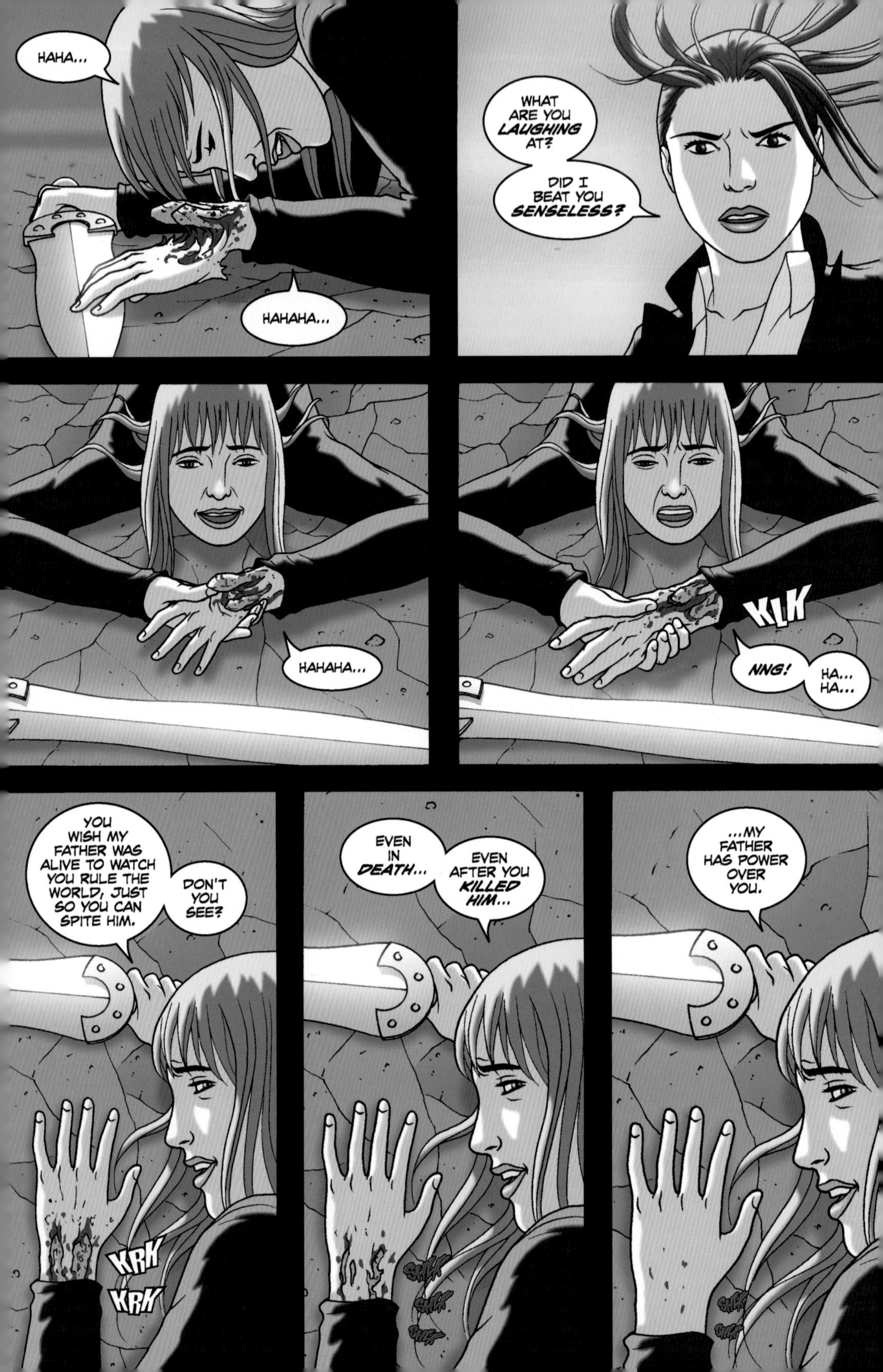
HAHA...
HAHAHA...
WHAT ARE YOU *LAUGHING* AT?
DID I BEAT YOU *SENSELESS?*
HAHAHA...
KLK
NNG!
HA... HA...
YOU WISH MY FATHER WAS ALIVE TO WATCH YOU RULE THE WORLD, JUST SO YOU CAN SPITE HIM.
DON'T YOU SEE?
KRK
KRK
EVEN IN *DEATH*...
EVEN AFTER YOU *KILLED HIM*...
SHLK
SHLK
SHLK
...MY FATHER HAS POWER OVER YOU.

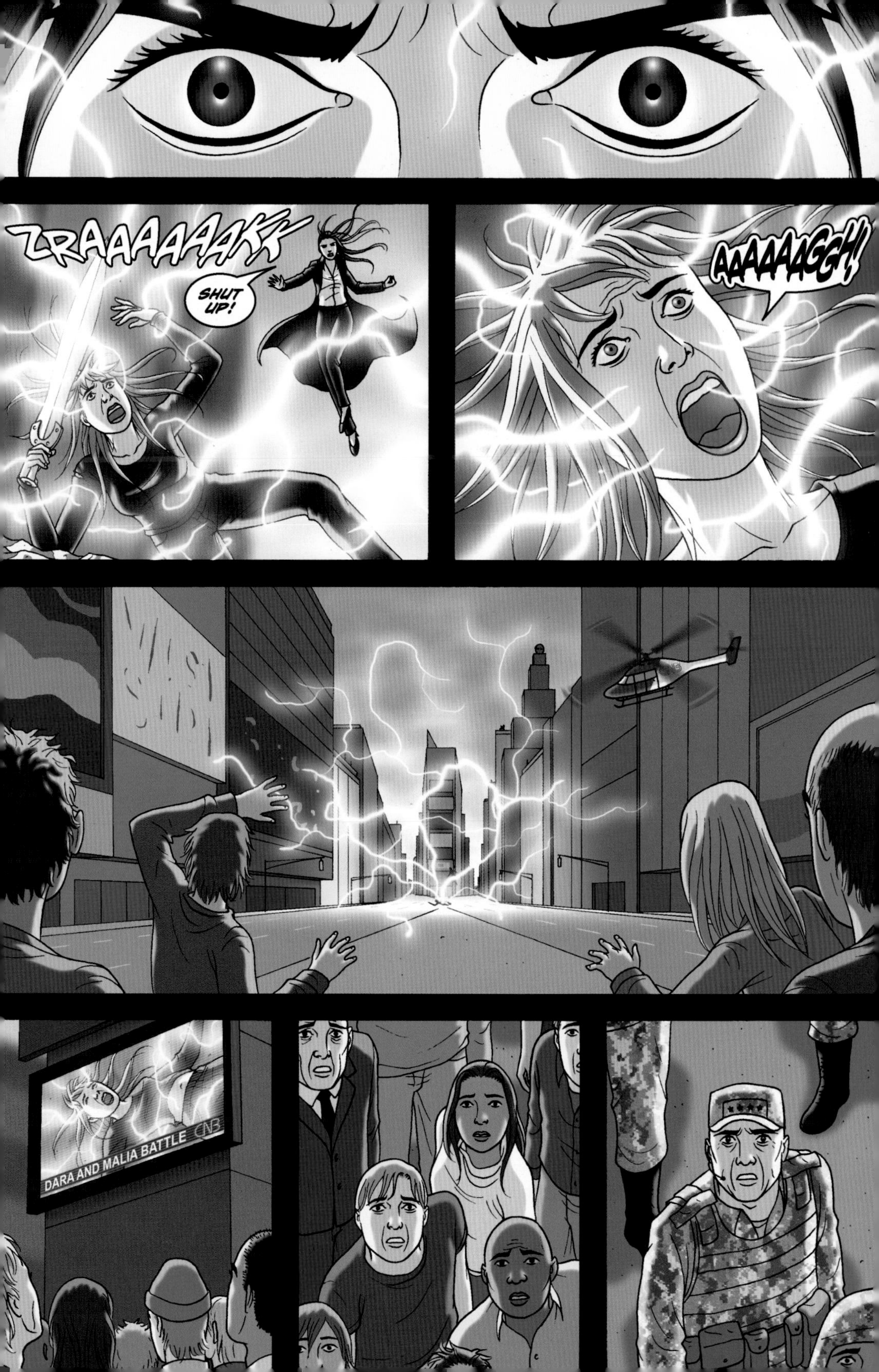
ZRAAAAAAKK
SHUT UP!
AAAAAAGGH!
DARA AND MALIA BATTLE
CNB

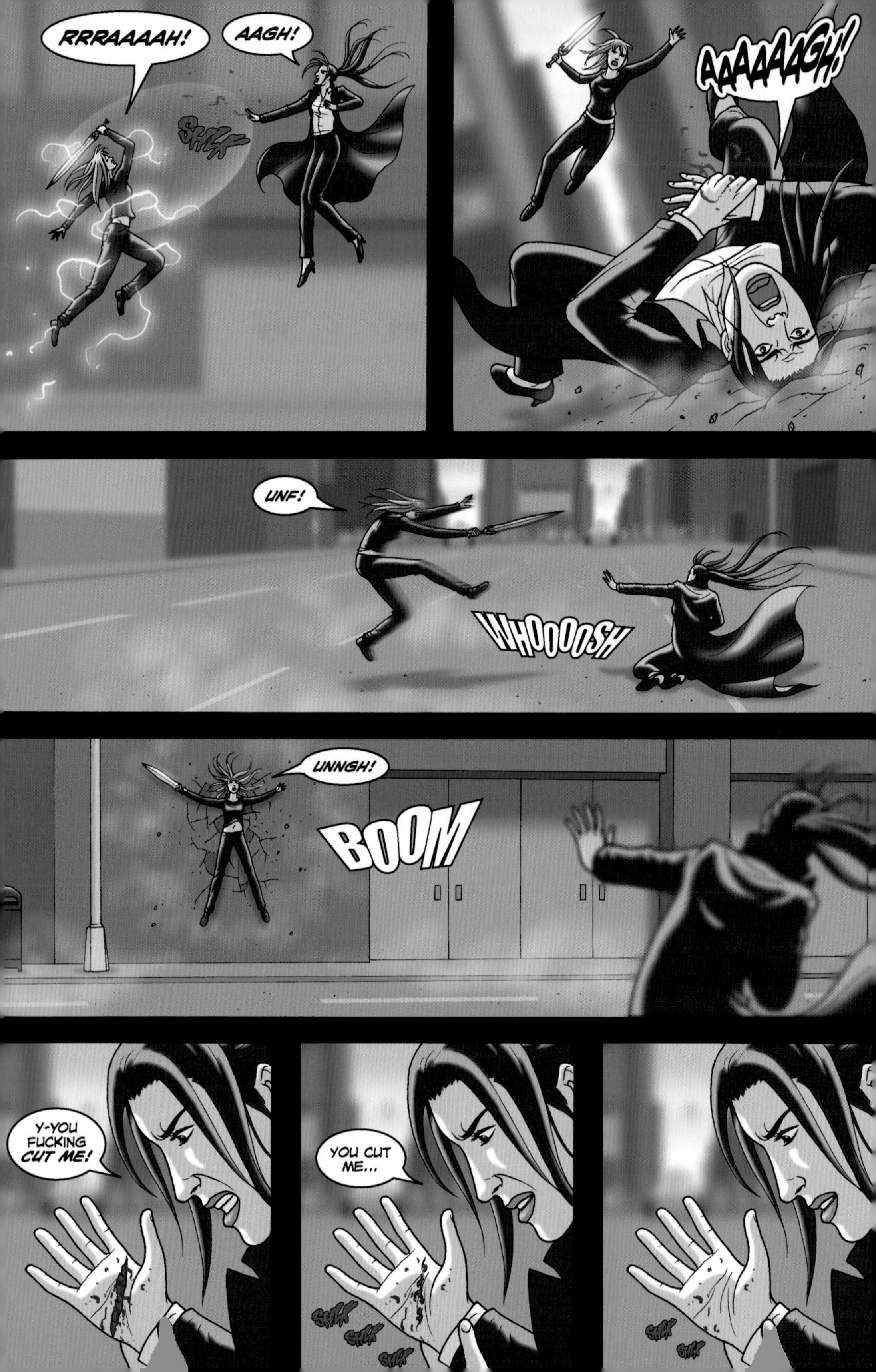
RRRAAAAAH!
AAGH!
SHLK
AAAAAAGH!
UNF!
WHOOOOOSH
UNNGH!
BOOM
Y-YOU FUCKING CUT ME!
YOU CUT ME...

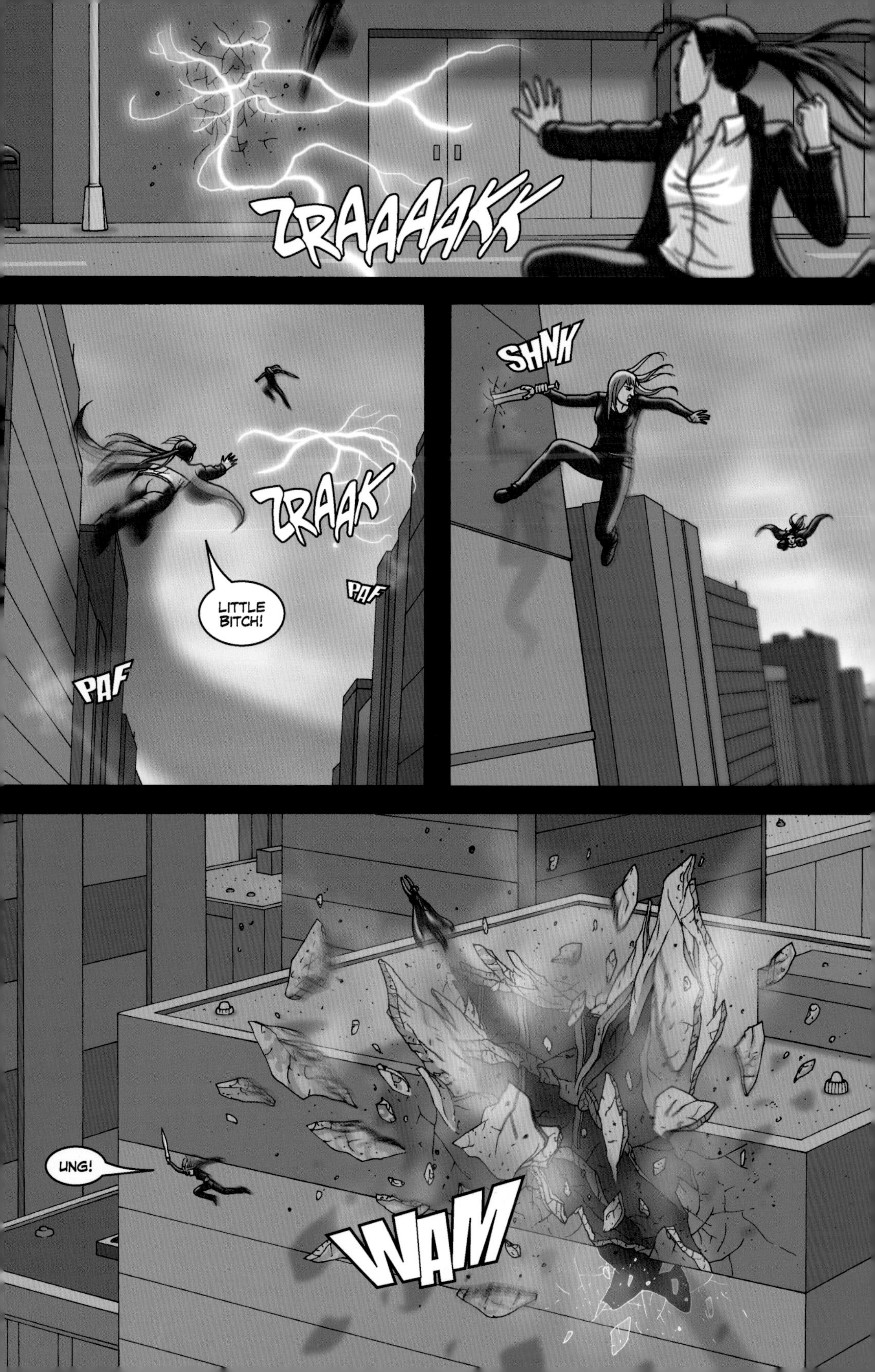
ZRAAAAKK
ZRAAK
LITTLE BITCH!
PAF
PAF
SHNK
UNG!
WAM

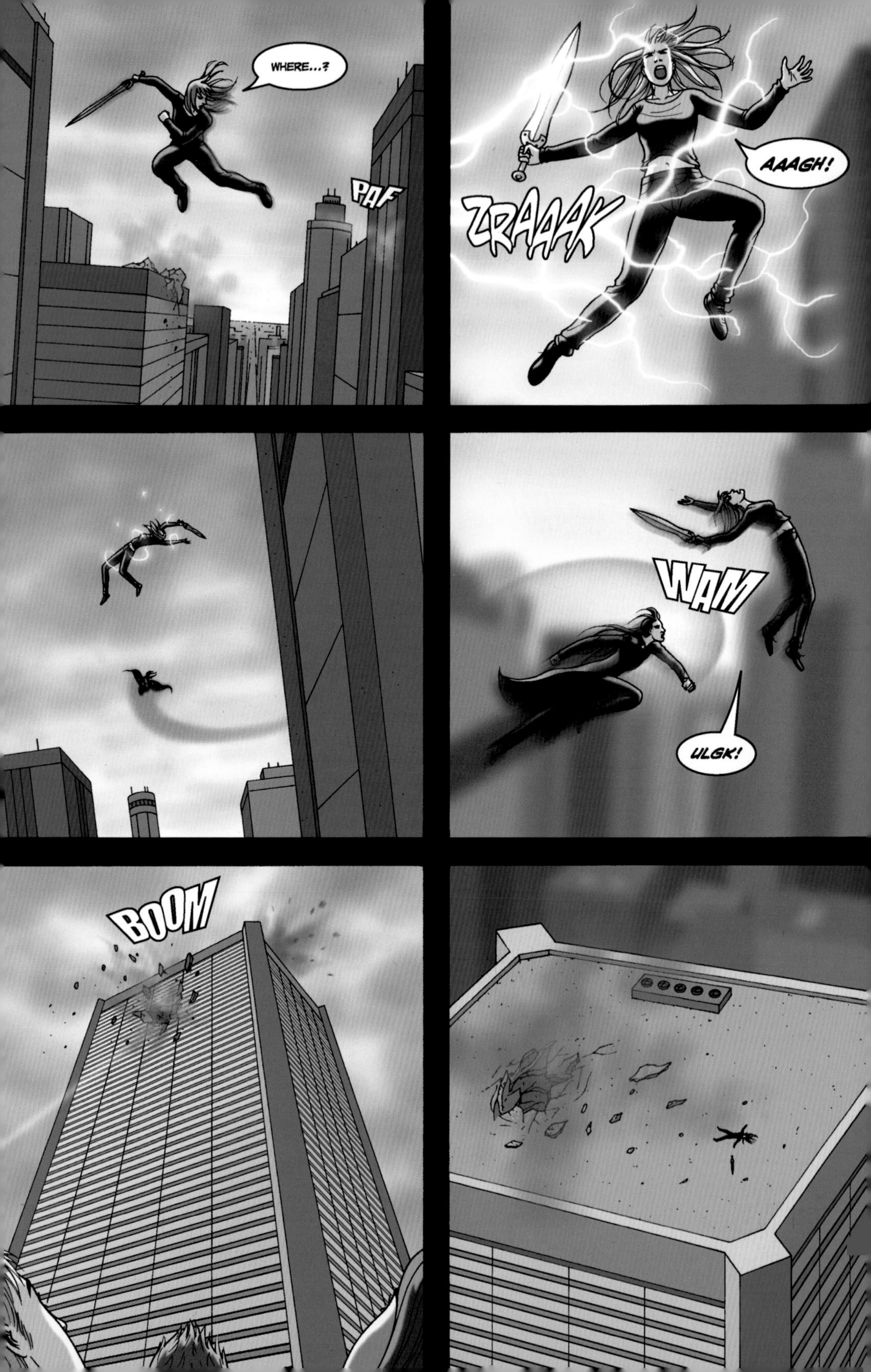
WHERE...?
PAF
ZRAAAK
AAAGH!
WAM
ULGK!
BOOM

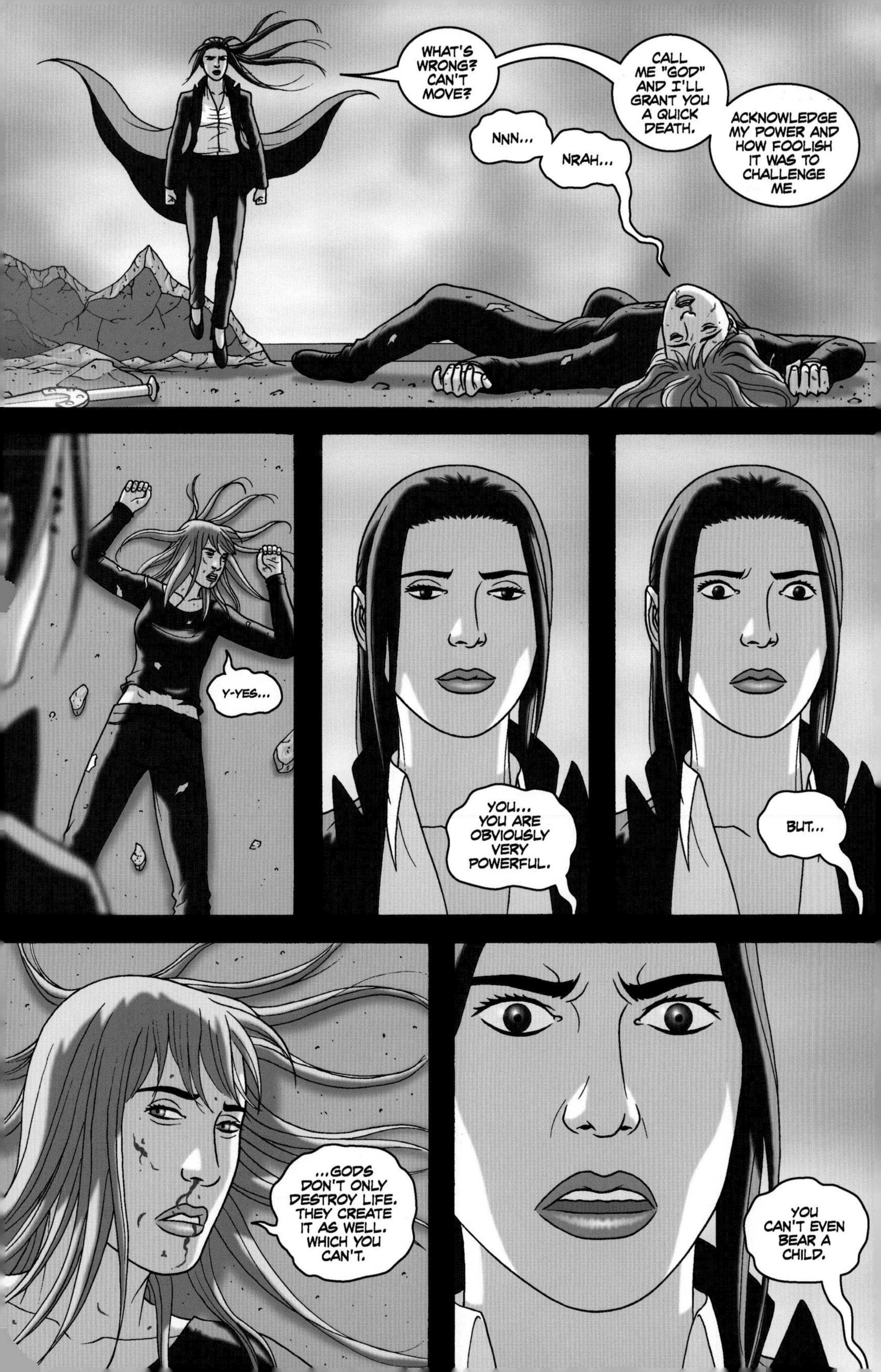
WHAT'S WRONG? CAN'T MOVE?
CALL ME "GOD" AND I'LL GRANT YOU A QUICK DEATH.
ACKNOWLEDGE MY POWER AND HOW FOOLISH IT WAS TO CHALLENGE ME.
NNN...
NRAH...
Y-YES...
YOU... YOU ARE OBVIOUSLY VERY POWERFUL.
BUT...
...GODS DON'T ONLY DESTROY LIFE. THEY CREATE IT AS WELL. WHICH YOU CAN'T.
YOU CAN'T EVEN BEAR A CHILD.

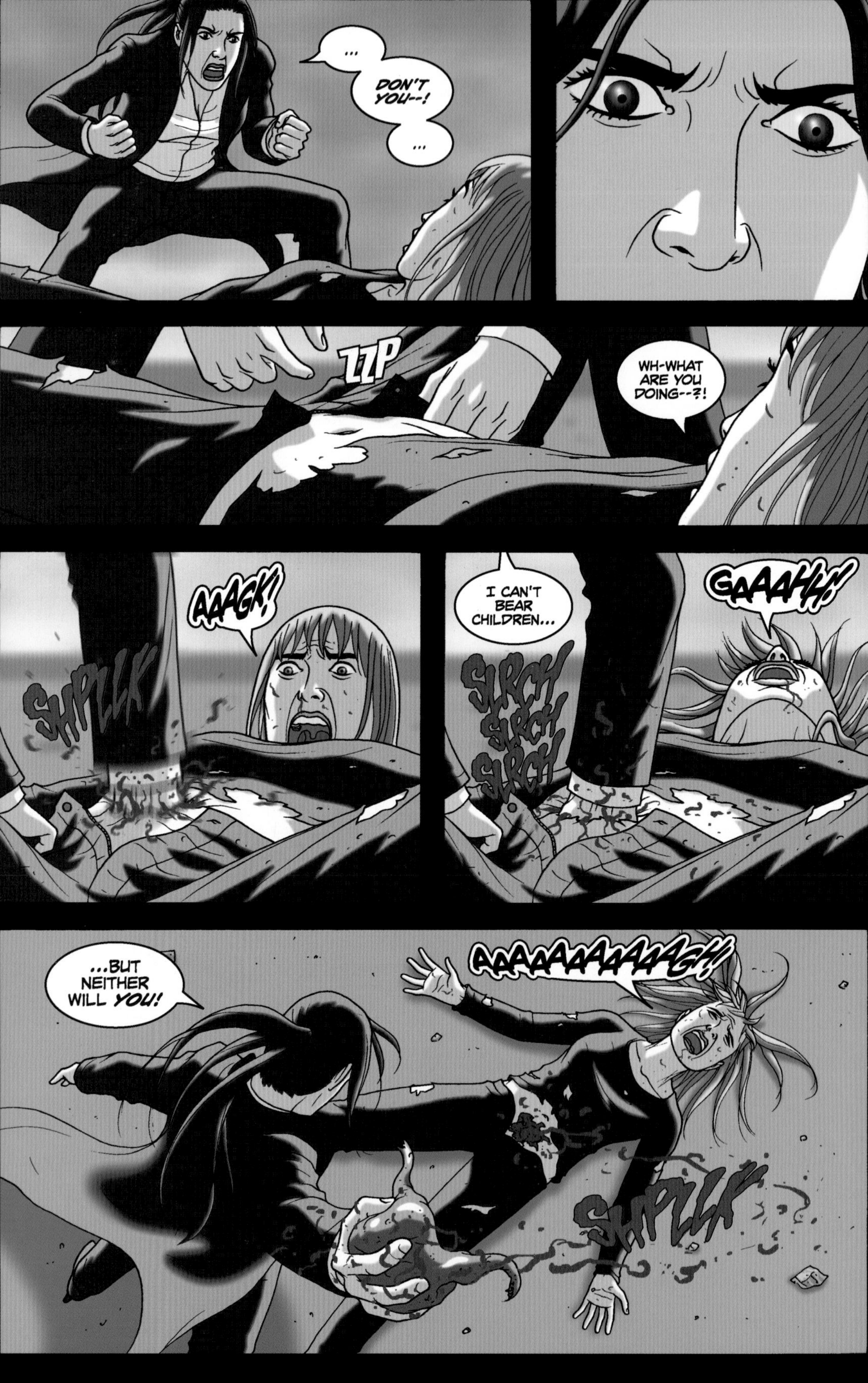
...
DON'T YOU--!
...
ZZP
WH-WHAT ARE YOU DOING--?!
AAAGK!
SHPLLK
I CAN'T BEAR CHILDREN...
GAAAHH!
SLRCH SLRCH SLRCH
...BUT NEITHER WILL YOU!
AAAAAAAAAAAGH!
SHPLLK

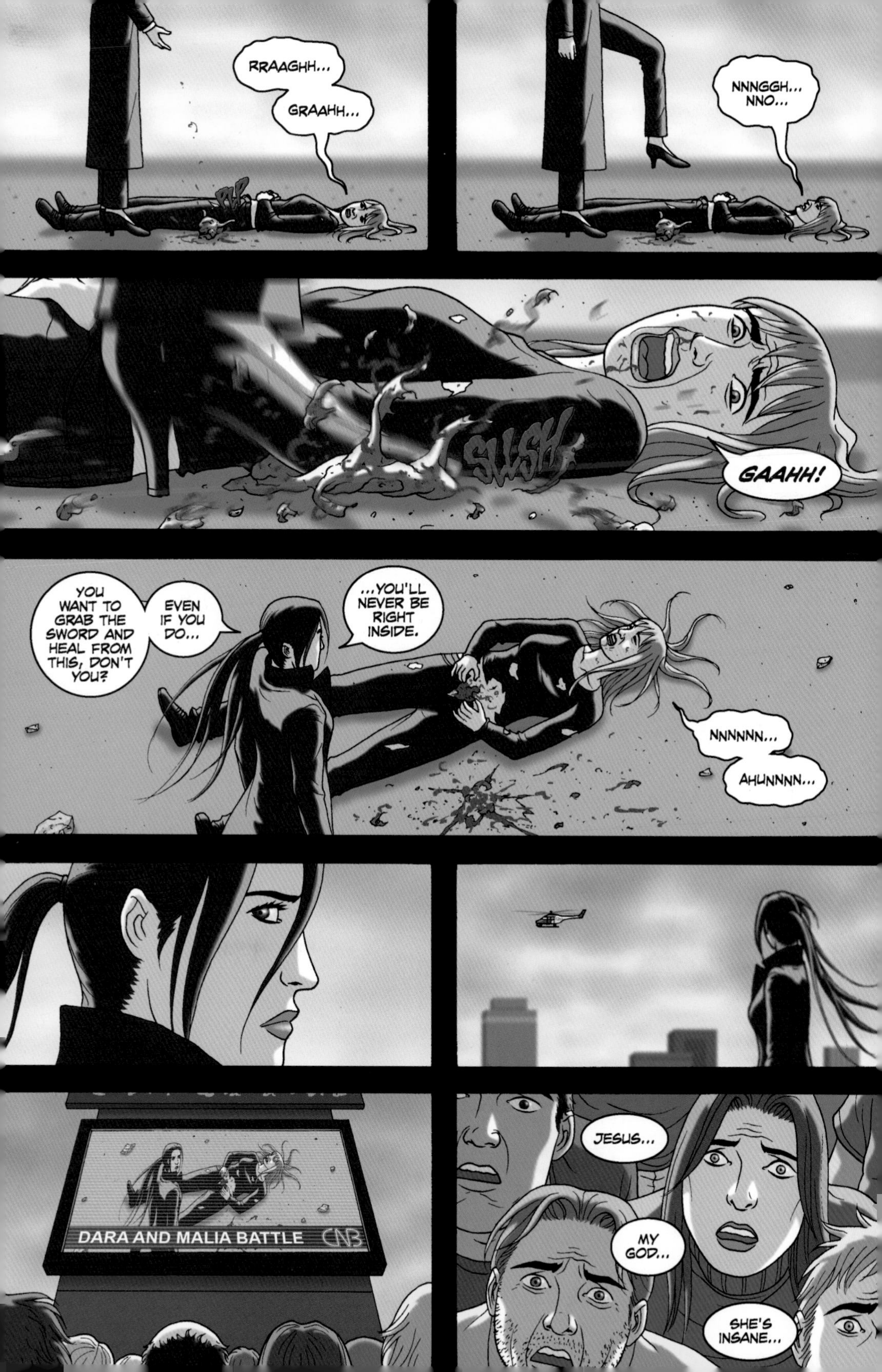
RRAAGHH...
GRAAHH...
NNNGGH... NNO...
SLISH
GAAHH!
YOU WANT TO GRAB THE SWORD AND HEAL FROM THIS, DON'T YOU?
EVEN IF YOU DO...
...YOU'LL NEVER BE RIGHT INSIDE.
NNNNNN...
AHUNNNN...
DARA AND MALIA BATTLE
CNB
JESUS...
MY GOD...
SHE'S INSANE...

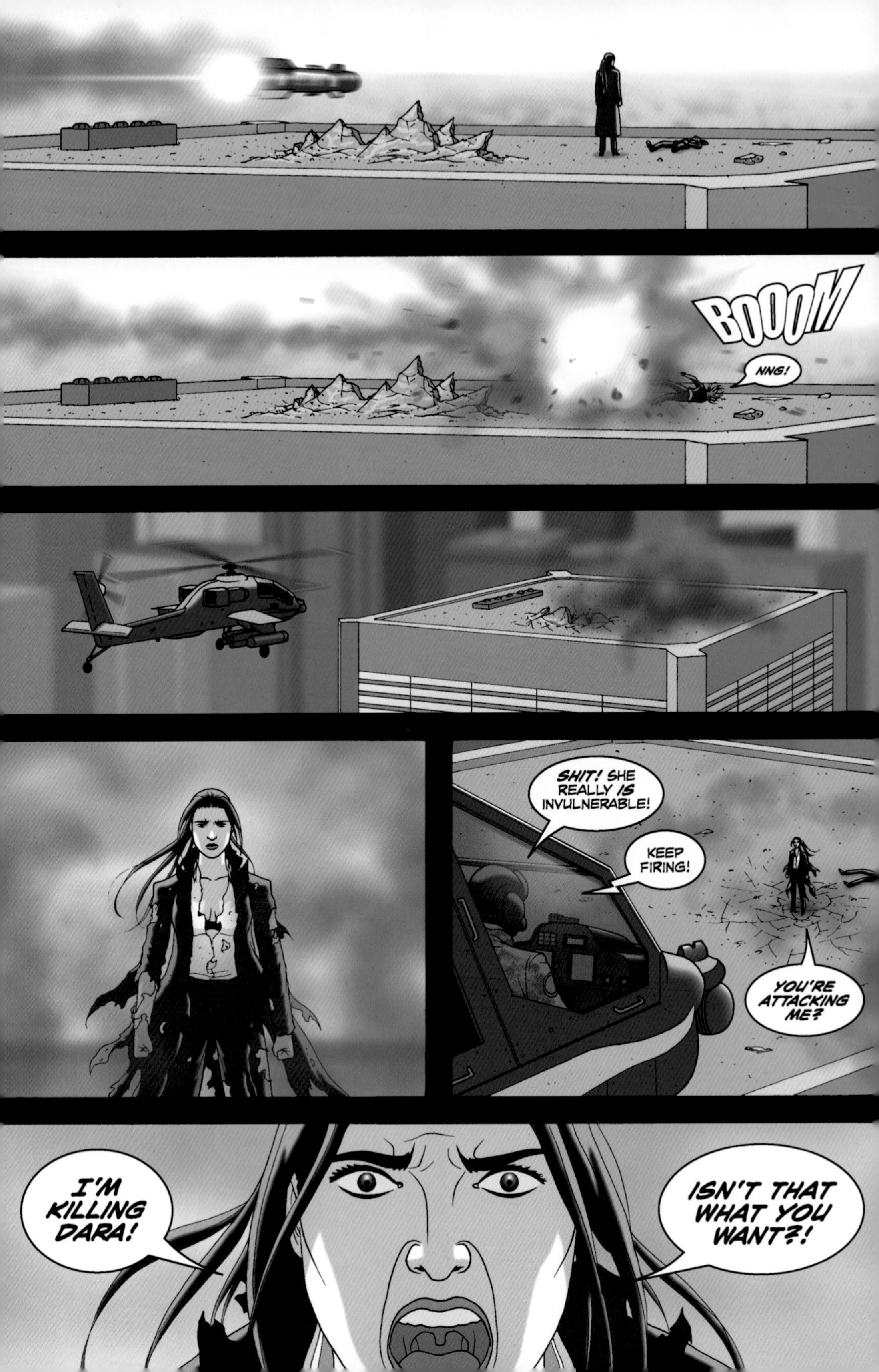
BOOOM
NNG!
SHIT! SHE REALLY IS INVULNERABLE!
KEEP FIRING!
YOU'RE ATTACKING ME?
I'M KILLING DARA!
ISN'T THAT WHAT YOU WANT?!

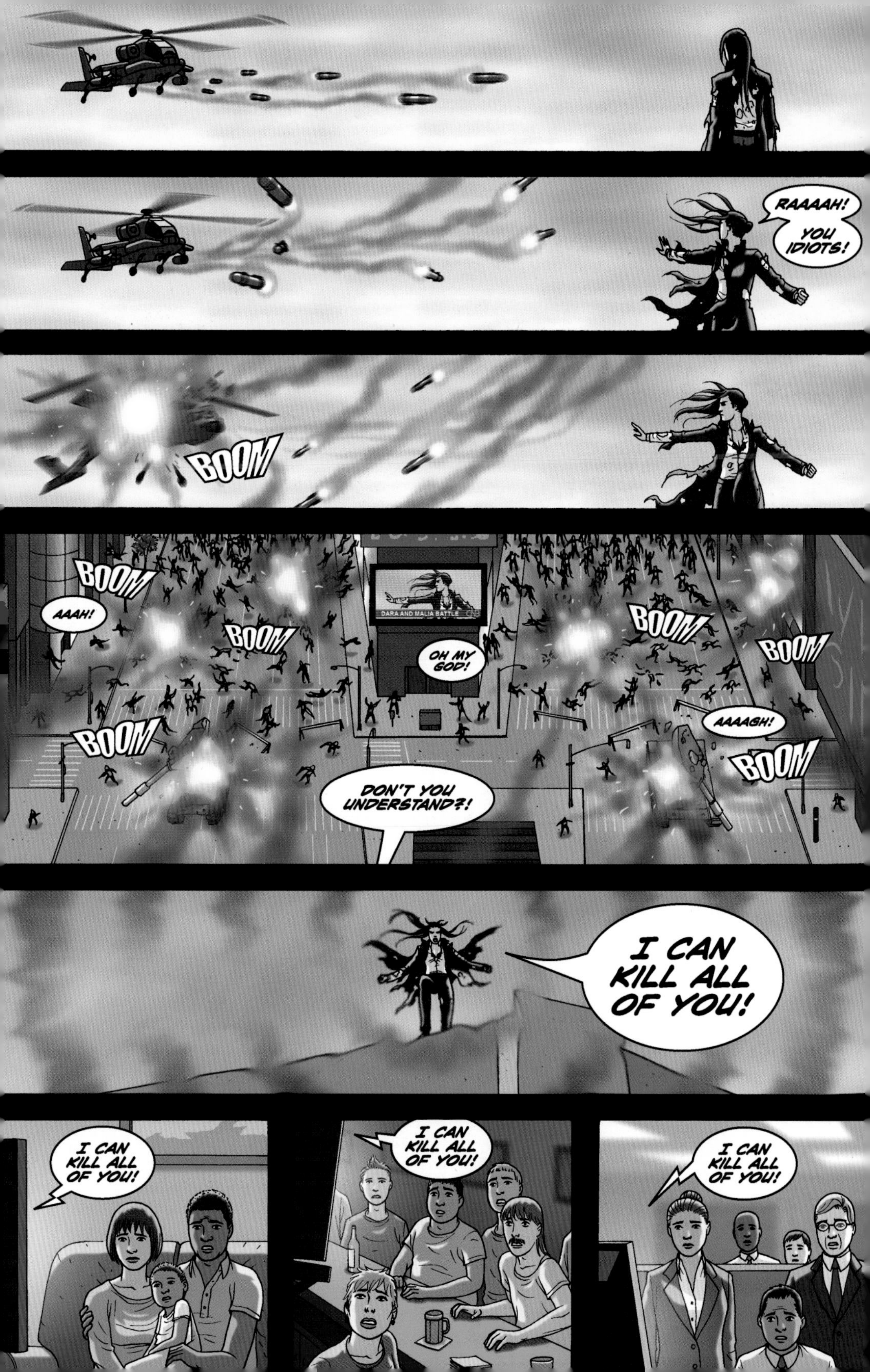
RAAAAH!
YOU IDIOTS!
BOOM
BOOM
AAAH!
BOOM
DARA AND MALIA BATTLE
OH MY GOD!
BOOM
BOOM
BOOM
AAAAGH!
BOOM
DON'T YOU UNDERSTAND?!
I CAN KILL ALL OF YOU!
I CAN KILL ALL OF YOU!
I CAN KILL ALL OF YOU!
I CAN KILL ALL OF YOU!

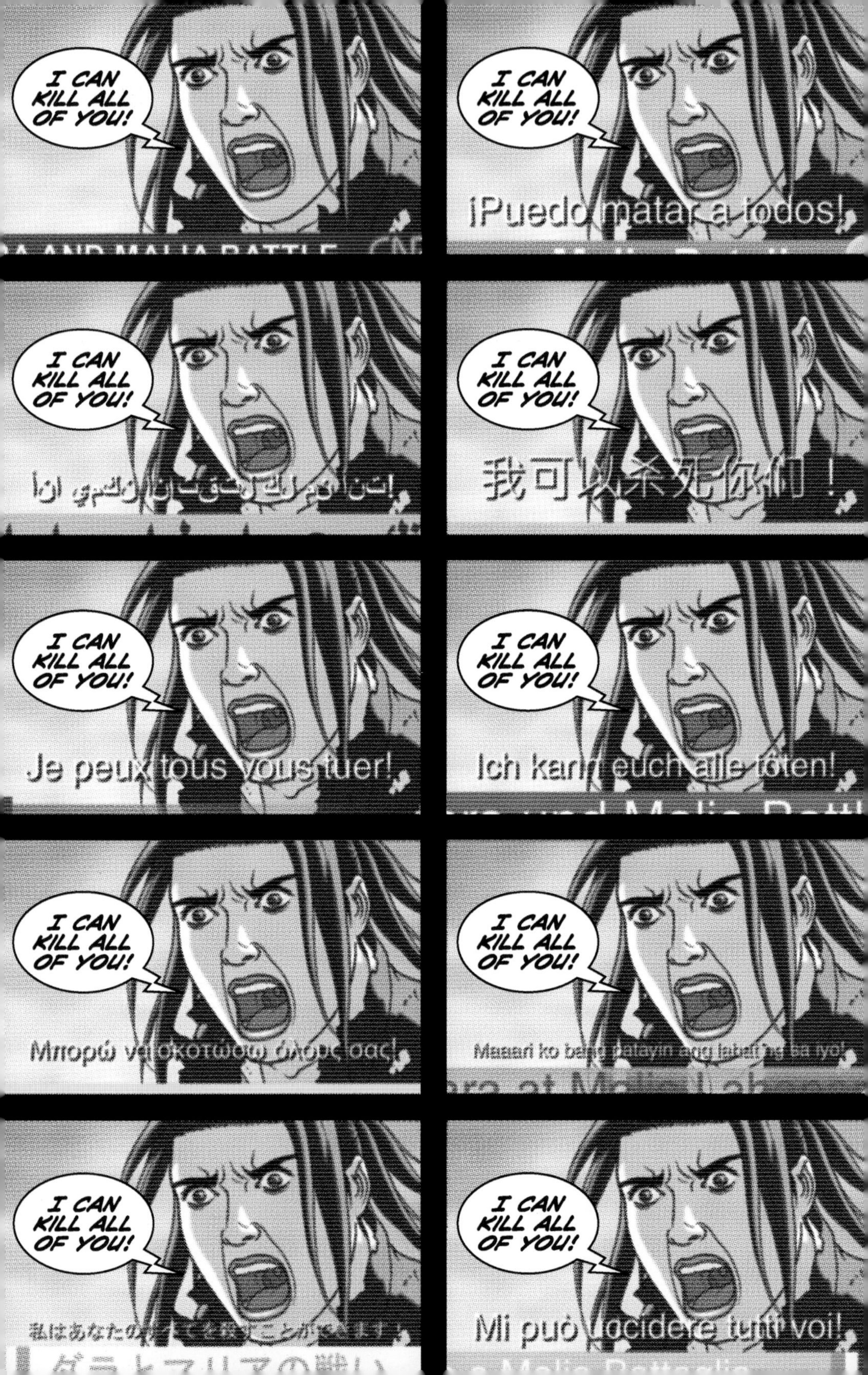
I CAN KILL ALL OF YOU!
I CAN KILL ALL OF YOU!
¡Puedo matar a todos!
I CAN KILL ALL OF YOU!
I CAN KILL ALL OF YOU!
我可以杀死你们！
I CAN KILL ALL OF YOU!
Je peux tous vous tuer!
I CAN KILL ALL OF YOU!
Ich kann euch alle töten!
I CAN KILL ALL OF YOU!
Μπορώ να σκοτώσω όλους σας!
I CAN KILL ALL OF YOU!
I CAN KILL ALL OF YOU!
I CAN KILL ALL OF YOU!
Mi può uccidere tutti voi!

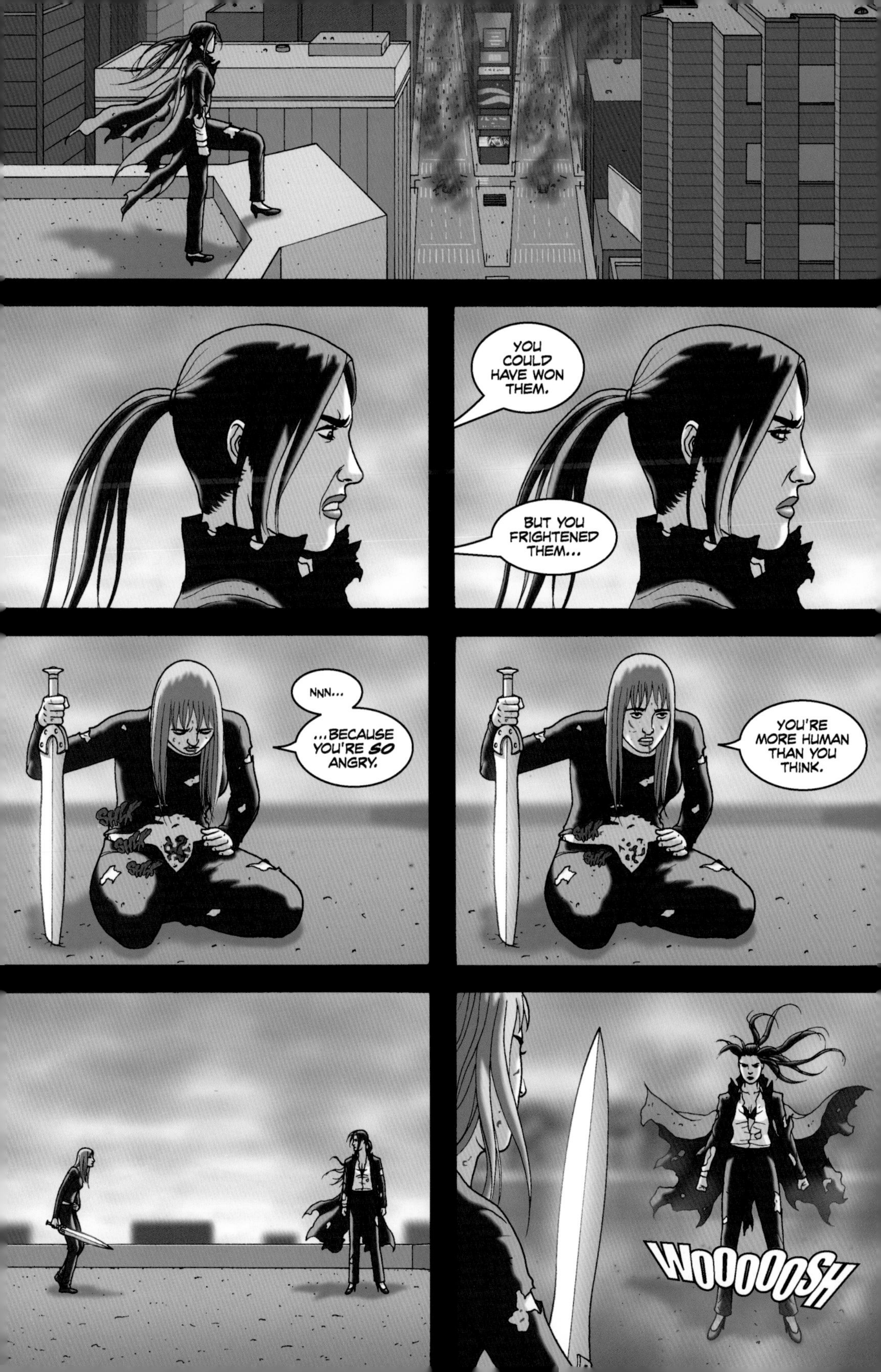
YOU COULD HAVE WON THEM.
BUT YOU FRIGHTENED THEM...
NNN...
...BECAUSE YOU'RE *SO* ANGRY.
YOU'RE MORE HUMAN THAN YOU THINK.
WOOOOOSH

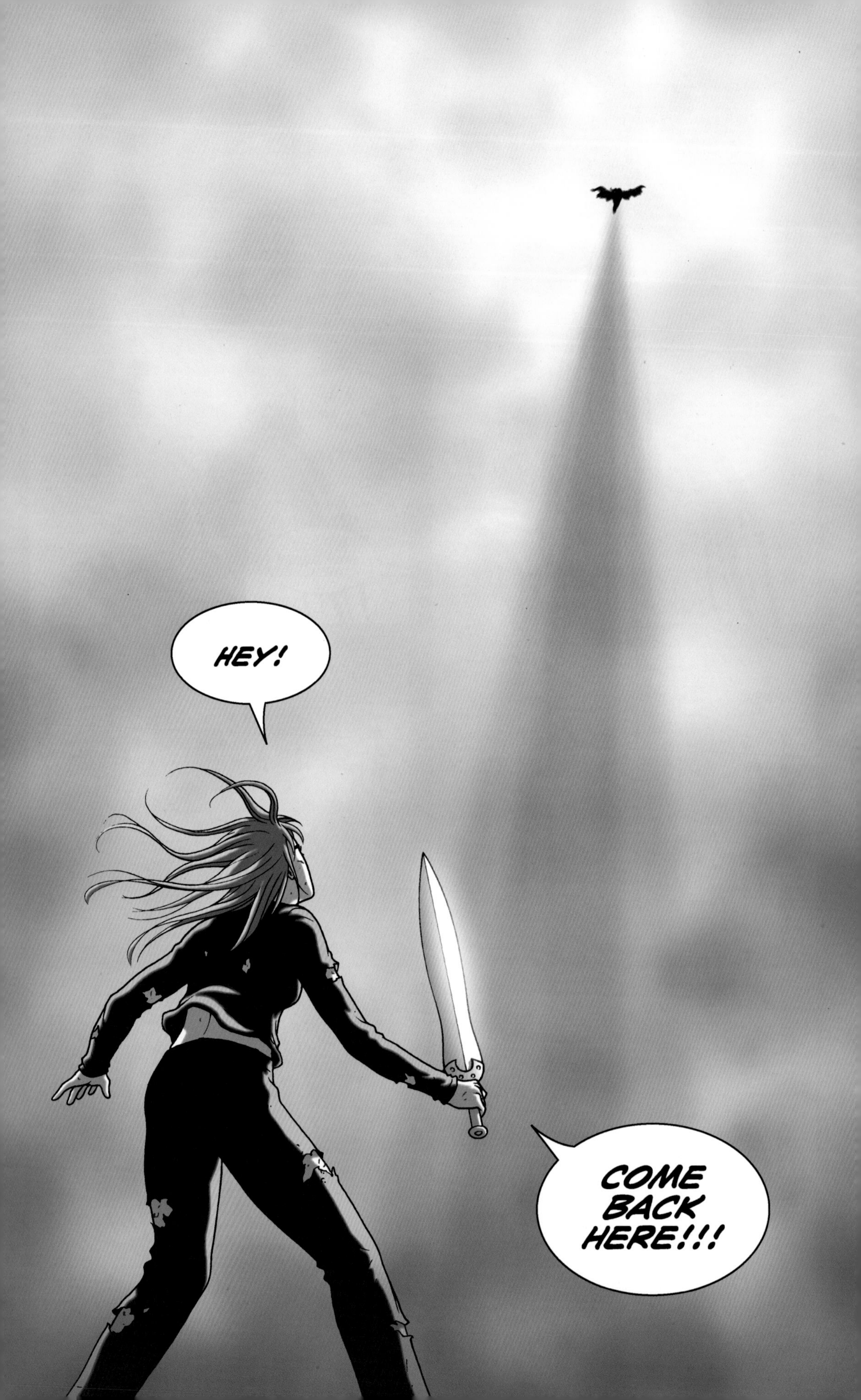
HEY!
COME BACK HERE!!!

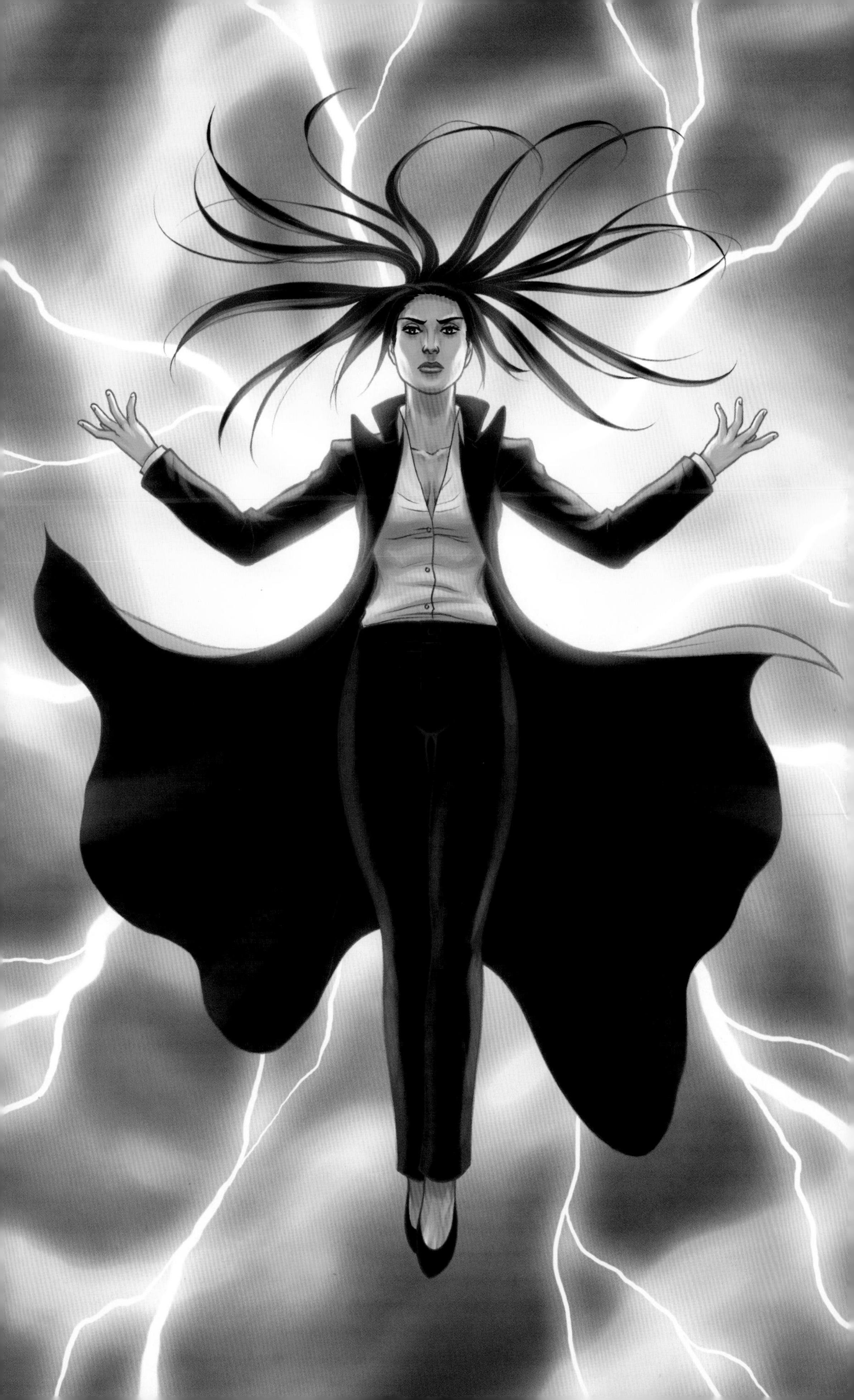

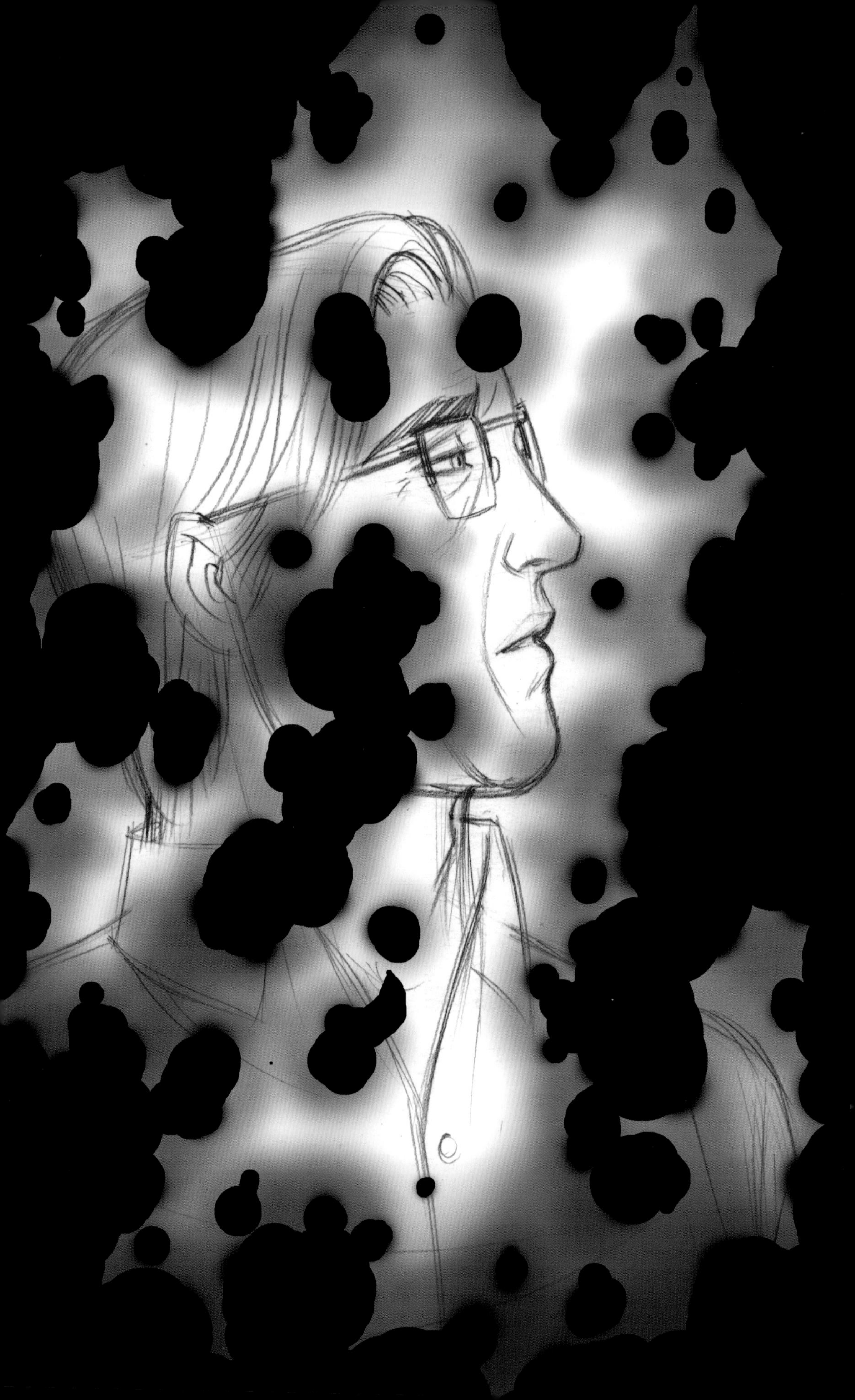

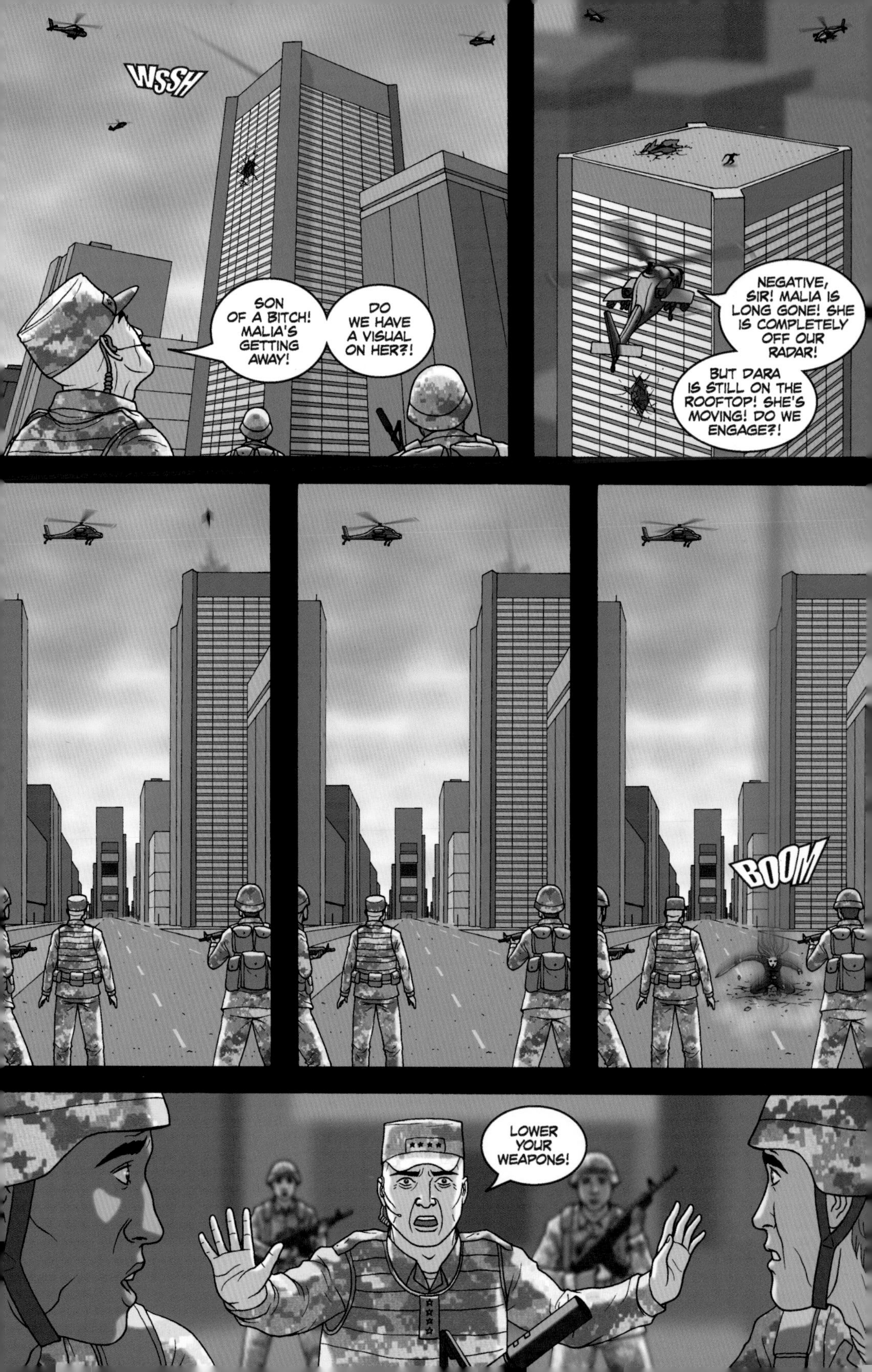
WSSH
SON OF A BITCH! MALIA'S GETTING AWAY!
DO WE HAVE A VISUAL ON HER?!
NEGATIVE, SIR! MALIA IS LONG GONE! SHE IS COMPLETELY OFF OUR RADAR!
BUT DARA IS STILL ON THE ROOFTOP! SHE'S MOVING! DO WE ENGAGE?!
BOOM
LOWER YOUR WEAPONS!

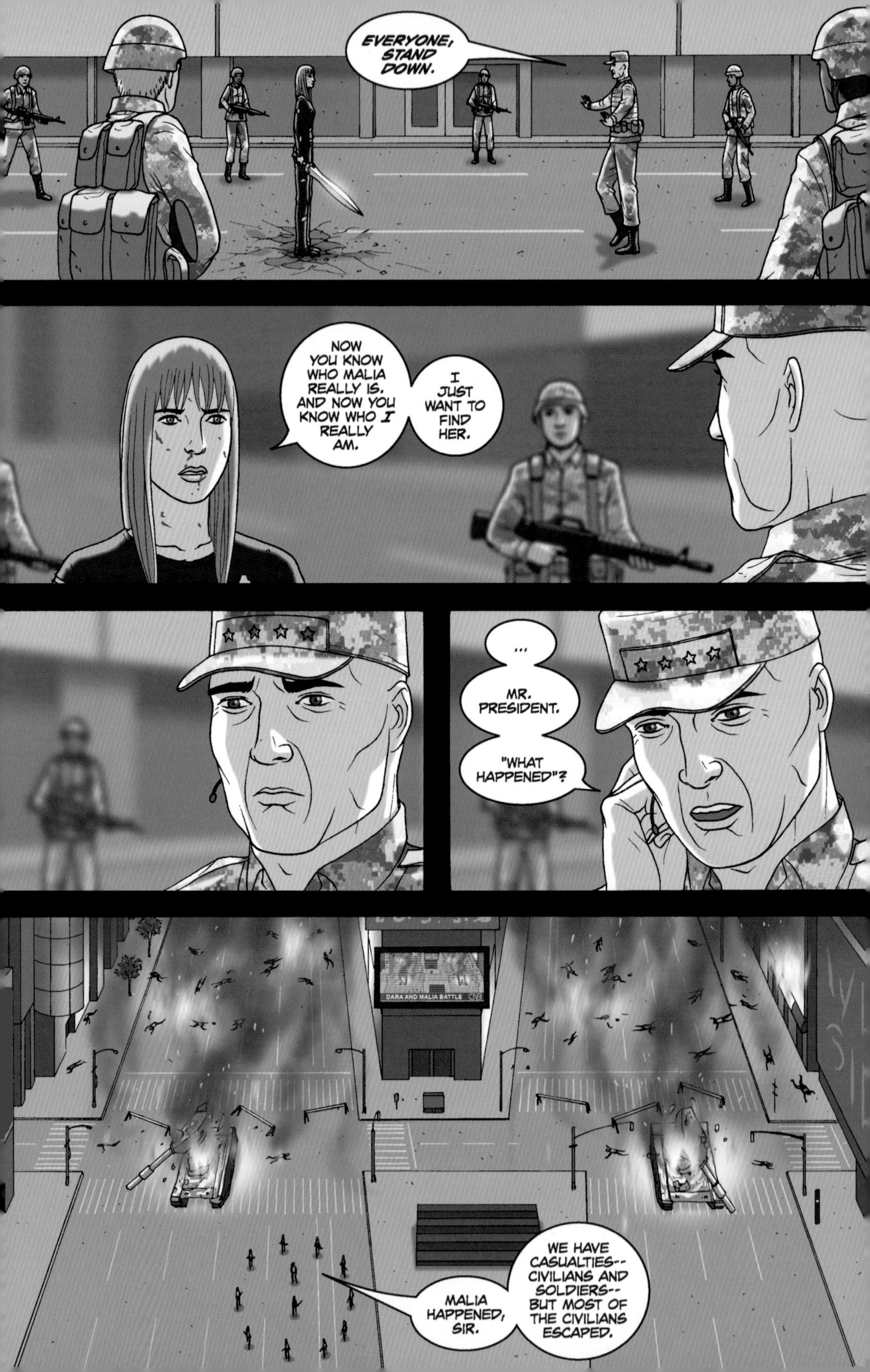
EVERYONE, STAND DOWN.
NOW YOU KNOW WHO MALIA REALLY IS. AND NOW YOU KNOW WHO *I* REALLY AM.
I JUST WANT TO FIND HER.
...
MR. PRESIDENT.
"WHAT HAPPENED"?
DARA AND MALIA BATTLE
MALIA HAPPENED, SIR.
WE HAVE CASUALTIES-- CIVILIANS AND SOLDIERS-- BUT MOST OF THE CIVILIANS ESCAPED.

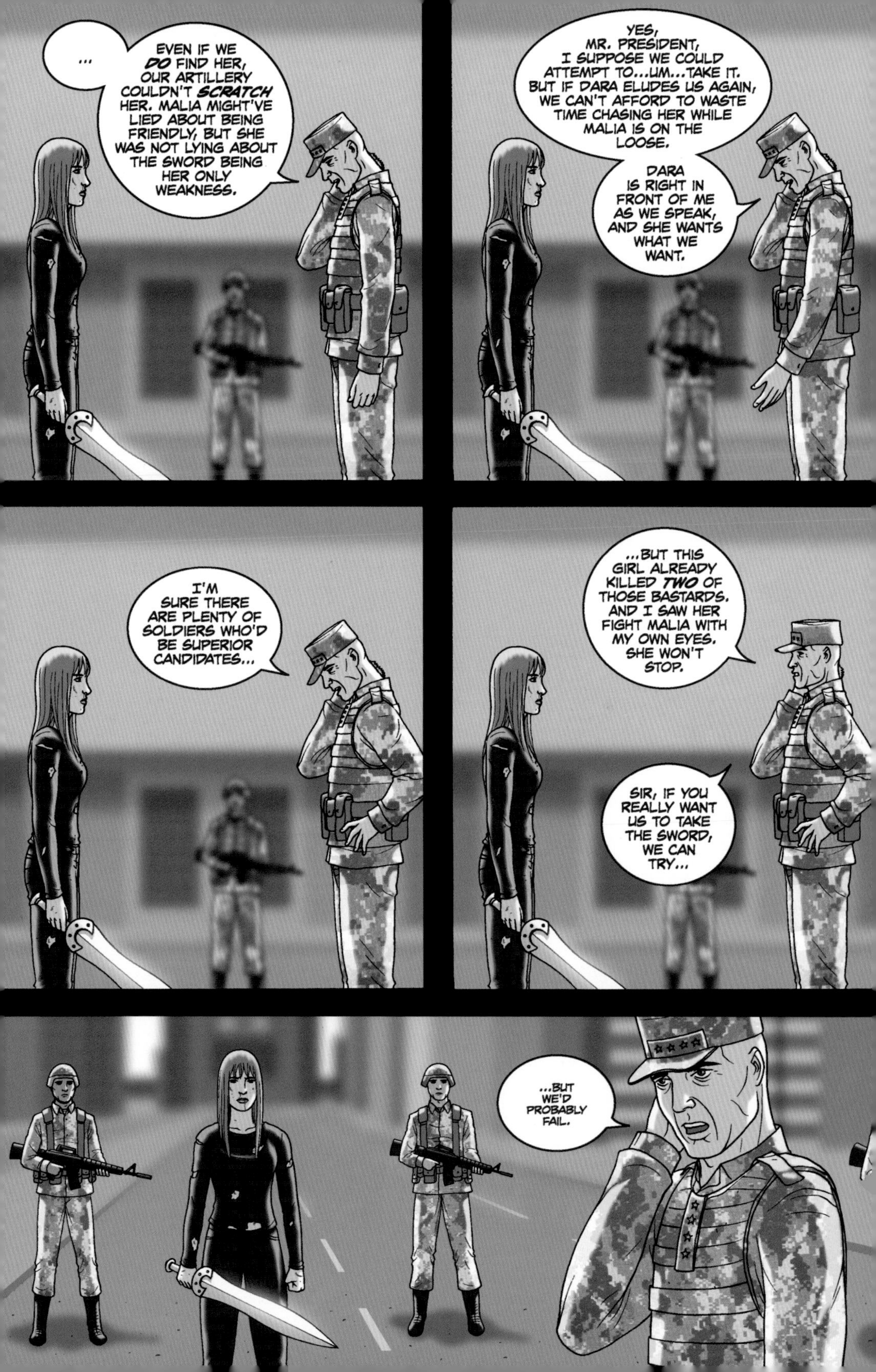
...
EVEN IF WE DO FIND HER, OUR ARTILLERY COULDN'T SCRATCH HER. MALIA MIGHT'VE LIED ABOUT BEING FRIENDLY, BUT SHE WAS NOT LYING ABOUT THE SWORD BEING HER ONLY WEAKNESS.
YES, MR. PRESIDENT, I SUPPOSE WE COULD ATTEMPT TO...UM...TAKE IT. BUT IF DARA ELUDES US AGAIN, WE CAN'T AFFORD TO WASTE TIME CHASING HER WHILE MALIA IS ON THE LOOSE.
DARA IS RIGHT IN FRONT OF ME AS WE SPEAK, AND SHE WANTS WHAT WE WANT.
I'M SURE THERE ARE PLENTY OF SOLDIERS WHO'D BE SUPERIOR CANDIDATES...
...BUT THIS GIRL ALREADY KILLED TWO OF THOSE BASTARDS. AND I SAW HER FIGHT MALIA WITH MY OWN EYES. SHE WON'T STOP.
SIR, IF YOU REALLY WANT US TO TAKE THE SWORD, WE CAN TRY...
...BUT WE'D PROBABLY FAIL.

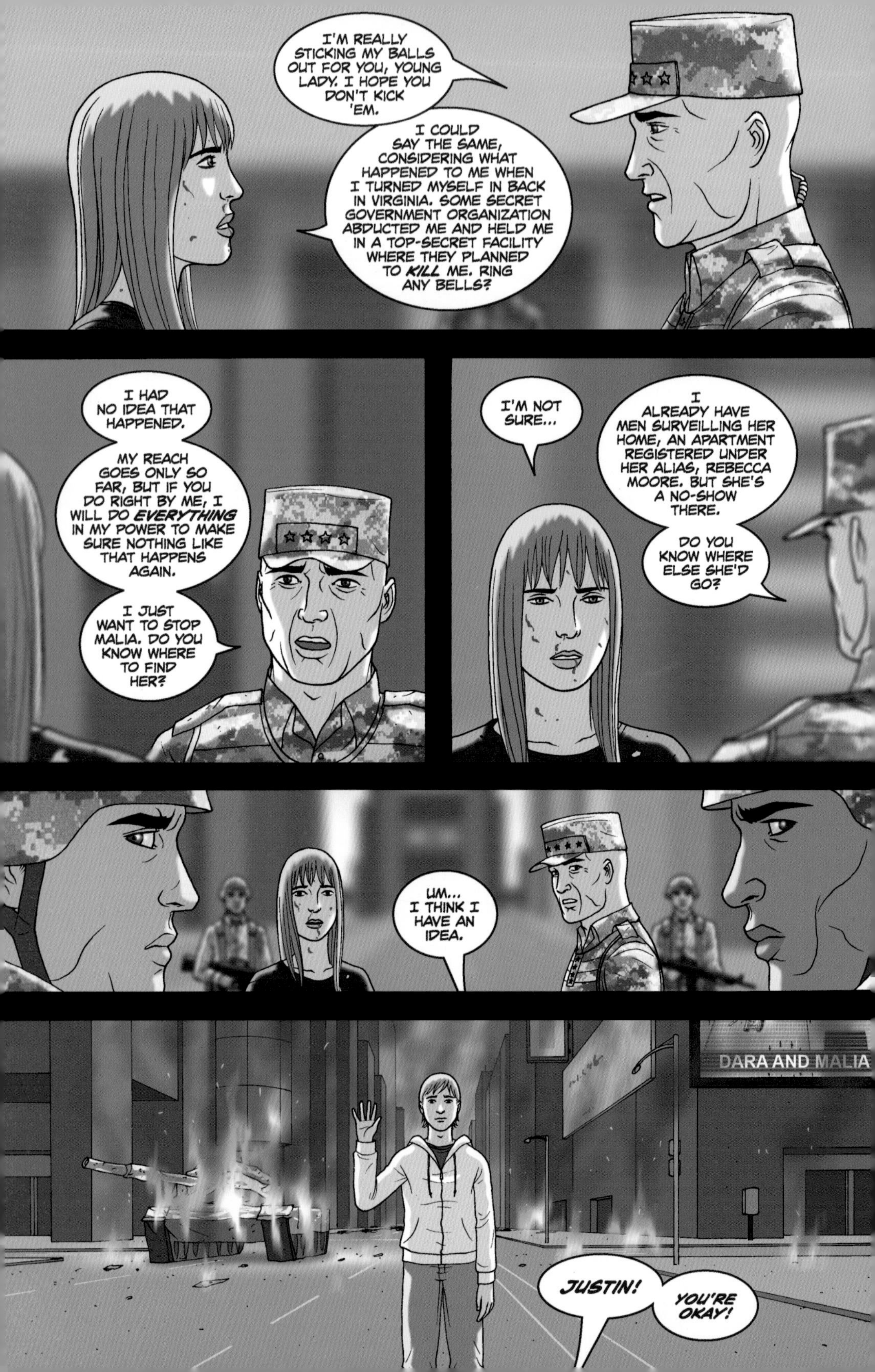
I'M REALLY STICKING MY BALLS OUT FOR YOU, YOUNG LADY. I HOPE YOU DON'T KICK 'EM.
I COULD SAY THE SAME, CONSIDERING WHAT HAPPENED TO ME WHEN I TURNED MYSELF IN BACK IN VIRGINIA. SOME SECRET GOVERNMENT ORGANIZATION ABDUCTED ME AND HELD ME IN A TOP-SECRET FACILITY WHERE THEY PLANNED TO *KILL* ME. RING ANY BELLS?
I HAD NO IDEA THAT HAPPENED.
MY REACH GOES ONLY SO FAR, BUT IF YOU DO RIGHT BY ME, I WILL DO *EVERYTHING* IN MY POWER TO MAKE SURE NOTHING LIKE THAT HAPPENS AGAIN.
I JUST WANT TO STOP MALIA. DO YOU KNOW WHERE TO FIND HER?
I'M NOT SURE...
I ALREADY HAVE MEN SURVEILLING HER HOME, AN APARTMENT REGISTERED UNDER HER ALIAS, REBECCA MOORE. BUT SHE'S A NO-SHOW THERE.
DO YOU KNOW WHERE ELSE SHE'D GO?
UM... I THINK I HAVE AN IDEA.
DARA AND MALIA
JUSTIN!
YOU'RE OKAY!

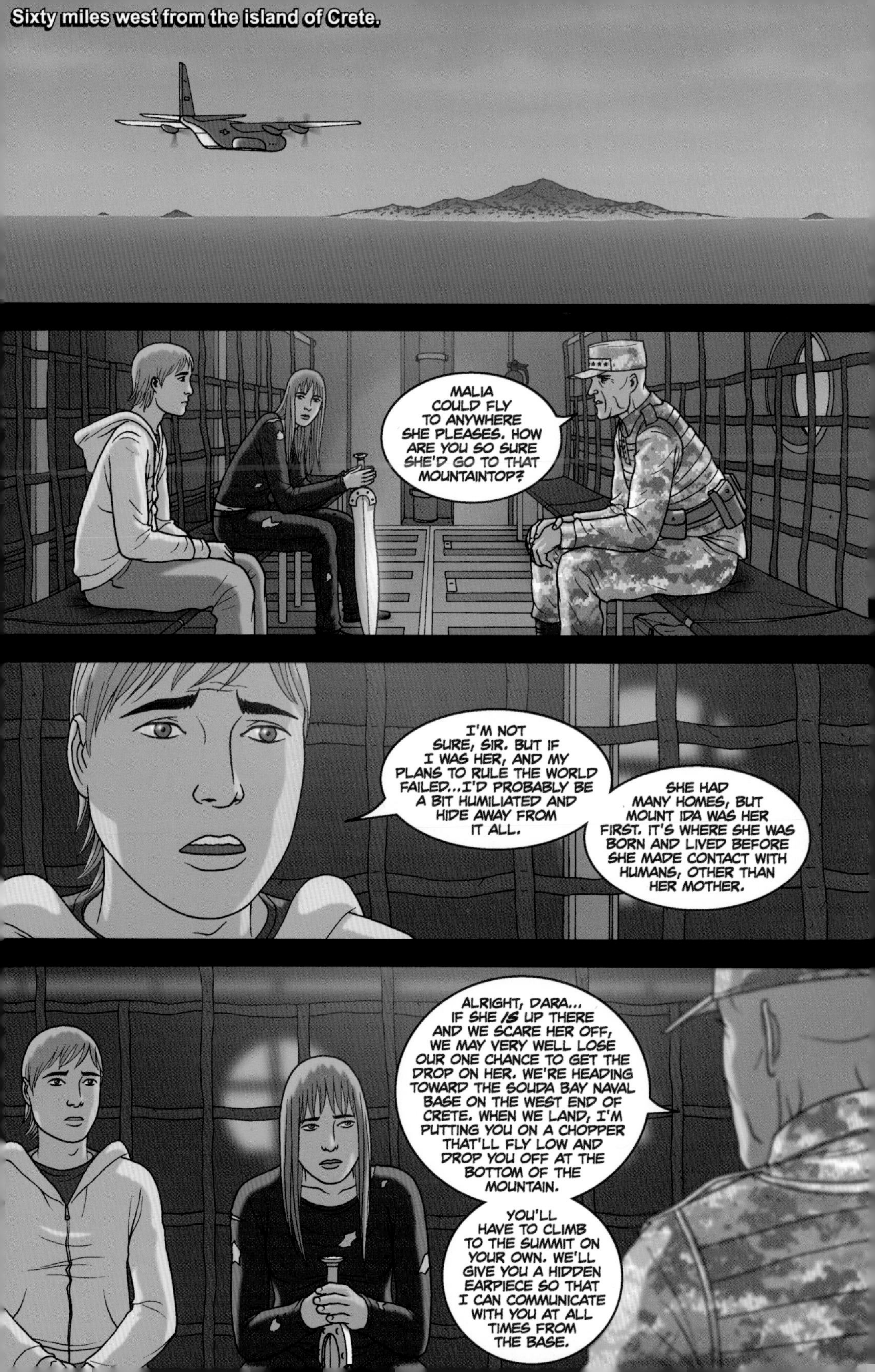
Sixty miles west from the island of Crete.
MALIA COULD FLY TO ANYWHERE SHE PLEASES. HOW ARE YOU SO SURE SHE'D GO TO THAT MOUNTAINTOP?
I'M NOT SURE, SIR. BUT IF I WAS HER, AND MY PLANS TO RULE THE WORLD FAILED...I'D PROBABLY BE A BIT HUMILIATED AND HIDE AWAY FROM IT ALL.
SHE HAD MANY HOMES, BUT MOUNT IDA WAS HER FIRST. IT'S WHERE SHE WAS BORN AND LIVED BEFORE SHE MADE CONTACT WITH HUMANS, OTHER THAN HER MOTHER.
ALRIGHT, DARA... IF SHE IS UP THERE AND WE SCARE HER OFF, WE MAY VERY WELL LOSE OUR ONE CHANCE TO GET THE DROP ON HER. WE'RE HEADING TOWARD THE SOUDA BAY NAVAL BASE ON THE WEST END OF CRETE. WHEN WE LAND, I'M PUTTING YOU ON A CHOPPER THAT'LL FLY LOW AND DROP YOU OFF AT THE BOTTOM OF THE MOUNTAIN.
YOU'LL HAVE TO CLIMB TO THE SUMMIT ON YOUR OWN. WE'LL GIVE YOU A HIDDEN EARPIECE SO THAT I CAN COMMUNICATE WITH YOU AT ALL TIMES FROM THE BASE.

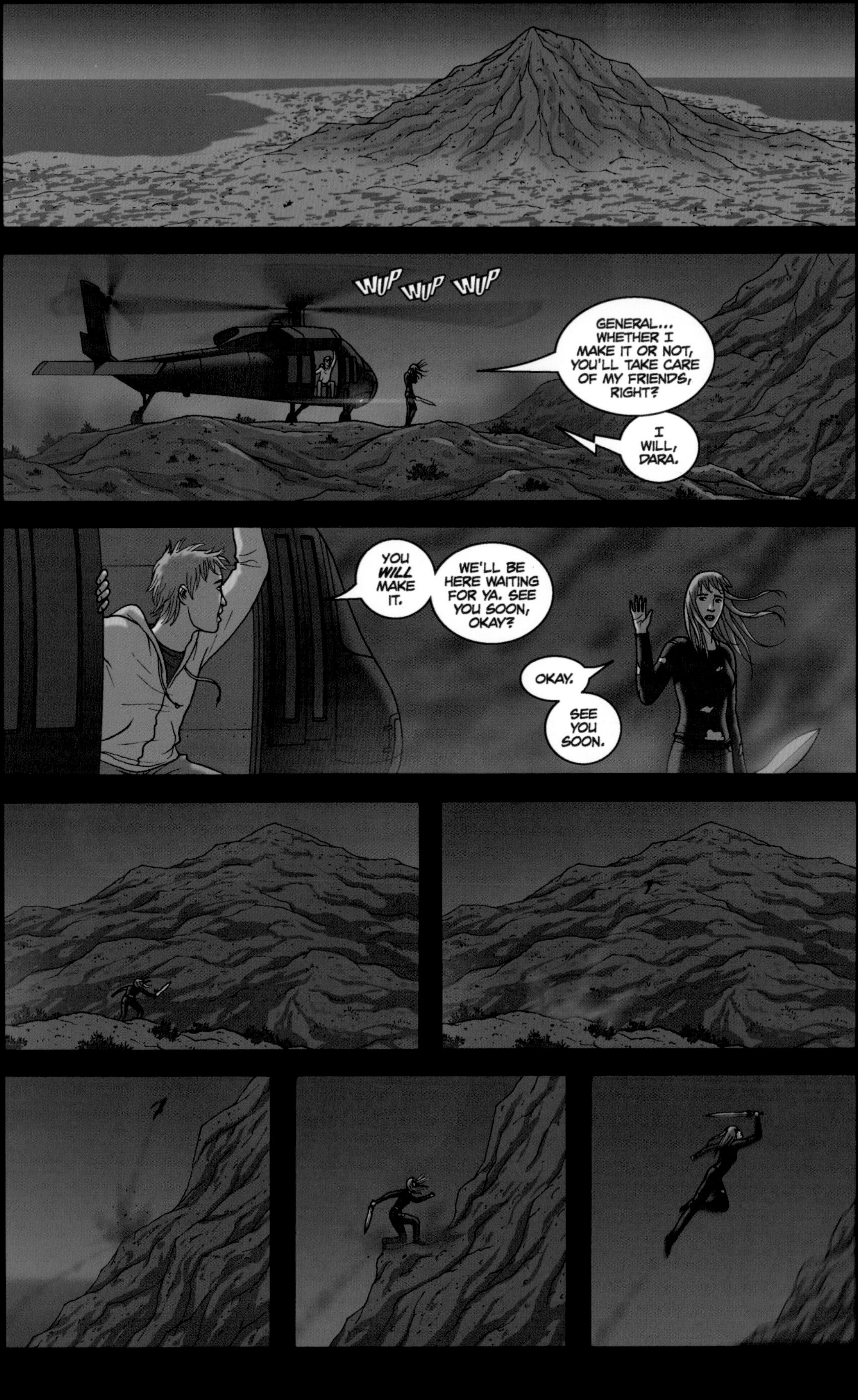
WUP WUP WUP
GENERAL... WHETHER I MAKE IT OR NOT, YOU'LL TAKE CARE OF MY FRIENDS, RIGHT?
I WILL, DARA.
YOU *WILL* MAKE IT.
WE'LL BE HERE WAITING FOR YA. SEE YOU SOON, OKAY?
OKAY.
SEE YOU SOON.

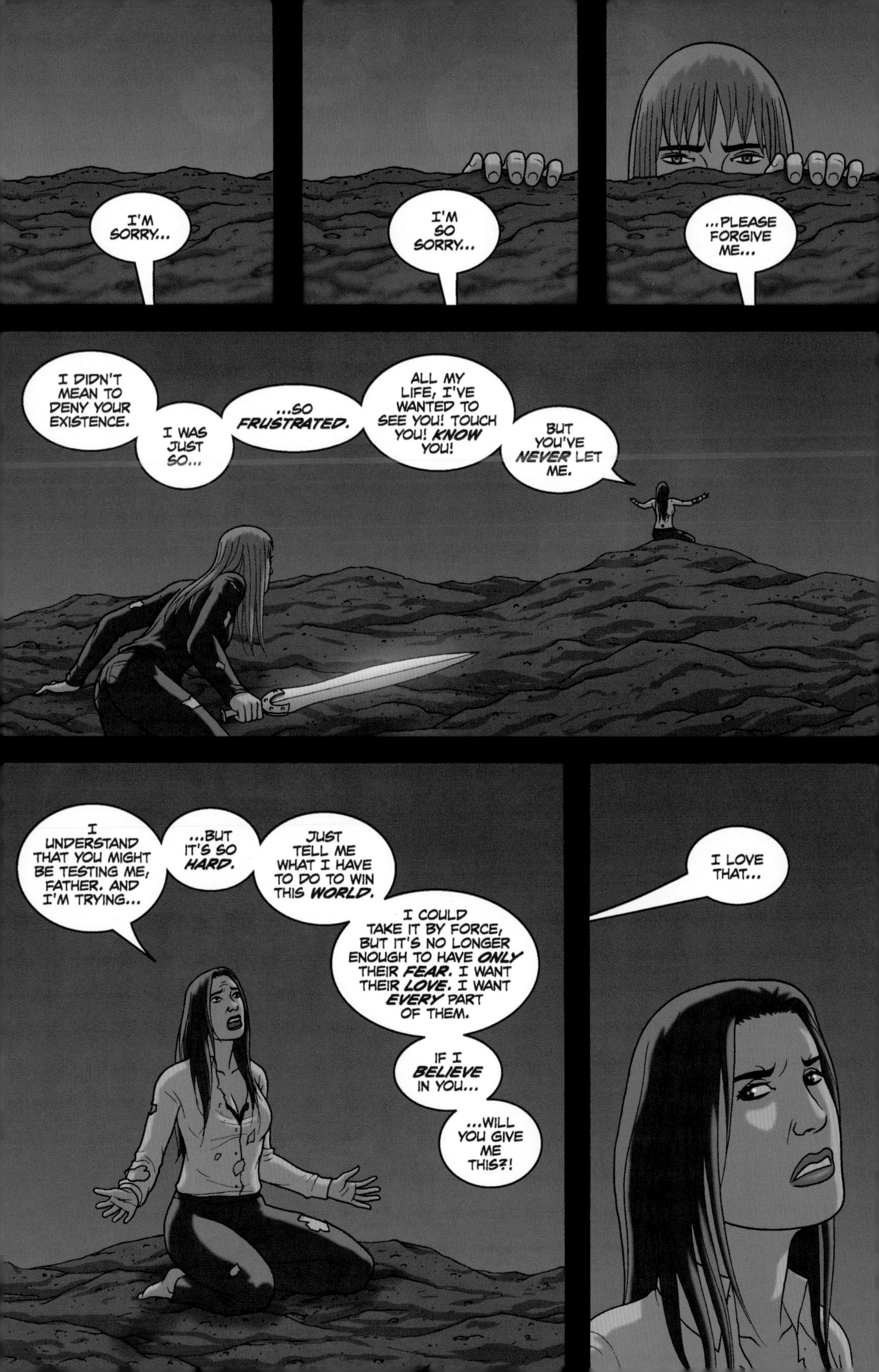
I'M SORRY...
I'M SO SORRY...
...PLEASE FORGIVE ME...
I DIDN'T MEAN TO DENY YOUR EXISTENCE.
I WAS JUST SO...
...SO FRUSTRATED.
ALL MY LIFE, I'VE WANTED TO SEE YOU! TOUCH YOU! KNOW YOU!
BUT YOU'VE NEVER LET ME.
I UNDERSTAND THAT YOU MIGHT BE TESTING ME, FATHER. AND I'M TRYING...
...BUT IT'S SO HARD.
JUST TELL ME WHAT I HAVE TO DO TO WIN THIS WORLD.
I COULD TAKE IT BY FORCE, BUT IT'S NO LONGER ENOUGH TO HAVE ONLY THEIR FEAR. I WANT THEIR LOVE. I WANT EVERY PART OF THEM.
IF I BELIEVE IN YOU...
...WILL YOU GIVE ME THIS?!
I LOVE THAT...

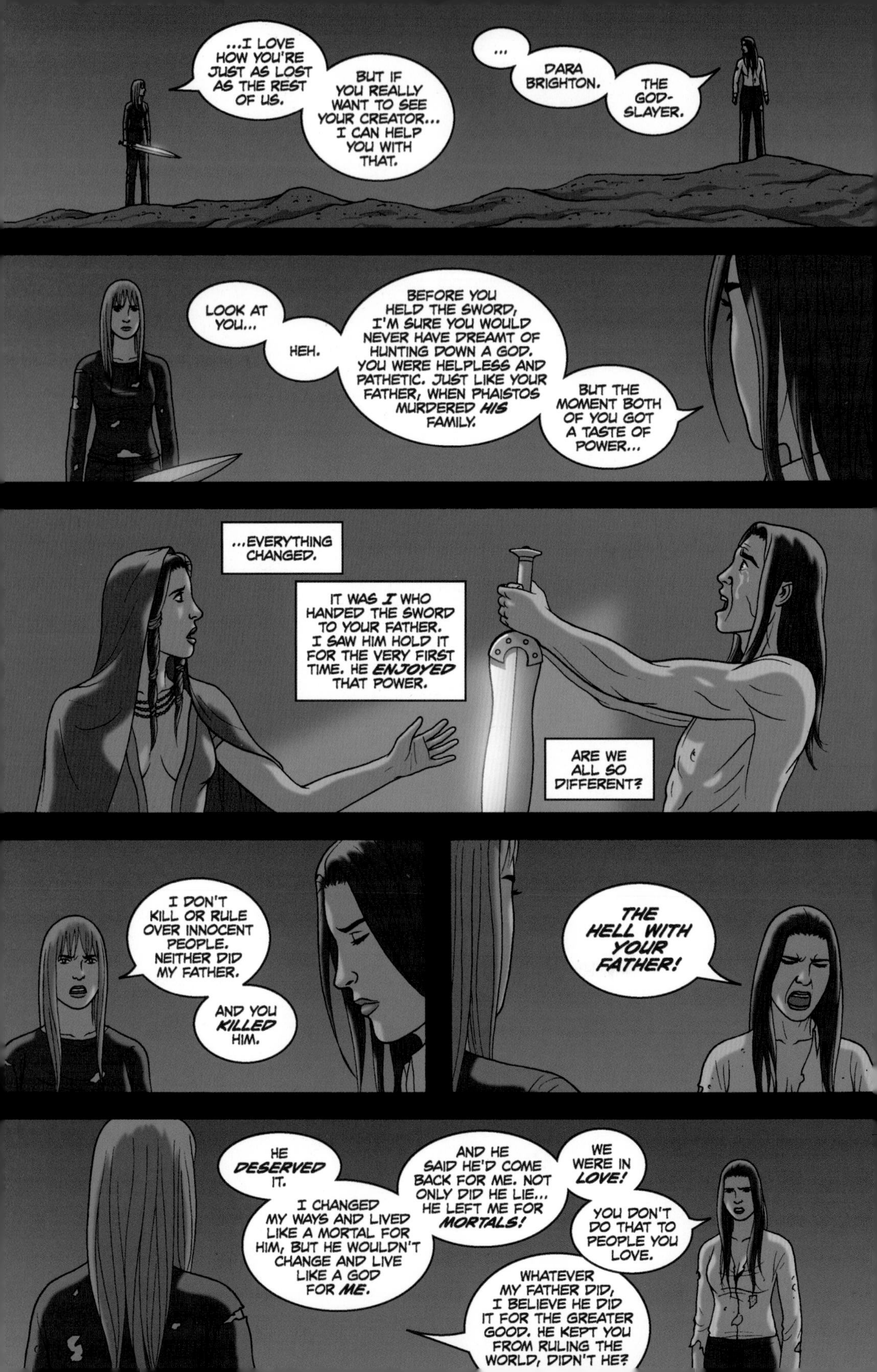

...I LOVE HOW YOU'RE JUST AS LOST AS THE REST OF US.
BUT IF YOU REALLY WANT TO SEE YOUR CREATOR... I CAN HELP YOU WITH THAT.
...
DARA BRIGHTON.
THE GOD-SLAYER.
LOOK AT YOU...
HEH.
BEFORE YOU HELD THE SWORD, I'M SURE YOU WOULD NEVER HAVE DREAMT OF HUNTING DOWN A GOD. YOU WERE HELPLESS AND PATHETIC. JUST LIKE YOUR FATHER, WHEN PHAISTOS MURDERED HIS FAMILY.
BUT THE MOMENT BOTH OF YOU GOT A TASTE OF POWER...
...EVERYTHING CHANGED.
IT WAS I WHO HANDED THE SWORD TO YOUR FATHER. I SAW HIM HOLD IT FOR THE VERY FIRST TIME. HE ENJOYED THAT POWER.
ARE WE ALL SO DIFFERENT?
I DON'T KILL OR RULE OVER INNOCENT PEOPLE. NEITHER DID MY FATHER.
AND YOU KILLED HIM.
THE HELL WITH YOUR FATHER!
HE DESERVED IT.
I CHANGED MY WAYS AND LIVED LIKE A MORTAL FOR HIM, BUT HE WOULDN'T CHANGE AND LIVE LIKE A GOD FOR ME.
AND HE SAID HE'D COME BACK FOR ME. NOT ONLY DID HE LIE... HE LEFT ME FOR MORTALS!
WE WERE IN LOVE!
YOU DON'T DO THAT TO PEOPLE YOU LOVE.
WHATEVER MY FATHER DID, I BELIEVE HE DID IT FOR THE GREATER GOOD. HE KEPT YOU FROM RULING THE WORLD, DIDN'T HE?

"GREATER GOOD."

I'M SURE YOU'D LIKE TO BELIEVE YOUR FATHER WAS A COURAGEOUS HERO, BUT CAN ANY OF US TRULY KNOW WHAT HIS INTENTIONS WERE?

MAYBE HIS REFUSAL TO RULE THE WORLD BY MY SIDE AND KILL MY BROTHERS HAD NOTHING TO DO WITH MORALS.

MAYBE HE WAS JUST A COWARD.

I KNOW WHAT YOU'RE TRYING TO DO, BUT IT WON'T WORK.

IF MY FATHER WAS A COWARD, WHY DID HE FACE PHAISTOS-- THE BIGGEST OF YOU FOUR--AND TAKE HIM DOWN BY HIMSELF.

IS THAT WHAT HE TOLD HIS CLASS?

HE USED "BIGGEST" TO DESCRIBE PHAISTOS?

HAHAHA!

...

PHAISTOS MAY HAVE BEEN THE MOST VICIOUS, BUT HE WAS CERTAINLY NOT THE BIGGEST. YOUR FATHER WAS SUCH A LYING BASTARD.

HE LIED TO EVERYONE IN HIS LIFE, INCLUDING YOU.

WHY WOULD YOU WANT TO AVENGE HIM?

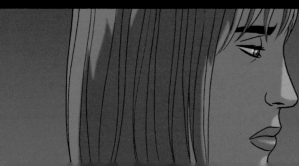

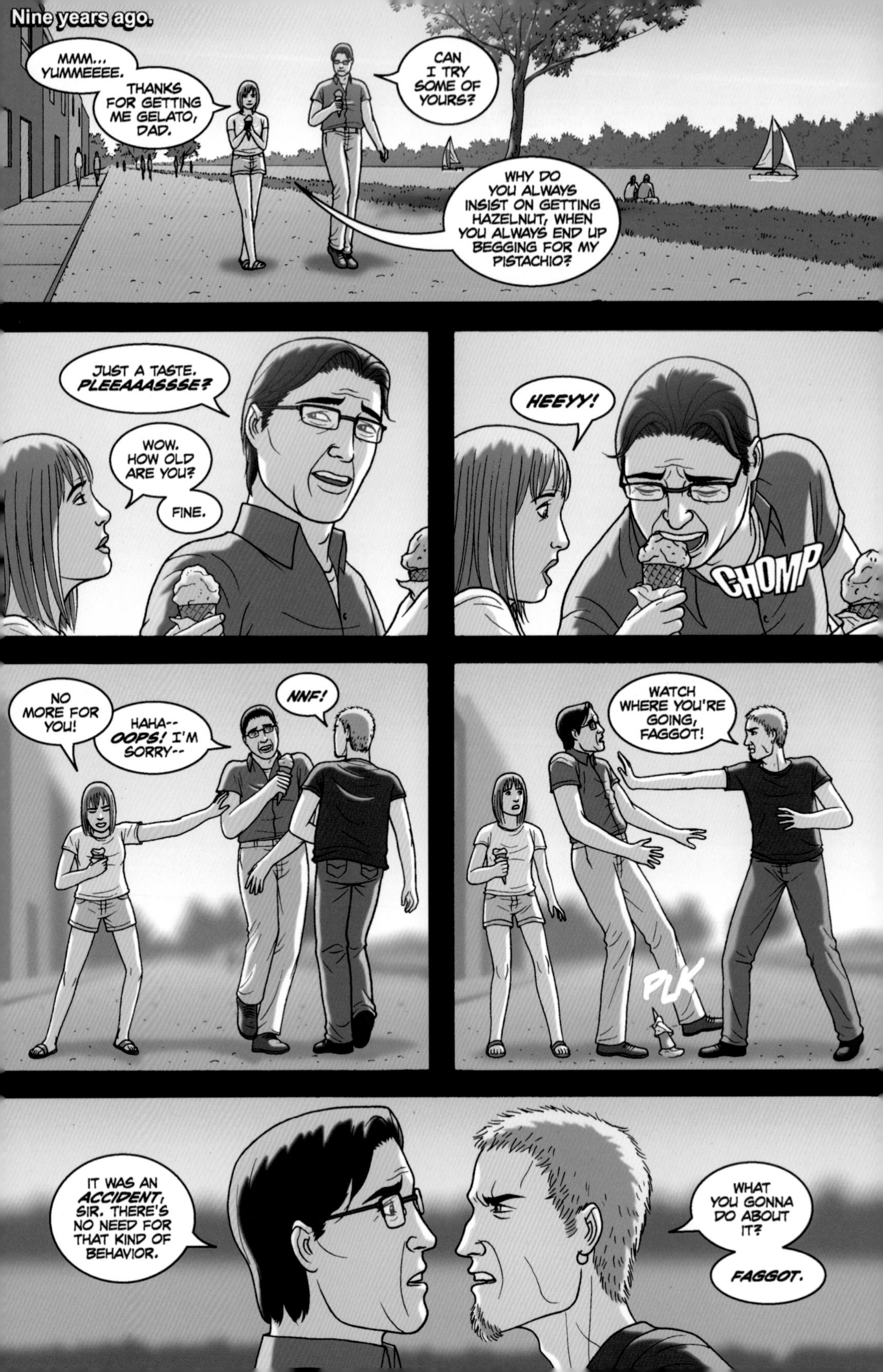
Nine years ago.
MMM... YUMMEEEE.
THANKS FOR GETTING ME GELATO, DAD.
CAN I TRY SOME OF YOURS?
WHY DO YOU ALWAYS INSIST ON GETTING HAZELNUT, WHEN YOU ALWAYS END UP BEGGING FOR MY PISTACHIO?
JUST A TASTE. PLEEAAASSSE?
WOW. HOW OLD ARE YOU?
FINE.
HEEYY!
CHOMP
NO MORE FOR YOU!
HAHA-- OOPS! I'M SORRY--
NNF!
WATCH WHERE YOU'RE GOING, FAGGOT!
PLK
IT WAS AN ACCIDENT, SIR. THERE'S NO NEED FOR THAT KIND OF BEHAVIOR.
WHAT YOU GONNA DO ABOUT IT?
FAGGOT.

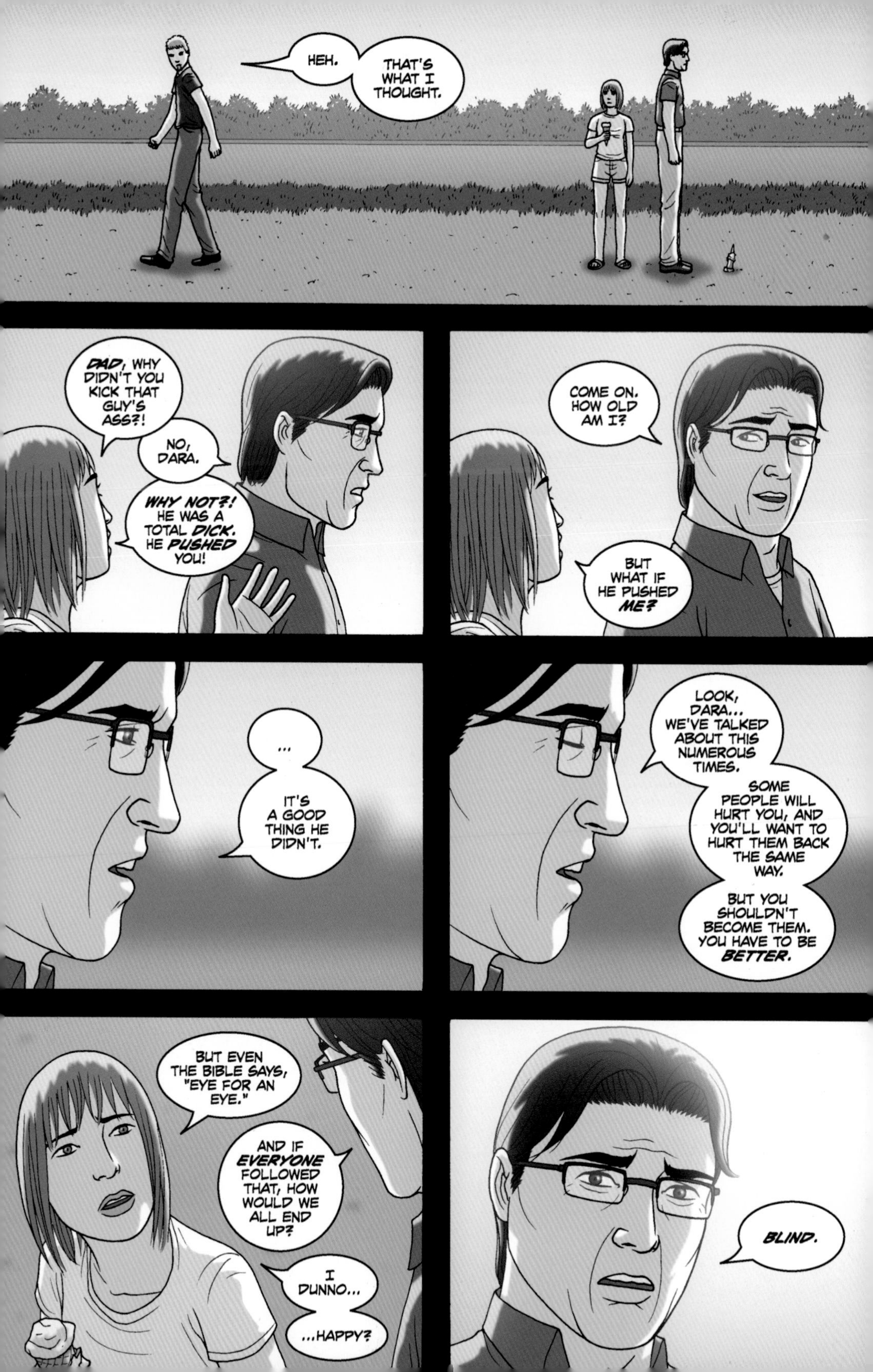
HEH.
THAT'S WHAT I THOUGHT.
DAD, WHY DIDN'T YOU KICK THAT GUY'S ASS?!
NO, DARA.
WHY NOT?! HE WAS A TOTAL DICK. HE PUSHED YOU!
COME ON. HOW OLD AM I?
BUT WHAT IF HE PUSHED ME?
...
IT'S A GOOD THING HE DIDN'T.
LOOK, DARA... WE'VE TALKED ABOUT THIS NUMEROUS TIMES.
SOME PEOPLE WILL HURT YOU, AND YOU'LL WANT TO HURT THEM BACK THE SAME WAY.
BUT YOU SHOULDN'T BECOME THEM. YOU HAVE TO BE BETTER.
BUT EVEN THE BIBLE SAYS, "EYE FOR AN EYE."
AND IF EVERYONE FOLLOWED THAT, HOW WOULD WE ALL END UP?
I DUNNO...
...HAPPY?
BLIND.

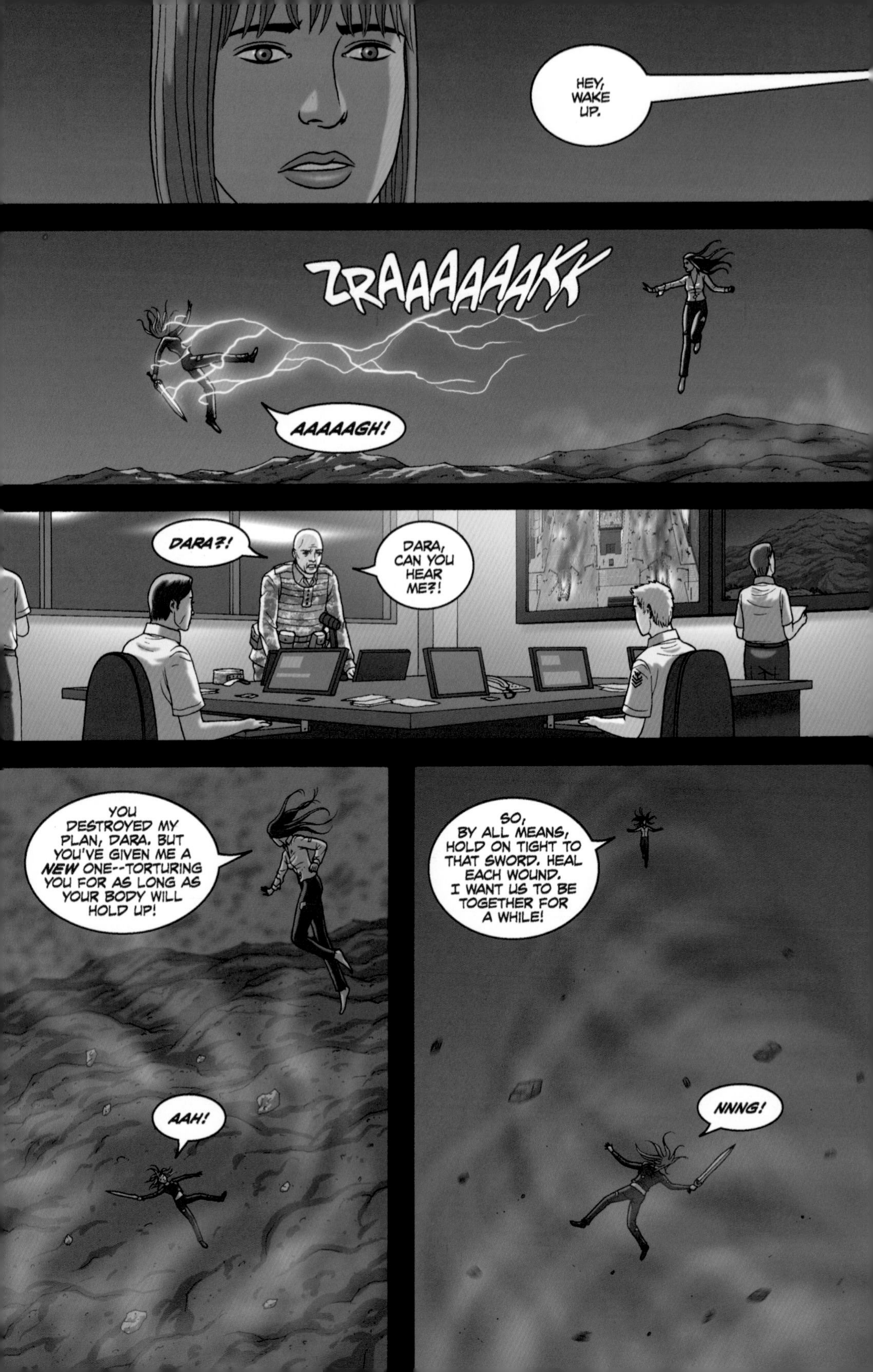
HEY, WAKE UP.
ZRAAAAAAAKK
AAAAAGH!
DARA?!
DARA, CAN YOU HEAR ME?!
YOU DESTROYED MY PLAN, DARA. BUT YOU'VE GIVEN ME A NEW ONE--TORTURING YOU FOR AS LONG AS YOUR BODY WILL HOLD UP!
AAH!
SO, BY ALL MEANS, HOLD ON TIGHT TO THAT SWORD. HEAL EACH WOUND. I WANT US TO BE TOGETHER FOR A WHILE!
NNNG!

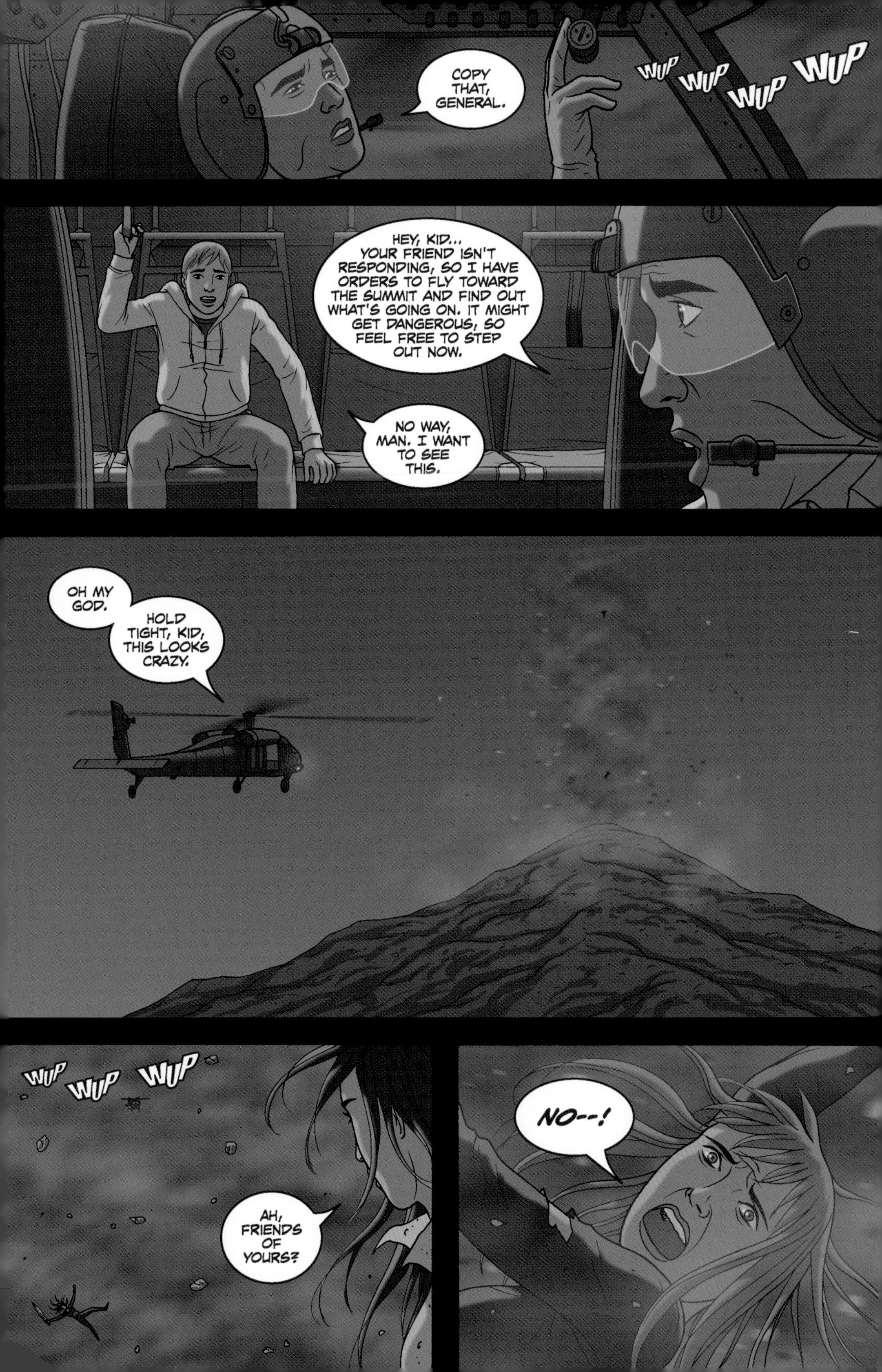
COPY THAT, GENERAL.
WUP WUP WUP WUP
HEY, KID... YOUR FRIEND ISN'T RESPONDING, SO I HAVE ORDERS TO FLY TOWARD THE SUMMIT AND FIND OUT WHAT'S GOING ON. IT MIGHT GET DANGEROUS, SO FEEL FREE TO STEP OUT NOW.
NO WAY, MAN. I WANT TO SEE THIS.
OH MY GOD.
HOLD TIGHT, KID, THIS LOOKS CRAZY.
WUP WUP WUP
AH, FRIENDS OF YOURS?
NO--!

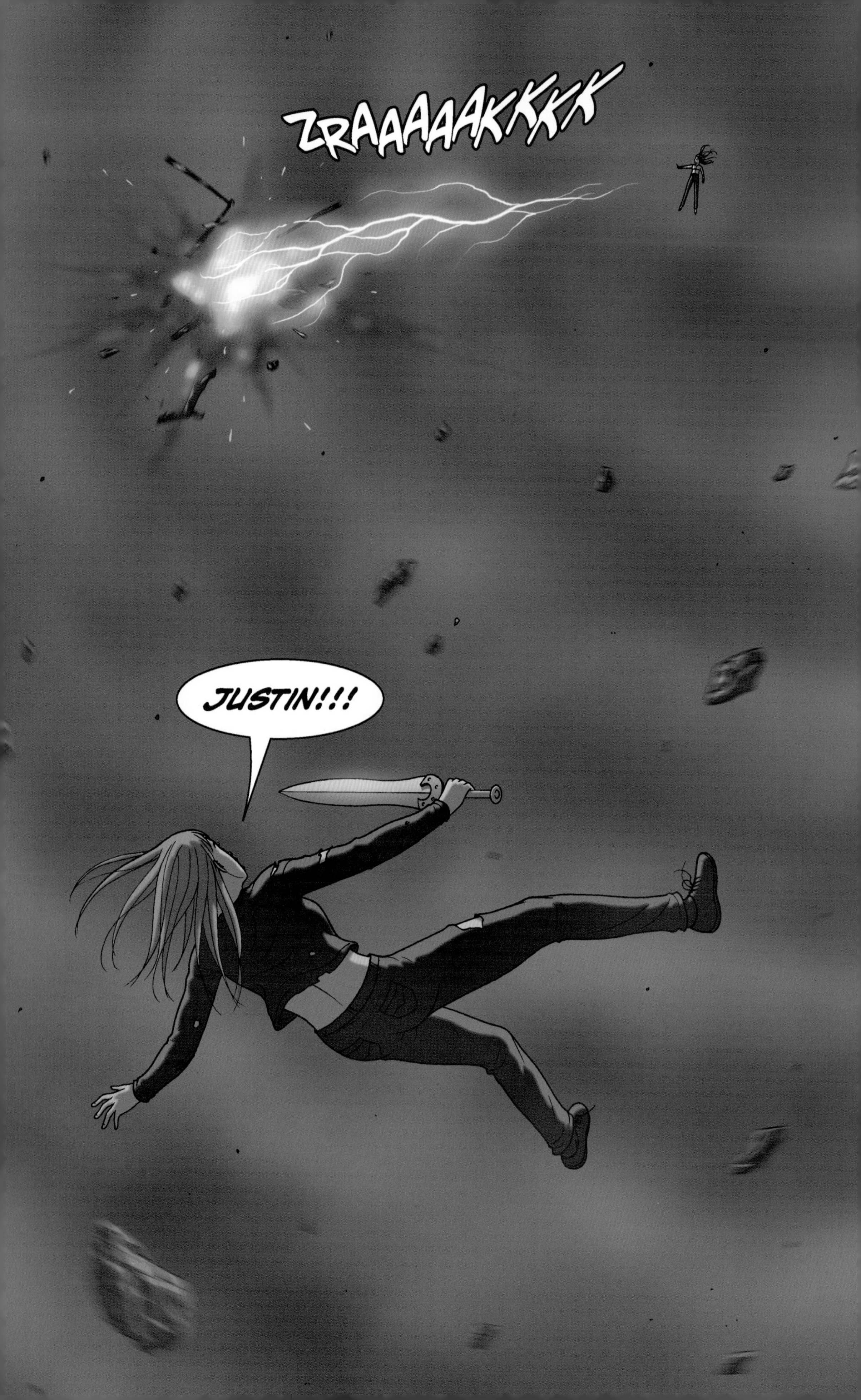
ZRAAAAAKKKK
JUSTIN!!!

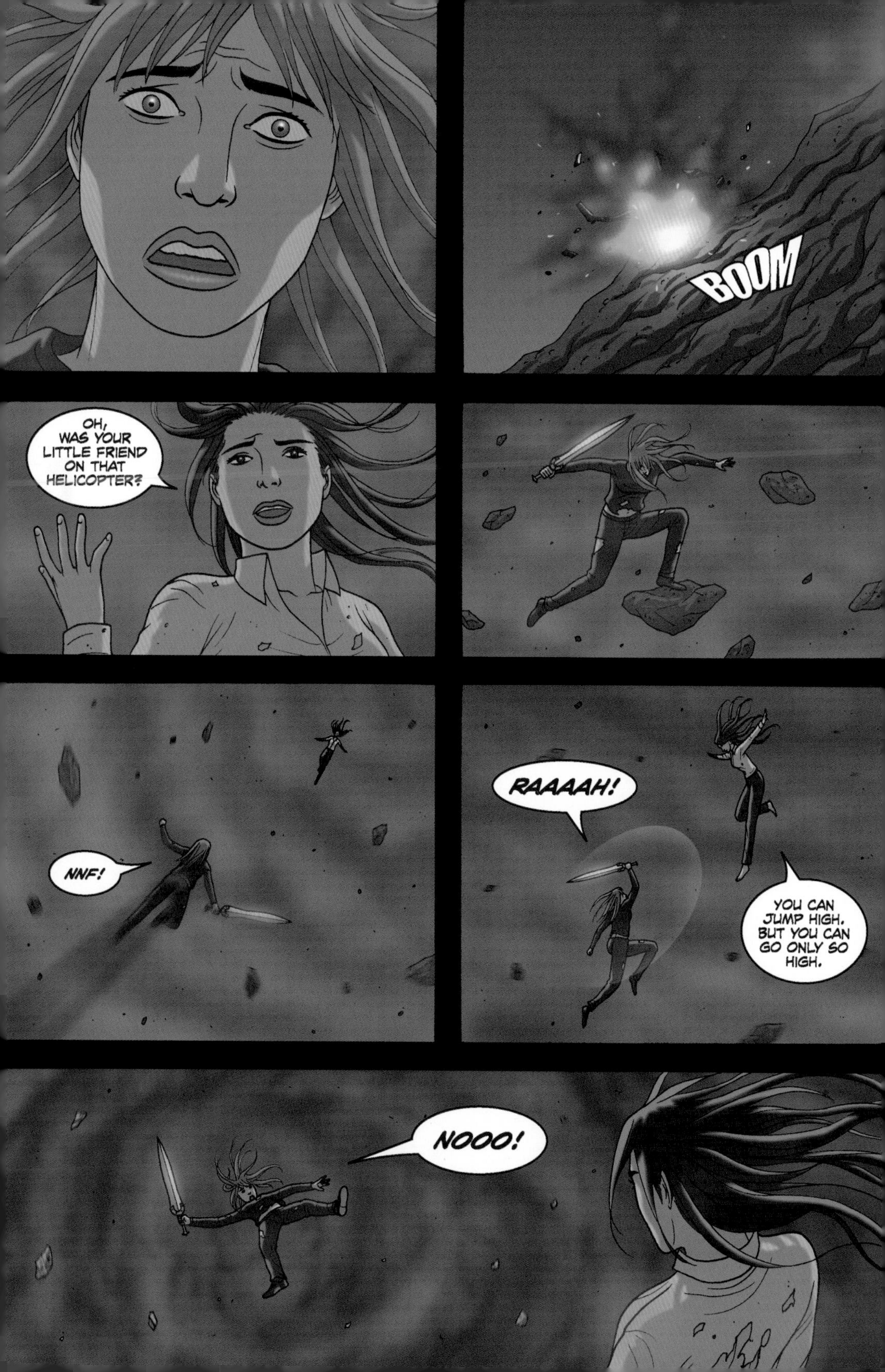
BOOM
OH, WAS YOUR LITTLE FRIEND ON THAT HELICOPTER?
NNF!
RAAAAH!
YOU CAN JUMP HIGH. BUT YOU CAN GO ONLY SO HIGH.
NOOO!

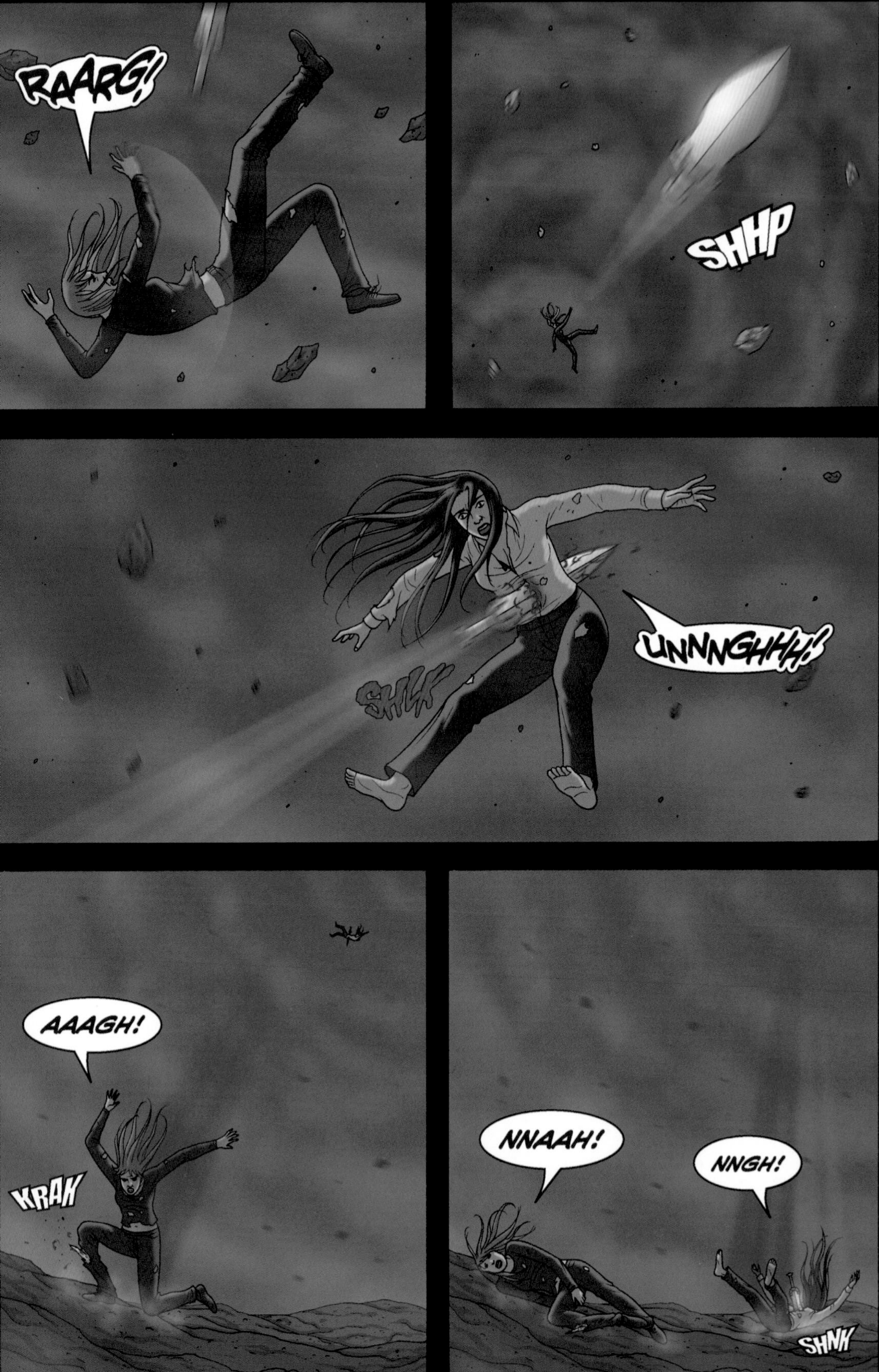
RAARG!
SHHP
UNNNGHHH!
SHLK
AAAGH!
KRAK
NNAAH!
NNGH!
SHNK

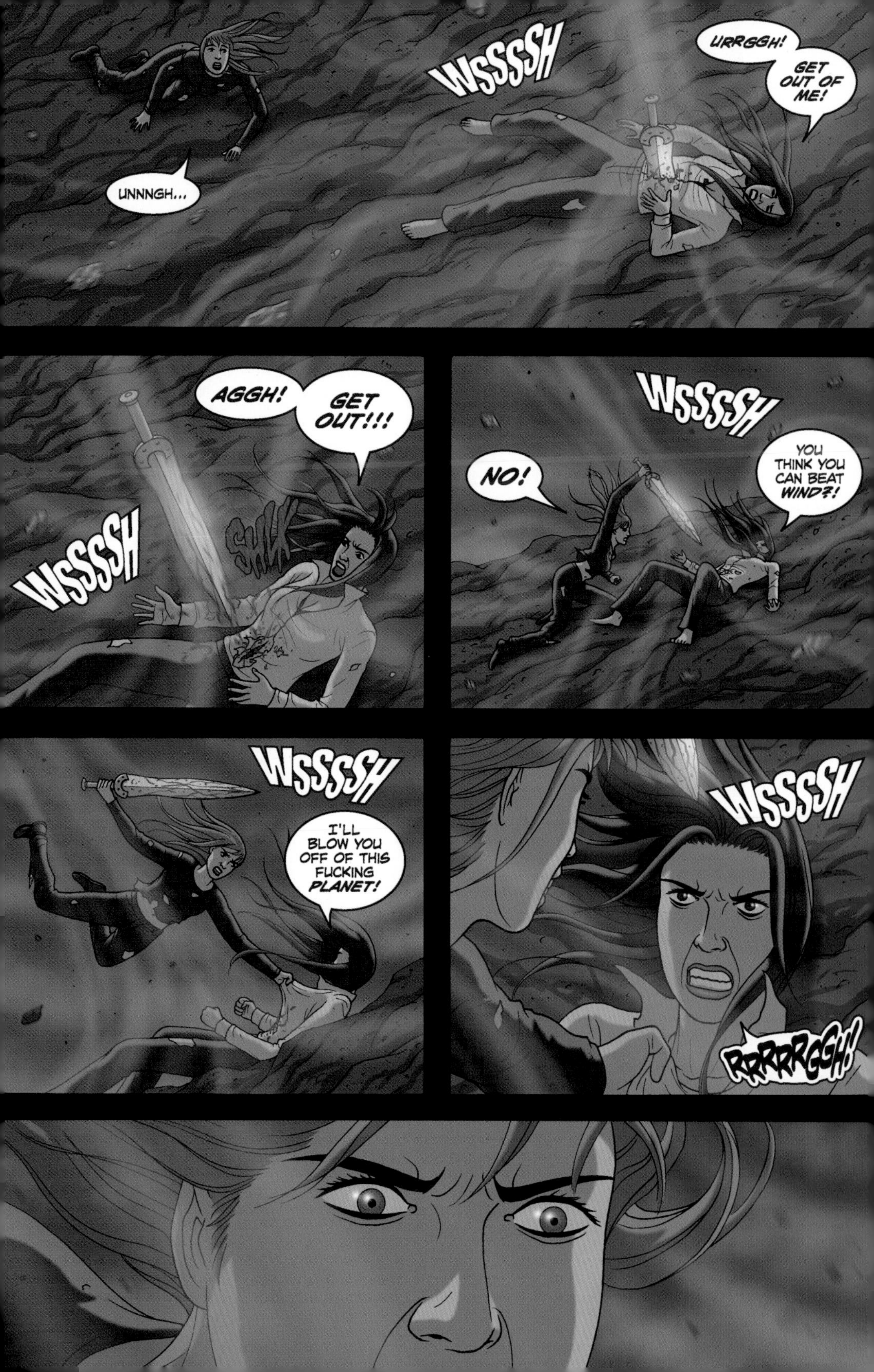

UNNNGH...
WSSSSH
URRGGH!
GET OUT OF ME!
AGGH!
GET OUT!!!
WSSSSH
SHK
WSSSSH
NO!
YOU THINK YOU CAN BEAT WIND?!
WSSSSH
I'LL BLOW YOU OFF OF THIS FUCKING PLANET!
WSSSSH
RRRRRGGH!

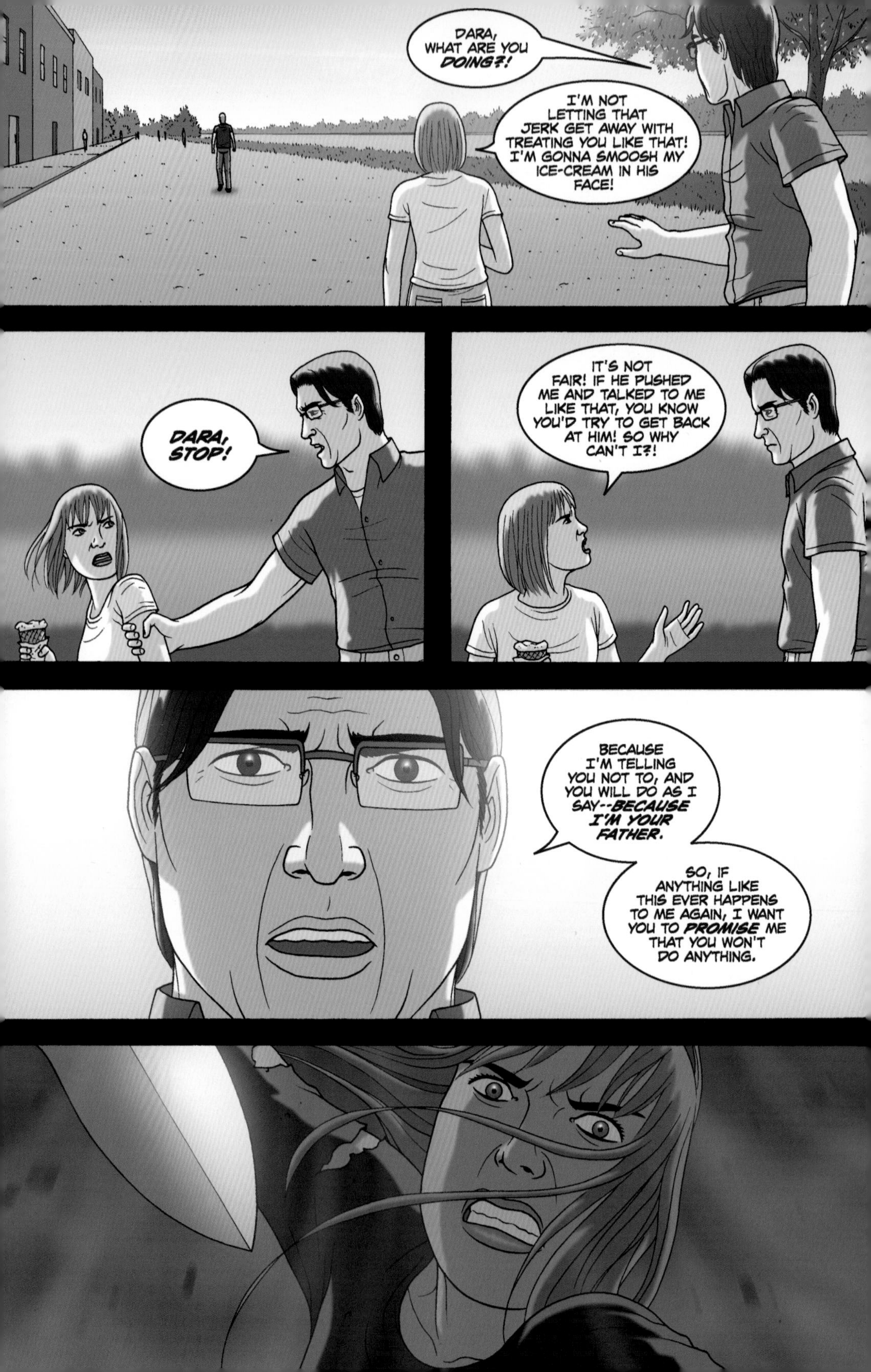
DARA, WHAT ARE YOU *DOING?!*
I'M NOT LETTING THAT JERK GET AWAY WITH TREATING YOU LIKE THAT! I'M GONNA SMOOSH MY ICE-CREAM IN HIS FACE!
DARA, STOP!
IT'S NOT FAIR! IF HE PUSHED ME AND TALKED TO ME LIKE THAT, YOU KNOW YOU'D TRY TO GET BACK AT HIM! SO WHY CAN'T I?!
BECAUSE I'M TELLING YOU NOT TO, AND YOU WILL DO AS I SAY--*BECAUSE I'M YOUR FATHER.*
SO, IF ANYTHING LIKE THIS EVER HAPPENS TO ME AGAIN, I WANT YOU TO *PROMISE* ME THAT YOU WON'T DO ANYTHING.

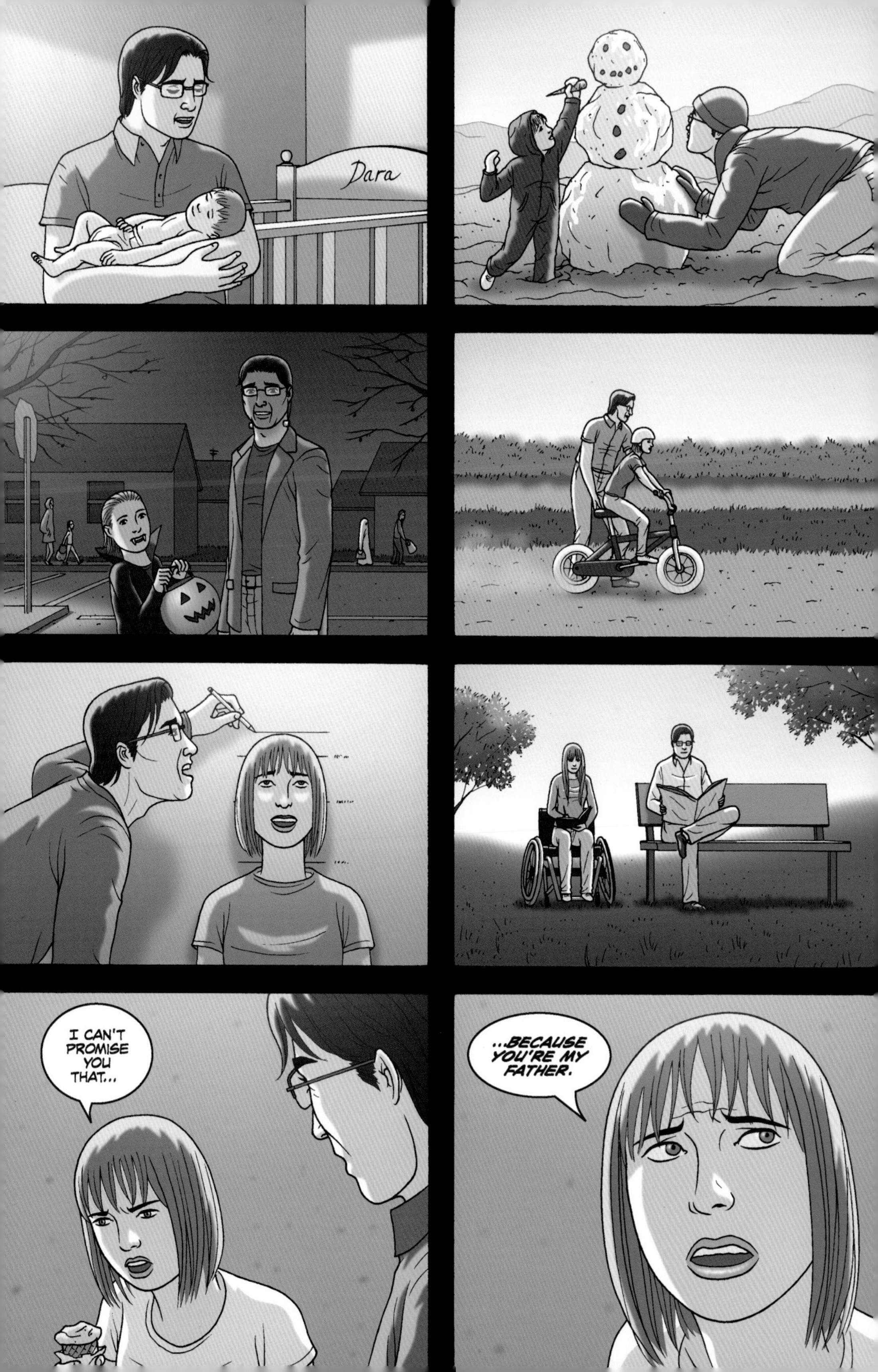
Dara
I CAN'T PROMISE YOU THAT...
...BECAUSE YOU'RE MY FATHER.

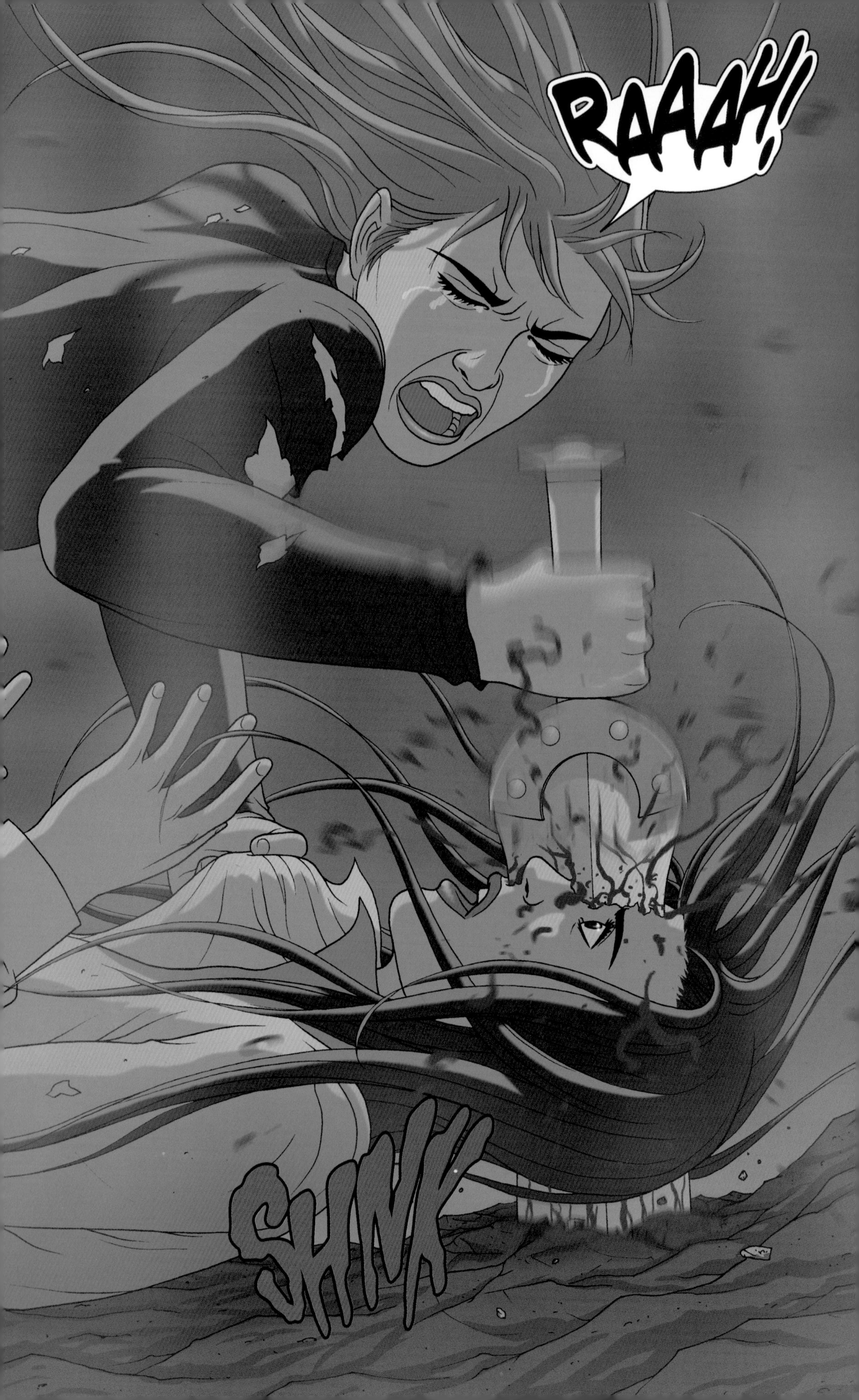
RAAAH!
SHINK

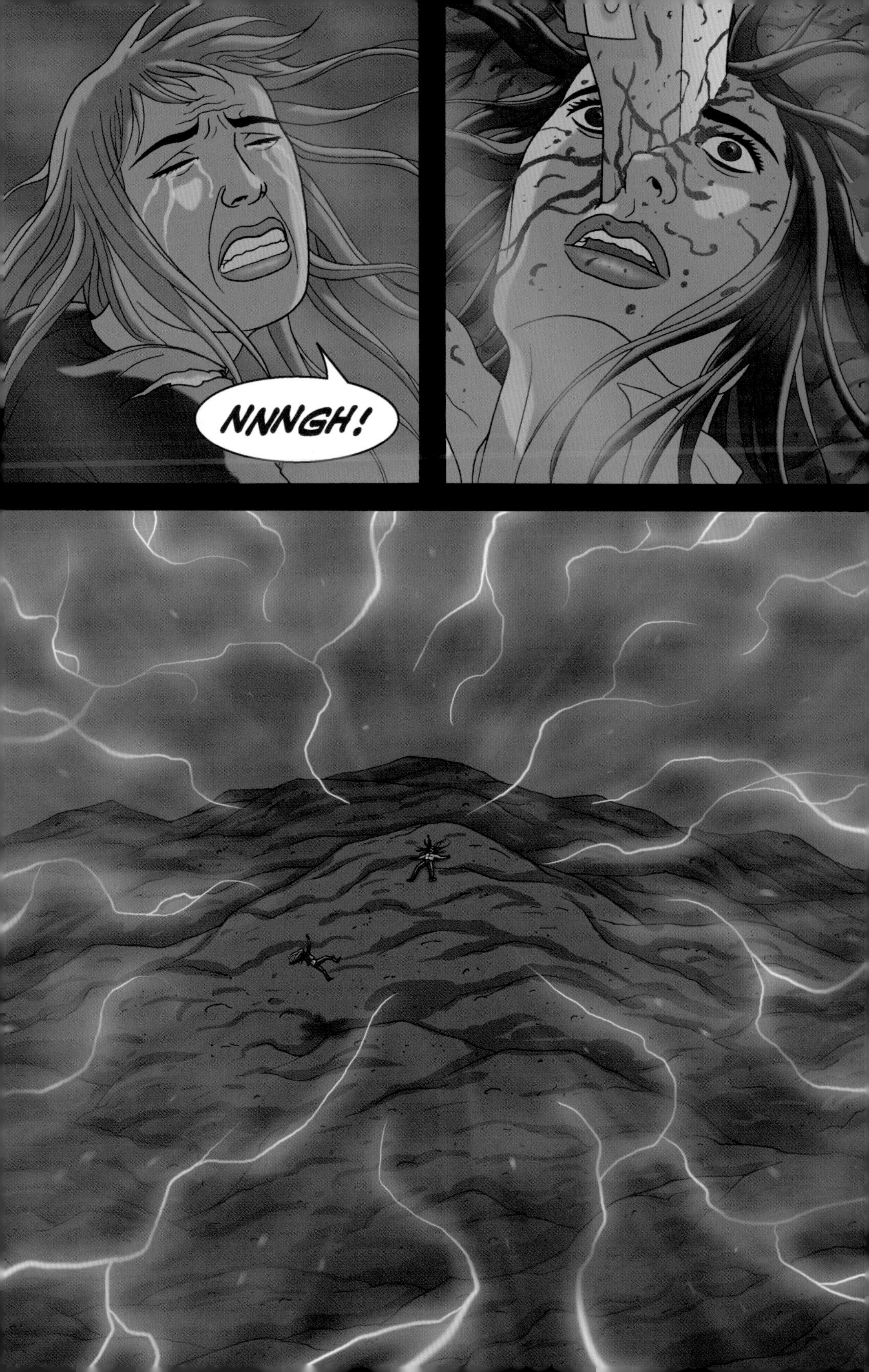
NNNGH!

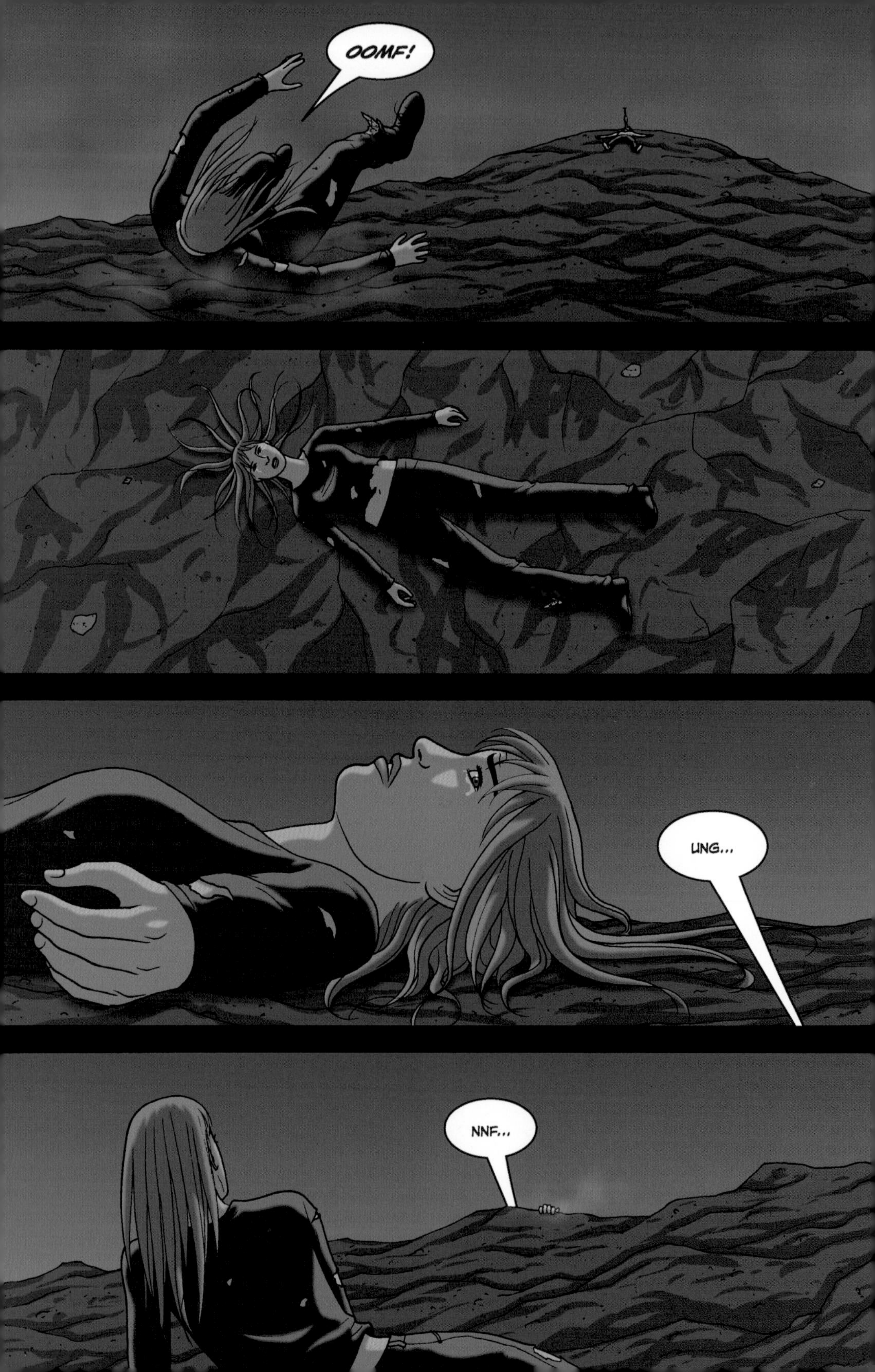
OOMF!
UNG...
NNF...

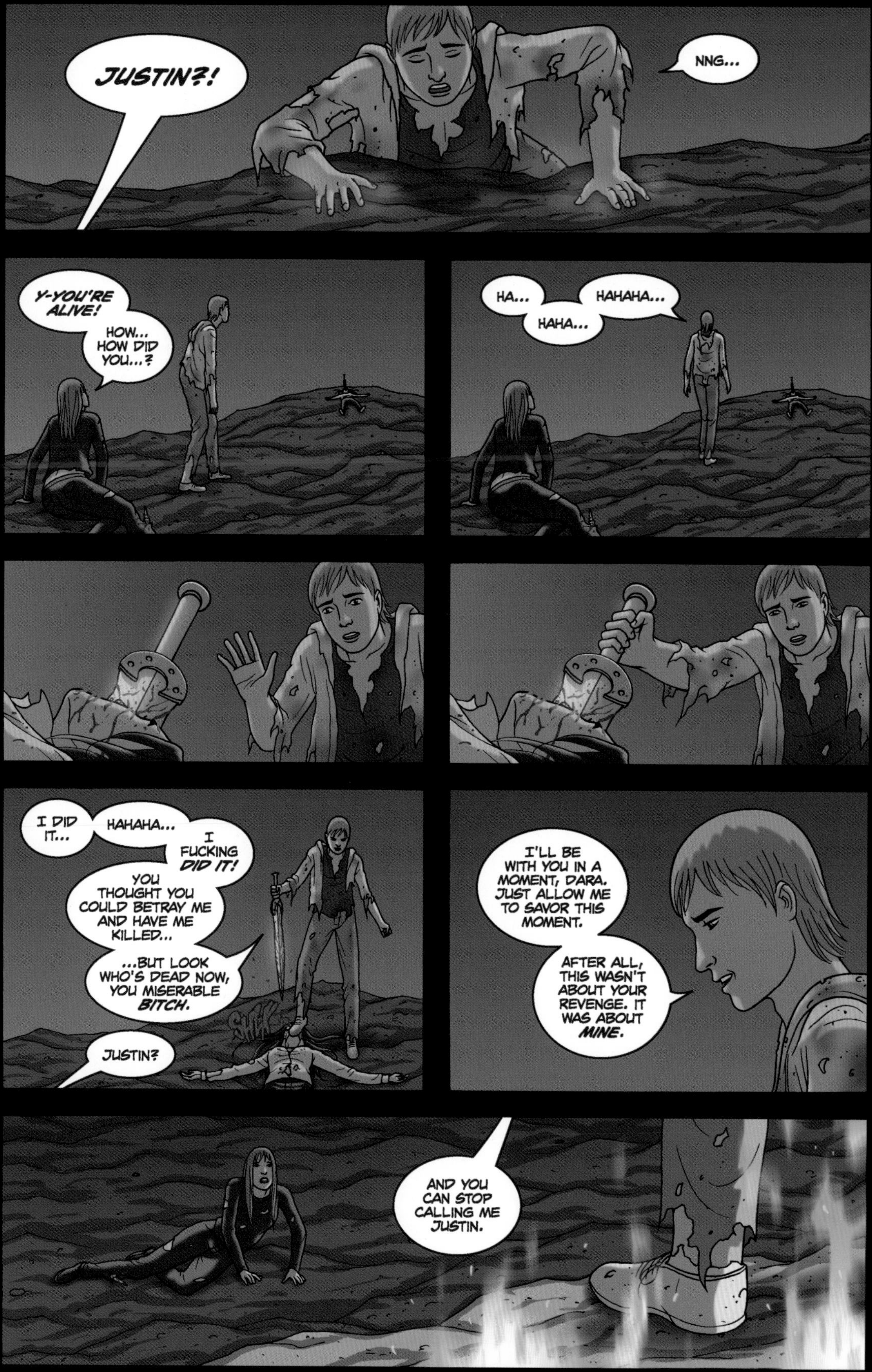
JUSTIN?!
NNG...
Y-YOU'RE ALIVE!
HOW... HOW DID YOU...?
HA...
HAHA...
HAHAHA...
I DID IT...
HAHAHA...
I FUCKING DID IT!
YOU THOUGHT YOU COULD BETRAY ME AND HAVE ME KILLED...
...BUT LOOK WHO'S DEAD NOW, YOU MISERABLE BITCH.
JUSTIN?
I'LL BE WITH YOU IN A MOMENT, DARA. JUST ALLOW ME TO SAVOR THIS MOMENT.
AFTER ALL, THIS WASN'T ABOUT YOUR REVENGE. IT WAS ABOUT MINE.
AND YOU CAN STOP CALLING ME JUSTIN.

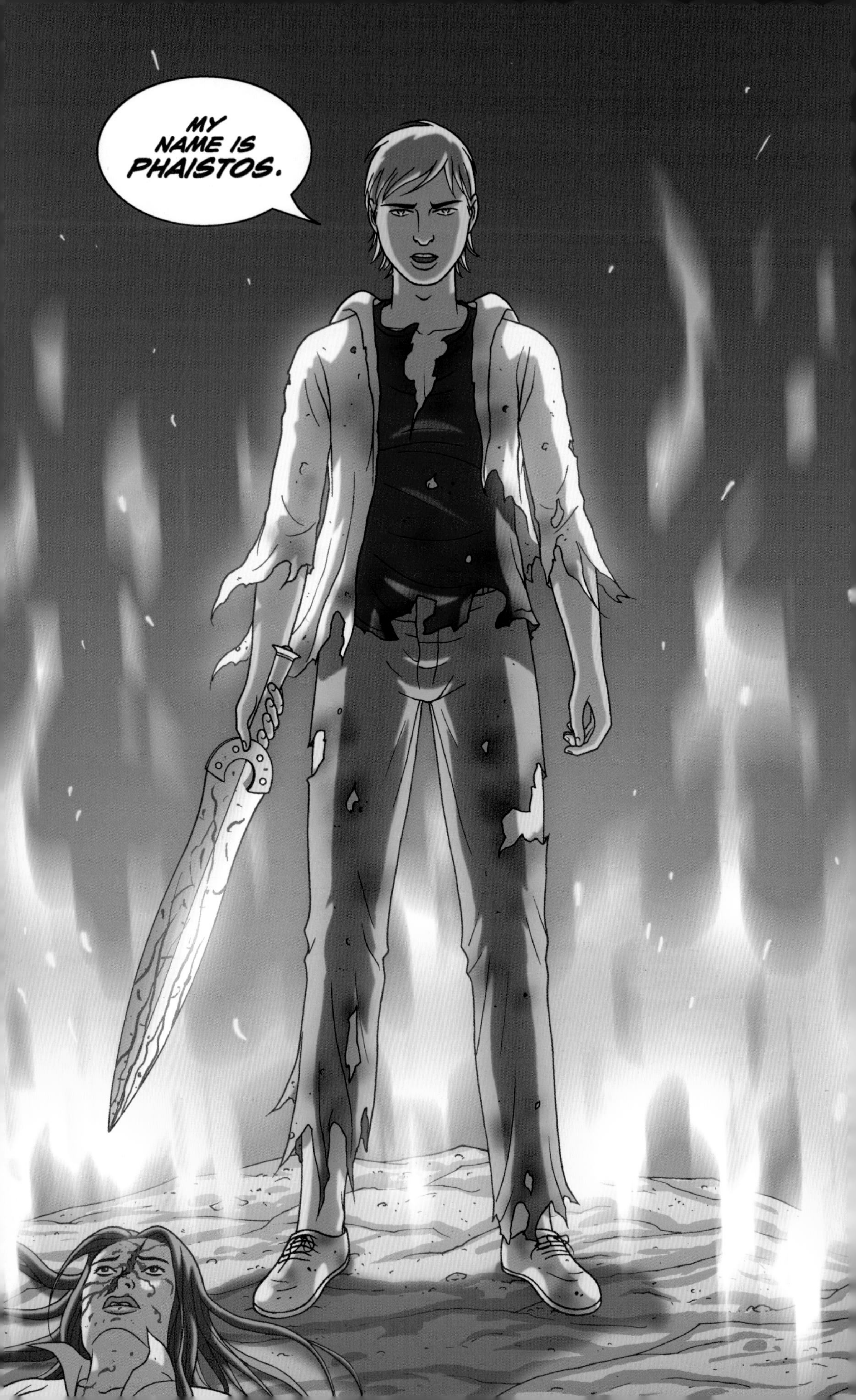
MY NAME IS PHAISTOS.

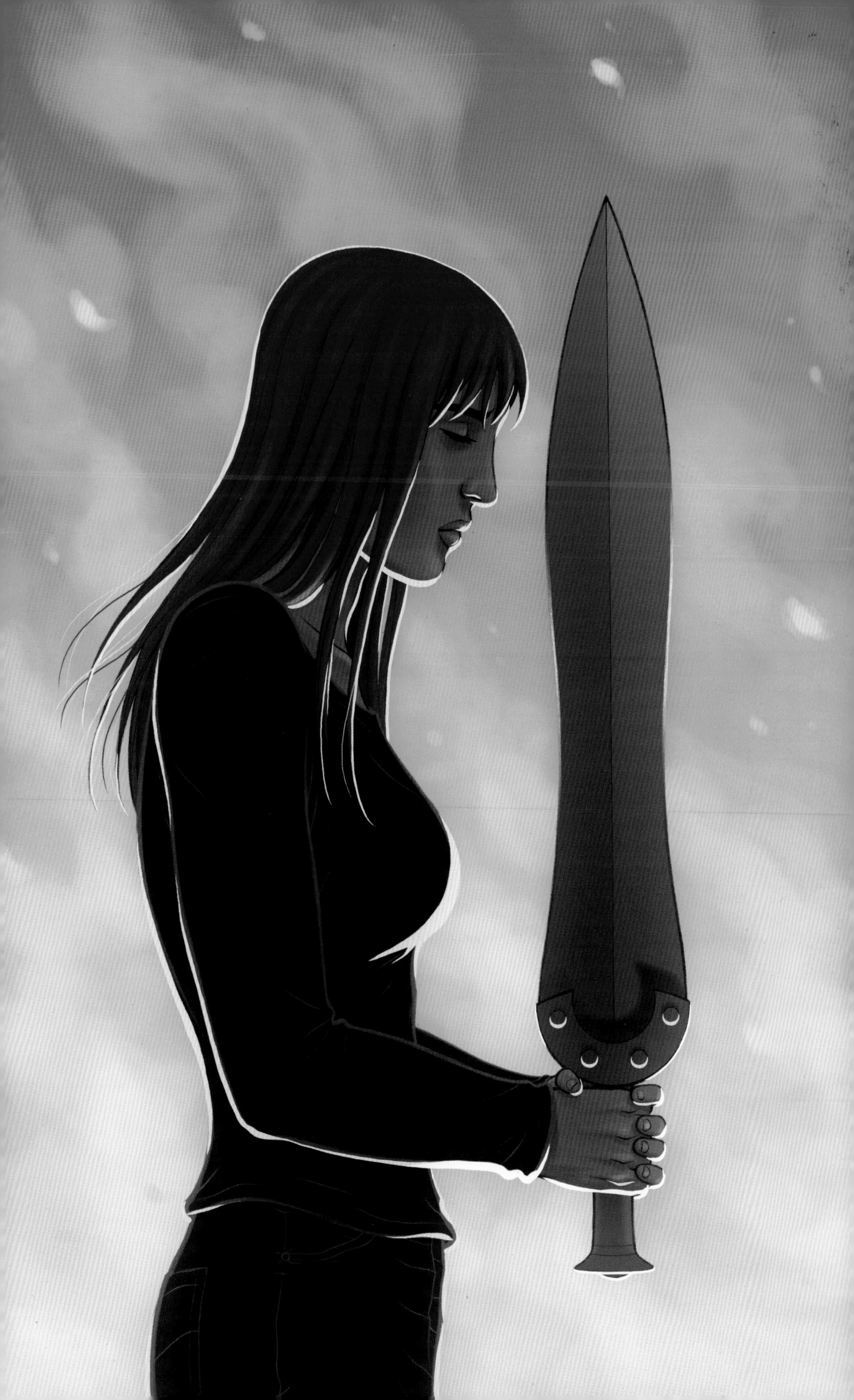

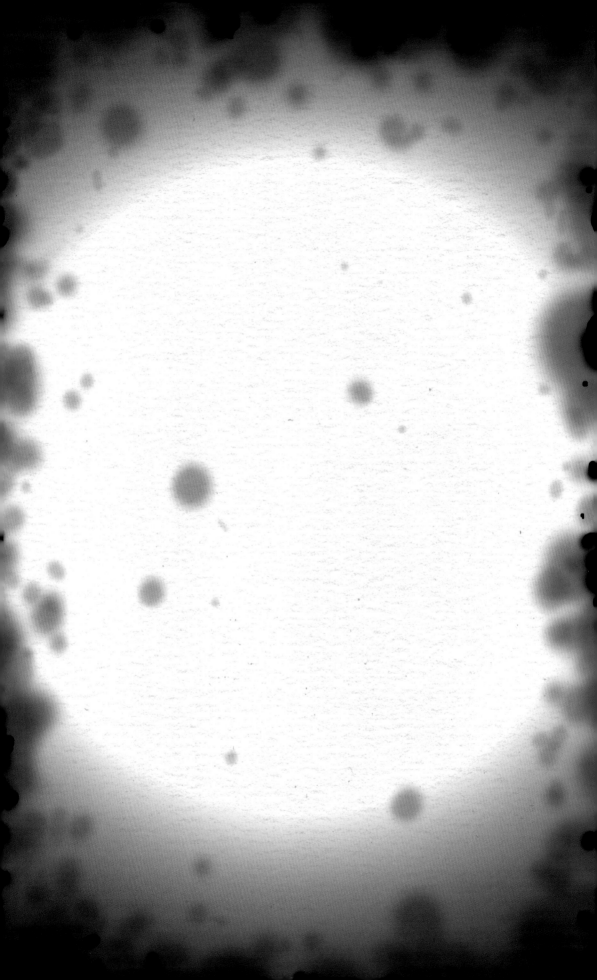

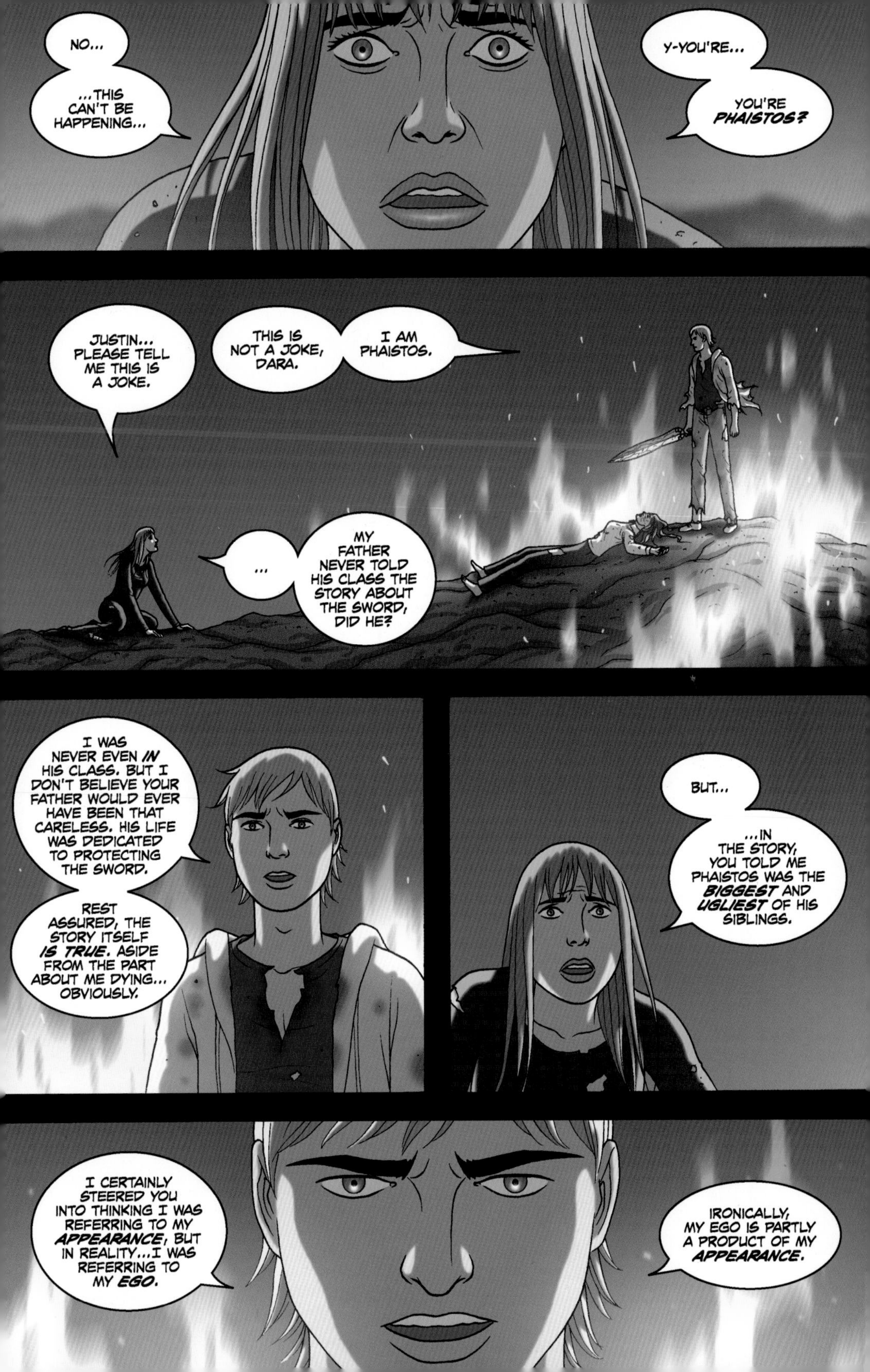
NO...
...THIS CAN'T BE HAPPENING...
Y-YOU'RE...
YOU'RE PHAISTOS?
JUSTIN... PLEASE TELL ME THIS IS A JOKE.
THIS IS NOT A JOKE, DARA.
I AM PHAISTOS.
...
MY FATHER NEVER TOLD HIS CLASS THE STORY ABOUT THE SWORD, DID HE?
I WAS NEVER EVEN IN HIS CLASS. BUT I DON'T BELIEVE YOUR FATHER WOULD EVER HAVE BEEN THAT CARELESS. HIS LIFE WAS DEDICATED TO PROTECTING THE SWORD.
REST ASSURED, THE STORY ITSELF IS TRUE. ASIDE FROM THE PART ABOUT ME DYING... OBVIOUSLY.
BUT...
...IN THE STORY, YOU TOLD ME PHAISTOS WAS THE BIGGEST AND UGLIEST OF HIS SIBLINGS.
I CERTAINLY STEERED YOU INTO THINKING I WAS REFERRING TO MY APPEARANCE, BUT IN REALITY...I WAS REFERRING TO MY EGO.
IRONICALLY, MY EGO IS PARTLY A PRODUCT OF MY APPEARANCE.

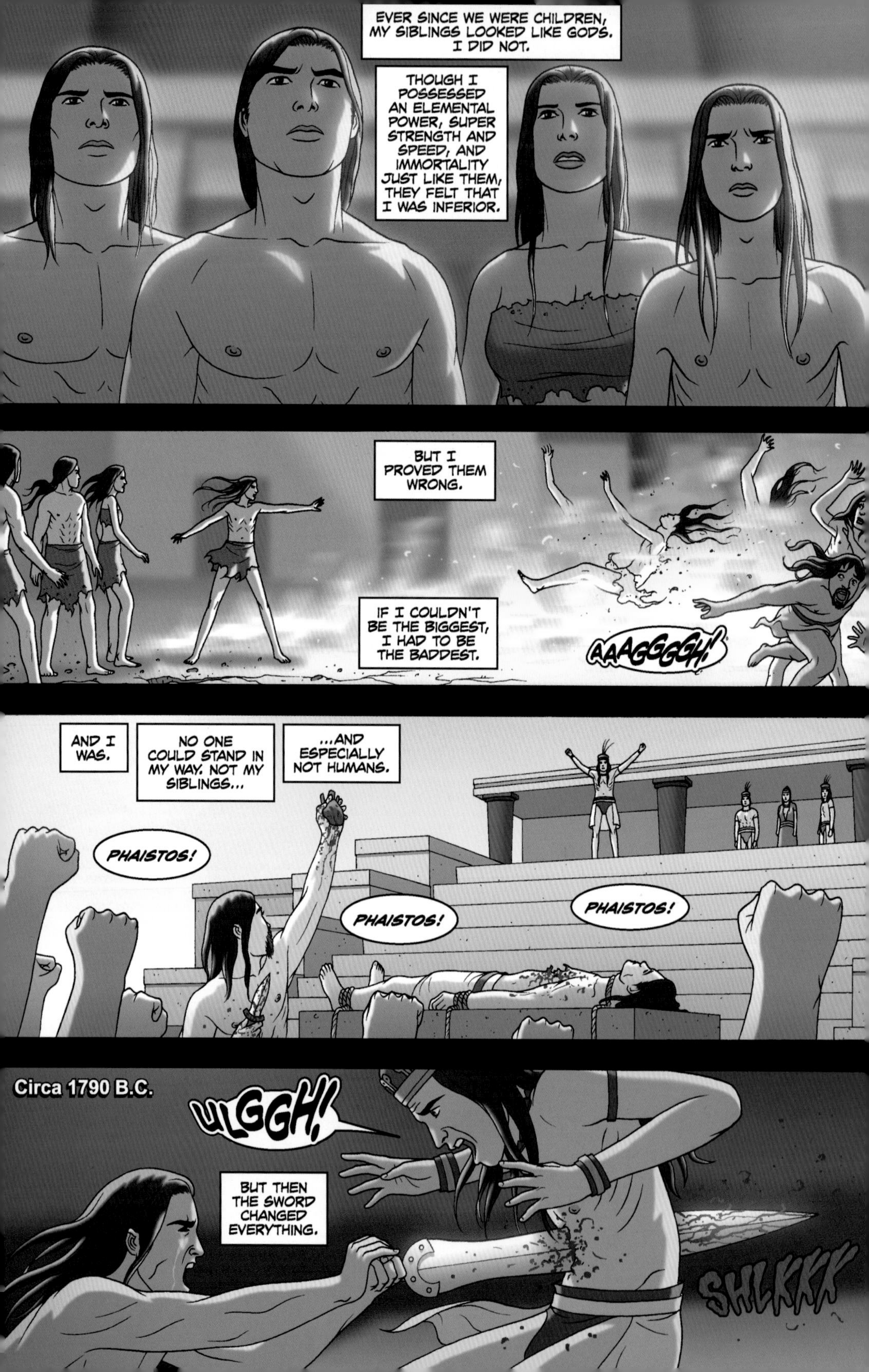
EVER SINCE WE WERE CHILDREN, MY SIBLINGS LOOKED LIKE GODS. I DID NOT.
THOUGH I POSSESSED AN ELEMENTAL POWER, SUPER STRENGTH AND SPEED, AND IMMORTALITY JUST LIKE THEM, THEY FELT THAT I WAS INFERIOR.
BUT I PROVED THEM WRONG.
IF I COULDN'T BE THE BIGGEST, I HAD TO BE THE BADDEST.
AAAGGGGH!
AND I WAS.
NO ONE COULD STAND IN MY WAY. NOT MY SIBLINGS...
...AND ESPECIALLY NOT HUMANS.
PHAISTOS!
PHAISTOS!
PHAISTOS!
Circa 1790 B.C.
ULGGH!
BUT THEN THE SWORD CHANGED EVERYTHING.
SHLKKK

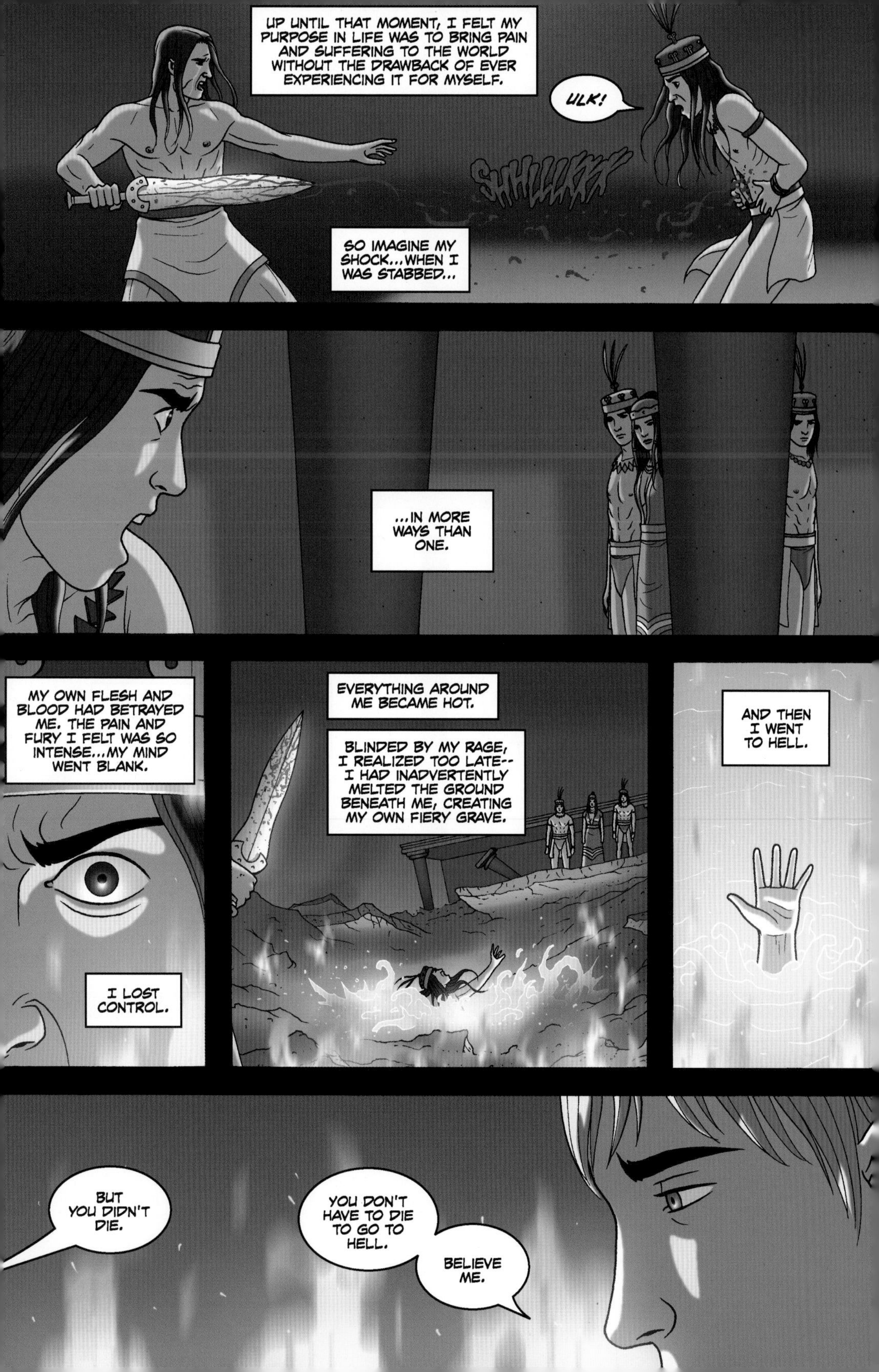
UP UNTIL THAT MOMENT, I FELT MY PURPOSE IN LIFE WAS TO BRING PAIN AND SUFFERING TO THE WORLD WITHOUT THE DRAWBACK OF EVER EXPERIENCING IT FOR MYSELF.
ULK!
SHHLLLKKK
SO IMAGINE MY SHOCK...WHEN I WAS STABBED...
...IN MORE WAYS THAN ONE.
MY OWN FLESH AND BLOOD HAD BETRAYED ME. THE PAIN AND FURY I FELT WAS SO INTENSE...MY MIND WENT BLANK.
I LOST CONTROL.
EVERYTHING AROUND ME BECAME HOT.
BLINDED BY MY RAGE, I REALIZED TOO LATE-- I HAD INADVERTENTLY MELTED THE GROUND BENEATH ME, CREATING MY OWN FIERY GRAVE.
AND THEN I WENT TO HELL.
BUT YOU DIDN'T DIE.
YOU DON'T HAVE TO DIE TO GO TO HELL.
BELIEVE ME.

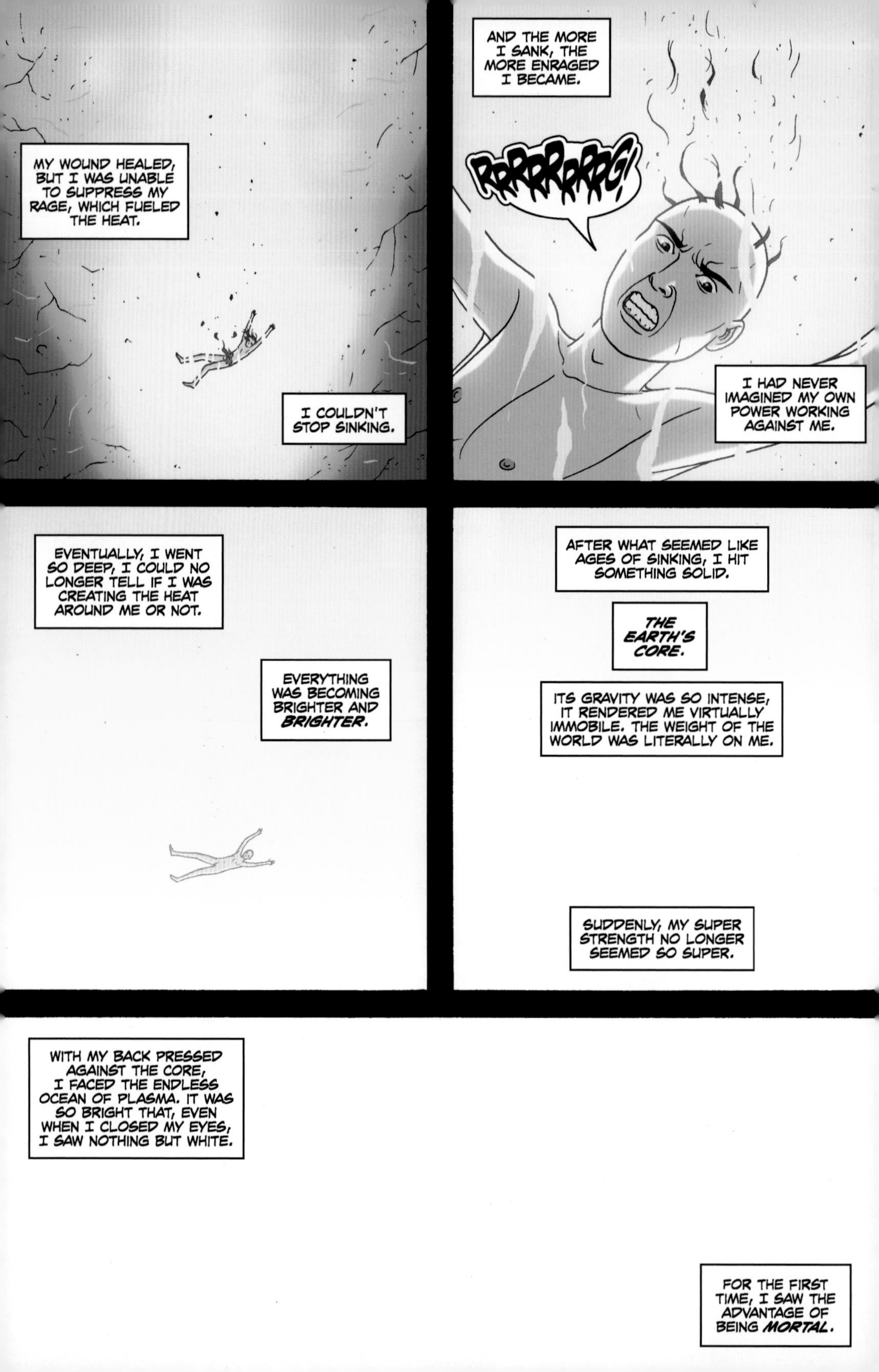
MY WOUND HEALED, BUT I WAS UNABLE TO SUPPRESS MY RAGE, WHICH FUELED THE HEAT.
I COULDN'T STOP SINKING.
AND THE MORE I SANK, THE MORE ENRAGED I BECAME.
RRRRRRRRG!
I HAD NEVER IMAGINED MY OWN POWER WORKING AGAINST ME.
EVENTUALLY, I WENT SO DEEP, I COULD NO LONGER TELL IF I WAS CREATING THE HEAT AROUND ME OR NOT.
EVERYTHING WAS BECOMING BRIGHTER AND BRIGHTER.
AFTER WHAT SEEMED LIKE AGES OF SINKING, I HIT SOMETHING SOLID.
THE EARTH'S CORE.
ITS GRAVITY WAS SO INTENSE, IT RENDERED ME VIRTUALLY IMMOBILE. THE WEIGHT OF THE WORLD WAS LITERALLY ON ME.
SUDDENLY, MY SUPER STRENGTH NO LONGER SEEMED SO SUPER.
WITH MY BACK PRESSED AGAINST THE CORE, I FACED THE ENDLESS OCEAN OF PLASMA. IT WAS SO BRIGHT THAT, EVEN WHEN I CLOSED MY EYES, I SAW NOTHING BUT WHITE.
FOR THE FIRST TIME, I SAW THE ADVANTAGE OF BEING MORTAL.

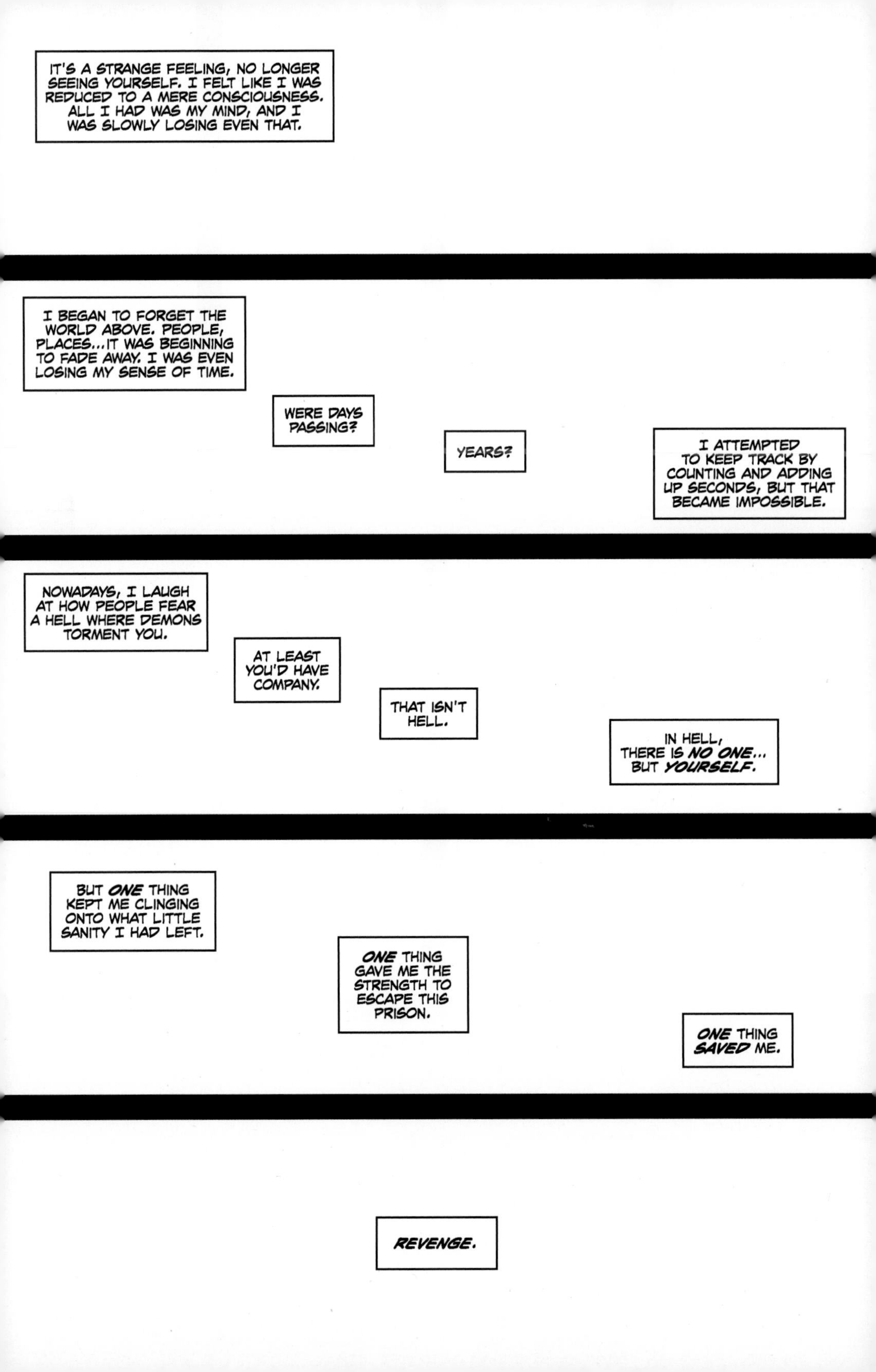
IT'S A STRANGE FEELING, NO LONGER SEEING YOURSELF. I FELT LIKE I WAS REDUCED TO A MERE CONSCIOUSNESS. ALL I HAD WAS MY MIND, AND I WAS SLOWLY LOSING EVEN THAT.
I BEGAN TO FORGET THE WORLD ABOVE. PEOPLE, PLACES...IT WAS BEGINNING TO FADE AWAY. I WAS EVEN LOSING MY SENSE OF TIME.
WERE DAYS PASSING?
YEARS?
I ATTEMPTED TO KEEP TRACK BY COUNTING AND ADDING UP SECONDS, BUT THAT BECAME IMPOSSIBLE.
NOWADAYS, I LAUGH AT HOW PEOPLE FEAR A HELL WHERE DEMONS TORMENT YOU.
AT LEAST YOU'D HAVE COMPANY.
THAT ISN'T HELL.
IN HELL, THERE IS *NO ONE*... BUT *YOURSELF*.
BUT *ONE* THING KEPT ME CLINGING ONTO WHAT LITTLE SANITY I HAD LEFT.
ONE THING GAVE ME THE STRENGTH TO ESCAPE THIS PRISON.
ONE THING *SAVED* ME.
REVENGE.

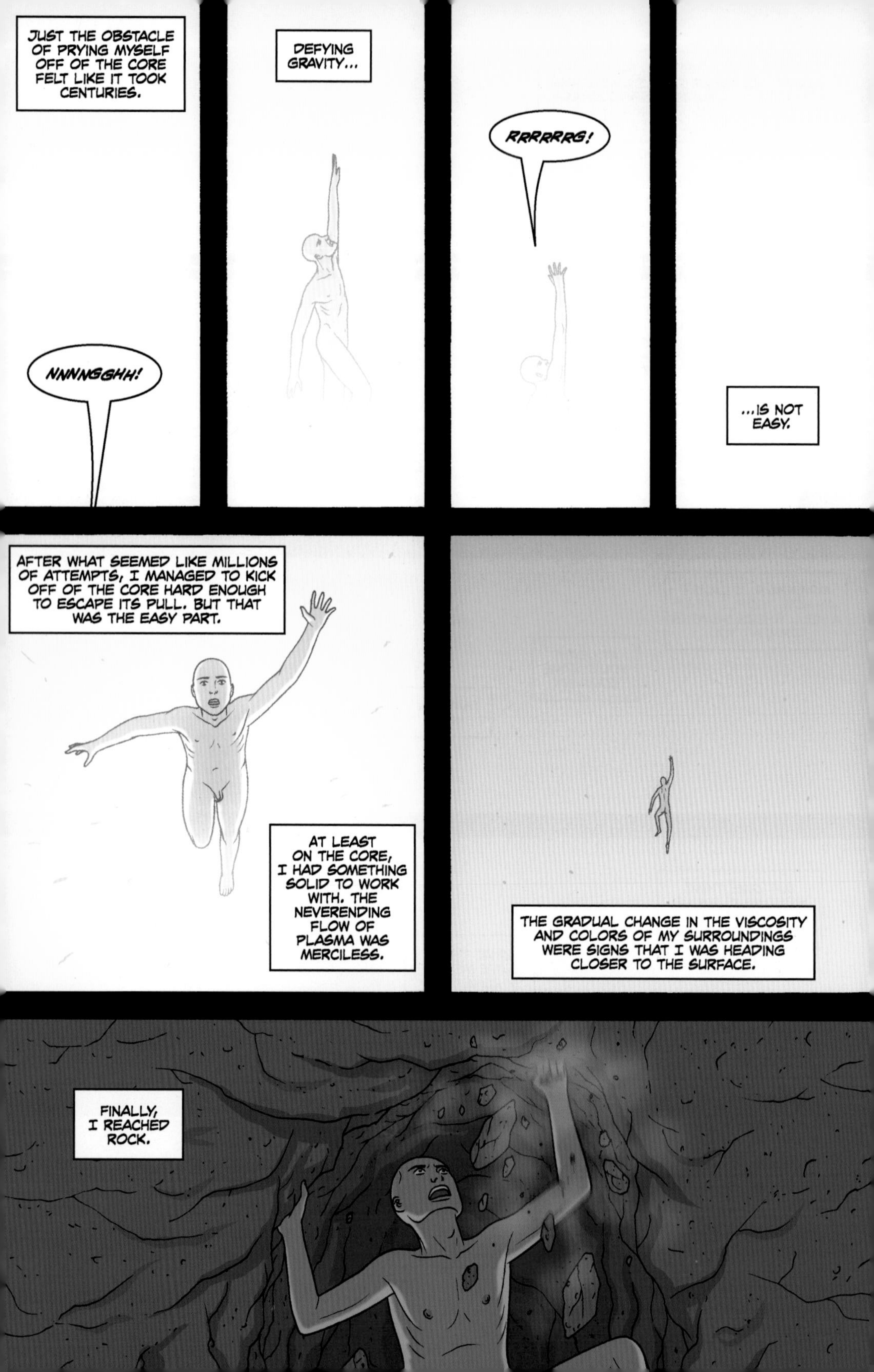
JUST THE OBSTACLE OF PRYING MYSELF OFF OF THE CORE FELT LIKE IT TOOK CENTURIES.
NNNNGGHH!
DEFYING GRAVITY...
RRRRRRG!
...IS NOT EASY.
AFTER WHAT SEEMED LIKE MILLIONS OF ATTEMPTS, I MANAGED TO KICK OFF OF THE CORE HARD ENOUGH TO ESCAPE ITS PULL. BUT THAT WAS THE EASY PART.
AT LEAST ON THE CORE, I HAD SOMETHING SOLID TO WORK WITH. THE NEVERENDING FLOW OF PLASMA WAS MERCILESS.
THE GRADUAL CHANGE IN THE VISCOSITY AND COLORS OF MY SURROUNDINGS WERE SIGNS THAT I WAS HEADING CLOSER TO THE SURFACE.
FINALLY, I REACHED ROCK.

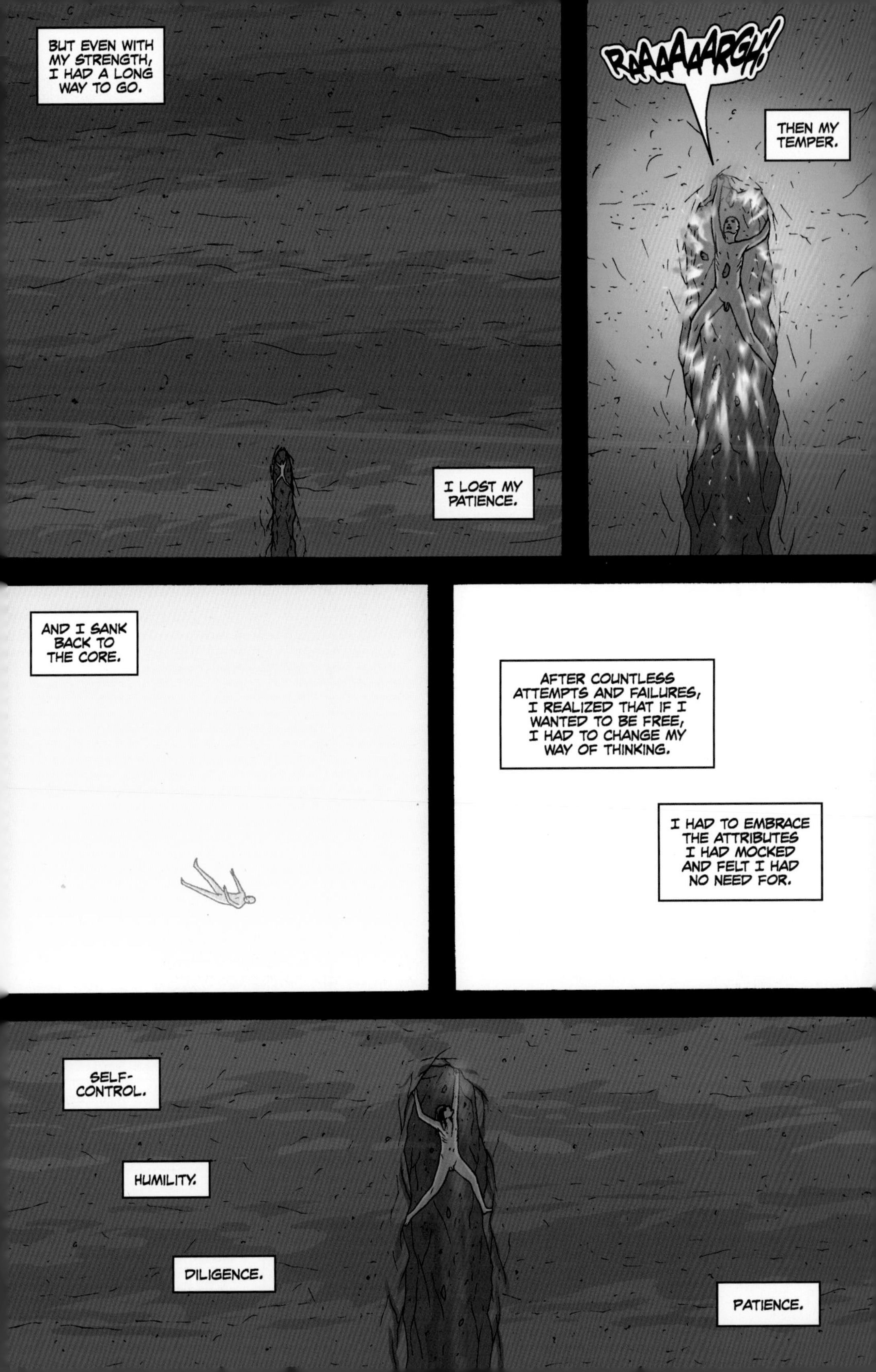
BUT EVEN WITH MY STRENGTH, I HAD A LONG WAY TO GO.
I LOST MY PATIENCE.
RAAAAAARGH!
THEN MY TEMPER.
AND I SANK BACK TO THE CORE.
AFTER COUNTLESS ATTEMPTS AND FAILURES, I REALIZED THAT IF I WANTED TO BE FREE, I HAD TO CHANGE MY WAY OF THINKING.
I HAD TO EMBRACE THE ATTRIBUTES I HAD MOCKED AND FELT I HAD NO NEED FOR.
SELF-CONTROL.
HUMILITY.
DILIGENCE.
PATIENCE.

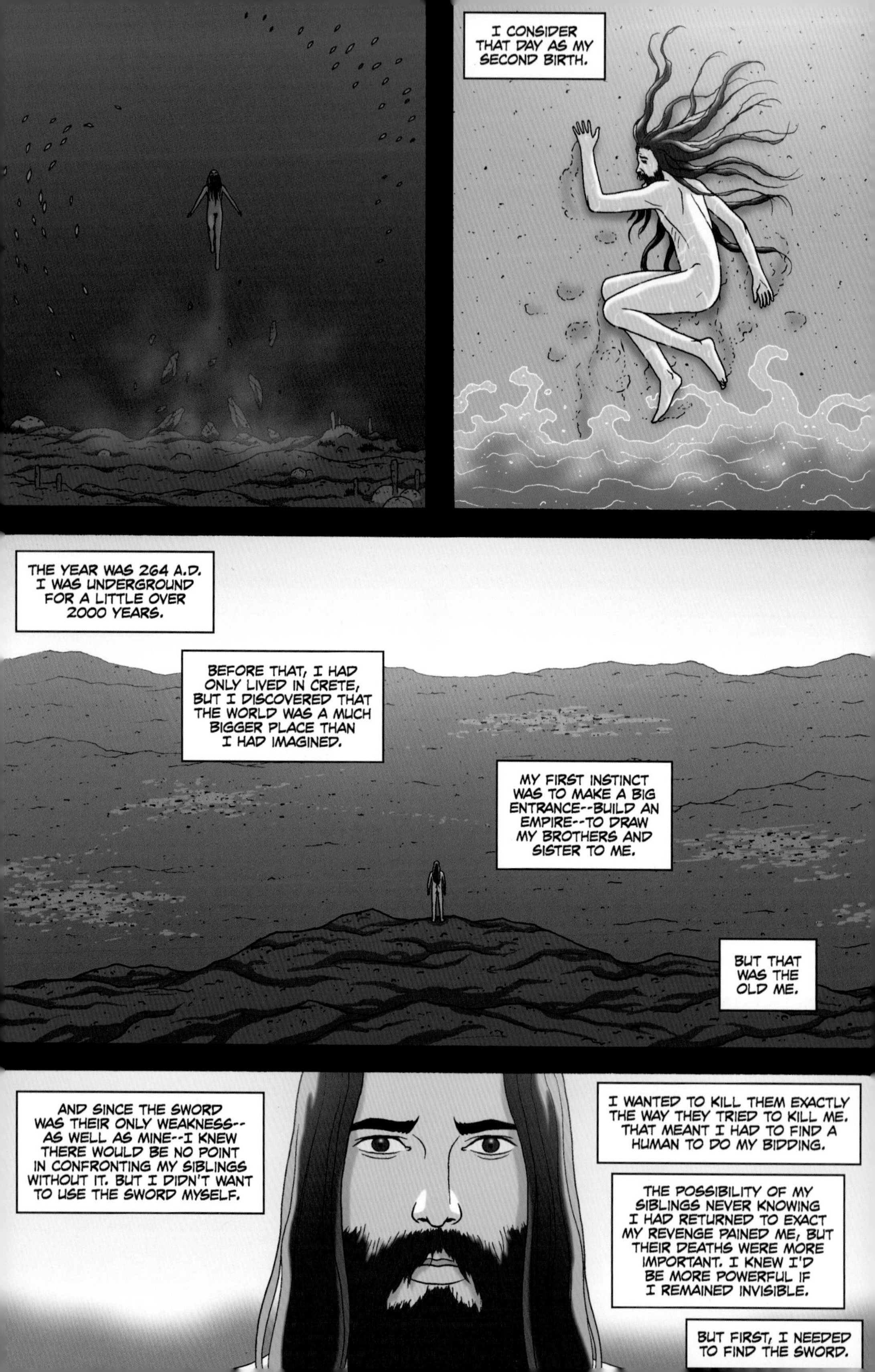
I CONSIDER THAT DAY AS MY SECOND BIRTH.
THE YEAR WAS 264 A.D. I WAS UNDERGROUND FOR A LITTLE OVER 2000 YEARS.
BEFORE THAT, I HAD ONLY LIVED IN CRETE, BUT I DISCOVERED THAT THE WORLD WAS A MUCH BIGGER PLACE THAN I HAD IMAGINED.
MY FIRST INSTINCT WAS TO MAKE A BIG ENTRANCE--BUILD AN EMPIRE--TO DRAW MY BROTHERS AND SISTER TO ME.
BUT THAT WAS THE OLD ME.
AND SINCE THE SWORD WAS THEIR ONLY WEAKNESS--AS WELL AS MINE--I KNEW THERE WOULD BE NO POINT IN CONFRONTING MY SIBLINGS WITHOUT IT. BUT I DIDN'T WANT TO USE THE SWORD MYSELF.
I WANTED TO KILL THEM EXACTLY THE WAY THEY TRIED TO KILL ME. THAT MEANT I HAD TO FIND A HUMAN TO DO MY BIDDING.
THE POSSIBILITY OF MY SIBLINGS NEVER KNOWING I HAD RETURNED TO EXACT MY REVENGE PAINED ME, BUT THEIR DEATHS WERE MORE IMPORTANT. I KNEW I'D BE MORE POWERFUL IF I REMAINED INVISIBLE.
BUT FIRST, I NEEDED TO FIND THE SWORD.

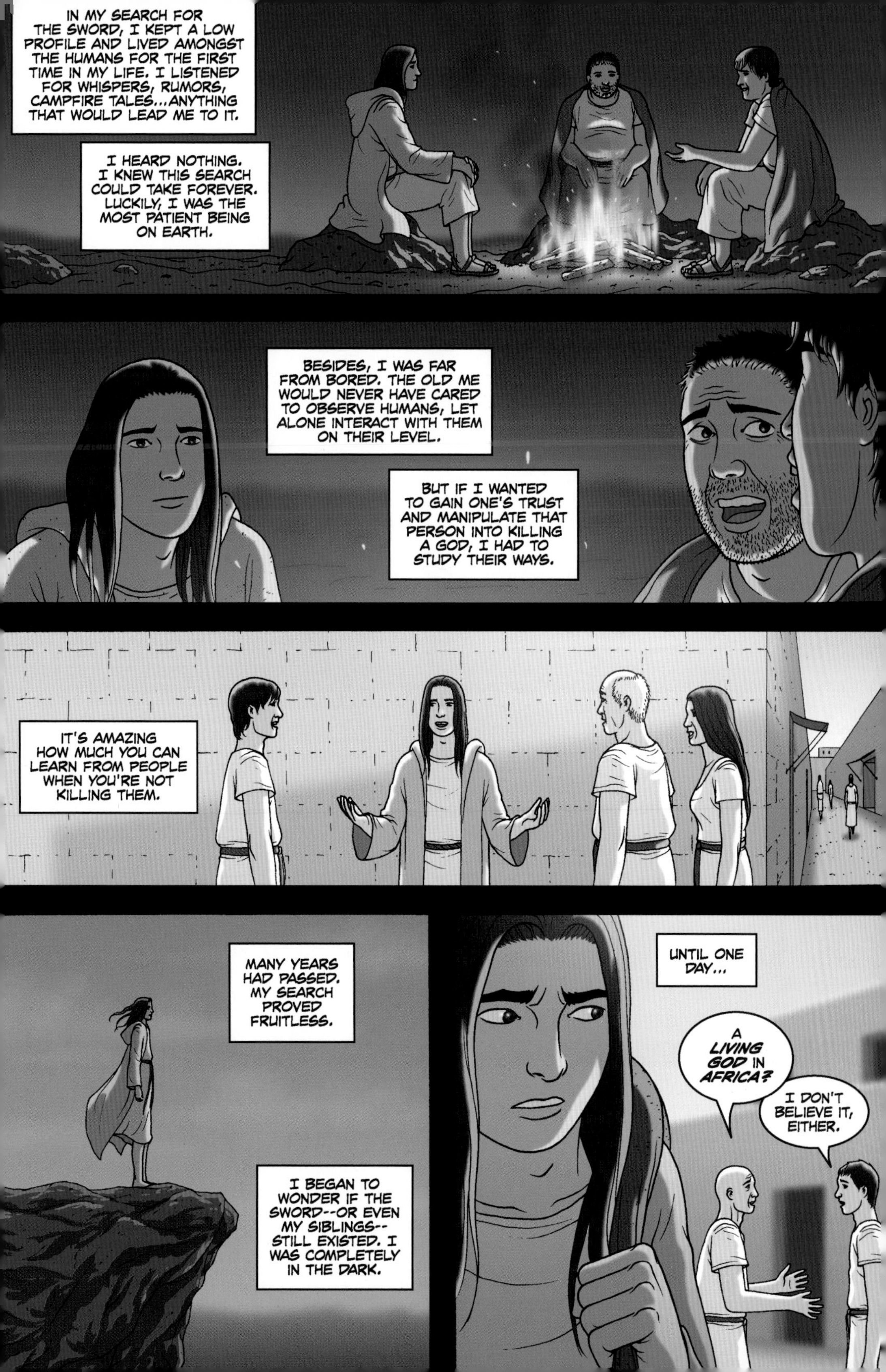
IN MY SEARCH FOR THE SWORD, I KEPT A LOW PROFILE AND LIVED AMONGST THE HUMANS FOR THE FIRST TIME IN MY LIFE. I LISTENED FOR WHISPERS, RUMORS, CAMPFIRE TALES...ANYTHING THAT WOULD LEAD ME TO IT.
I HEARD NOTHING. I KNEW THIS SEARCH COULD TAKE FOREVER. LUCKILY, I WAS THE MOST PATIENT BEING ON EARTH.
BESIDES, I WAS FAR FROM BORED. THE OLD ME WOULD NEVER HAVE CARED TO OBSERVE HUMANS, LET ALONE INTERACT WITH THEM ON THEIR LEVEL.
BUT IF I WANTED TO GAIN ONE'S TRUST AND MANIPULATE THAT PERSON INTO KILLING A GOD, I HAD TO STUDY THEIR WAYS.
IT'S AMAZING HOW MUCH YOU CAN LEARN FROM PEOPLE WHEN YOU'RE NOT KILLING THEM.
MANY YEARS HAD PASSED. MY SEARCH PROVED FRUITLESS.
I BEGAN TO WONDER IF THE SWORD--OR EVEN MY SIBLINGS--STILL EXISTED. I WAS COMPLETELY IN THE DARK.
UNTIL ONE DAY...
A *LIVING GOD* IN *AFRICA?*
I DON'T BELIEVE IT, EITHER.

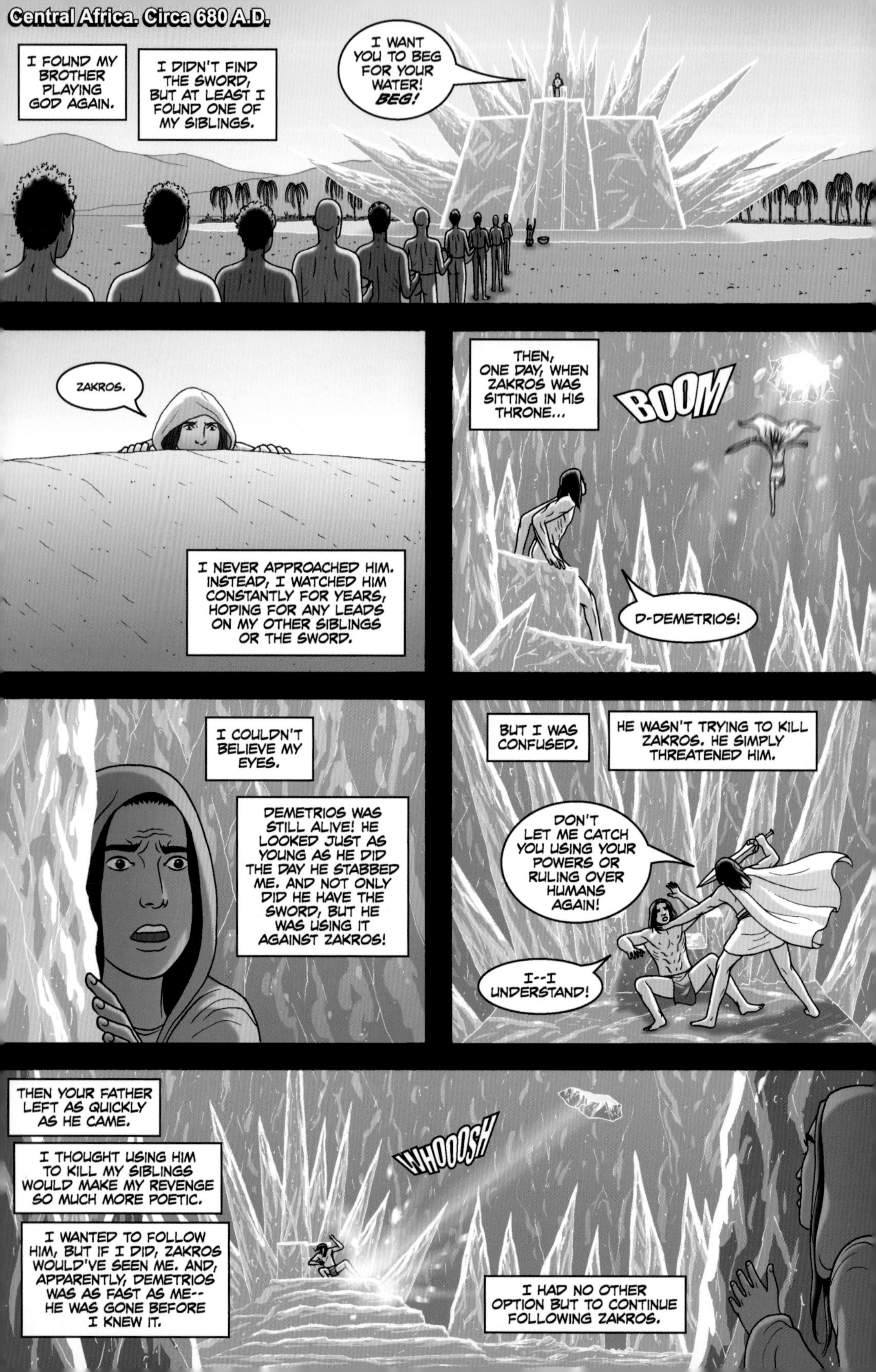
Central Africa. Circa 680 A.D.
I FOUND MY BROTHER PLAYING GOD AGAIN.
I DIDN'T FIND THE SWORD, BUT AT LEAST I FOUND ONE OF MY SIBLINGS.
I WANT YOU TO BEG FOR YOUR WATER! BEG!
ZAKROS.
I NEVER APPROACHED HIM. INSTEAD, I WATCHED HIM CONSTANTLY FOR YEARS, HOPING FOR ANY LEADS ON MY OTHER SIBLINGS OR THE SWORD.
THEN, ONE DAY, WHEN ZAKROS WAS SITTING IN HIS THRONE...
BOOM
D-DEMETRIOS!
I COULDN'T BELIEVE MY EYES.
DEMETRIOS WAS STILL ALIVE! HE LOOKED JUST AS YOUNG AS HE DID THE DAY HE STABBED ME. AND NOT ONLY DID HE HAVE THE SWORD, BUT HE WAS USING IT AGAINST ZAKROS!
BUT I WAS CONFUSED.
HE WASN'T TRYING TO KILL ZAKROS. HE SIMPLY THREATENED HIM.
DON'T LET ME CATCH YOU USING YOUR POWERS OR RULING OVER HUMANS AGAIN!
I--I UNDERSTAND!
THEN YOUR FATHER LEFT AS QUICKLY AS HE CAME.
I THOUGHT USING HIM TO KILL MY SIBLINGS WOULD MAKE MY REVENGE SO MUCH MORE POETIC.
I WANTED TO FOLLOW HIM, BUT IF I DID, ZAKROS WOULD'VE SEEN ME. AND, APPARENTLY, DEMETRIOS WAS AS FAST AS ME-- HE WAS GONE BEFORE I KNEW IT.
WHOOOSH
I HAD NO OTHER OPTION BUT TO CONTINUE FOLLOWING ZAKROS.

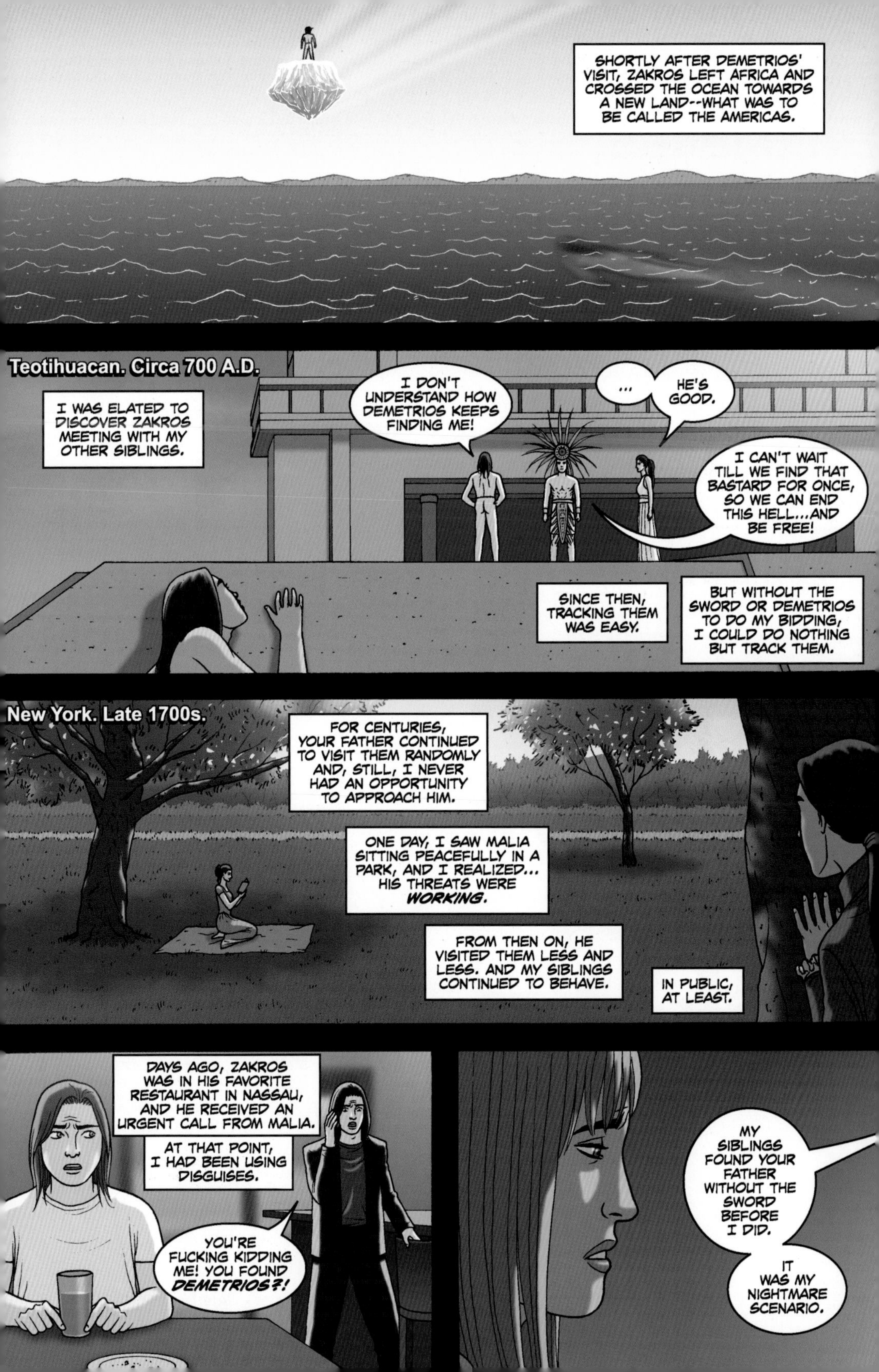

SHORTLY AFTER DEMETRIOS' VISIT, ZAKROS LEFT AFRICA AND CROSSED THE OCEAN TOWARDS A NEW LAND--WHAT WAS TO BE CALLED THE AMERICAS.
Teotihuacan. Circa 700 A.D.
I WAS ELATED TO DISCOVER ZAKROS MEETING WITH MY OTHER SIBLINGS.
I DON'T UNDERSTAND HOW DEMETRIOS KEEPS FINDING ME!
...
HE'S GOOD.
I CAN'T WAIT TILL WE FIND THAT BASTARD FOR ONCE, SO WE CAN END THIS HELL...AND BE FREE!
SINCE THEN, TRACKING THEM WAS EASY.
BUT WITHOUT THE SWORD OR DEMETRIOS TO DO MY BIDDING, I COULD DO NOTHING BUT TRACK THEM.
New York. Late 1700s.
FOR CENTURIES, YOUR FATHER CONTINUED TO VISIT THEM RANDOMLY AND, STILL, I NEVER HAD AN OPPORTUNITY TO APPROACH HIM.
ONE DAY, I SAW MALIA SITTING PEACEFULLY IN A PARK, AND I REALIZED... HIS THREATS WERE *WORKING*.
FROM THEN ON, HE VISITED THEM LESS AND LESS. AND MY SIBLINGS CONTINUED TO BEHAVE.
IN PUBLIC, AT LEAST.
DAYS AGO, ZAKROS WAS IN HIS FAVORITE RESTAURANT IN NASSAU, AND HE RECEIVED AN URGENT CALL FROM MALIA.
AT THAT POINT, I HAD BEEN USING DISGUISES.
YOU'RE FUCKING KIDDING ME! YOU FOUND *DEMETRIOS?!*
MY SIBLINGS FOUND YOUR FATHER WITHOUT THE SWORD BEFORE I DID.
IT WAS MY NIGHTMARE SCENARIO.

I'LL TAKE THE FRONT DOOR. YOU TWO ENTER THROUGH THE BACK.

I WATCHED THEM MURDER YOUR FAMILY, ONE BY ONE.

AFTER HUNDREDS OF YEARS OF SEARCHING FOR DEMETRIOS, WATCHING MALIA TORTURE HIM WAS *PAINFUL*.

I WANTED TO DO *SOMETHING*.

LUCKILY, MALIA ZAPPED AN ELECTRICAL OUTLET, CREATING A FIRE.

ZRT

ZZZRMMMM

I INTENSIFIED IT TO TRY TO MAKE THEM LEAVE. I WAS DESPERATE.

ZRT

BUT DEMETRIOS WAS DEAD, AND ANY HOPE FOR MY PERFECT REVENGE DIED WITH HIM.

AHUH.

AHUH.

NO...

THEN, YOU REMAINED.

I WAS SO DISTRAUGHT OVER LOSING DEMETRIOS THAT I REFUSED TO LEAVE WITH NOTHING. I WANTED TO SAVE YOU SO I COULD AT LEAST ASK YOU IF YOU KNEW WHERE THE SWORD WAS.

JUST KILL THE GIRL SO WE CAN GET OUT OF HERE.

I CONCENTRATED THE FIRE ONTO THE CEILING AND LET IT COLLAPSE ON YOU. IT WAS THE ONLY WAY I COULD THINK OF KEEPING YOU ALIVE.

AND NOT ONLY WAS I SURPISED TO SEE YOU SURVIVE...

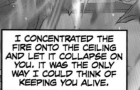

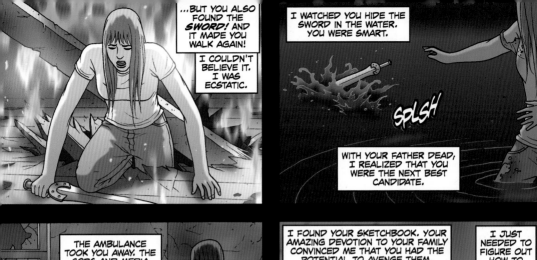

...BUT YOU ALSO FOUND THE *SWORD!* AND IT MADE YOU WALK AGAIN!

I COULDN'T BELIEVE IT. I WAS ECSTATIC.

I WATCHED YOU HIDE THE SWORD IN THE WATER. YOU WERE SMART.

SPLSH

WITH YOUR FATHER DEAD, I REALIZED THAT YOU WERE THE NEXT BEST CANDIDATE.

THE AMBULANCE TOOK YOU AWAY. THE COPS AND MEDIA FINALLY LEFT THE CRIME SCENE, BUT I STAYED BEHIND. I FORAGED THROUGH YOUR ROOM TO LEARN ABOUT YOU.

I FOUND YOUR SKETCHBOOK. YOUR AMAZING DEVOTION TO YOUR FAMILY CONVINCED ME THAT YOU HAD THE POTENTIAL TO AVENGE THEM.

I JUST NEEDED TO FIGURE OUT HOW TO APPROACH YOU.

YOUR FAMILY'S FUNERAL BECAME THE PERFECT OPPORTUNITY.

I'M SO SORRY ABOUT YOUR LOSS. YOUR FATHER'S CREATIVE WRITING CLASS HONESTLY CHANGED MY LIFE.

YEAH, HE COULD MAKE UP THE GREATEST STORIES OUT OF NOWHERE.

IT'S JUST A SHAME THAT HE NEVER PUBLISHED ANYTHING.

THE NIGHT BEFORE THE FUNERAL, I GOT A HOTEL ROOM AND USED ANOTHER DISGUISE THAT I THOUGHT YOU WOULD FIND MORE APPEALING-- JUSTIN FOREMAN, ONE OF THE MANY ALIASES IN MY REPERTOIRE THAT I USED TO TRACK MALIA IN NEW YORK.

JUSTIN NOW HOLDS A SPECIAL PLACE IN MY HEART. HE REPRESENTS HOW YOUR FATHER *DECEIVED ME.*

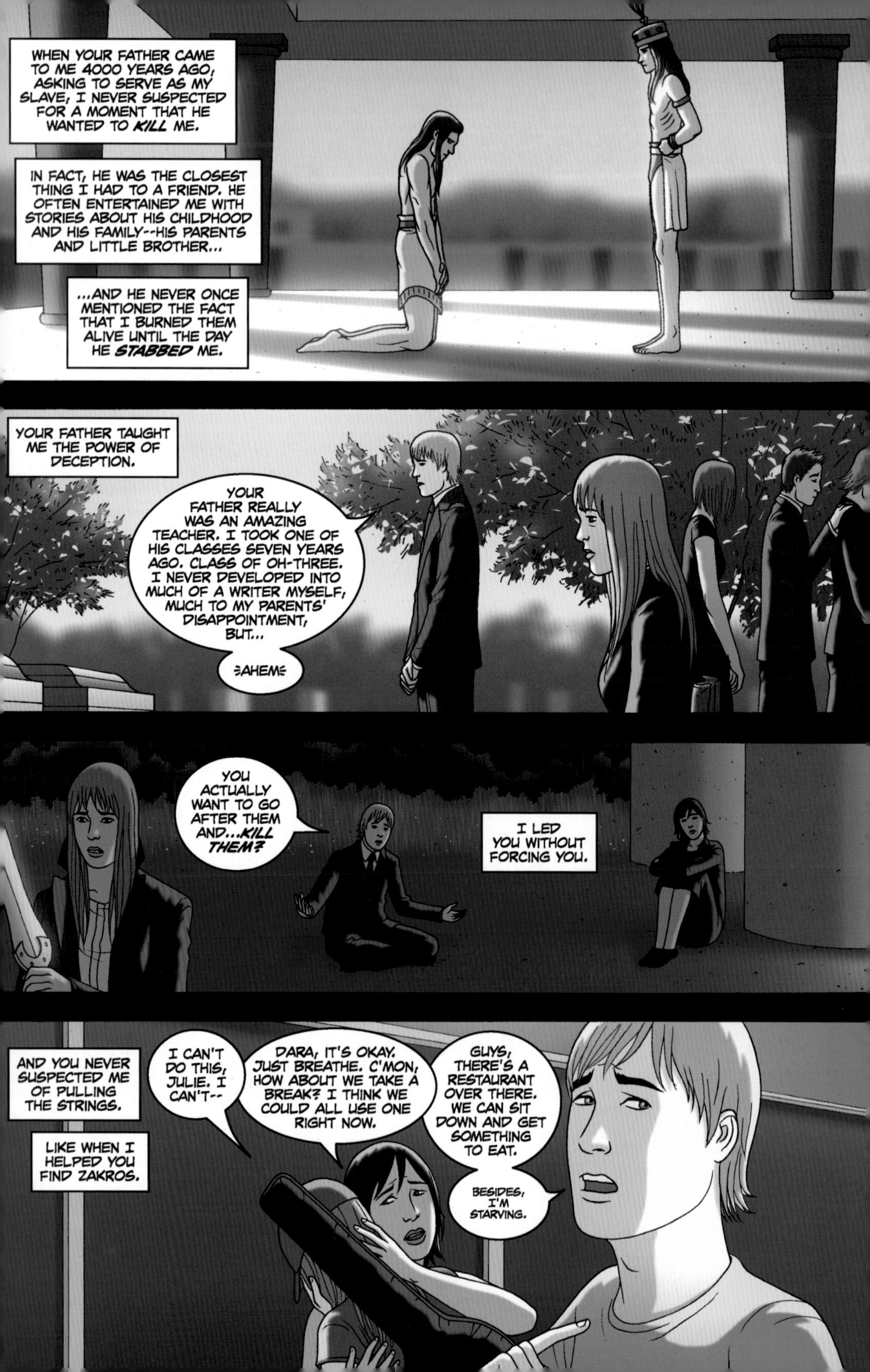
WHEN YOUR FATHER CAME TO ME 4000 YEARS AGO, ASKING TO SERVE AS MY SLAVE, I NEVER SUSPECTED FOR A MOMENT THAT HE WANTED TO KILL ME.
IN FACT, HE WAS THE CLOSEST THING I HAD TO A FRIEND. HE OFTEN ENTERTAINED ME WITH STORIES ABOUT HIS CHILDHOOD AND HIS FAMILY--HIS PARENTS AND LITTLE BROTHER...
...AND HE NEVER ONCE MENTIONED THE FACT THAT I BURNED THEM ALIVE UNTIL THE DAY HE STABBED ME.
YOUR FATHER TAUGHT ME THE POWER OF DECEPTION.
YOUR FATHER REALLY WAS AN AMAZING TEACHER. I TOOK ONE OF HIS CLASSES SEVEN YEARS AGO. CLASS OF OH-THREE. I NEVER DEVELOPED INTO MUCH OF A WRITER MYSELF, MUCH TO MY PARENTS' DISAPPOINTMENT, BUT...
AHEM
YOU ACTUALLY WANT TO GO AFTER THEM AND...KILL THEM?
I LED YOU WITHOUT FORCING YOU.
AND YOU NEVER SUSPECTED ME OF PULLING THE STRINGS.
LIKE WHEN I HELPED YOU FIND ZAKROS.
I CAN'T DO THIS, JULIE. I CAN'T--
DARA, IT'S OKAY. JUST BREATHE. C'MON, HOW ABOUT WE TAKE A BREAK? I THINK WE COULD ALL USE ONE RIGHT NOW.
GUYS, THERE'S A RESTAURANT OVER THERE. WE CAN SIT DOWN AND GET SOMETHING TO EAT.
BESIDES, I'M STARVING.

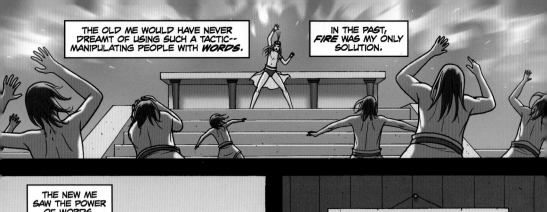

THE OLD ME WOULD HAVE NEVER DREAMT OF USING SUCH A TACTIC--MANIPULATING PEOPLE WITH *WORDS.*
IN THE PAST, *FIRE* WAS MY ONLY SOLUTION.
THE NEW ME SAW THE POWER OF WORDS.
ONLY A COUPLE STRUNG TOGETHER CAN BRING *UNITY*...
MARRY ME
WHITES ONLY
...OR *DIVISION.*
WORDS CAN CREATE AN ENTIRE WORLD...
...FOR *THIS* LIFE...
We the People
...AND THE *NEXT.*
AND THEY CAN MOTIVATE A YOUNG GIRL TO SEEK REVENGE AGAINST GODS.

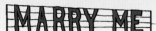

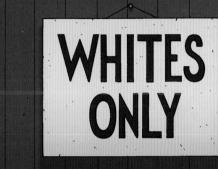

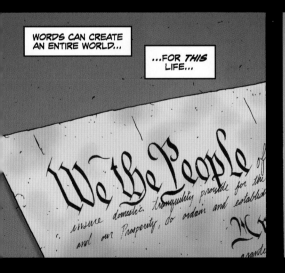

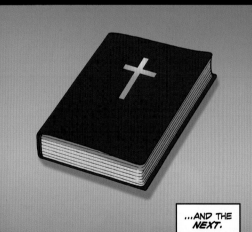

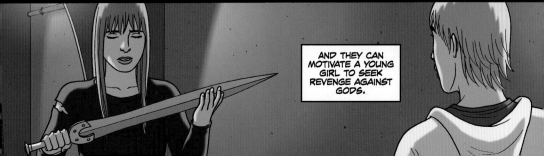

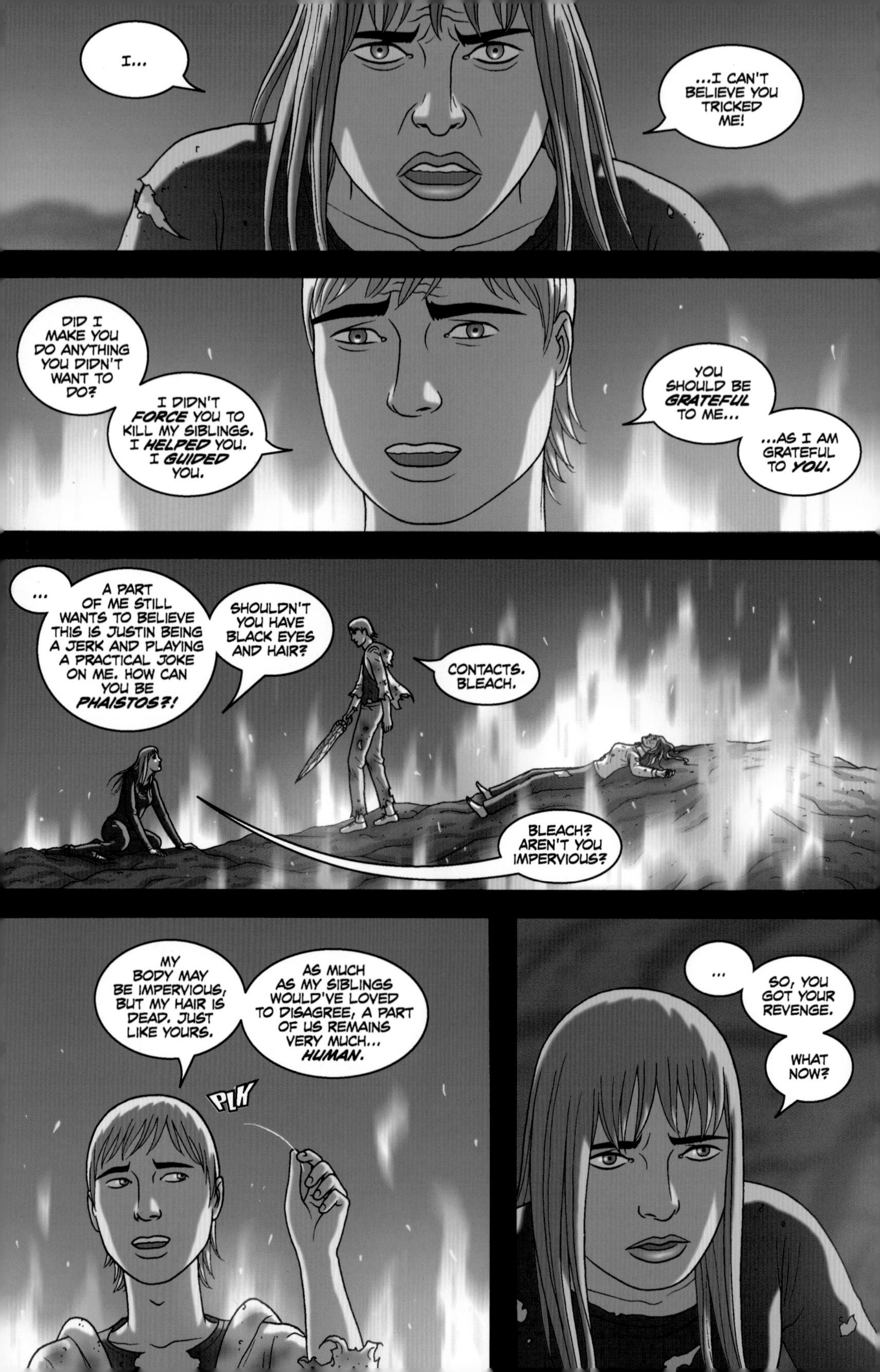
I...
...I CAN'T BELIEVE YOU TRICKED ME!
DID I MAKE YOU DO ANYTHING YOU DIDN'T WANT TO DO?
I DIDN'T *FORCE* YOU TO KILL MY SIBLINGS. I *HELPED* YOU. I *GUIDED* YOU.
YOU SHOULD BE *GRATEFUL* TO ME...
...AS I AM GRATEFUL TO *YOU*.
...
A PART OF ME STILL WANTS TO BELIEVE THIS IS JUSTIN BEING A JERK AND PLAYING A PRACTICAL JOKE ON ME. HOW CAN YOU BE *PHAISTOS?!*
SHOULDN'T YOU HAVE BLACK EYES AND HAIR?
CONTACTS. BLEACH.
BLEACH? AREN'T YOU IMPERVIOUS?
MY BODY MAY BE IMPERVIOUS, BUT MY HAIR IS DEAD. JUST LIKE YOURS.
AS MUCH AS MY SIBLINGS WOULD'VE LOVED TO DISAGREE, A PART OF US REMAINS VERY MUCH... *HUMAN*.
PLK
...
SO, YOU GOT YOUR REVENGE.
WHAT NOW?

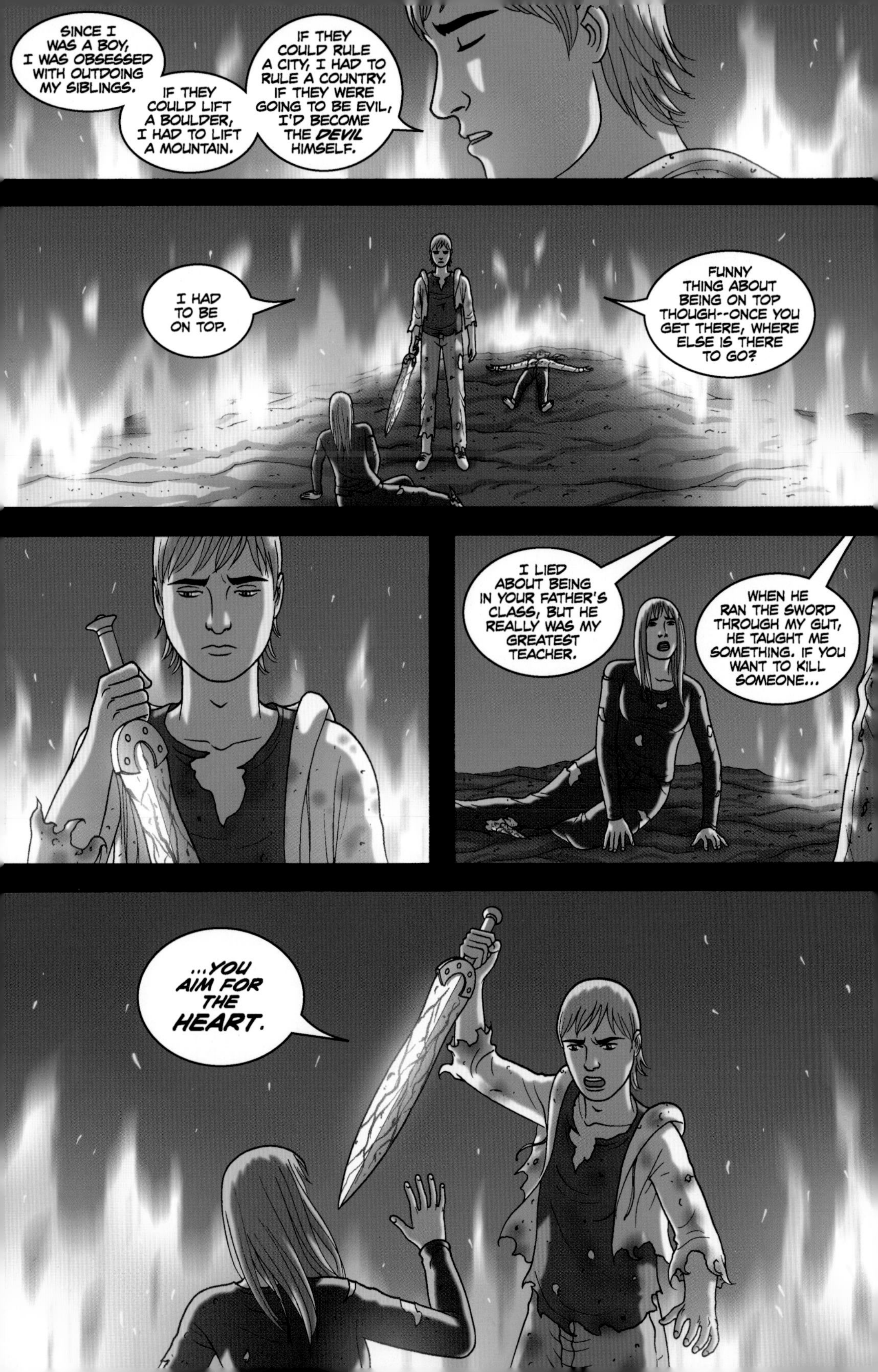
SINCE I WAS A BOY, I WAS OBSESSED WITH OUTDOING MY SIBLINGS.
IF THEY COULD LIFT A BOULDER, I HAD TO LIFT A MOUNTAIN.
IF THEY COULD RULE A CITY, I HAD TO RULE A COUNTRY. IF THEY WERE GOING TO BE EVIL, I'D BECOME THE *DEVIL* HIMSELF.
I HAD TO BE ON TOP.
FUNNY THING ABOUT BEING ON TOP THOUGH--ONCE YOU GET THERE, WHERE ELSE IS THERE TO GO?
I LIED ABOUT BEING IN YOUR FATHER'S CLASS, BUT HE REALLY WAS MY GREATEST TEACHER.
WHEN HE RAN THE SWORD THROUGH MY GUT, HE TAUGHT ME SOMETHING. IF YOU WANT TO KILL SOMEONE...
...YOU AIM FOR THE HEART.

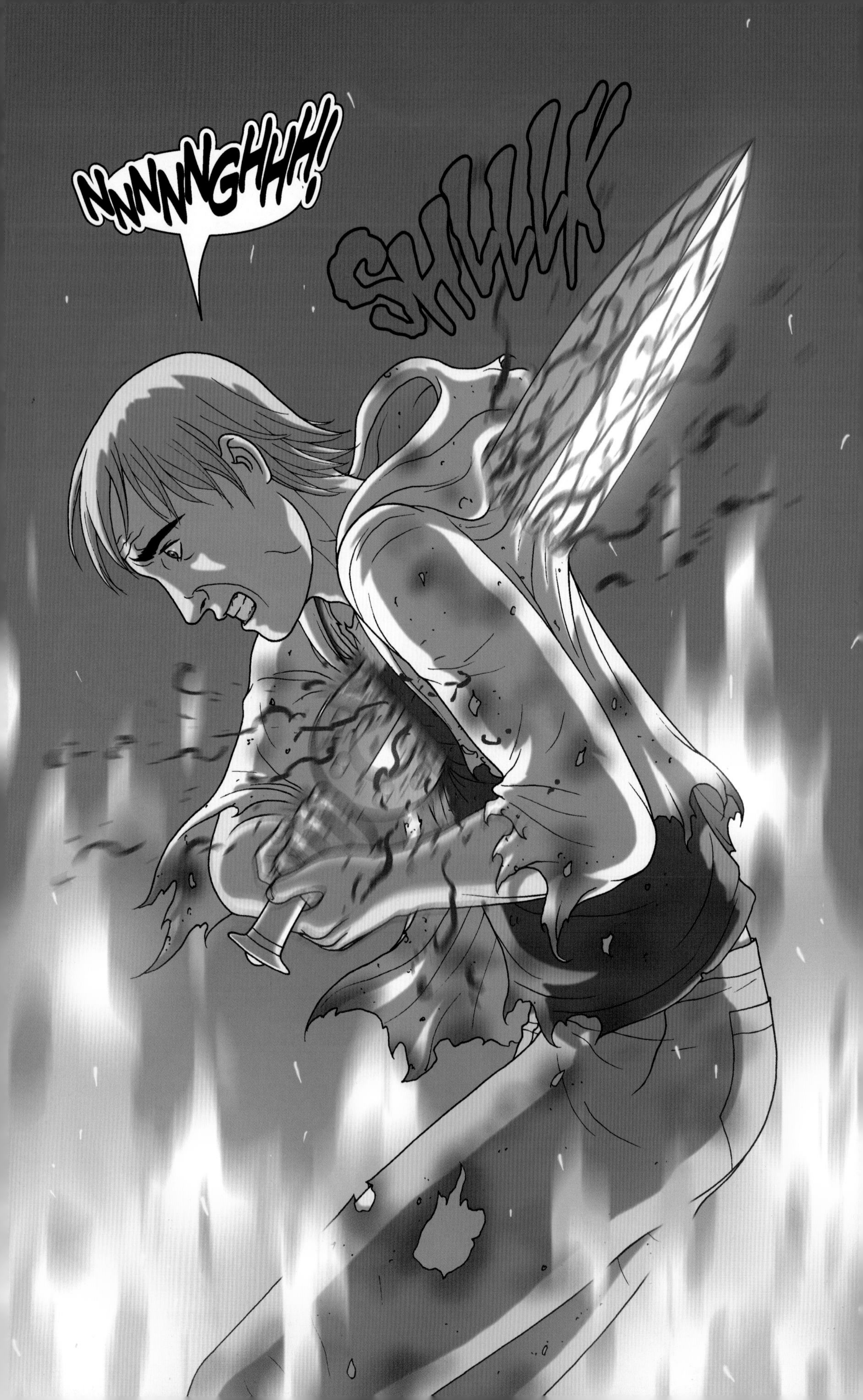
NNNNNGHHH!
SHLLLK

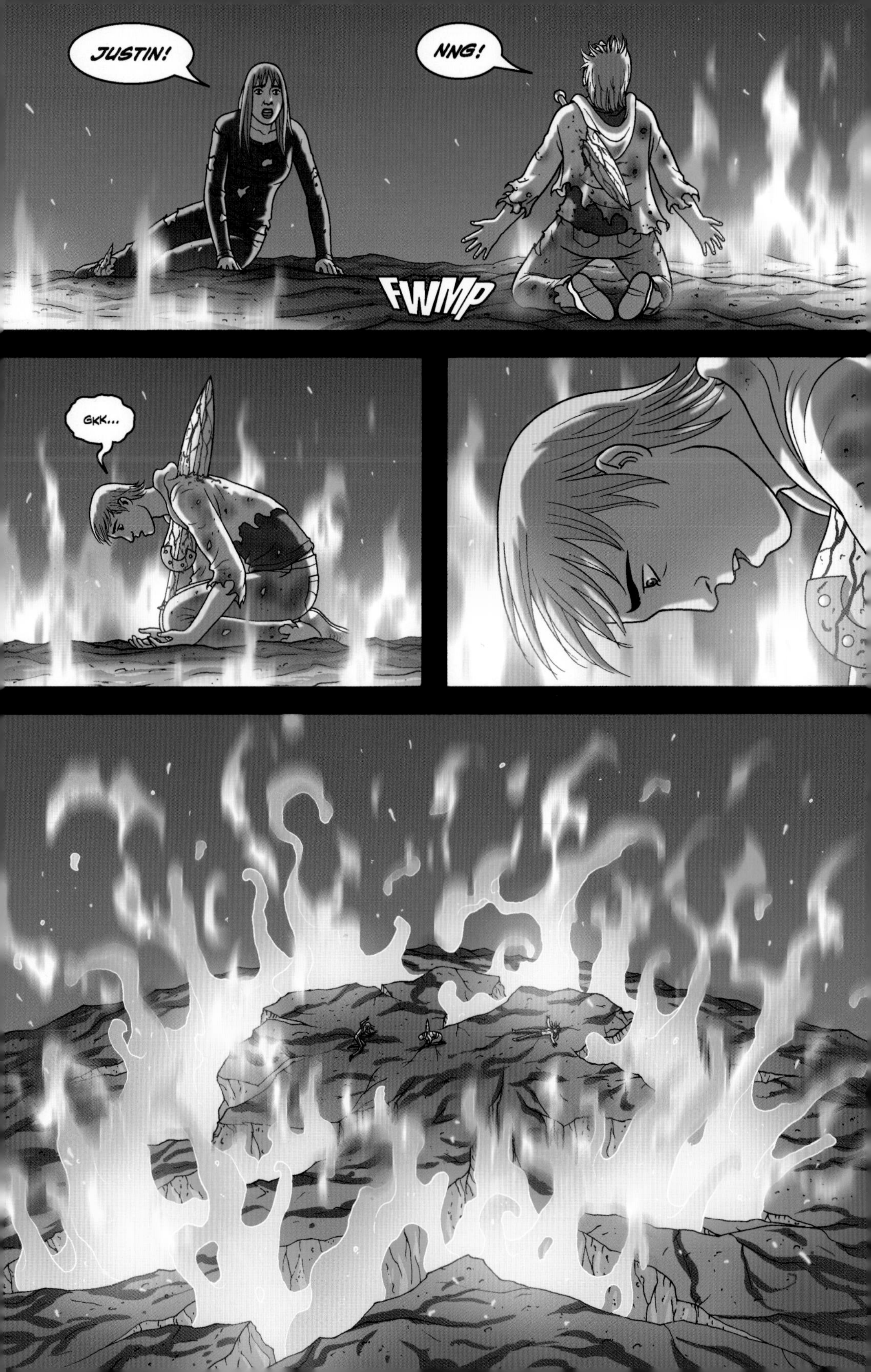
JUSTIN!
NNG!
FWMP
GKK...

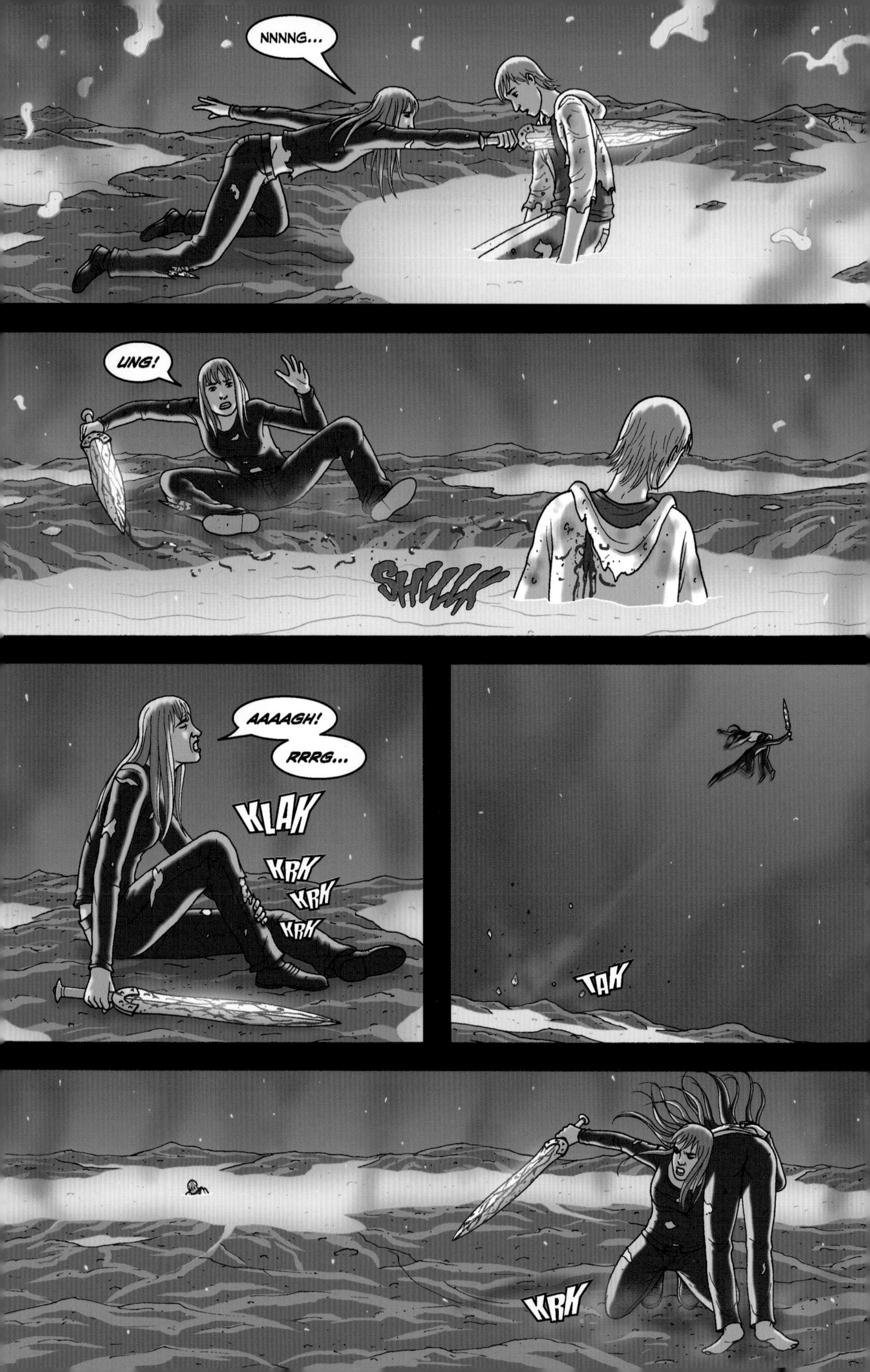
NNNNG...
UNG!
SHLLK
AAAAGH!
RRRG...
KLAK
KRK
KRK
KRK
TAK
KRK

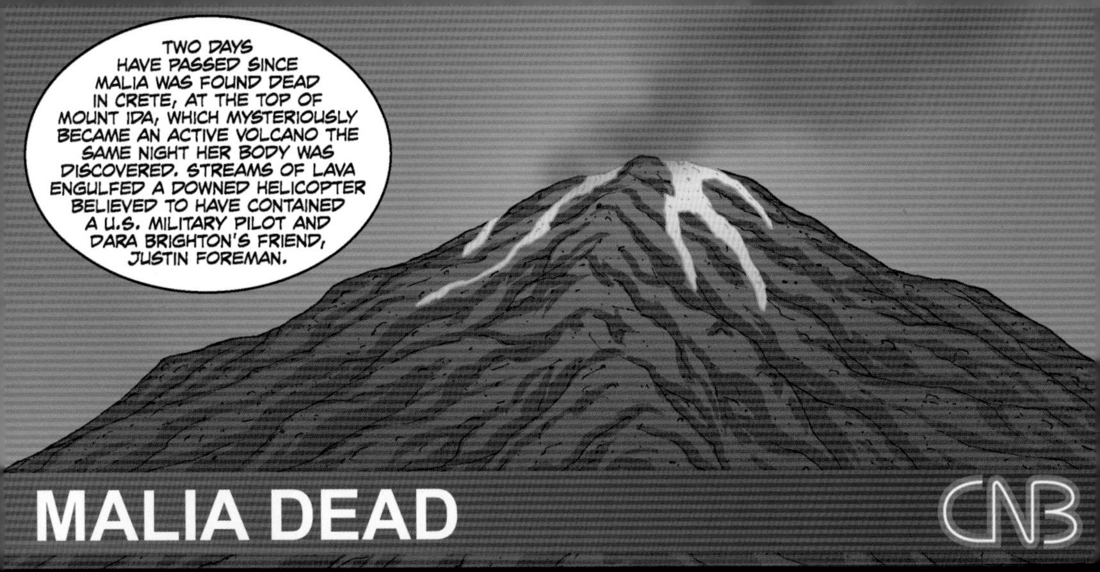
TWO DAYS HAVE PASSED SINCE MALIA WAS FOUND DEAD IN CRETE, AT THE TOP OF MOUNT IDA, WHICH MYSTERIOUSLY BECAME AN ACTIVE VOLCANO THE SAME NIGHT HER BODY WAS DISCOVERED. STREAMS OF LAVA ENGULFED A DOWNED HELICOPTER BELIEVED TO HAVE CONTAINED A U.S. MILITARY PILOT AND DARA BRIGHTON'S FRIEND, JUSTIN FOREMAN.
MALIA DEAD
CNB

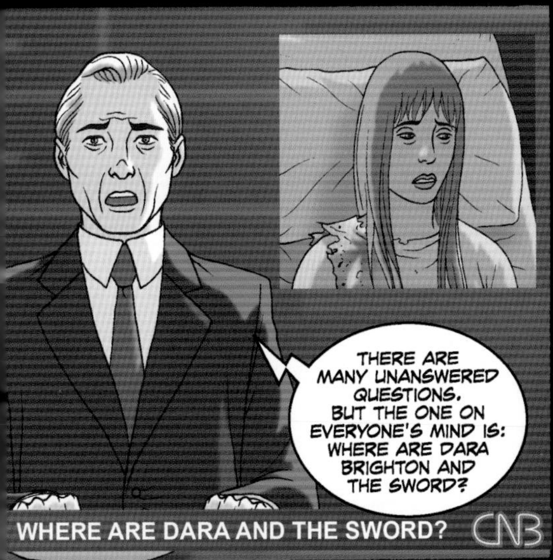
THERE ARE MANY UNANSWERED QUESTIONS. BUT THE ONE ON EVERYONE'S MIND IS: WHERE ARE DARA BRIGHTON AND THE SWORD?
WHERE ARE DARA AND THE SWORD?
CNB

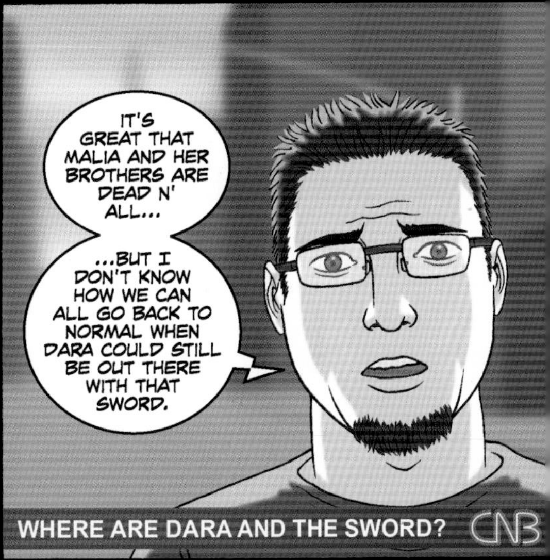
IT'S GREAT THAT MALIA AND HER BROTHERS ARE DEAD N' ALL...
...BUT I DON'T KNOW HOW WE CAN ALL GO BACK TO NORMAL WHEN DARA COULD STILL BE OUT THERE WITH THAT SWORD.
WHERE ARE DARA AND THE SWORD?
CNB

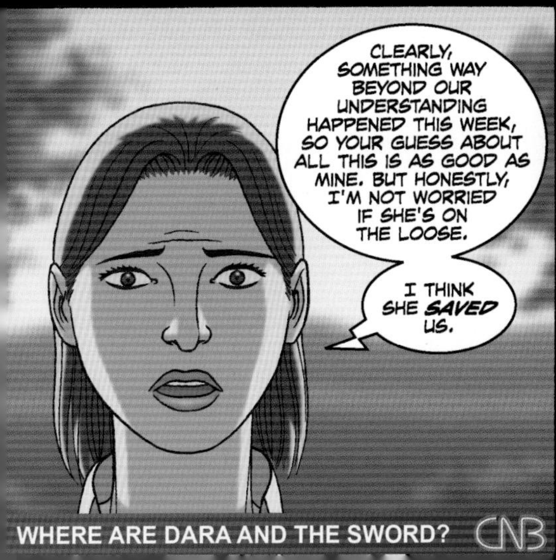
CLEARLY, SOMETHING WAY BEYOND OUR UNDERSTANDING HAPPENED THIS WEEK, SO YOUR GUESS ABOUT ALL THIS IS AS GOOD AS MINE. BUT HONESTLY, I'M NOT WORRIED IF SHE'S ON THE LOOSE.
I THINK SHE SAVED US.
WHERE ARE DARA AND THE SWORD?
CNB

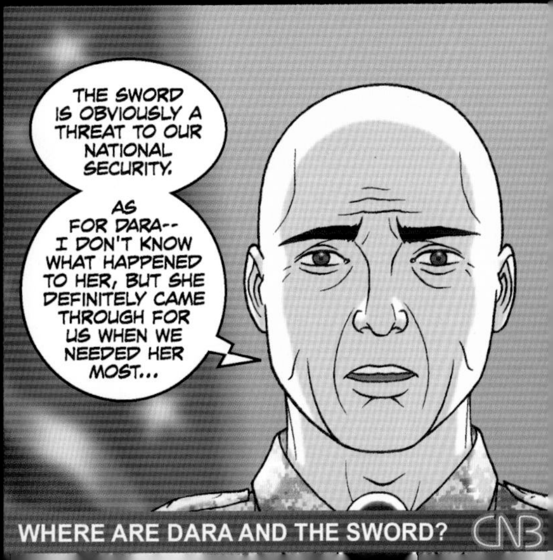
THE SWORD IS OBVIOUSLY A THREAT TO OUR NATIONAL SECURITY.
AS FOR DARA-- I DON'T KNOW WHAT HAPPENED TO HER, BUT SHE DEFINITELY CAME THROUGH FOR US WHEN WE NEEDED HER MOST...
WHERE ARE DARA AND THE SWORD?
CNB

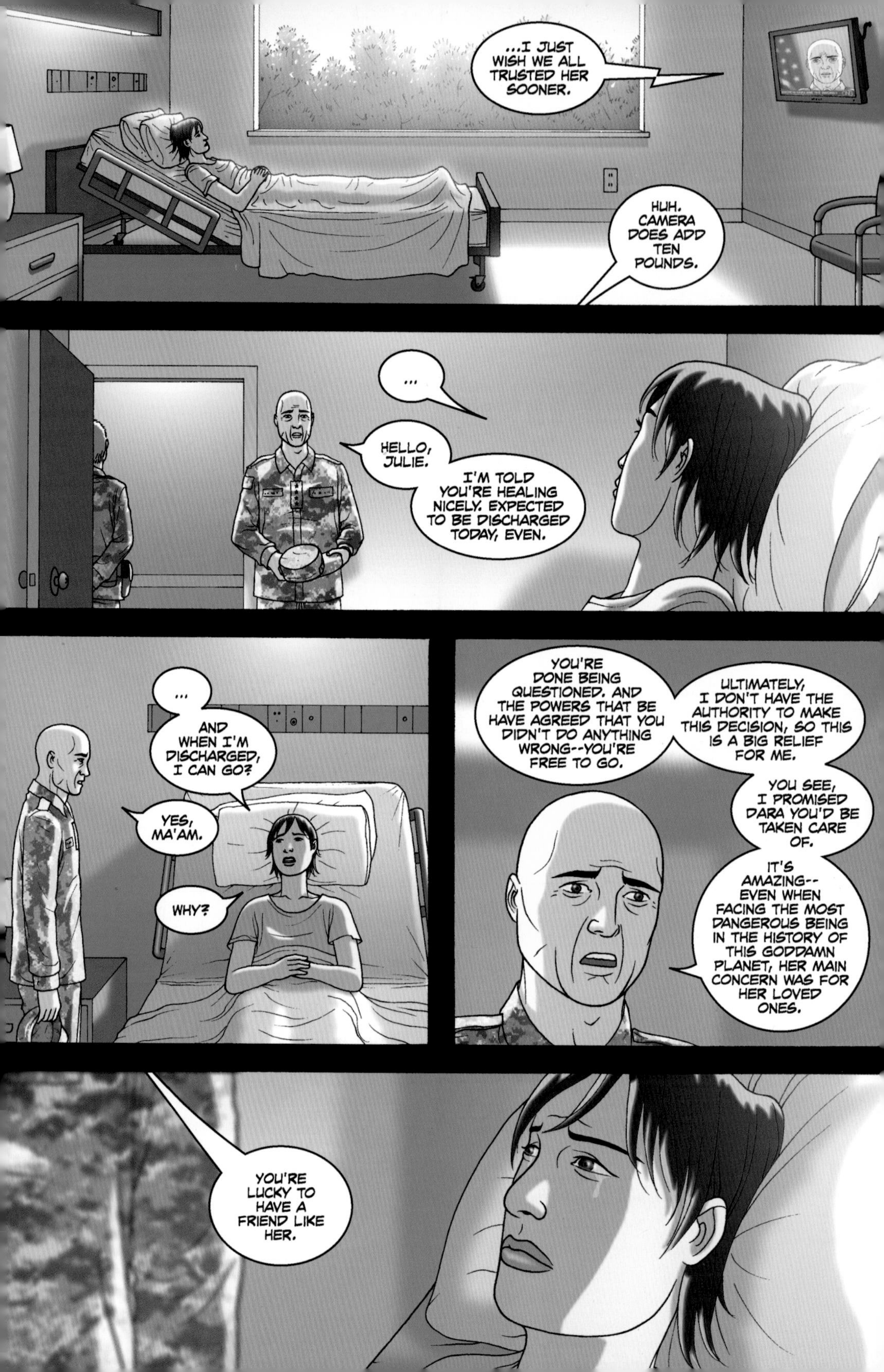
...I JUST WISH WE ALL TRUSTED HER SOONER.
HUH. CAMERA DOES ADD TEN POUNDS.
...
HELLO, JULIE.
I'M TOLD YOU'RE HEALING NICELY. EXPECTED TO BE DISCHARGED TODAY, EVEN.
...
AND WHEN I'M DISCHARGED, I CAN GO?
YES, MA'AM.
WHY?
YOU'RE DONE BEING QUESTIONED. AND THE POWERS THAT BE HAVE AGREED THAT YOU DIDN'T DO ANYTHING WRONG--YOU'RE FREE TO GO.
ULTIMATELY, I DON'T HAVE THE AUTHORITY TO MAKE THIS DECISION, SO THIS IS A BIG RELIEF FOR ME.
YOU SEE, I PROMISED DARA YOU'D BE TAKEN CARE OF.
IT'S AMAZING--EVEN WHEN FACING THE MOST DANGEROUS BEING IN THE HISTORY OF THIS GODDAMN PLANET, HER MAIN CONCERN WAS FOR HER LOVED ONES.
YOU'RE LUCKY TO HAVE A FRIEND LIKE HER.

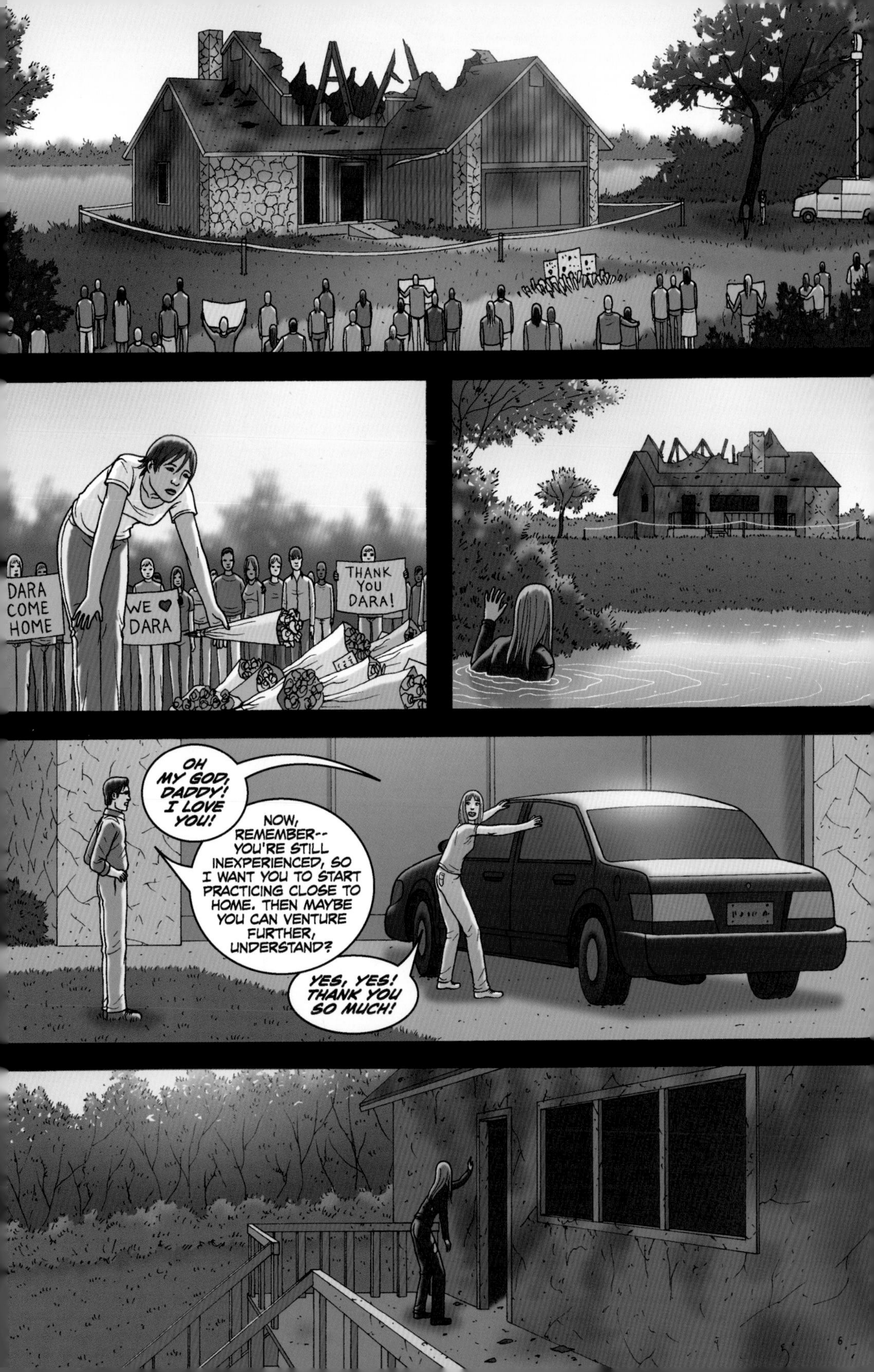

DARA COME HOME
WE ♥ DARA
THANK YOU DARA!
OH MY GOD, DADDY! I LOVE YOU!
NOW, REMEMBER-- YOU'RE STILL INEXPERIENCED, SO I WANT YOU TO START PRACTICING CLOSE TO HOME. THEN MAYBE YOU CAN VENTURE FURTHER, UNDERSTAND?
YES, YES! THANK YOU SO MUCH!

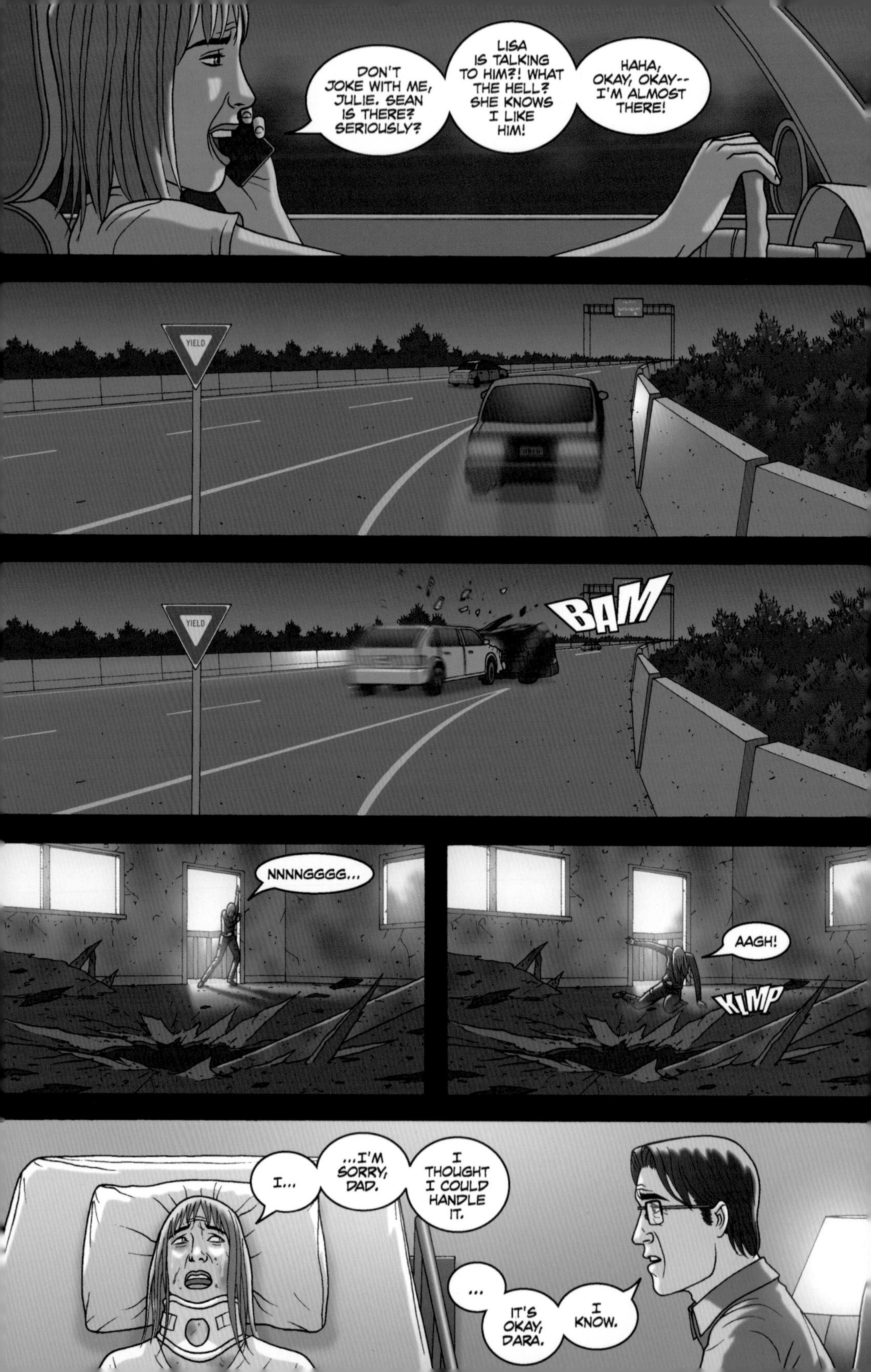
DON'T JOKE WITH ME, JULIE. SEAN IS THERE? SERIOUSLY?
LISA IS TALKING TO HIM?! WHAT THE HELL? SHE KNOWS I LIKE HIM!
HAHA, OKAY, OKAY-- I'M ALMOST THERE!
YIELD
YIELD
BAM
NNNNGGGG...
AAGH!
KLMP
I...
...I'M SORRY, DAD.
I THOUGHT I COULD HANDLE IT.
...
IT'S OKAY, DARA.
I KNOW.

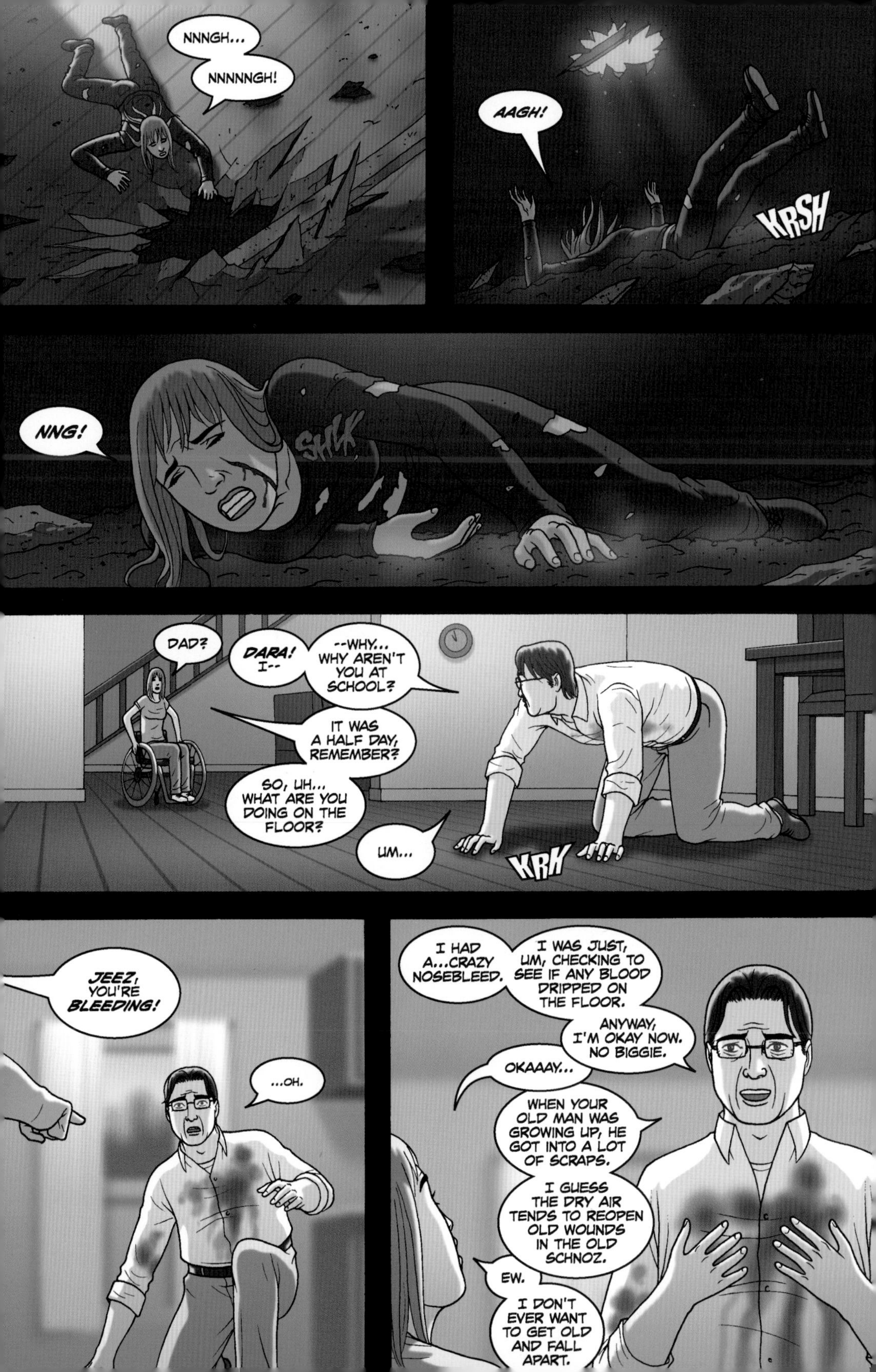
NNNGH...
NNNNNGH!
AAGH!
KRSH
NNG!
SHLK
DAD?
DARA! I--
--WHY... WHY AREN'T YOU AT SCHOOL?
IT WAS A HALF DAY, REMEMBER?
SO, UH... WHAT ARE YOU DOING ON THE FLOOR?
UM...
KRK
JEEZ, YOU'RE BLEEDING!
...OH.
I HAD A...CRAZY NOSEBLEED.
I WAS JUST, UM, CHECKING TO SEE IF ANY BLOOD DRIPPED ON THE FLOOR.
ANYWAY, I'M OKAY NOW. NO BIGGIE.
OKAAAY...
WHEN YOUR OLD MAN WAS GROWING UP, HE GOT INTO A LOT OF SCRAPS.
I GUESS THE DRY AIR TENDS TO REOPEN OLD WOUNDS IN THE OLD SCHNOZ.
EW.
I DON'T EVER WANT TO GET OLD AND FALL APART.

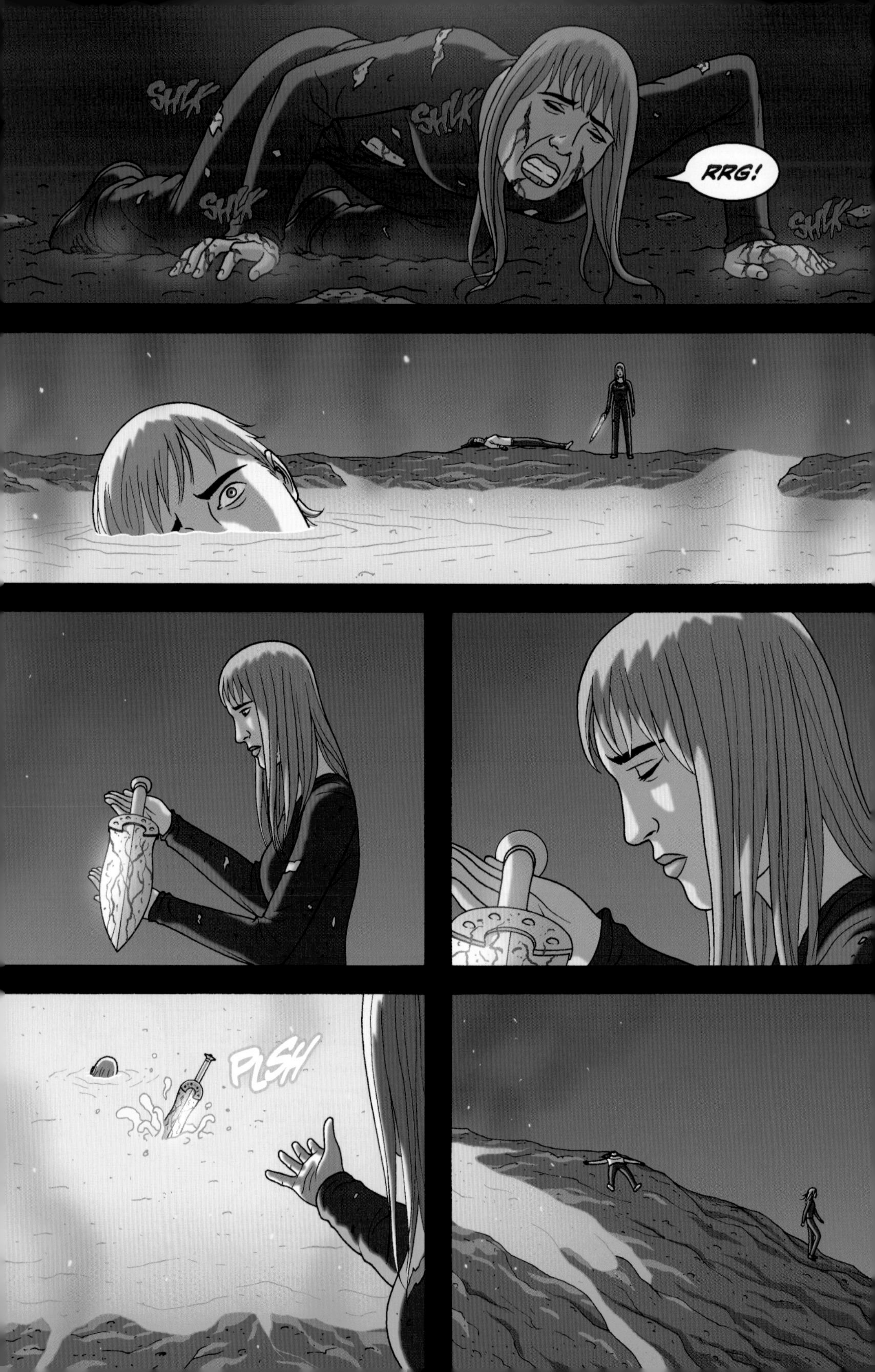
SHLK
SHLK
SHLK
RRG!
SHLK
PLSH

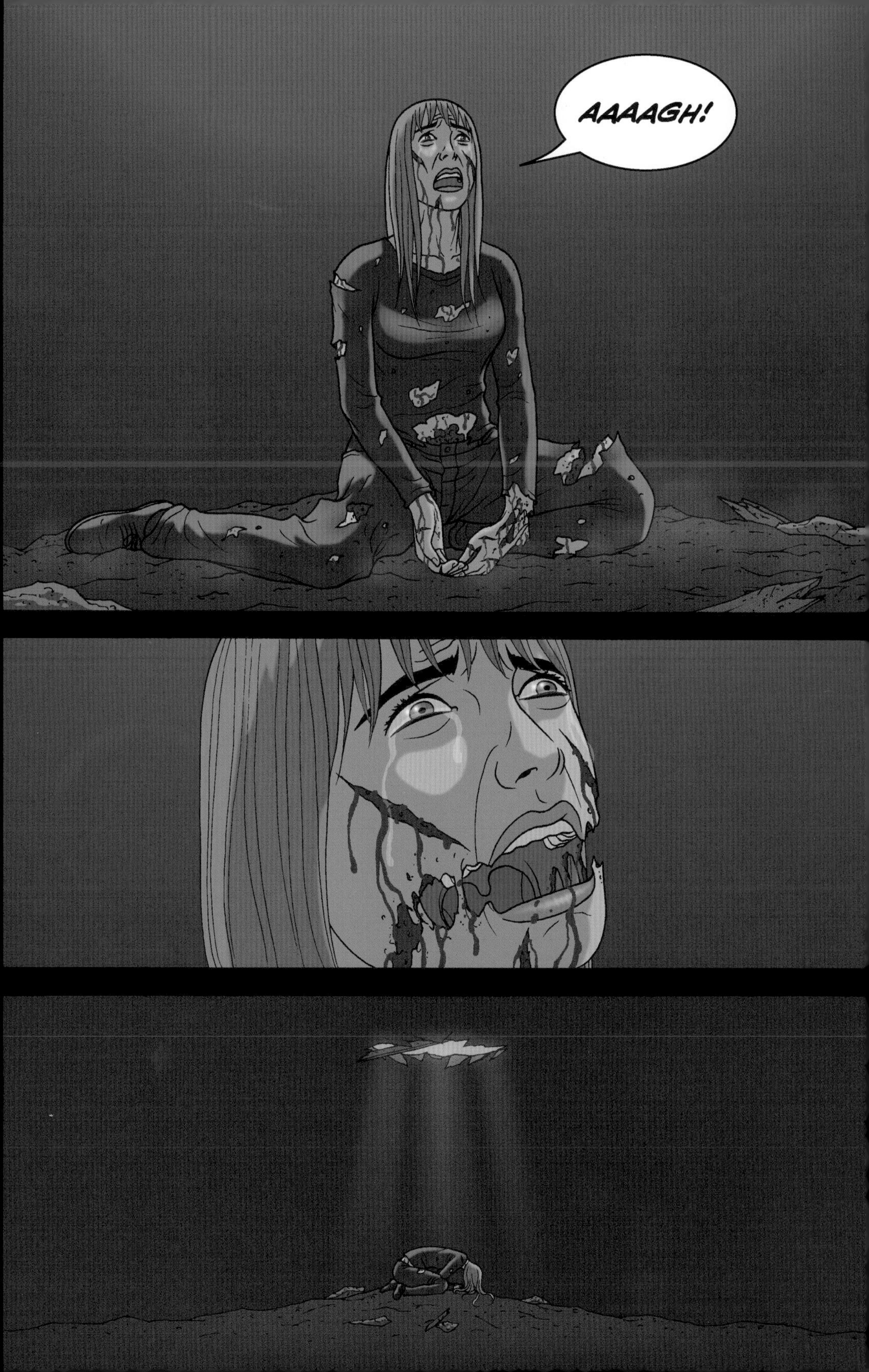
AAAAGH!

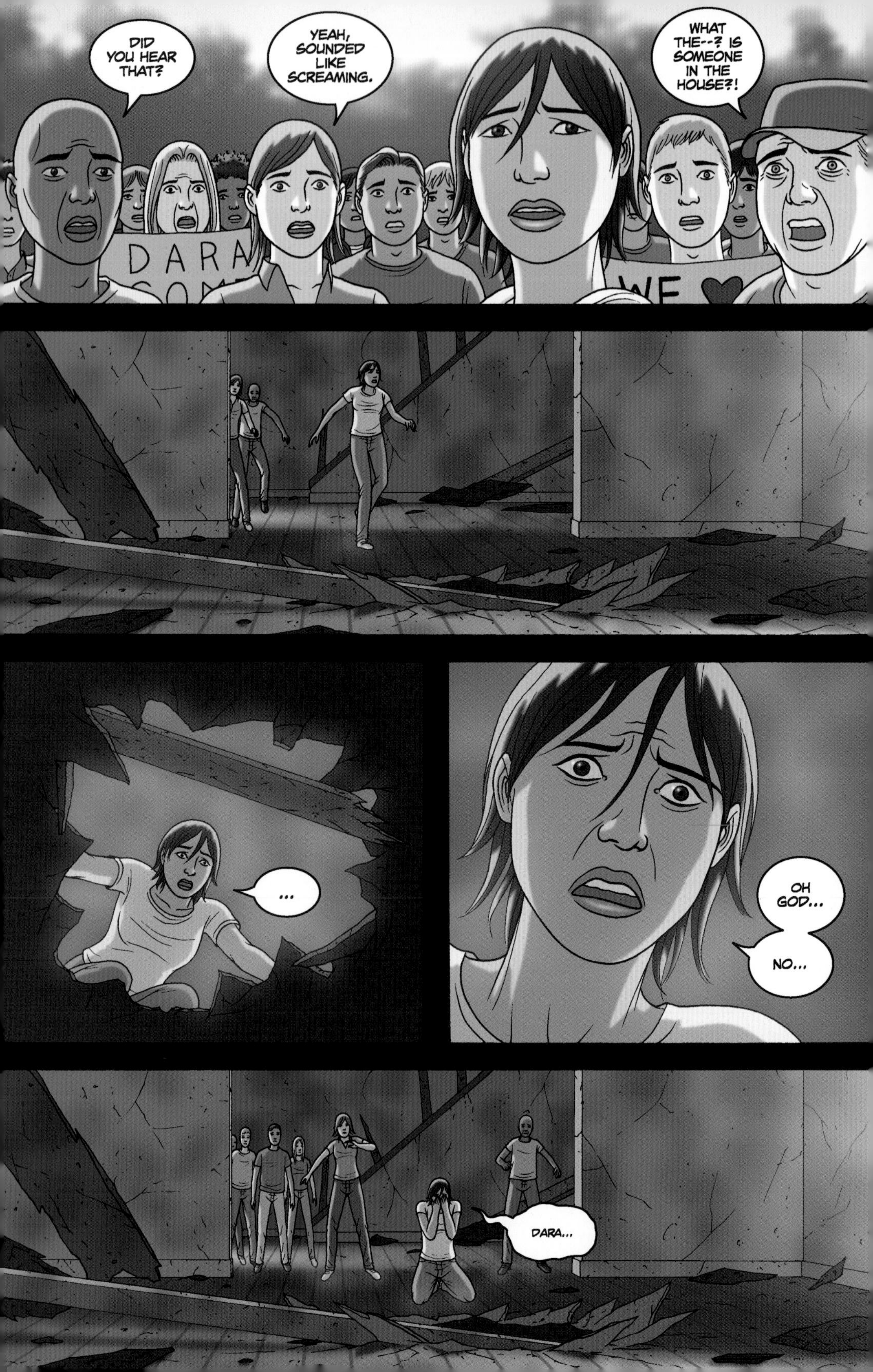
DID YOU HEAR THAT?
YEAH, SOUNDED LIKE SCREAMING.
WHAT THE--? IS SOMEONE IN THE HOUSE?!
DARA
WE
...
OH GOD...
NO...
DARA...

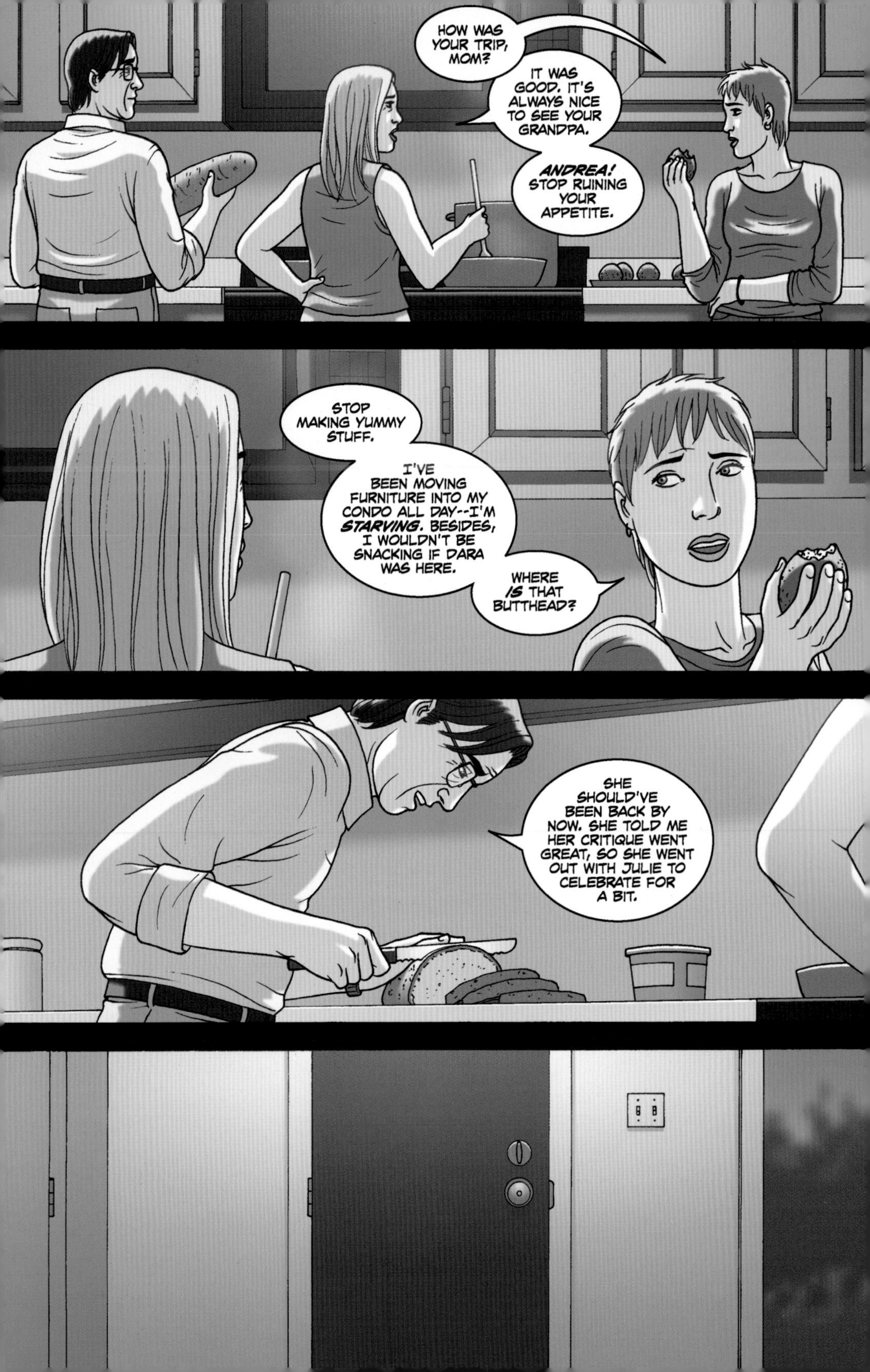
HOW WAS YOUR TRIP, MOM?
IT WAS GOOD. IT'S ALWAYS NICE TO SEE YOUR GRANDPA.
ANDREA! STOP RUINING YOUR APPETITE.
STOP MAKING YUMMY STUFF.
I'VE BEEN MOVING FURNITURE INTO MY CONDO ALL DAY--I'M STARVING. BESIDES, I WOULDN'T BE SNACKING IF DARA WAS HERE.
WHERE IS THAT BUTTHEAD?
SHE SHOULD'VE BEEN BACK BY NOW. SHE TOLD ME HER CRITIQUE WENT GREAT, SO SHE WENT OUT WITH JULIE TO CELEBRATE FOR A BIT.

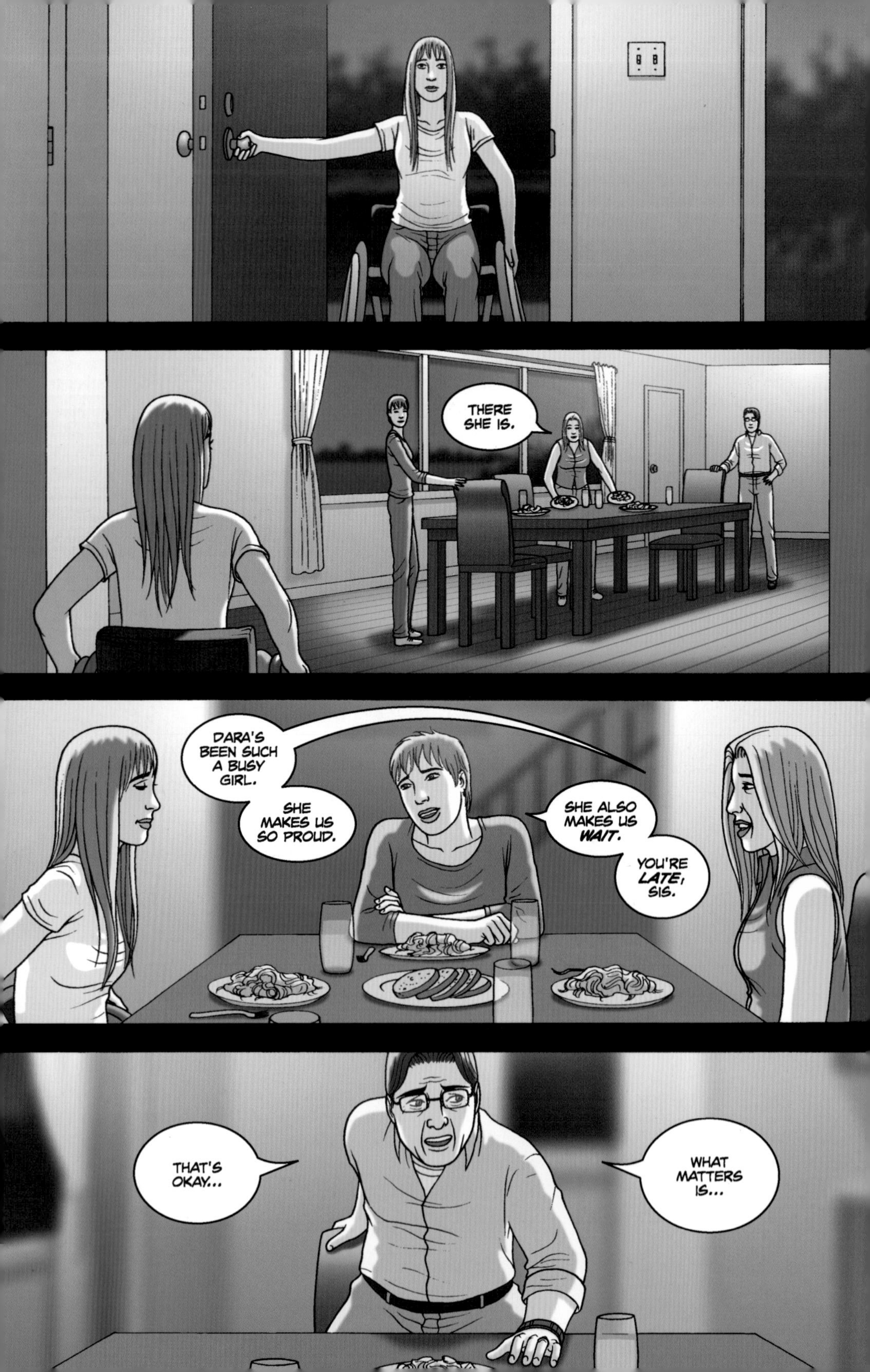
THERE SHE IS.
DARA'S BEEN SUCH A BUSY GIRL.
SHE MAKES US SO PROUD.
SHE ALSO MAKES US WAIT.
YOU'RE LATE, SIS.
THAT'S OKAY...
WHAT MATTERS IS...

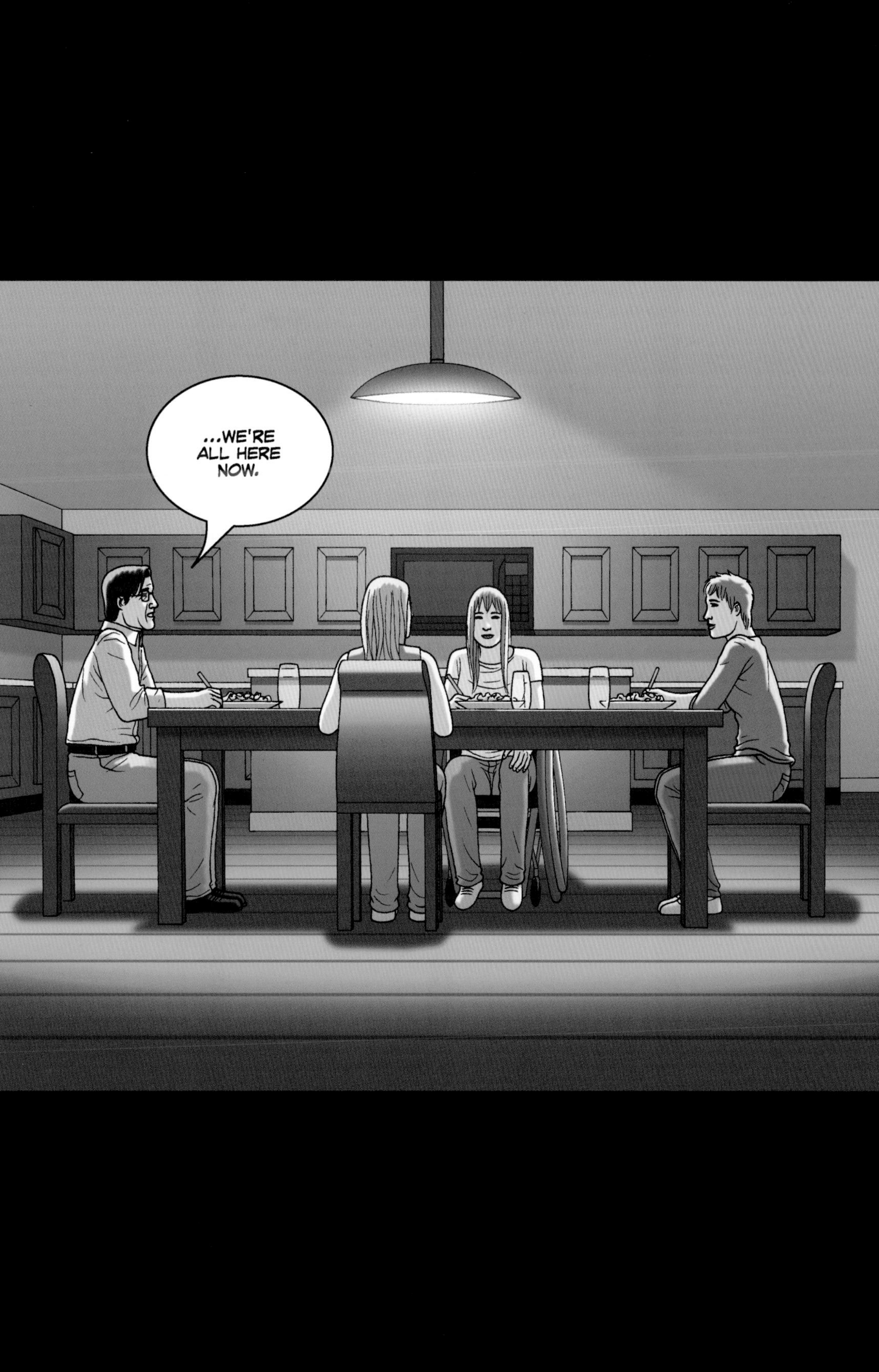
...WE'RE ALL HERE NOW.

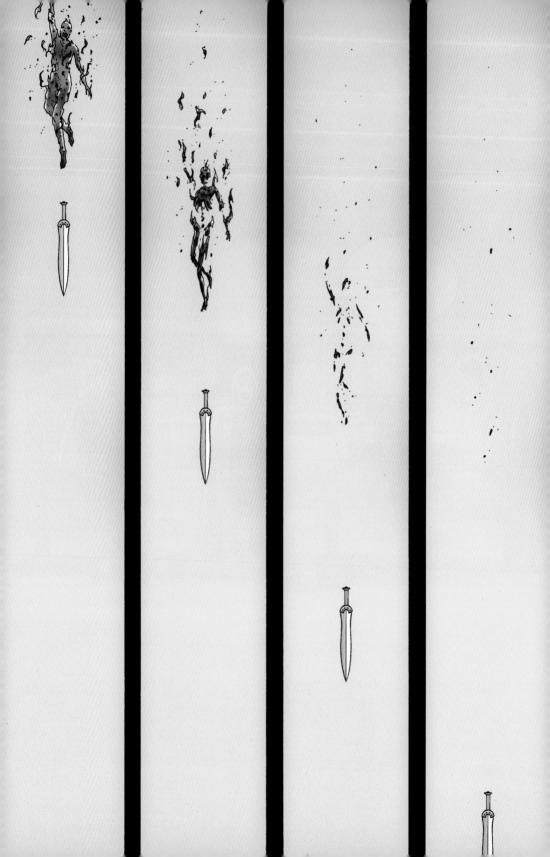

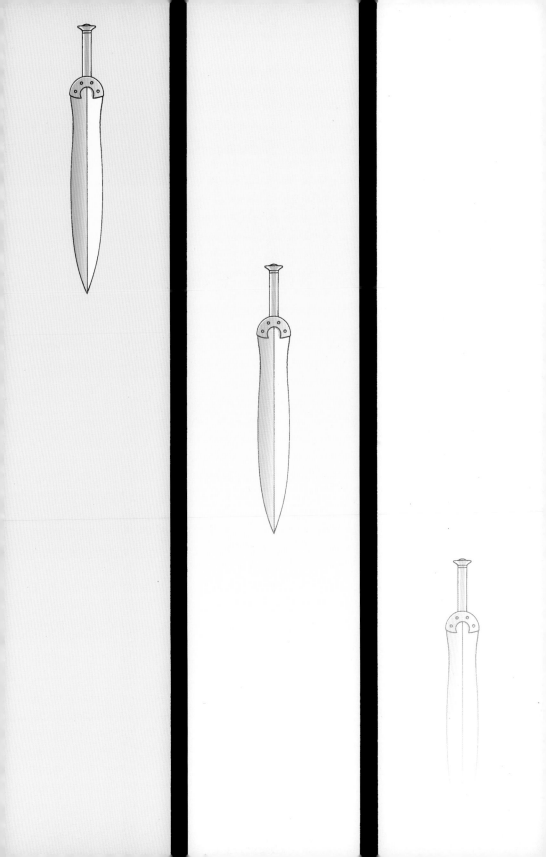